Revolution!

Cuba '58

a novel by

kent barker

First Printing in Paperback, 2013

ISBN 978-0-9568421-0-7

Published by KBP
Watermill House
Mill Street
Cranbrook
Kent TN17 4HL

www.kentbarker.co.uk/PUBLISHING/

The Author:

Kent Barker is a writer, journalist and broadcaster.

Over the past 30 years he has visited the Caribbean many times, reporting for the BBC and ITN from Jamaica, Barbados, Turks and Caicos, Virgin Islands and the Bahamas.

But it wasn't until 2004 that he discovered Cuba. He immediately became fascinated by the country's history and in particular its extraordinary relationship with the USA in the 1950s, and by the rebels who brought down Batista.

For Celia,

whose adventurous spirit took us
to Cuba in the first place

Contents

Prologue – Old Year.

Ok, ok so it's not actually 1958 yet. We've still got another month until the start of that extraordinary year. But the thing is that Joe has to be in Havana on 10th December 1957 because that's when the Hotel Riviera has its grandiose opening. And Joe needs to be there for that. Partly because much else of what happens to him stems from it and partly because it's such a bizarre event. I mean here we are in a poverty stricken Caribbean country with Castro and Guevara running around in the hills beating up Batista's troops ... while El Presidente himself is doling out huge spondulics to the Mafia to build him a new Casino. Not that Havana is actually short of casinos. There are dozens of them. And since Meyer Lansky and his mob – well the mob actually – started running them about five years ago they are actually honest. I mean, really, who except Batista would think of bringing in America's most notorious gangster to clean up his corrupt gambling dens? The thing is that once the punters start to realise a casino is bent they stop going there. And once they realise all Cuba's casinos are bent they stop going there at all. And if your only other exports are sugar and cigars then you're in trouble. Now the thing about Meyer Lansky is that he understood this. He understood that you can make quite a nice little profit from a casino that is absolutely above board, honest, decent and legal. In fact you will make more money in the long run from an honest table than a dishonest one. And apart from the odd rubbing out of opponents and, during prohibition, running a mass bootleg import business, most of what Meyer Lansky has done has been legal. Well, nearly legal anyway. Legal but not overly respectable. And to Lansky the Hotel Riviera represents respectability. It also represents good business. After all a sizable chunk of the $14 million the project cost has been bankrolled by Batista's government. Good business, incidentally, for Batista who finds $3 million in a Swiss bank account in his name and reputedly receives 50% of Havana's gambling profits thereafter. But we're getting ahead of ourselves. All we need to know for now is that Joe Lyons has just arrived in Havana. He travelled on a freighter out of Miami. Full of bright new American cars. Caddys and Olds and Packards and Chevvies. All with tail fins that would grace a space ship. Then I promise we'll move right along to '58 just as soon as we can.

2

REVOLUTION - CUBA '58.

Part 1

Winter

Chapter 1.

It's the smell of the city that assaults him. Yes, Havana attacks the other senses. It's noisy, it's colourful, it's hot. But the smell is different. Different to Miami. Different to New York. And certainly different to Deptford. It's hibiscus and jasmine and lemon, mixed with sea salt and exhaust fumes. But there's another odour on the mid-evening breeze that's not so pleasant. Joe sniffs twice trying to place it. He's walking down a narrow side street looking up at the elegant colonial buildings with their ornate wrought iron balconies and carved wooden doors. The smell is getting stronger and, as he turns the corner, it blasts him full in the face. At first he can't make sense of the scene he's witnessing ... and then can't believe it. The road he's turned into is wide and lined with trees and lampposts. Traffic moves down it at a sedate pace. There are few pedestrians, and none on his side. There's something wrong. Something incongruous. Something mal-odorous. And then he looks up and his gaze is transfixed. It's swaying gently in the soft wind. A body. On the end of a rope. Hanging from a lamppost. A ghastly gallows. As he's staring at this sight, made all the more extraordinary by the normality of its surroundings and its proximity to the centre of a major city, he registers the sound of a siren in the distance. And beneath the lamppost bearing its strange fruit, a pick-up tuck screeches to a stop. Two men hurriedly extend a ladder from the back of the truck, resting its top rung against the arm of the makeshift gibbet. One climbs up and, with a single swipe of a long knife, cuts the rope. The body falls neatly into the back of the pick-up. But as the man scrambles down the ladder the siren, whose wail has been steadily increasing, reveals itself as belonging to a large black and white Oldsmobile tearing down the road. The driver guns the pick-up's engine. The ladder is retracted and stowed. A fist bangs on the roof of the driver's cab, tyres scream and the vehicle shoots off. But the Olds with the wailing siren is upon them. One of the men in the back of the truck raises an arm. Joe sees a pistol in his hand and instinctively moves backwards towards cover. One, two, then a volley of shots ring out as the pick-up vanishes in cloud of dust and smoke, closely pursued by the black and white saloon. Within seconds all is normal again. The traffic resumes its leisurely homeward journey, pedestrians walk on by. Only the smell is left. The lingering smell of a decaying corpse, now partly masked by the stench of burned tyre rubber.

§§§§§

It's heading for one of those dreamy Caribbean sunsets with a few fluffy white clouds hanging around waiting for the right moment to turn flamingo-pink. The sun is just low enough to be glinting on the water and reflecting a strange luminosity onto the distant crescent of buildings across the Havana Bay to Joe's right.

Straight ahead stands the white lighthouse on the low cliffs guarding the entrance to the harbour. At its base the severe stone walls of the Moro fortress descend to the water.

Joe is leaning over the forward rail of the grubby Miami freighter, grabbing his first sight of Cuba. Later he'll remember it as being one of those rare moments in life when you know you've touched, just fleetingly, some higher plane of contentment. It's the potent mixture of the excitement of adventure and trepidation of the unknown, set against the sublime beauty of a tropical sunset. It sends a thrill almost sexual in intensity down the spine.

Is that what Joe is after, adventure? Perhaps. Though he probably wouldn't see it that way himself. He's just restless. Testosterone-fuelled, young-man-will-travel restless. And what better a destination than Cuba. Current capital of world sleaze. Throbbing with rum, rumba and sex. The playground of rich Americans who hop down from New York or Washington or Miami pouring their dollars into an impoverished peasant economy and buying just about anything or anybody they want. Not, that this is Joe's reason for coming. No he's just earning a few bucks to keep him on the road. He'd no intention of coming to the Caribbean at all until, escaping the Northern winter, he'd

Greyhounded down to Florida and answered the small-ad in the Miami Herald. *"Delivery Drivers Wanted"*. Delivery to where? To Havana. The American expats there, along with the 5,000 tourists a week, need transport. So dozens of great gasoline-guzzling, chrome-plated, tail-finned, gleaming-new Oldsmobiles and Pontiacs and Chevrolets and Cadillacs are shipped weekly out of Miami on ferries and freighters. Most are pre-ordered and Joe's job is to drive them from the docks to their new owners, generally in the US residential districts of Vededo.

"But I don't speak a word of Spanish," he protests to the Drive-away boss.

"So who does? Cuba's virtually A US colony. Everyone speaks American." And he hands Joe a bunch of keys. "That Dodge there," he says, "that one's special. You deliver that one first. And the keys go personally to the owner. Top floor Hotel National. Ask for Mr Lansky. Everyone knows him."

So with the flamingo clouds fading, the freighter containing Mr Lansky's new Dodge edges slowly up the harbour entrance where it berths. "Cars will be ready on the dock by 10.00 tomorrow morning" says the Mate to Joe and the other drivers.

Joe walks down the gangplank, sniffs the warm crepuscular air and looks round at the mass of humanity on the quay-side. Before he's actually set foot on Cuban soil he's assailed by four or five youths thrusting, amazingly, neatly printed visiting cards into his hand.

"You need room?"

"Very cheap room, very clean".

"Good apartment in Vieja – old town - come see."

Joe fancies the idea of an apartment. After all who knows how long he might stay. So he gives the nod to a good looking teen-ager, thin with olive skin and black hair.

"I carry your bag. It's OK. Is not far. Where you from?" And he pushes Joe proudly through the quayside crowd as if he's won him as a prize in some game of lotto.

With the light fading Havana's waterfront looks both romantic and menacing. Street lights are dim or non existent. Horse drawn carts vie with bicycles, motor bikes and big American cars for road space. Joe's guide negotiates a gap for them to cross the street and they walk over cobbles across a square dominated by a lowering church. Up one alley, down another, now it's people who pose the problem. Sitting on door-steps, standing in groups, strolling, hurrying, offering wares, basically blocking the way. But our pair push through and on into another large square surrounded by grand dilapidated buildings.

"Here. Up here." And the young man leads Joe through an open gateway into a courtyard sprouting exotic plants, some reaching up to the first tier of balconies that surround the atrium. Up one, two, three flights of stairs they climb. On each level families are gathered outside drinking, smoking, eating, talking. There's Latin dance music coming from one open doorway. A woman is taking washing off a line. Joe's companion pushes open a door and shouts loudly in Spanish.

A motherly woman comes over wiping her hands and offers Joe a barrage of what he assumes to be welcome. "Do you speak English?" he asks. She shakes her head. "Is OK I speak for her" says the youth. "And Maria, she speak English very good. She give you lessons if you want. Maria live across from you. She home soon."

In fact when Joe sees his quarters it appears that Maria lives even nearer than had been suggested. His 'apartment' turns out to be one room with a door leading off from the balcony round the internal stair-well. But it has an interior connecting door to what he is told is Maria's room. Joe also has a window looking out onto the street for which he's just paid extra. It certainly wasn't for the furniture. There's an old iron bedstead with a sagging mattress, a single chair, a small table, a washstand with bowl and a rickety wardrobe. The only light comes from an unshaded pendant in the centre of the ceiling boasting, what Joe estimates, is a 20 watt bulb.

He puts down his bag, bounces on the bed to test the springs, and determines to go out straight away to find beer and food and, with a little luck, a sultry Cuban woman. Instead he's about to stumble on the macabre scene of a corpse being cut from a lamp-post and an ensuing gun fight.

8

Chapter 2

It seems that Maria is prepared to teach rather more than Spanish.

Joe looks at her as she straddles him on the bed. It's that languorous post-coital moment when calm has returned but bodies are still united. He can hardly believe his luck. Quite apart from the fact that she has a fabulous body, she took absolutely no seducing whatsoever. Almost the reverse. It was his second evening in Havana. He'd been standing overlooking the stair-well outside his room staring down on the plants below when this vision appeared. The one good thing, he reflected, of being four flights up is that, if you want to take advantage of watching the ascent of a beautiful Cuban girl then it's going to take her some time to arrive at the top.

At that stage of course he didn't know she was Maria. He just knew he was in love. Though it's true there is only the finest of lines between love and lust in Joe's vocabulary. On the last flight up she was watching him watching her. And before she reached the top step she presented him with a huge smile.

"You must be José. Concha told me you were here. Phew … those stairs. Pleased to meet you. I'm Maria."

And she walks along the balcony a goddess; dark hair glowing, cappuccino skin gleaming, breasts bouncing. Joe holds out his hand and is rewarded with an electric smooth touch in response.

He can't quite recall how, within twenty-four hours, he was touching not her hand but her whole body. He remembered she'd wasted no time in negotiating what he thought was a rather large fee for language lessons. But right at that moment he wasn't going to turn her down for anything.

And he remembered when he'd explained his entire Spanish vocabulary consisted of the one word 'cerveza' she'd suggested they'd better start the next evening. And he'd been rather surprised when, as they sat down for their first lesson in her room, she'd suggested they begin by learning the names for different parts of the body. *Brazo* for arm had seemed ok, as had *mano* - hand, and *cabeza* and *pierna*. But her *pechos* had taken him a bit by surprise, especially when she moved his hand onto them. And by the time she was fondling his *pene* and, not long afterwards he was moving it into her *coño*, he was thinking that linguistics really wasn't that bad a subject after all… and as they kissed an infuriating snatch of the current Broadway hit kept resurfacing in his mind. Maria, Maria. I've just kissed a girl named Maria!

§§§§§

Entwined in the warm evening air with Maria dozing in his arms Joe reflects that, all in all, it has been a pretty damn good start to his trip. I mean he's got a job and now, apparently, a girl.

Chapter 3

Joe had, as planned, collected the Dodge from the wharf. Now, rather nervously in the foreign city traffic, he is driving it northwards to the Malecon – that wide curving embankment that separates the city from the bay. Attractive three story houses in an array of pastel colours line the left hand side of the highway. In the distance cranes tower over the skyline showing a sizable building programme round the city centre. The Hotel Nacional comes into view well before the Dodge gets there. Two high towers, ten stories apiece, set on top of a small rise, a commanding position. And the building itself seems like some medieval fortress. The long approach is lined with palm trees. A succession of tennis courts lead down to the left. Swanky cars crowd the lavish entrance.

The contrast with the surrounding area could not be more marked. In the two blocks Joe had travelled since turning off the Malecon, he'd seen barefoot raged-clothed children playing in the street among litter and dirt, dodging between rusting derelict cars.

But here is unembarrassed luxury. Red carpets and uniformed commissioners ease the paths of the expensive Americans. Inside the lobby waiters rush back and forth with silver trays of drinks. Splashing and laughter comes from the poolside, and beyond guests stroll on manicured lawns under mature trees.

Directed by the receptionist, Joe makes his way past signs for Wilbur Clark's Havana Casino, to the lift where he presses the top button. It appears there are only four rooms on the entire floor though it soon transpires that each is a suite larger than most people's apartments. The door to the Lansky suite is opened by a large and unpleasant looking man.

"Yeah" he growls.

"I'm here to deliver Mr Lansky's car"

"Yeah. Well gi'us the keys then."

"I was told to deliver them to Mr Lansky personally"

"Well I don't give a fuck what you was told. I'm telling you to give them here".

The conversation has started on a decidedly bad note. Joe is disliking this gorilla more with every word he uttered. Some deep rooted subconscious objection to being told what to is taking hold. Adrenaline is welling, hackles are rising. Joe fights to remain calm.

"Wouldn't it just be possible for me to see Mr Lansky for a moment so I can just hand him the keys personally. It's what I'm being paid to do. It's my instructions. I'm trying to do my job properly. Is there any particular reason why I shouldn't actually see him?"

"Yeah there is. Cause I say to hand over the keys now. And you're beginning to piss me off. So why don't you do it NOW."

Joe thinks for a second. He's standing at an open door with a huge angry and increasingly aggressive man in front of him who's clearly some sort of bodyguard. He probably could just hand over the keys and walk away. But by now he's damned if he's going to. On the other hand refusing to do so is clearly going to cause problems. He can hardly turn round and press the lift button and stand there waiting for it to arrive all the time smiling nicely at the goon. But at that moment fate takes a hand, and an extremely short dapper looking man appears behind the oaf and asks what's happening.

"Jerk here's refusing to hand over your car keys"

Lansky looks at Joe. Joe looks at Lansky. Joe smiles his best English smile and without thinking what he's doing blurts out: "Shalom". Perhaps it was the small mezuzah above the door buzzer. Perhaps it's the skull-cap the little man is wearing. Perhaps it's fate. But it works instantly and completely. A reciprocal smile breaks across his face.

"Let the boy in won't you" he says. And the gorilla puts on his most gruesome scowl and steps aside. "Come in, come in. You've got my Dodge then. Good. Good. Haven't had a new car for years. How is it? You come out on the boat with it? I ask Angelo in Miami to make sure it's looked after properly.

"Meyer", he says, "Meyer I'll send someone down with it personally."

Lansky has led the way through to a room with a large tidy desk and a panoramic view of Havana Bay and the city centre.

"Wow, what a view." says Joe rather at a loss for anything else to say under the barrage of Lansky's welcome.

"Oh that's nothing you wait until you see the view from *my* hotel. The Riviera. Twenty-one-stories, 440-rooms. Look you can see it from here."

And he points out of the window to a modernistic high-rise half a mile away, with balconies apparently cantilevered out of thin air. "It's the largest casino-hotel in Cuba - or anywhere in the world outside of Vegas. The official opening's next week. I've got Ginger Rogers starring in the Cabaret. You won't believe what it cost to get that dame down here. You must come. You will come won't you?"

He looks up into Joe's eyes with a stare that seems to be assessing his soul. It's a weird sensation. This little Jewish man with an accent from the Lower East Side, starring at the young Englishman who's about as Jewish as the Archbishop of Canterbury.

"I'd love to come." says Joe, holding his gaze. "But if you're opening a new hotel you might need some extra staff. Are there any jobs going?"

Lansky avoids the question: "How old are you?"

"Twenty-one"

"Been in the military?"

"Yes, I did two years National Service".

"I've got a boy your age" says Lansky. Then, clearly immensely proud, he pulls out a photograph of a young man in a military uniform. "He's at Westpoint you know. What did you do? Where did you serve?"

Joe gives Lansky a potted version of his military career. Posted to Cyprus straight after training and from there sent in to Suez to take back the canal after Nasser's nationalisation.

"Yes you Limey's really screwed Israel didn't you?" says Lansky. "You persuade her to invade Sinai promising her control of the canal zone and then **you** invade saying you're trying to keep

13

Israel and Egypt apart! It's no wonder the UN kicked your ass out of there."

Joe is not certain how to respond to this. "Not exactly my call," he says tactfully. "I was just a squaddie doing the job. I'm not sure that Egypt should have taken the canal in the first place, and I'm not sure we and the French had any business invading without a UN mandate. But surely if anyone screwed anyone surely it was Uncle Sam not supporting either Israel or us?"

Lansky again looks at him carefully and smiles as if satisfied by the response.

"So what else did you do in the army?" he asks.

"Oh a bit of boxing and studied a bit of engineering"

"Go to college?"

"No, I left school soon after 17 and worked for a bit before getting my service papers". Joe is beginning to wonder where this is leading. Why should this little man be so interested in his background? It felt as if he was being interviewed for a job, but he didn't even know if any job existed. And why had Lansky seemed so bizarrely proud of his new hotel, or that his son was at Westpoint.

"Ok" says Lansky "Give us a call tomorrow and I'll see if there's any work I can find for you. You seem OK." And he waves him out. In the corridor the muscleman appears.

"A boxer" he sneers. "What sort of boxer. You couldn't punch shit off a fly".

Joe finally loses it: "What the hell is it with you. I've never seen your ugly face in my life before and you seem determined to give me grief. Yes I did a bit of boxing. I was alright. Not good enough to go pro. But I used to spar with some on the circuit including a couple of heavyweights. So arseholes like you don't impress me one bit." And he turns to push past the man who is half blocking the way to the front door.
Next moment he's flying backwards into Lansky's office under the force of a hefty open hand punch.

"Boys, boys" says Lansky. If you want to play, play outside, do."

"Any time" says Joe.

"How about now?" says his adversary.

14

"OK".

Joe, for all his bravado, begins to wonder what he's this is sensible. The man in front of him is enormous, with fists like proverbial plates of ham. And there's an ugly bulge under his jacket suggesting a shoulder holster. But Joe can't really back out now despite the fear knotting his stomach. So he sidles round a central table keeping the big man at bay while he tries to puzzle out a strategy. The bodyguard simply ignores the table, upends it and pushes it aside. A blue Chinese vase crashes to the floor and smashes in pieces.

"Whoa! Wait up." says Lansky. "Not now. Not here. You'll break all the fake Ming. Go outside. In fact you can wait until this afternoon. I got some associates dropping round. We'll come along and risk a couple of bucks on the outcome. Let's say 3 o'clock at the bottom tennis court. Now, Big Tony, let the Limey out nicely."

Tony grunts and allows Joe free passage to the front door. In the lift on the way down Joe wonders what the hell he's let himself in for.

§§§§§

Two forty-five and Joe's staring through the wire mesh around the hotel's bottom court where two attractive American girls are playing rather average tennis. He focuses on their bodies, admiring long legs and lithe thighs. There's that familiar knot growing in his stomach. It's like that before every fight he's ever had. Boxers call it butterflies. To him it's more like someone mixing concrete in his colon. "Use it," Bob used to say. And Joe's back, waiting to climb into the ring in the big upstairs gym at the Thomas a'Becket pub in the Old Kent Road. "Use the adrenaline. It's what's going to get your muscles moving. It's what's going to keep your reflexes keen. It's not fear it's power. Now think who you're fighting. What are his weaknesses? What are your strengths? How are you going to use *them* to exploit his weaknesses?"

15

Bob's words are still echoing round his head when he sees the group walking down the path. The diminutive Lansky dwarfed by Big Tony, a half dozen other men all in sharp suits following behind. Joe looks at Tony's feet and sees, to his satisfaction, he's still wearing his leather brogues. Joe's been out and bought some sneakers with rubber soles which should give him more purchase on the tarmac. The group arrives. The girls on court look up surprised at the sudden interest in their game. Lansky motions them over whispers something and slips a large denomination bill. They hurriedly pack up their tennis gear and leave.

On court Lansky outlines the rules. Ten minutes. No rounds. Keep to one end of the court. No hitting or kicking if a man's down. Only a knock-out is decisive. Lansky himself will do the count. Other than that anything goes.

Joe is only half listening. Mostly he's sizing up his opponent. And Big Tony is some size. Probably 6ft 2 and at least 18 stone. Joe's giving him 3 inches and the best part of five stone. But the American's older, possibly 30, and he's jowley and already beginning to sweat in the December afternoon sun. He'll be wanting to finish it quickly and he'll be reckoning that one decent punch will do it. So I've got to keep out of his way and wear him down thinks Joe.

And before he really knows it Big Tony's lumbering up to him. He's faster than Joe expects. A right comes crashing in towards his head. Joe leans back in the nick of time and it whistles past. Tony wastes not a moment and is moving in again. Joe's feet feel like lead. His heart's racing. His hands are sweating. Then suddenly the adrenaline reaches his feet. One moment he's treading water the next he dancing on air. His right's up in a classic boxer's guard. He's skipping, feinting, moving, dancing round the big man. He hasn't thrown a punch yet. Tony has unleashed three of four. They've all missed. Joe tries a tentative left jab and is surprised when it connects with something. But instantly he's back out of range and out of danger. Now let him come to me thinks Joe. Let him make the running. Let him think he's got the initiative. Out of the corner of his eye Joe can see the men in suits gesticulating and waving. And he can hear several shouting: "come on Big Tony, squash the punk". Tony's on him again. A left and a right pound in. One connects glancingly with Joe's shoulder. But it leaves the big man open. Joe jabs two lefts in rapid succession, ducks low and backs off to safety. Two in the face. Not hard, but it will make him more cautious. Thomas a'Becket Bob's words come back to him, "Body blows tire your opponent. Hits to the head anger him. You don't want your man angry until he's tired. When he's tired he'll be scared 'cause he knows he tired and then you want him angry so he'll make mistakes."

The words buzz round Joe's head as he flashes another left in the direction of the jowly face. As he expects Tony moves back easily avoiding the blow, but his guard's down and he's not expecting Joe's left-right-left to the chest and stomach. Better hits. More muscle. Tony feels them. Joe's back out or range. Skipping round. Again he waits for the big man to make the move. **He'll** go for the body now thinks Joe. Hurt him a little bit whispers Bob from another continent. Joe lets the big man's punch connect with his stomach. But his muscles are balled tight as iron and though it's a meaty blow it doesn't harm. But the right to Tony's nose does. Joe sees his eyes water and follows up at once. A left upper-cut to the flabby exposed stomach and a right hook to the face which lands satisfyingly on the point of the nose. There's a crack and blood begins to flow. Right thinks Joe first blood to me. But now he'll be dangerous. What would I do? He looks at his opponent and in a flash he knows. This isn't a man who's used to playing by the rules. But I've been making him play my mine. So now he'll play dirty. And even as the thought forms and he starts to move away, Tony's leather brogue lashes out and connects with Joe's crotch. His knees sag and he's down on the tarmac spread-eagled across the service line. You stupid stupid bastard he says to himself you should have seen that coming. Wake up. And instinctively he rolls over and away as the same mighty foot whistles a quarter of an inch past his face. OK. So what happened to the no kicking a man if he's down rule then? Done it once he'll do it again. Almost in slow-motion he sees the foot raise behind and swing in a low powerful arch heading straight for his face. Somehow he frees an arm and grabs for the shoe pushing it away from his face and then onwards and upwards. Tony's off balance. Tony's wobbling. His one foot left on the ground is slipping. Joe's rising with a brown heel on one hand. Tony's going down. Going down hard. The harder they are the bigger the fall thinks Joe as Tony topples and crashes down on his back.

It's the time Joe needs to recuperate, regather, regroup. He's up on his feet. Backing off. Watching. Listening. And he hears at least one voice from among the men in suits urging him on. "Finish him off. Kick the shit out of him. Do it. Do it now". But Joe keeps his distance and waits for Big Tony to lever himself up. Once up though Joe wastes no time. He's in like a panther. Jab, jab, punch. Back again. In again. Now it's a real scrap, but Joe's getting in four good hard hits to Tony's one weak blow. Yet another to the nose. The blood's flowing freely now. A red stain down the white shirt. One, two, three to the stomach. It's not Tony, it's the Thomas a'Becket punchbag. Bob's got his shoulder against it. "Come on now, put your heart into it," he's shouting. Joe's hitting seventh heaven out of his punchbag opponent but he's just not going down. His arms hang limply by his side, the strength to lift them evaporated. Two blows to the jaw hurts Joe's knuckles more than Big Tony. He's rooted to the spot. Eighteen stone of putty. Defenseless yet utterly unbending. Joe puts a leg out behind him and pushes him backwards. Tripped up and overbalanced he crashes to the ground. Every ounce of strength gone. Joe steps back, takes out his handkerchief pads his sweating face and raw knuckles. He walks slowly over to Lansky and his group. Large sums of money are changing hands. All, it seems, in the little man's favour. He claps Joe on the back and introduces him to his associates: "Santo Trafficante, 'Black Jack' Thomas McGinty, Wilbur Clark, Moe Dalitz, and my brother Jake".

"You've done me proud my son," he says and peels off a hundred dollar bill. "Here, this is for you. I gave them ten-to-one against you winning. I've been telling Big Tony for months he was getting flabby and needs to sharpen up. Now use some of that to buy yourself a suit. Make sure it's linen. Light colour will do. You'll need shirts and tie and shoes too. And meet me at the

Riviera tomorrow morning. 11.00 and we'll see what we can find for you to do...."

§§§§§

So here's Joe, walking up the Malecon, sun shining, waves lapping, light dappling, traffic purring past. A hundred dollars in his pocket. A sizable sum. Many a Cuban could live for a year on that. And Joe's got prospects. He's hooked up with Havana's top hotel and casino owner who seems to have taken a shine to him. And although he doesn't yet know it, Joe's heading for Maria, and Maria's bed and, through Maria, an introduction to Cuba's destiny.

Chapter 4

Close up the Riviera looks like one of those great modernistic Miami Beach hotels which, in Miami Beach, look fine, even elegant, but even in the new Havana looked decidedly out of place.

Angular and futuristic it sweeps back from the Malecon in a sort of great "Y". From a distance is appears to Joe to be made of Turquoise. As he gets nearer he can see why. It is in fact clad in a turquoise coloured mosaic. Cantilevered balconies grace each extremity of the "Y". Next to the building itself is a large structure that looks for all the world like a giant egg. But it is as if a dinosaur has had an unfortunate liaison with Faberge, for this egg is covered in gold mosaic.

Joe has arrived early. Maria had to be at work by 8.00 in a factory round the back of Havana's massive domed capital building – more like down-town Washington DC that a Caribbean country but perhaps accurately reflecting the fact that Uncle Sam all but owns this tropical island outright.

Walking together through the narrow streets of the old city she had been less than impressed when Joe told her that he might be working for Meyer Lansky. "He's so far up Batista's arse he can see daylight through his teeth" she had said, surprising him with her graphic vocabulary. "They're corrupt those people. All those fucking Americans. Absolutely corrupt. They keep Batista in power and make him rich while he fucks the country and keeps everyone poor. They'll be the first to go come the revolution."

Joe had thought this just a figure of speech but as he looked at her as she crossed the street with morning sunlight dappling her skin, he saw extraordinary passion in her face. But if he was surprised at her outburst of political rhetoric he said nothing. He was still in that euphoric state of new sexual liaison. Even holding her hand provided an electrical charge. They seemed to be walking on air as they floated through the early morning crowds. In part it may have been lack of sleep. Maria had proved an enthusiastic lover but even she, after their third bout had drifted into unconsciousness. Not Joe. He had lain awake looking at her in the dim light. Watching her breasts as they rose and fell gently with her breathing. Running his hand gently up her thigh and nuzzling between her legs, stroking her soft hair. He'd never seen such female perfection and never had such time to luxuriate in it.

So in a semi trance he walks into the Riviera and asks at the reception desk for Mr Lansky. Since the hotel was not yet officially open there's no receptionist on duty, but a man with an Mid West American accent shouts through the ornate lobby asking if anyone knows where Meyer is. Joe has some trouble working out the effect of the furnishings. There are at once grandiose and gaudy. Magnificent, modernistic yet monstrous. The vast chandelier looks more like a series of flying saucers heralding an alien invasion that a sensible source of illumination.

Lansky is located in the kitchen and Joe is dispatched to find him there. It is, in fact, more like an ocean of stainless steel and the diminutive hotel owner bobs up and down among the pots and pans and ranges and refrigerators. "Good casinos serve good food," he says and proudly shows Joe over every inch of his empire displaying a surprising knowledge not just of utensils and ingredients, but of the number and range of covers that can be catered for. "This is the engine room of the ship," he expounds, "If we get the kitchen right everything else will work. Everyone knows that Meyer Lansky can run a good casino, but a good kitchen....!"

After some twenty minutes of the tour in which Joe feels more like a public health inspector than a putative employee, he cautiously raises the subject of work. "How's the knuckles?" responds Lansky "Bit sore today I should think. You sure gave Big Tony a pasting. You know how to handle yourself. Ever used a gun?" Joe mutters something about firearms training in national service. "Good, good." says Lansky. "You'll need protection. These fucking revolutionaries. Never know what they're going to do next. The president's got them by the balls and he's squeezing hard, but they keep popping up all over the place. And they don't seem to like the US of A that much. Stupid bastards. Without us this country wouldn't be worth diddly squat. I'll want you to do some driving for me. Few people here and there. The odd delivery. That sort of thing. But it would be best if you had a piece. Just in case. Big Tony'll sort you out. Don't worry about him any more. He's a pussy really when you get to know him."

Joe leaves the Riviera still in a dream. He is at the wheel of Lansky's new Dodge again but this time with the little man in the back. "Why did you get a Dodge?" he asks. "Wouldn't a Caddy have been more your thing." "Ostentatious crap" replies Lansky. The dodge is just as good a car. But it doesn't stand out. It doesn't raise it's fucking head up and say look how much fucking money I've got. I've always run Dodges. Ever since Prohibition in New York when you didn't want too many people looking at you or checking what you got in the trunk".

As they sweep North up the Malecon Joe reflects on the contradictions of the man in the back seat. He had just built himself perhaps the most ostentatious hotel in Havana with more gold leaf and glitter per square inch than a Rocco palace, and yet here he is extolling the virtues of perhaps the dullest car on an Island brimming with primary coloured chromium plated examples of Detroit's most exuberant creations.

Joe drops him off at the Nacional where Lansky habitually takes lunch over a poolside meeting with his associates. He'd given Joe a list of locations in the city he'd need to know and suggested he spend the afternoon driving around and getting the topography sorted. Then at 11.00 that evening he was to collect a gentleman from the hotel and accompany him to the Shanghai nightclub. "The show will sure open your eyes and put hairs on your chest," said Lansky cryptically.

So Joe sets out to explore the city with the aid of a hotel map and almost immediately gets lost. The old town round the port where he's living is a warren of tiny streets and alleys. Just to the West, separated by the vast domed Capitol is Central Havana, and further West still is Vadado, the new Americanised area with towering hotels and apartments rising out of shanty-towns and slums. Way down to the South is the airport along avenues lined with trees and fading colonial architecture. And dotted throughout this miasma are the nightclubs and casinos and brothels Joe has to get to know. He finds the Tropicana on his way back from the airport. It's set in a vast estate with two huge stages and hundreds

22

of tables set out in the open air. It prides itself as the largest and most beautiful nightclub in the world and promises chorus lines of 50 dancers. A poster shows Nat King Cole as a recent headline attraction.

Next Joe locates the San Souci, set in a recently renovated Spanish Villa, and then the Monmartre in a former indoor dog track. Both promise imported American showgirls and elaborate productions. As he drives past ragged children on the streets and roadside vendors of cheap food he wonders at the society that can accommodate such luxury and such poverty in such close proximity.

On his way back to meet Maria from her factory he's held up in a traffic jam. Police cars, ambulances and fire trucks siren past. He asks an American in a car in front what's happening. "Just another bomb from those damn pinko revolutionaries," he replies. "It's like this every week. The more bombs they plant the more the police crack down and the more the police crack down the more bombs they plant."

Maria is pleased to see him and impressed with the Dodge. She leans back luxuriating in the plush leather and tunes the radio to some rumba. "But can you afford to be seen in a Yankee imperialist's car?" jokes Joe.

"Lansky's not so much an imperialist as a mobster," she replies. "You know Batista brought him and Benny Segal in to clean up the casinos. It's like handing them the keys to the treasury. Where do the profits go? Straight to Lansky's bank account in Miami and Batista's in Switzerland."

"Do you really mind me working for him?" asks Joe.

"Not for the moment. It might be useful" she replies enigmatically. "Anyway I'd love to see Ginger Rodgers. I hear she's at the opening of the Riviera next week. Can you get me a ticket?"

Joe looks at her with amazement. This strikingly beautiful woman who works for her living in a dingy cigar factory; lives in a cheap apartment on the fourth floor of an old town tenement, teaches him English while fucking him senseless, and preaches revolution while trying to get in to the newest casino in town. "Erm I'll ask Meyer" he says limply.

23

§§§§§

Just before eleven Joe is in his new linen suit outside the flunkied entrance to the Hotel Nacional. High rollers dripping with Rolex's and their escorts dripping with diamonds are headed in for Wilbur Clark's casino, the Café Parisien night club, or the Terrace bar that connects the two.

Joe is escorting a Lansky associate from Vegas who apparently wants to import a little Cuban-style sex to the strip. Five minutes in the Shanghi and they both realise that even in liberal Navada this would be a little too rich for Mid-Western blood.

The nightclub is in a decidedly shady looking theatre in Chinatown. Not far, in fact, from the Cohiba cigar factory from where Joe collected Maria earlier. They pay $1.25 for the best seats and tip the doorman a buck to get in the front row. "We don't want to miss any little detail do we?" says Joe's companion with a leer.

The theatre is larger than it looks from the outside with perhaps 800 seats divided between the stalls and the balcony. The audience is exclusively male, though Joe supposes there might be some women in the darkened boxes to either side of the stage, and of every nationality colour and hue imaginable.

As they enter there's a movie playing on a large and rather threadbare screen. It's not exactly subtle. Two women are sucking a man's cock, both contriving to show as much of their naked bodies as possible.

Joe has only once seen pornography like it, at a stag-night for a friend of a friend in London. But that was coy compared to this.

The audience seems rather unimpressed. The house lights are three quarters on. Most people seem to be talking about something other than the artistic merits of the cinematography. Drinks are being served. After a while the lights go down for the main cabaret.

A band starts playing a Latin rhythm from the orchestra pit. The curtain rises with a flourish to reveal a stage filled with young women posing on a succession of platforms. They're wearing shorts and bras, but as the tempo of the music changes to a fast rumba they troop forward to the front of the stage, off the come the bras and out come perhaps 30 pairs of breasts, small, large and medium, white brown and black, pert , sexy, saggy, or sorry.

These are paraded demurely for the audience for a few minutes until they return to the back of the stage and the curtain comes down again. Joe and the man from Vegas exchange glances as if to say that was pretty tame when the band provides a thunderous fanfare and the curtain rises again.

This time the girls seem to have discarded their shorts as well and are now hidden from total exposure only by a series of twirling parasols. But like the male member, a parasol can go down as well as up. And as the chorus line parades front stage, down they go and it rapidly becomes apparent that either the seamstress was on strike or the management parsimonious because someone forgot to provide the girls with g-strings.

It is, for Joe, something of an eye-opener. His sexual experience pre-Maria was limited to a knee trembler with the local goer in Deptford and a visit to a rather sordid squaddies whorehouse in Cyprus. Now here he is, staring straight up 30 completely exposed female crotches as they parade for him just above his eye level. If it's the kind of thing you want to see, he reflects, then it is certainly worth the extra dollar for the ring-side seat.

In a flash the lights are out and the curtain down, but not for long. The band is getting steamed up and the curtain rises for a pas de deux Apache-style with a couple
called Conchita Lopez and Alfred Romero who also seems to be the choreographer. He's clearly given himself the choice part of the act because as he whirls his partner around he systematically removes layers of her clothing. Finally the missing g-string appears as Conchita is left wearing nothing but it and a scanty bra. Alfred, obviously wishing to preserve his sensibilities, leaves the stage while his partner, perhaps still feeling overdressed, removes

the last two articles to stand statuesque and completely nude in front of a few hundred applauding men.

The series of tableaux that follow demonstrate, if nothing else, that the theatre's wardrobe mistress must have been severely underemployed. There are no costumes to speak of. Just naked women in different poses dotted around the stage.

After a while Joe and his companion head to the bar where they seek out the owner of the Shanghi, Jose Orozco Garcia, a paunchy, affable fellow with a big cigar and the tailoring of a syndicate hood, complete with fedora.

"Nothing's too good for our customers" he tells the Texan. "We change the show every day and we've got 60 girls and a dozen men employed all year round. The biggest problem in a country like Cuba is finding enough girls willing to appear naked. But we never miss a performance except …. except for revolutions."

Later, around 3.00 am, Joe climbs the stairs up to his room and creeps quietly in. But next door Maria is either sleeping lightly or was waiting for him. No sooner is he in bed than there's a quiet knock on his door and she slips in, as naked as any of the chorus girls he's been watching. When he tells her of his evening she says simply, "Silly boy. If you want to see a fanny you can see mine any time. And without having to pay $1.20."

Chapter 5

Joe's duties as Lansky's driver in the week before the Riviera opens seem varied and unpredictable. He's back and forward to the airport several times a day, and shuttling between the Monmartre and the Monseigneur Casino which Meyer also appears to own or run in association with brother Jake. Joe also meets Mrs Lansky. A bright, vivacious, somewhat loud, New Yorker in her early 50's with green eyes, blonde hair and a garish dress sense that seems to favour bright red. She's called Thelma, though everyone knows her as Teddy, and she's even shorter than Lansky, perhaps five foot nothing Joe estimates,

Teddy loves to shop and she has Joe waiting interminably outside Havana's smartest stores before she emerges with assorted packages and parcels. She confides to Joe that she married Meyer in Havana exactly ten years ago and hints that she'd rather prefer to be home in New York, or at least in Miami, but that there are one or two legal niceties that currently make that a bit difficult.

In the evenings Joe is involved in rehearsals for the opening of the Riviera's casino, housed in the giant Faberge egg next to the Hotel. It's a complex process. A dapper Italian named Dino Cellini is in charge of the croupiers that run the Roulette Black Jack and Crap tables in the centre of the room. He's been training young Cubans for the work and has recruited doctors vets and even an airline pilot, all of whom expect to earn more in a month in the Casino that they can in a year of indigenous employment. Round the edge of the room are lines of slot machines. A senior official of Batista's government personally oversees their installation and makes his own arrangements for removing the proceeds.

Joe is sent off to order a Tuxedo – anyone working in the casino is expected to be in evening dress, and has a surprisingly un-acrimonious interview with Big Tony who, as Lansky predicted, is now perfectly friendly. The big man hefts out a suitcase from a cupboard and opens it to reveal an assortment of two dozen or so revolvers and automatics. Joe handles a few and chooses a lightweight .22 which fits relatively inconspicuously inside his breast pocket. He's given a few hundred rounds of ammunition and told to present himself at the local barracks where, on production of a ten dollar bill, a certain sergeant will take him to a firing range and give him a refresher course on small arms handling.

On his way back from this encounter Joe begins to wonder about the line of work he's fallen into. It is undoubtedly glamorous. He's running about town in a brand new car, moving seamlessly in and out of the top hotels commissioning suits and dinner jackets from fashionable tailors, and having to escort people to probably the most uninhibited sex shows in the world.

But just why does his employer seem to be universally regarded as the US's top mobster? Why does he appear to be hand in glove with the head of an extremely repressive political regime? And, above all, in what circumstances and on whom might Joe be expected to use his new automatic?

But there is not a lot of time to ponder on such reflections. Every waking hour belongs to Meyer, and most sleeping ones to Maria. She is, decidedly, another enigma. He still can't believe she really exists. She is bright, witty and sexy and could, presumably, have the pick of any man she wanted. So why pick him? After all he's not much of a catch. A traveller passing through. A young Englishman with few social graces and, before he started working for Lansky, hardy a penny to his name. Handsome enough, Joe supposes surveying himself in the mirror, in a rather craggy post-acne sort of way. But frankly not film star features. Why had Maria been so eager and so quick to seduce him? He didn't doubt that she liked him well enough – especially in bed. She spoke little about her work at the factory. He gathered she'd started as one of the teams of cigar rollers and worked her way up into some sort of lower managerial position, but she didn't care to talk much about it. In fact every facet of Maria seems to have some secret buried behind it. One day, he thinks, he'll come home and the next-door room will be empty and Conchita will say Maria? Maria who?

But for the moment there's seems nothing for it but to submit to her rampant sexual desires and get on with his Spanish lessons. He is, in fact, finding the language less hard that he expected. It may be that he has a natural ear, or it may be that Maria is a natural teacher. Certainly her technique of bringing him to within an inch of an orgasm while he conjugates irregular verbs or demanding he recites a new vocabulary list before granting him entry is unconventional, and possibly not practised in too many of the top language schools. But it certainly seems to work.

Politically too Maria is hard to fathom. Certainly she hates Americans, or at least the sort of American economic imperialism that appears so prevalent in Cuba. And she also clearly hates the president, Batista. But whenever Joe tries to engage her in a political discussion, she seems oddly coy and generally turns the tables, quizzing Joe about his views. Not that he has many. In Britain his background had been staunch working-class Labour. The army had provided a wider perspective, and sought to inculcate a more right-wing "my country right or wrong" ethos. To be honest, Joe has given the politics of his new host country little thought. He is certainly struck by the enormous disparity between extreme wealth and abject poverty that he can see on the streets every day. But how it came to be and what to do about it are not issues at the forefront of his mind.

When Joe asks Lansky if there would be any chance of his girlfriend coming along to the opening night, the little man thinks for a moment and then says: "Why sure. In fact she can accompany a friend of mine. Teddy will be there and it's best if this friend and she doesn't meet. So perhaps your girl and mine can keep each other company".

The knowledge that Meyer Lansky has a mistress makes him, to Joe, rather more human. The man is a puzzle. Small, Jewish, fervently pro Israel, he habitually wears light grey stay-pressed trousers, matching grey socks, and sombre shirts worn outside his trousers. His lack of stature – he's perhaps 5ft 3ins – is more than compensated for by a magnetic personality and an aura of power. He has a remarkable head for figures – Joe has been surprised by his statistical grasp of any subject from the amount of gas the car will consume on any given journey, to the percentage that the gaming tables at the Monmartre will produce on any particular evening. He appears to carry everything in his head. Joe has never seen him with an attaché case or notebook. And yet he seems able to stitch up deals with the Cuban president, and has a reputation as "chairman of the board" of American organised crime, apparently controlling most of the gambling in Havana. He's personable, affable, even friendly and given to surprising busts of homespun philosophy. As they walked round the Riviera Casino floor he told Joe: "There's no such thing as a lucky gambler. There are just winners and losers, The winners are those who control the game."

Try as he may Joe can't see anything particularly illegal in what Lansky does. Yes several of his men are expected to carry guns. But then they are also often carrying very large sums of cash from the gaming tables. The whole point about the Lansky clean-up operation in Havana is that is stamped out illegal or sharp practices. To Joe he appears simply a successful businessman - a hotelier and a casino operator. And, on the 10th December 1958, the host at the glitzy opening of his proudest venture, the Riviera.

The press and the TV are out in force. Limmos and red carpets usher people who are famous or who simply look famous into the lobby. A huge orchestra has been assembled. Lansky is bobbing around the complex of kitchens checking and rechecking the menus. "Miss" Rogers, the star of the night, has been holed up in an upstairs suite with her retinue waiting for her cue to take to the stage of the Copa room. The Riviera Room restaurant is packed and appreciative diners praise the best steaks in Cuba.

Joe's duties are to be available to run any errands for Jake Lansky who's been brought in for the night from the Nacional to oversee operations. Early on there was little to do and, feeling rather uncomfortable in his new dinner jacket, he hung around waiting for the arrival of Maria and Carmen, Lansky's "moll" as Maria had unkindly dubbed her.

They arrived in a down-at-heel looking taxi around 9.00 but immediately had the photographers glancing up and popping a few protective flash bulbs in case they turned out to be famous. They certainly looked the part. Maria had acquired an extremely low cut evening dress and high heels which accentuated her backside and give it a delightful wriggle as she walked. Carmen was more demurely attired but equally beautiful. Where Maria had Cuba's distinctive Spanish light brown skin, Carmen boasted the darker West Indian hue. Her fuller figure seemed to be straining to escape from her white gown.

Joe proudly took their arms and escorted them in to small side table in the Copa room and summoned waiters to provide Daiquiris and Mojitos.

Now the party seems to be going with a swing. The casino is packed. The one-armed bandits are rattling round the side of the room. Stacks of chips are being raked this way and that. America's most serious high rolling gamblers seem to have assembled in Havana for the occasion. Dino Cellini is bobbing about checking his croupiers and ostentatiously kissing the ladies' hands.

Back in the Copa room the orchestra is reaching a crescendo, the house lights dim, and the powerful follow-spot picks out the star of the evening, the great Ginger Rodgers, as she is heralded to the stage.

Without Fred Astair some of the frisson may have been missing, but much of the Rogers magic remains as she heads a lavishly choreographed floor show. Perhaps her singing is not quite in the Judy Garland league, but Meyer Lansky's famous remark to Joe, picked up by an eavesdropping reporter, that "she sure can wiggle her ass but can't sing a goddam note" seems a bit unfair.

§§§§§

So there, as 1957 draws to a close, in the air-conditioned cool of a sultry Havana night, rich Americans and elite Cubans are downing rum cocktails and dancing the night away. The country's latest multi-million dollar hotel has opened, financed by American underworld money and hefty subventions from the Batista government. Tourists line up at airports in Miami and

31

Washington and New York to fly down to the 'Paris' of the Caribbean. Some will think nothing of writing cheques for $20,000 or $30,000 to cover a night at the tables. Everyone is on the gravy train and as the rhythms of the rumba waft out over the palm trees and pools there seems to be no end in sight.

Revolution Cuba '58

PART 2

New Year

Chapter 6

At the end of the line of traffic Joe pulls the car over and gets out. Traffic jams are not uncommon in Havana, but the worst occur when the military is involved. It's sometimes hard to reconcile the liberal lifestyle of Americans in Cuba with the fact that the government is, by any other name, a military dictatorship.

It's January 2nd. The festive season has come and gone in a flash. Somehow Joe feels that Christmas isn't Christmas if you're sitting round a swimming pool in 80 degree heat being served iced rum cocktails. All his childhood Christmases were spent in front of a coal fire in a front room in Deptford with adults drinking Stout or India Pale Ale. The memory of Tolly Cobbald floods back as he gazes at a bikini-clad blonde on a recliner. The beer came in an elegant clear-glass quart bottle on whose neck was a small oval label bearing the name of the brewer above the outline of a slender naked woman. Post-war Britain was rather short on naked women. The new look covered female legs in folds of material. Advertisements for underwear were coy and far between. Before discovering the National Geographic magazine with pictures of bare-breasted African tribeswomen, or summoning up courage to buy copies of the naturists' monthly, Health and Efficiency with it's clean living Scandinavian buttocks and breasts, the tiny Tolly Cobbald nude was, for an adolescent male, about as exciting as it got.

Here in Havana, by contrast, sex is everywhere on show, and everywhere for sale. Hardly a street passes without a tout offering pornographic postcards. Every hotel bar and lobby has girls hanging about looking for business. At dusk, like bats coming out for their evening feed, the main roads and boulevards are lined with women waiting for passing trade. On collecting an "associate" from the airport on Christmas Eve Joe was asked to drive straight to the nearby Casa Marina. The American said he'd be about an hour and suggested Joe come in and wait inside. From the front it looked just like any other rather run down colonial mansion, inside it had the distinctive bordello dim-red-lights and cheap-perfume-and-semen smell. But where most cat houses have a range of ages on offer here there were only two: young and very young. The girls, and for once the term was appropriate, paraded in front of the clients wearing either nothing or less. Some had breasts and pubic hair but most had merely adolescent bumps and downy fluff. Each had that hooker's vacant expression that is a mixture of come-on and total indifference but these pubescents looked as if they wanted a doll to play with rather than a man. Perhaps 13 year-olds are what some elderly males most crave but not a 21-year old like Joe, and he was already feeling sickened by the whole tawdry experience when the madam, thinking he too was a punter, offered him a selection of "guaranteed" virgins to deflower for a small extra price. He decided to wait in the car.

§§§§§

Later, after she'd returned from midnight mass, he recounted the experience to Maria. They were lying on the bed as they exchanged gifts and shared a bottle of champagne he'd bought to celebrate the season. "They should have been at home with their families, wrapping presents and waiting for Santa to arrive" he said. "I used to love Christmas it was a chance to spend a bit of time with my dad and assorted uncles and aunts and cousins. The thought of those kids stuck in that place over Christmas is just awful. Where do they all come from?"

There's a flash in Maria's eyes. "Mainly they get them from orphanages, but some families are so poor in Cuba the only way to feed the other children is to sell the daughters off to work in the city. Of course they never say it's for prostitution, but most parents must know in their hearts that it is. Someone estimated that more than 12,000 women in Cuba earn their living that way. That fucking Batista's no more than a pimp. He's selling his nation's daughters to the Yankee imperialists for sex and keeps the rest of us in poverty. Only one in six women in this country has a job. Fucking Americans own all our mines, half our sugar

36

production, half our railways and almost all the utilities ..." As she trails off Joe wonders at the anger welling inside this beautiful woman. Suddenly his smiling happy bubbly sexy simple Maria is an angry firebrand orator with an unexpected grasp of political rhetoric and sociological statistics.

So it's nine days later and Joe is stuck in a traffic jam. He walks up the stationary line of cars to see what the problem is. As he suspected there's the Army blocking the road. Then into view comes a procession ... a line of women clad entirely in black. And behind them, more and more women marching silently and slowly along the main road. In front two hold aloft a banner saying simply "Stop The Murder Of Our Sons".

A crowd has gathered, held back by the soldiers and Joe asks around until he can find someone who speaks enough English to explain what's going on.

"A year ago the bodies of four boys including a 14 year old were found in a deserted building in Santiago. They'd been tortured and murdered. The secret police picked them up a few days earlier and accused them of revolutionary activities which was nonsense. This year the mother of one boy, William Soler, has asked women in every city in Cuba to march in protest."

"Did they ever find who killed them," asked Joe.

"Everyone knew who did it but no one was ever arrested. No one is ever arrested. Hundreds of people disappear and either they are never seen again or their bodies are found beaten and tortured, Batista's thugs have freedom to do what they want and no-one can stop them. The judges are appointed by Batista, the Army is run by Batista, the police are controlled by Batista. And Batista says it's all to stop the revolutionaries. Huh. Some revolutionaries. A few men with beards running round the hills in *Oriente,* in the east, with old guns and no ammunition. And he sends his best troops to rout them out and they can't find them. It's pathetic."

A couple of soldiers are beginning to take an interest in their conversation, and suddenly Joe's informant has vanished into the crowd. He turns his attention back to the procession passing in front. Suddenly he sees a woman who looks just like Maria. He looks again and sees that it is, indeed, she. There among the women in black. Walking slowly and silently and proudly. Making her point. Taking a stand.

That evening he tells her he saw her in the procession. And asks her how she came to be involved. She pauses and without answering asks him how much he knows about the 'opposition'.

"Only that there are a bunch of men with beards running around in the hills evading the troops."

"It's rather more than that," she says. "On July 26 five years ago -1953 - a lawyer called Fidel Castro led a small group opposed to Batista in an attack on a military garrison in Santiago called Moncada. It wasn't a great success. 50 were killed and Fidel, his brother and some others were arrested and put in jail. But it showed everyone that thy COULD oppose the government.

"While he was in prison opposition groups started up all over Cuba and particularly here in Havana at the university. But they all had different ideas of what to do about Batista and what sort of government they wanted to see in his place. You mustn't forget that this is the third time that Batista has seized power here because almost every other regime has been as bad or worse than his military dictatorship. Anyway finally they had to let Fidel out of jail and he went off to Mexico with a group of other exiled supporters. That's where he formed the July 26th Movement. And he got FEU – the Federation of University Students – to go over there and they signed a pact. It called for the 'unity of all the revolutionary, moral and civic forces of the nation - students, workers youth organisations and all men of dignity so they will support the struggle which will end in victory or our death'."

That passionate expression that Joe had noticed before radiates from Maria's face as she recites the revolutionary rhetoric. "But how did you get involved?" he asked her, "And how involved are you?"

"My brother was a student at the university. He was best friends with Jose Antonio Echevarria the student leader. But he was impatient. He wouldn't wait for Fidel to come back from Mexico with guns and men. He left his studies and went off to Santiago and joined Frank Pais who was leading the opposition there. At the end of 1956 Fidel and Raul and the others were due to land in *Oriente* from a boat they'd bought in Mexico. They should have been there on 30th November but they were held up. Frank and my brother started an uprising in Santiago. Frank was OK but my brother was wounded and then captured and killed. My whole family was devastated, but my mother most of all. They were just simple people, bakers from Bayamo, but she was so angry about what was happening she set off to join the rebels who had scattered into the mountains of the Sierra Maestra. It took her weeks to find them, and then as she had no gun and as, back then, there were no women in the Sierra, they wouldn't let her stay. But they did let her ...."

Maria trailed off. "I'm sorry. You know it's not that I don't trust you. But so many lives are at risk, it's probably better if you don't know too much. In fact the way we are all set up means that no-one knows more than a handful of other people who are involved."

"You say 'we'. You mean you are one of them?

"It depends what you mean by one *of them*? If you mean do I believe in getting rid of that bastard that's ruining my country and killing and torturing my brothers and sisters, then yes, I'm one of them. If you mean am I about to join Fidel and Raul and Che in the Sierra, and start shooting soldiers, then no I am not. I am not sure I believe that killing people is right ... even in a right cause. And I'm not at all sure I could do it myself."

"So what do you do? Joe asked.

"I recruit people to the cause. I raise money. I march. At the moment I'm trying to infiltrate the enemy ..." she said turning and putting her arms round Joe and kissing him gently.

"Me. The enemy?"

"Well you work for those bastard Yankees that are screwing my country"

"How is Meyer Lansky screwing Cuba? He's bringing millions of dollars in here and helping to attract hundreds of thousands of tourists."

"Dollars that are going straight to Batista and his henchmen, and tourists that are distorting the economy and raping young girls."

"And where do you think the money that you collect for the rebels goes? Joe asked.

39

"To provide food and clothing".

"And guns?"

"Yes probably. And guns. If they didn't have guns they'd be slaughtered by the army."

"But I thought you didn't believe in killing people. The guns you buy kill people."

"And I though we were talking about the American Imperialists and sex-perverts that YOU are supporting. You seem to have subtly changed the subject. Western lap-dog."

Maria smiles her sexiest smile, kneels on the bed opposite Joe and slowly undoes the buttons of her blouse.

"Not lap dog", says Joe. "Sex fiend please …"

Chapter 7

Meyer Lansky is away in the States for much of January so Joe is working to his brother Jake. Jake has none of the charisma of his elder brother, but is a solid lieutenant overseeing the day to day running of the Lansky businesses. He seems to trust his brother's judgement in Joe and gives him increasingly responsible tasks to perform. Many seem to involve moving large sums of cash around.

Joe has been studying how the finances of a casino work. First punters are encouraged to use cash with a small charge levied for personal cheques. At the end of the evening all the takings from all the tables are collected and counted in a back-room. The money is then split into two piles. Joe is unsure exactly how this division is made, but he suspects that one pile represents the actual operating costs of the casino: wages, pay-offs, rent to the hotel, small element of profit etc. This sum is banked. The other pile of cash is the 'bunce' which simply disappears. Since no one keeps records of how much is gambled in any given evening, the legitimate or 'declared' sum for tax or other official purposes is generally much much lower than the actual sum.

Joe is curious about how they trust the cheques. Many are for large sums of money sometimes up to $50,000. One night Jake asks him to drive a Casino employee known to all as "Dusty" Peters to the airport early the following morning. As they're heading south from Vadedo Joe asks him where he's off to and Dusty fills in another piece of the jigsaw. "I get the first flight to Miami and go straight to the bank and deposit last night's cheques. We're good customers so the bank runs a special on each cheque. By the end of the day we know if there are any that haven't cleared and I bring them back on the evening flight and we have a little word with the people concerned. "

If Joe is interested to know what that 'little word' is, he soon finds out. A dapper young Cuban called Norbeta Pena habitually hangs around the Riviera casino throughout the evening. He is a graduate of the Cellini croupier school but has now been assigned to other duties which he describes as 'credit control'. One evening Joe is told to help him. Dusty, back from Miami, seeks out Norbeta and hands him two or three cheques. Norbeta checks the hotel registry finds two room numbers he needs, and asks one of the receptionists to phone round the other hotels in town for a third name. He checks that Joe is carrying. "Just in case. You won't need it. But it's best to have some insurance". Up they go in the lift and knock on the door of room 803. A Texan, just out of the shower, answers. Norbeta apologises for disturbing him and explains that there seems to be some mix up at the bank, and the man's cheque has not been honoured. The Texan is embarrassed and cross. He invites them in and sits them down. The cheque is for ten grand. "I've got eight thou here" he says, and pulls out two rolls of notes. "But what about tonight? I was planning on recouping my losses at the tables."

Norbeta asks if there is anyone in the Texan's party who will counter sign a credit note for him until he can sort things out with his bank the next day. And they arrange to meet in the Casino later to discuss the arrangement. The whole interview has taken four minutes. The American is visibly relieved. "The worst thing for a gambler" says Norbeta in the lift on the way back down, "is not to be able to gamble. That guy comes down here two or three times a year. He used to go to Wilbur's at the Nacional, now he comes to the Riviera. We've never had any credit problems with him before so I'm not worried. But this next guy is different. I don't know him at all."

The second punter also covers his cheque with cash but is told firmly that it is a cash only arrangement from then on. If he wants to write a cheque and wait until it clears, the management will be delighted to hold that sum and to allow him to sign markers up to that limit, but no credit. The arrangement seems acceptable and Joe and Norberta are soon on their way across town to chase down the third defaulter. This time they seem to be too late. He's checked out of his hotel. Norberta's on the phone to the airport. In quick fire Spanish he asks the authorities to check if he's left the country and, if not, to detain him if he tries. Joe picks up the phrase "the usual arrangement".

"But what happens if he's already gone?" asks Joe.

"Well, we'll wait until he tries to come back into the country, and we'll let all the other casinos in town know to be on the look-out. If it was a really big sum of money then Mr Lansky might pay a percentage to some 'debt collectors' in the States who would make him realise that there was no option BUT to pay up."

"Have you ever had to use any muscle here?" asks Joe.

"Almost never. As I say there's one thing a gambler fears more than anything else, and that's being blacklisted."

"And what about locals, do you give them credit?"

" The cashiers are instructed to take a local cheque up to $100 without arguing. They don't bounce."

"Never?"

"Never so far. After all what sensible Cuban would risk having El Presidente's men coming after them to collect?"

Later Joe watches Norberto in action on the floor. A cashier will discretely approach him nod towards the gentleman who asking to sign a credit marker. Nine times out of ten the Cuban knows them and gives a yes or no on the spot. Occasionally he goes to have a quiet word with the man in question. Checks his name, where he's staying, what other casinos he frequents etc. Early in the evening the Texan approaches Norberto and introduces a friend who shakes the Cuban's hand. Afterwards Norberto give the nod to the cashier, and shortly afterwards the Texan comes away with a pile of chips and heads to the blackjack table.

Joe quickly realises that there is far more going on in the hushed surroundings of the Casino than he first thought. There are the high rollers. Generally quiet, sober, serious, well dressed. Playing a system. Playing the percentages. Expecting to win over a period of time. They'll move from one casino to another, from one country to another. For them it's not a hobby it's a way of life. A profession. Then there are the wealthy amateurs. On vacation in Havana. Wives, girlfriends, mistresses either discretely behind them at the table, or next door watching the cabaret. These men are mostly rather less sober. They'll have had rum cocktails at 6.00, wine or beer with diner and will now be sipping champagne or brandy or 15 year old Havana Club. Consequently they're less cautious. They'll play on instinct or hunch – getting increasingly excited as the stakes rise. And the more they lose, the more they'll risk trying to get it back. And then there are the neophytes, the Casino virgins who can't afford to lose much at all. Mostly they'll bet low to keep their stash of chips going as long as possible. When the money's gone, they'll go. Together these men – and it is men 19 times out of 20 - make the casinos rich. But the casinos work for their money. To start with they have to create the right atmosphere. The lighting has to be subdued but not dingy. There needs to be relative quiet. Only the whir and tinkle of the slot machines disturbs the hush in the Riviera. Drunks are discretely and politely removed. Prostitutes are barred. But there are a surprising number of people lounging around watching. At first Joe thought they were punters waiting for the right moment to join a table. Later he realised they are casino employees keeping a careful eye on the punters and the croupiers. While Norberto keeps tabs on the high rollers, his underlings are watching the amateurs and the first timers, heading off problems before they occur. Ready to move in at once if a croupier signals that something may be wrong. It is, concedes Joe, a pretty slick operation.

Later, in bed, with Maria sleeping gently beside him, he considers the huge sums of money changing hands and begins to think of Maria's brother, and little William Soler, and the Barbudos in the hills with clapped out guns. Despite all her hard work campaigning and money raising Maria collects only comparatively tiny amounts for the opposition movement. He stares for a moment at her classic profile and watches her breasts rise and fall with her breathing. As he falls asleep he fleetingly considers if there might be some way to divert a bit of the wealth from the Riviera to the rebels. After all, if the Lansky brothers are financing Batista and his army thugs, it would surely only be fair for the Lanskys to help finance the Castro brothers and the opposition?

Chapter 8

Joe and Maria are walking hand in hand on the Malecon at dusk. It's magic. The sun is setting over the new high rise hotels to the West. The last iridescent light is bouncing off the bay and dappling the pastel painted houses across the road to their left. Early evening lights begin to pepper the windows. Down-at-hoof nags clatter along behind traps relaying romantic tourists to bars and restaurants. Snatches of Latin music waft over the warm air.

"Why me?" Joe wants to know. "Why did you choose me? Or do you give your body to every stray Englishman who moves in next door and asks for language lessons?"

"I thought you had a nice smile" replies Maria laughing, and then adds more seriously: "And I thought you might be useful".

"Useful?"

"Yes useful"

"How?"

Maria stops and pushes him up against the concrete breakwater and envelopes him in her arms. "Don't take this the wrong way, but I thought you might be able to help us. You're not American, but you're American enough to be able to move in and out of the western hotels without suspicion. We didn't know precisely what you might be able to do, but it had been decided to try to recruit a European."

"Have I been recruited then."

"That depends on you. This is not your country so I don't expect you to feel the anger for what's happening in the same way that I do, but I would hope you would understand the injustice and the cruelty and why we have no option but to fight for our freedom."

"Who do you want freedom from? Batista or Uncle Sam."

"Both. They're one and the same."

"No I don't think they are. Let me tell you about the America *I* know. It starts when you sail into New York past the statue of Liberty. You know the mantra about the huddled masses. But there's a lot of truth in it. They really have welcomed millions of poor, homeless, persecuted, oppressed people from over the world, but particularly from Europe. When Hitler and the Nazis were on the rampage in the 30s it was America who provided a sanctuary for the Jews. And before that. Lansky and his family fled from the pogroms of the Russian Tzars and arrived in America to make a new life. I was brought up with religious and political freedom as a historic right in England. But we were stuck in a class system that was almost as oppressive. But in America they pride themselves in 'can do'. Anyone can do anything they put their mind to regardless of their background. Go from log cabin to president. From shoe-shine boy to head of the corporation..."

Joe is getting carried away with his own eloquence. Maria is smiling at him sadly.

"Yes, can do" she says. "Tell that to the negroes in the South. Can ride on the bus but only in the back seats. Tell that to the Indians on the plains. Can live in a reservation 'cause we've slaughtered all your buffalo. And *Lansky*. You use Lansky as an example of American sanctuary. He shat on the very doorstep that welcomed him. He ignored every rule and law of the new country that gave him such a generous opportunities. If the stories are anything to go by he killed, robbed, threatened, and cheated his way to the top. Top of what? Top of a crime syndicate that's bigger than US Steel. And just what has the US done in Latin America? Some jingoistic president called Munroe produces a doctrine that says they have a right to interfere in anything in the US's back yard. And that includes organising revolutions to overthrow other people's democratically elected governments. Or here, shelling out millions of dollars to prop up corrupt regimes. Where do you think Batista gets his tanks, and planes, and ships and the rest of his military supplies? From fucking America that's where. It was in the paper this week. America has just announced *another* million dollars in military aid for this year. And what will that money be spent on. Killing and torturing 14 year old children that's what."

She pauses for breath. And Joe studies her beauty in the fading light and his heart lurches. Before he even fully realises it he's crossed a threshold. "How much money do you need to raise for your rebels?"

Maria thinks for a moment. "Well, obviously as much as possible. Why, have you bought a lotto ticket?"

"No but I've an idea how you might be able to win some money at roulette or blackjack."

She looks at him sadly. Now I know you're crazy she says. You know you can't win. You know the odds are always against you."

"No, you can't win if you are betting with your money. But you could try betting with Lansky's."

§§§§§

The idea he outlines has to be put before a local committee and afterwards Joe is taken to meet one of the leaders of city's July 26th Movement, known universally as M.26/7. Much secrecy and subterfuge surrounds his whereabouts. Maria provides an address in Centro Havana. There Joe's handed an envelope with another address in the old city. But when he gets there it doesn't exist. As he's staring up at the house numbers, an anonymous man approaches him and offers him dirty postcards. This is such a regular occurrence on Havana streets that Joe, as usual, simply ignores him. To engage in conversation generally results in increased pestering. But this man is persistent, and among his quick fire patter Joe makes out the words "if you post now, should arrive on 26th July. So he asks the man if he's got any other postcards for sale and agrees to accompany him back to his room. They set off down a small alleyway, through first one courtyard and then another. Finally, when Joe is completely disoriented they slip through an opening into an apparently deserted building. On the right, behind some wooden scaffolding a sheet of canvass covers a hidden door. The postcard seller knocks three times and disappears, telling Joe to wait. A few moments later a small

47

observation hole in the door opens and a pair of eyes look at Joe and then behind him and to left and right. Finally the door is unbolted and Joe slips into the semi-darkness. The door closes and he's trapped in a small corridor. "I'm sorry but I have to check you over" says a voice, and Joe is quickly and expertly frisked. His automatic is removed from his inside pocket almost before realises it and he's ushered upstairs.

The man he is to meet greets him from a couch in then centre of a sparsely furnished room with piles of books covering the floor.

"Please forgive me for not getting up. I've just had an operation. I ran into a little problem a few months back and it's taking rather a long time to recover. I'm Faure. You must be Joe. Maria's told me a good deal about you."

Joe brings up a chair and, before sitting, is dispatched to fetch iced tea from a battered looking fridge in a corner of the room which serves as a kitchen area.

"It's probably an anathema to an Englishman to be offered *cold* tea" says Faure, "But I find it refreshing."

"I'm surprised at you," says Joe "I thought iced tea was an American invention. I may have to report you for succumbing to cultural imperialism."

Faure laughs at Joe's pleasantry and instantly the two men feel a rapport.

"I'm sorry about the cloak and dagger business of getting you here. My comrades who are being extremely generous of their time during my convalescence insist on it. The fewer people who know exactly where I am the better. "

"Do you mind me asking what was the nature of the little 'problem' you ran into?" asks Joe.

"Just about a year ago things were looking pretty bad for Fidel in the mountains. They'd lost three quarters of the original force that arrived from Mexico in the first battle after the Granma landed. So the last dozen or so retreated into the hills expecting to find the peasants – the *Gajerios* - welcoming them with open arms. But the locals were so frightened of Batista's thugs and so suspicious of this bunch of amateur revolutionaries that most refused to help and some even became spies for the army.

"From down here in the *llano*, the plains, it looked as if Fidel's *sierra* revolution had petered out so we conceived a bold plan which we thought would result in the complete decapitation of the regime. We knew whereabouts in the presidential palace Batista was quartered and we thought that if enough of us attacked at once, his guards would be too surprised to resist. Plus we arranged to take over the radio station, Radio Reloj, to call the country to arms and to bring out the people.

"It was 3.30 on March 13. I was with the first group of about 100 that stormed the palace. For us in the movement it was the happiest day of our lives. We vowed that no one would back down until we had succeeded."

Faure paused, looking into the distance, remembering.

"So what happened?" asked Joe.

"It all started well. Afterwards Batista claimed he knew of the plot but he couldn't have known when it was to happen because we did surprise the place guards. But they are well trained and they fought back strongly. I was shot and wounded in the first moments of the attack and had to crawl back from the palace gates. But some did get through. They fought their way up two flights of stairs. But the rat Batista had fled to the third floor and there were no stairs up to his eyrie, only a lift. The thing is it didn't matter whether we got him straight away. As long as we held the wing of the palace with him as our hostage, we had won."

"But hang on" says Joe, " surely you weren't expecting to hold onto a part of the presidential palace with fewer than 100 men. Did you have machine guns? Did you have grenades? Rifles? What?"

"No. Just hand guns and machetes and knives. But we had re-enforcements. Or at least we should have had. There were two other groups who were due to back us up. But they never arrived. Afterwards they claimed there were too many police and troops surrounding the area after the alarm went up. Me, I think they were cowards. And their cowardice cost us dear. We lost 35 comrades in the battle, but many many more in the following days. The secret police arrested and tortured innocent students and opponents of the regime whether or not they had been

49

involved. They killed at least 70 including Pelayo Cuervo who was a lawyer and elected opposition politician."

"Fidel at least must have been pleased when he heard of what you'd attempted?"

"No, that's the sad part. He was furious. He called it a useless expenditure of blood and said if he'd wanted Batista killed he'd could have done it himself. And after a year of sitting in various safe houses waiting to recover I am beginning to see it his way. If Batista had been killed it would have given the Army generals every excuse to mount a full-blown military coup and to rule as a junta. There's precious little democracy or freedom in Cuba under Batista, but under the butcher Cowley or the psycopath Chaviano it would be even worse."

"Well, at least you must have galvanised the opposition. Shown that it could be done. That it was a cause worth fighting for?"

Faure smiled sadly. "No it didn't work like that. It actually got Batista a lot of sympathy from the Americans and other ex-pats here. It encouraged Washington to support his regime with even more military aid. And amazingly the CTC, the Cuban Workers Confederation, were so fearful of their jobs that they actually marched in support of the bastard."

"So what do you do next?"

"Well I actually think Fidel is right. We have to win a psychological revolution before we can win a military one. The majority of the people and also a large part of the army has got to believe that we can provide not just an alternative but a better government than Batista.'

"Surely there is another group you have to convince too?" says Joe.

"Who?"

"The people in Washington. You don't want them swinging in behind Batista, which they might do if they think Cuba is becoming a back door for communism to enter the States. And the people who will influence Washington are the US corporations who own your economy. If they think their interests will be threatened by a revolution, they'll be lobbying their senators and congressmen to send a couple of warships into the

Miami Straights, and for extra troops to be stationed in Guantanamo Bay.

Faure looks thoughtful. "Yes you're right. And I believe Fidel also thinks like that. He's already started inviting American Journalists up into the *sierras*. He got some really good coverage last year in the New York Times from a guy called Matthews. Fidel had a total of about 30 troops at the time. But he kept talking about his 'divisions' and getting spurious messages delivered from apparently far flung rebel strongholds and Mathews reported that there were hundreds of them up there."

"But what he needs most of all is guns or money for guns." says Faure. "And we understand that you might be able to help provide them."

Chapter 9

It's three weeks later. The arrangements are made. The time has come to try out the plan.

It's not been easy getting the necessary paperwork in place. But July 26 members working in the banks and the civil service have risked their jobs to help. The first to be targeted is the Riviera. It's 8.00. Early for the casino, but a few pre-dinner gamblers are at the tables. A Cuban couple walk up to the cashier and in Spanish the man explains it's his girl-friend's birthday and he's promised her she can try her luck at Roulette. But he hasn't enough cash. Will they take a cheque? How much for? $100. The cheque is from the main national bank in Havana. The man's ID looks good. The cashier hands over $100 worth of chips and the couple move towards the tables. As the evening progresses other couples and single men come in, each cashing a cheque for a relatively small amount. The same thing is happening at the Monmartre, the Nacional and the Monsignieur. More Cubans than usual perhaps, but always cashing cheques under the house limit and always offering proper looking ID.

Later, when quizzed, the cashier at the Riviera agrees that night there were perhaps an unusual number of locals cashing cheques. But seven or eight? Throughout the entire evening? And a total of less that $600 when US punters were writing single cheques for $6,000? And the house rules do say he's allowed to cash local cheques for up to $100 without referring them to management don't they? Trouble is, Jake Lansky tells him, the Americans $6,000 cheques were honoured. None of the local ones for $80 or $100 were. The banks claimed that the accounts simply didn't exist. Every casino in town in which the Lnaskys have an interest has also been targeted.

"How much did we lose?" Joe asks Norberto the next night as the scam is discussed in the casino's back rooms. Only about $2000 and some of that wasn't a real loss because we got it back at the tables. But mostly they bet very low and very conservatively and never lost more than half their stake. And two or three had the luck running with them and won quite well. But it's not the money so much as the principle. Meyer is not going to like the idea that he's been done."

"$1460. Clear. " Says Maria. It's brilliant. You're brilliant. It worked perfectly. It would take us months to raise that sort of money from donations. When can we do it again?"

"You can't" says Joe. "It's just too risky. They'll be suspicious of any local cheques from now on, and they'll be particularly on the look-out for forged birth certificates and ID cards. Lansky will have the police checking the civil servants who arranged the false ID. No that was a one off."

It appears that Joe himself is not above suspicion. Meyer Lansky returns from Miami and is, as Norberto predicts, furious. "It's not the money," he says to anyone who will listen, "it's the principle. No one gets one over on Meyer Lansky." Joe is summoned to his office on the top floor of the Riviera and quizzed about what he knows. It's soon apparent that Lansky thinks the scam was a criminal job, but any local employees or employees with local connections like Joe are going to be watched.

Gambling on a double bluff Joe asks Lansky if it's not possible that the theft was politically motivated. Perhaps even organised by the rebels.

"Rebels" shouts Lansky, "Those two bit commie wierdos up in the hills. They couldn't steal rum from a distillery let alone rip off Meyer Lansky."

Jo pursues it. "But surely they must have supporters here in the city? It's quite wide spread the opposition isn't it?

"They're nothing. I was speaking to the president just the other day, and he told me they had no support to speak of. And anyway he's planning a big army operation this spring which will winkle them out of the hills once and for all."

"But what if they did overthrow President Batista?" Joe asks "Surely that would be pretty serious for you and the hotel business."

Lansky looks up sharply in amazement: "I though you were a bright kid" he says "But you sure 'aint being too bright at the moment. It doesn't matter a fig who's running the country here. Could be ex-president Socarras, could be Fulgencio Batista, could be Colonel Fermin Cowley or even Fidel bloody Castro himself. They're all going to need American support. They're all going to need American dollars, and they're all going to need American Tourists. And that's what I provide. And if there is any doubt about it I simply offer the new president or his supporters a cut off the tables or a bigger take from the slot machines. That's the real world. Not some starry-eyed pinko–inspired idea of a better, fairer society. Now this girl of yours. Local isn't she?"

Joe nods.

"Carmen liked her. Says she can be trusted."

Joe smiles to himself remembering the pains Maria had taken to disguise herself before walking in to the Monsignor with a colleague from the cigar factory, clutching her worthless cheque and forged ID.

"Get her to ask around. See if there's any word about who ripped me off. Someone must know. It was quite a well planned operation. Fact I would have been proud to have run a scam like that myself when I was younger."

Joe is working hard to conceal a smirk.

" Now, about Carmen" continues Lansky. She's got family down in a town called Trinidad on the south of the Island. Likes to visit them, hates trains and busses. Thought you might take her down. Get out of the city for a few days. See a bit of the island. You can stay in the Hotel Ronda. I'm told it's clean but nothing special. And there are a couple of errands you can run for me while you're down there. If your girl can get away you can take her too."

Joe reports back to Maria about Batista's planned offensive against the Sierra rebels, and asks her if she fancies a trip to Trinidad with Carmen.

"Can't do it" she says. "I can't just take time off from the factory like that. But you go. And be careful of Carmen. I think she fancies you a bit. I don't particularly mind if you screw her, but I don't think it would do your prospects with Lansky much good ."

Joe is fairly amazed and slightly shocked by this as he mulls it over later. Firstly he's never met anyone for whom sexual fidelity seems as unimportant as it does for Maria. He'd be pretty devastated if he found she was sleeping with another man. Secondly the idea that Carmen might fancy him, even a bit, is rather arousing. She is, after all, extremely beautiful. And extremely black. And black women have always featured in Joe's fantasies.

But as it turns out nothing immediately comes of the planned trip. It's not mentioned again and the round of odd jobs and driving around town continues. Under Maria's tuition Joe is now pretty fluent in Spanish even if his accent leaves something to be desired. In his spare time he's introduced to other M26/7 supporters or sympathisers, and even goes to a couple of low level political meetings at the university. One person he doesn't see again is Faure. "He left town" says Maria when asked, but wont be drawn on where he's gone.

One unexpected meeting is with Maria's mother Lydia. It's late at night. Maria, in Joe's bed, hears a noise from her room next door. She wakes Joe quietly and demands he go and see what it is. Conscious of the possible danger of secret police Joe takes his little automatic and pads naked across the room to the connecting door. There's no doubt there's someone in the room beyond. So he throws open the door enters swiftly moves to one side and pans the room with the gun in his outstretched arms. The trouble is it's so dark that Joe can hardly make out a thing. Then suddenly the overhead light is switched on temporarily blinding him. When he can see again there's a small middle-aged woman holding a revolver pointing at his head. They stare at each other down the barrels of their respective guns for a moment before she speaks:

"If I were Mae West I suppose I'd be asking you which one was the real gun" and she looks down at his penis hanging rather limply between his legs. From next door Maria shouts: "Lydia?" "Yes," replies the gunwoman, "it's me. There seems to be a man here pointing his piece at me."

Maria, also naked, and shaking with laughter comes through from the far room. "You can put the gun down Joe. And let me introduce you to my mother."

55

With surreal formality the naked man and the somewhat grubbily clothed woman lower their guns, advance to each other and shake hands. "Nice to meet you," says Joe. Next time you if you give us a little warning of your visit I'll make sure I'm better prepared."

As Maria reaches for a wrap and a bottle of Havana Club she sends Joe back to his room for shorts and to forage in Conchita's fridge for some ice. He assures Lydia she can talk freely in front of him and retells the story Joe's casino scam. Lydia responds with the latest news from the Sierra Maestra.

"It's like a complete village up there now. Che has organised a butcher's shop, a leather workshop and they've even started rolling their own cigars. They've got a printing press and are working on a radio transmitter. Whenever I'm there I'm in charge of baking bread. He's also started making uniforms for the rebels and the first thing he designed a new army cap. It was hilarious. Che proudly presented the first one to Fidel at a meeting of the *Commandantes*. Raul was there and Camilo and Juan Almeida. The thing is the cap looked exactly like a bus driver's cap and they all burst out laughing. Che was quite crestfallen. He ended up giving it away to the Mayor of Manzanillo who was visiting the camp."

"Isn't it dangerous to have all those facilities set up in one place?" asked Joe. "Surely it makes it an easy target for the army?"

"The army never goes up there any more. It doesn't dare. They send planes over all the time, but the village is well hidden under the trees. Che says part of the reason is to keep the morale of his troops up, but it's partly for the local *Gaujeros* who have now come over completely to our side. Che's done deals with them to buy their food and livestock at guaranteed prices so they have a proper income between the sugar harvests. They can also get their cigars and bread in the village. And he's started free medical sessions. They all bring their children along to see him when they are ill. But he says that most of the problems are due to bad diet not illness at all."

"What about the attack on Pino Del Agua?" asks Maria. "I heard it was only a half success."

"Well we captured more than 40 guns, took half a dozen prisoners and wiped out a complete patrol. But there was a disagreement between Fidel and Che over the attack. You remember those twenty-three rebels the army said had been killed last month in battle. Well it just wasn't true. They were prisoners. They were taken from jail in Santiago up into the foothills and massacred by the troops. Che was so angry he wanted to wipe out the whole army garrison at Pio. It started well enough. We overran the guard posts and killed the sentries, and we took out a patrol of reinforcements. But the troops rallied and held us up. Camillo was wounded trying to get to a captured machine gun. Che begged Fidel to let him go for an all out assault on the camp and set fire to it. Fidel sent two more platoons but he forbad Che from leading them into the battle himself. It was too dangerous he said and Che was too important to the cause to sacrifice himself in this fight. Well, Che said that he wasn't going to send his troops into a dangerous battle if he couldn't lead them. So they reluctantly agreed to withdraw the following morning."

"The newspaper said that Che had been wounded" said Maria.

"Not true. He wasn't hurt at all. And Camillo's wounds though quite bad were not life threatening. But the same newspaper reported that the army had five casualties as a result of "skirmishes". Well, we know we killed 18, and we think it may have been as high as 25. And what the paper didn't report was that next the army rounded up 13 peasants and just murdered them. They had nothing to do with the battle at all. They weren't even with the rebels. They were just innocent bystanders."

"So what are you doing here now?" asked Joe.

"I'm bringing copies of El Cuban Libre, the rebels' newspaper, to be distributed in the city with our account of the battle, and I've also got messages for some of the movement's leadership in Havana."

"And we've got a message for you take back to them," said Maria. Joe is working for Meyer Lansky who as you know is close to Batista. Well according to Lansky the army is preparing for a major assault on the Sierra later in the spring."

Joe leaves the two women sipping rum and reminiscing in Maria's dimly lit room and goes back to his bed. He sleepily realises another milestone has been passed. He's been taking part in discussions with two members of the underground movement about how to overthrow a Latin American government. And far from worrying him, he actually finds the experience rather exciting.

§§§§§

Next evening   Joe is delivering a package to one of Lansky's associates at the Hotel Nacional. It's a hot evening and the man is at the poolside bar sipping a Mojito. That unsurpassed evening light is bathing the city. Waiters scurry about with trays. Attractive American teenage girls flirt with college boys around the sun loungers. A late swimmer splashes in the water. A band is playing Cuban tunes. Palm trees sway in the breeze. Lights are coming on in that rapid tropical transition from day to night. And Joe gazes at this idyllic scene and thinks of Lydia up in the mountains baking bread for the rebels before going into battle beside them. He thinks of Batista's troops rounding up peasants and gunning them down. As he thinks of Che Guevera and Fidel Castro and Camilo Cienfuegos, grimy, sweaty, bearded, eating stewed goat round the camp-fire, he sees freshly shaven, newly showered tourists preparing to shovel down T-bone steaks and gather round the gaming tables before taking in the cabaret and dancing. Which, he asks himself, is the real world? And which does he really want to be part of?

Chapter 10

Joe is walking down the Rampa on a hot sunny morning with nothing much to do but look at the crowds gathering in the markets and the expensive American cars pulling out of the new brutalistic Hilton Hotel. He sees a poster on a billboard advertising a forthcoming *Gran Premio* race meeting and a list of international stars who will be in Cuba to take part. Among them is Britain's Sterling Moss and Argentina's Juan Manuel Fangio. A wild idea forms in his head which he mentions to Maria that evening. Again she says she must refer it to the local committee and promises an answer later that evening.

Joe is late back from the Casino, but Maria is still up, and there are two others with her. They like Joe's idea and think it could produce just the publicity coup they are seeking, but they're not sue how to bring it off.

The discussions carry on in to the night, and next day Joe seeks a meeting with Meyer Lansky.

"I noticed Juan Manuel Fangio will be in town at the end of the week" he says.

"Who the fuck's he?" asks Lansky.

"Probably the most famous racing driver in the world," says Joe. "I thought it might give you some useful publicity if you were to invite him to the Casino and give him couple of hundred bucks worth of chips on the house. He's a really big noise and the press will be following him everywhere. A decent endorsement from Fangio would be like gold. Plus I'd say just about everyone here would like to meet him."

Later, when Lansky has ascertained that Fangio is as big as Joe says he is, he agrees to the idea, gets an invitation typed out and has Joe deliver it to Fangio's agent who's already in town.

Thus it is that on the following Friday night Joe, in Lansky's Dodge, pulls up outside the Hilton and ushers the famous Argentine into the front seat. It's only a matter of half a mile or so from the Hilton to the Riviera, but Joe offers Fangio a quick look around the night time city. So they set off left down the Rampa and after another couple of lefts end up at the Capitol. Up to the Parque Central and over the Avenue Del Misiones the going is slow because of the evening crowds, but before they can cut out onto the Malecon the traffiic grinds to a halt altogether. A cart appears to have lost a wheel and its horse is beginning to panic.

"I know a short cut" says Joe, diving off left down a dark alley. Then: "damn there's a car blocking our way. We'll have to go back" But before he can engage reverse another car pulls into the alley, screeches to a stop behind the Dodge and four men get out carrying guns. Joe is out of the driver's door in a flash, reaching for his automatic. Before he can raise it he feels a blow to the side of his head. His gun fires into the air. He can feel blood tricking down his cheek. From the ground he sees Fangio escorted at gunpoint out of the Dodge and into the stationary car in front. One man peels off, jumps into the car behind and reverses swiftly back up the alley.

Joe picks himself up and walks back to the Avenue looking for a phone.

"So where is he now?" asks the police captain, clearly none too pleased that a major international celebrity appears to have been kidnapped from the centre of his city.

"So where the fuck is he now?" asks Lansky when Joe reports back. Joe gives the same reply he offered the policeman. "I've no idea. I just saw them bundle him into the back of a car. It didn't have its lights on. I couldn't see its number plate. I didn't even get a good look at the men, though I think they looked more Cuban than American."

"I sure hope so" says Lansky. "I sure don't want any rival mobs down here making like it's Chicago's south side in the 20s. Oh, and by the way, great publicity Joe. The man's lifted out of *my* car on the way to *my* Hotel while he's *my* guest. I'm seriously unimpressed."

"So where is he now?" Joe asks Maria that night as she bathes the superficial cut over his right temple.

"In a safe house drinking rum, eating steak and being fed revolutionary propaganda" she says. "It all went like clockwork. I'm proud of you. We've delivered the communiqué to the newspapers, and sent a briefing to all the international journalists in the city. It should be all over the front pages by tomorrow morning."

And indeed it is. Along with details of all the murders and atrocities that Batista's forces are alleged to have carried out. The communiqué demands a public renunciation of his methods from the president before the hostage is released.

The race is delayed in the hope the authorities can find the star driver. But there's no sign. When it does get underway a Cuban skids on a patch of oil, ploughs into the crowds killing four onlookers and injuring 50. When the Movement releases Fangio immediately afterwards, he's reported saying his kidnapping may have saved his life and he tells journalists that his captors had been friendly and his treatment warm and cordial.

Whether it's the Fangio fiasco, or whether Carmen's need to visit her relatives has become urgent Joe doesn't know. But the previously postponed trip is suddenly on again. Jake Lansky gives Joe his instructions. "I'd like you back within the week, but this is Carmen's trip so you'd better take your lead from her. And don't forget the army is everywhere so you can expect to get held up."

Joe is disappointed. It will mean missing the forthcoming Latin American Super Featherweight title fight in Havana between Joe Brown and the local champ "Babe" Echevarria. But there's nothing for it. Next morning Joe collects Carmen and two large suitcases from a small but elegant modern apartment out in Mirimar, Havana's newest residential area. Here Batista has had mechanical diggers carve out Florida-style marinas for the yacht and motor cruiser set. It's the sort of place where Hemmingway would feel at home, but has probably never visited.

Carmen seems pleased to see him, talking nineteen to the dozen, alternating between Spanish and English. She is wearing a loose flowery frock with buttons down the front that shows off her full figure.

They drive back along the Malecon and through the brand new tunnel that Batista has built to link the city with Casablanca and Cojimar and the miles of soft white sanded tourist beaches. But they turn off onto the ring road. Sign posts are few and far between. Outside the city centre the main traffic seems to consist of lumbering trucks belching out black fumes and horse pulled carts overloaded with sugar canes. Carmen relaxes and starts to quiz Joe about himself and what he's doing.

He tells her how restless he was after his national service. He didn't want to stay in the army. He wasn't very good with the discipline. But civilian life seemed dull. He'd hung around South London for a few months and then decide to blow his savings on a third class ticket across the Atlantic. New York had thrilled him. The sheer size and energy of the place, and the extraordinary mix of nationalities and races. He picked up some work down on the docks off the Hudson River where the liners berth, and rented a room on West 43rd street, down by the Port Authority building. It was at the southern end of Hells Kitchen, the very area where the musical West Side Story was set. But with winter coming on he decided to migrate south and was told work was easy to find in Florida. But what about Carmen? How had she got to know Lansky?

She explains she had been born in Cuban Trinidad. Her family had been in sugar for ever, first as slaves, then as planters, then overseers of the big plantations and then step by step as smallholders and finally land owners themselves. By the time it came to her father's generation they had 50 acres and were a fairly prosperous middle class family. "Though if you're black you can never really be middle class in Cuba."

"Is there really so much prejudice?" asked Joe.

"No, not like in America, but Cuba was a Spanish colony and the Blacks were slaves, brought over from Africa to cut the cane. And although the slaves were freed and Cuba got independence from Spain and all races were theoretically equal in the new Cuba, views remained entrenched."

"So who were your friends as a kid in Trinidad? Black, Spanish, Mulatto? "

"Well Trinidad is different from most other areas it's got a much higher black population than elsewhere. But at school I played with kids from all backgrounds. It's just that somehow the Spanish-white children always thought they were better than the rest of us. Even if they were dirt poor and we were better off."

"So why did you leave for Havana?"

"As you will see there's nothing in Trinidad apart from some pretty houses and a few tourists. The only opportunities for a girl is to find a husband and start breeding. And I fancied some adventure."

"So what were you doing in Havana when you met Lansky?"

Carmen doesn't answer immediately and her natural smile fades a little at the memories. "It's not that easy for a single black girl in Havana. Somehow the office and shop jobs go to others. I'd been there nearly a month and I was running out of money and I met this man who said he could find work for me as a dancer. Well, it was silly. I'd never had a dancing lesson in my life. But the sort of dancing he meant didn't require any experience except for what you do naturally last thing at night?"

"What's that?" says Joe naively.

"Getting undressed of course."

"Oh." Joe paused. "And did you do it?"

"Yes. I had no option. It was a bit of a shock at first. I mean I was brought up as a Catholic and had a pretty sheltered childhood. Nobody else had ever seen my body except my mother when I was a baby. And suddenly I was stripping off and parading myself before a room full of men every night."

"Did you hate it?"

"Funnily enough no. Once I'd got over the shyness I felt rather powerful. I mean there were all these men all fantasising about having sex with me. And there I was a few feet from them, showing off the very parts of myself they most wanted, and yet they couldn't have me. Couldn't touch me. I had control over them. But then I made a mistake."

"What was that".

"I fell for a man"

"That's so bad?"

"He was. He was the one who had introduced me to the night-club. He found me a room, and then started visiting me after the show. I was just a country girl and I thought he loved me and wanted me for myself. But once he'd had me ... and he was my first ... once I'd given myself to him I found he wanted me to go

63

with other men for money. It was awful. He kept on and on and on. And I was fixated on him and in the end I agreed. Well you can imagine the rest. Soon I was turning tricks for him every night after the show and he never made love to me himself. Just made me suck his dick occasionally. "

"And he kept all the money?" asked Joe.

"Yes, almost all. I had to beg him if I wanted anything, even sanitary towels or condoms."

"So how did you get away?"

"Sometimes my 'clients' used to take me back to their hotels after the show and one night after I'd fucked one of them I stopped at the bar for a beer before going home. And there were a couple of other working girls there obviously waiting for business. So I waited too and was amazed how quickly I got picked up. This American came in, looked round the bar, came straight up to me asked me how much. Half an hour later I was in the bar again and twenty minutes after that I was on my back under another humping Yank. But this time when I came down stairs the night manager of the Hotel wanted a chat. It seemed that I had to pay him a percentage to be allowed to operate there and give him a freebie every few days. But since I was getting the cash directly and could charge more in the hotel than in the club I was much better off. So the next night I left the show and my pimp and my room and started working the hotels."

The Dodge is now heading down highway A1 – the main tarmaced road that connects the West and East of the Island. Joe is starting to feel rather horny listening to Carmen's sexual history. The thought of her naked body parading on the stage or being humped by a succession of men has given him an erection. She herself has relaxed back into the comfortable seat and with the breeze whistling in from the window has undone the top and the bottom buttons on her dress. An innocent way to keep cool or a calculated come-on? Joe is unsure, but the result is an alluring depth of cleavage above and provocative glimpse of sexy black thigh below.

He remembers Maria's averred lack of jealousy but also her warning about interfering with Lasky's 'property'. But what's a red-blooded male to do? Surely it's up to Carmen. After all she's a big girl. And in all the right places.

"So is that how you met Lansky, in the bar?" he asks eventually.

"Yes, but not as a punter. He was bored one evening and simply wanted to talk. He bought me a couple of drinks and told me about his boyhood in Poland and on the Lower East side. In fact I lost a lot of money that night. Missed at least three tricks."

"So how did you er … get together ?" asked Joe.

"It was months later. We bumped into each other a couple of times. And then it seemed he actually came looking for me. And I told him I couldn't spend all evening talking because it was costing me money, and he pulled out $100 bill and said as a businessman he understood and he hoped that would cover my losses. Well, of course it was far more than I'd make in a week so I was happy to talk as long as he wanted. But to answer your question, we never did really get together until much later. He didn't seem to want sex much. One night when his wife was away he invited me up to his suite for a drink and said how he didn't much like sleeping alone. And I though, ok here we go. But he meant sleeping. He handed me a wrap and told me to put it on in the bathroom. When I came in he was in pyjamas, and he really did just want to cuddle. "

"All night?"

"All night. 'Course I tried to get him interested but he wasn't up for it"

"Literally." Laughed Joe.

Carmen laughed too.

"Sorry but I just can't imagine being in bed with you and not wanting to jump on top of you" says Joe.

"By the look of you you can't even be in the same car as me without wanting to jump me" says Carmen looking at Joe's crotch where the bulge is now quite evident. "I've always felt sorry for men. I mean it's so obvious when they want it. And they just don't seem to be able to control themselves."

"Yes it's hard" says Joe. And they both burst out laughing.

Joe risks a friendly pat on her thigh followed by a little squeeze. Innocent enough or a gentle come on? She would have to decide and make the next move. It's not long in coming.

Carmen slides over on the bench seat and puts her left arm round Joe's neck, resting her right hand lightly on his thigh. Slowly she starts massaging the nape of his neck while her other hand squeezes his thigh, tantalisingly close to his cock, but never quite touching it. "Just concentrate on your driving," she says.

This is easier said than done for the next moment she undoes two more buttons at the bottom of her dress and guides Joe's right hand between her legs. He explores upwards expecting to encounter a barrier of panties but finds instead his finger has slid straight into her sex. It's an electrifying moment. To know she's been sitting there for the past hour with no knickers. Available at any moment. He rubs his finger in and out of her and up and over her clitoris. She moans slightly and eases down in the seat, opening her legs to give him easier access. He moves his hand faster and faster and she comes quickly, head thrown back, eyes closed with a groan and a series of small shudders. Before he's even removed his hand, she's undoing his belt and unbuttoning his fly. Her hand delves beneath his pants and clasps firmly round his penis. Then she eases it out of its confinement and fondles it slowly. He's struggling to concentrate on the road ahead as her hand moves up and down. Just as he feels his orgasm rising he sees the roadblock ahead.

"No, stop," he pants "Soldiers…"

Chapter   11

Carmen looks up from her task and says "Oh shit". There's not time for Joe to get his wilting cock back into his pants, let alone to button his fly or do up his belt. Instead he pulls his shirt tails out and over his trousers to cover his crotch, and stands on the brakes. Carmen gets one bottom button of her dress done up, but then, surprisingly, undoes another top button. Her breasts are now all but revealed down to the nipples and it's clear that panties were not the only item of underwear she decided to forgo that morning.

The soldier looks round the inside of the car until his eyes light on the nearly exposed breasts. Then as if in the grip of a powerful magnet his gaze is held fixed.

"Where are you going," he stammers

"Trinidad," says Joe.

"Where have you come from?"

"Havana," says Joe.

"Why are you going to Trinidad?"

"It's our honeymoon" says Carmen to Joe's complete surprise. "We just got married yesterday".

"Will you get out of the car and open the trunk" says the soldier to Joe.

This is a decidedly unwelcome command. If Joe opens the door and stands up   nothing will stop his trousers falling to his ankles and exposing his now limp dick sticking out of his underpants. But Carmen is equal to the challenge. "It's OK honey" she says. "I'll show the nice soldier what we've got." And indeed revealing as much leg and cleavage as she can, she slides out of the car, walks right round the front to the side where the soldier is standing. Giving him her sexiest smile, she brushes past him and shimmies to the rear of the Dodge. As the soldier's eyes follow her, transfixed, Joe hastily readjusts his member and his trousers.

Clearly it's not every day this squaddie on road-block duty gets to stop and oggle a goddess like Carmen. And he's clearly in

67

no hurry to conclude the experience. He rummages around in the boot to little or no effect except to get Carmen to bend over in the hope perhaps that one or both breasts will finally break free of their slender bounds for his delectation. So Joe gets out and fumbles for a five dollar bill. It's a ludicrously large amount for a road-side bribe and he's fairly sure that one dollar would have served just as well. But he's in a hurry to get on, and hopes that Carmen will be in a hurry to get on with what she started a mile or so back.

The soldier has a momentary monetary tussle with his conscience, weighing up perhaps whether he might be able to find a half legitimate excuse to arrest the pair of them; hold them in separate cells; force the girl to strip for him and then and then have rampant sex with her for the rest of the day without being caught; court-martialled; cashiered; castrated and, in all probability, killed by his commanding officer. Against this is the certain knowledge of $5 which will buy him a box of cigars, a quart of Rum, a screw at the local brothel in Matanzas, as well as enabling him to give his wife enough extra cash to keep her off his back for a week. Sadly there's no contest. He pockets the greenback, closes the trunk, thanks the couple for their co-operation and risks the very slightest of caresses of Carmen's back-side as she walks back to the car. So slight that he can plausibly deny it ever happened, but firm enough to stoke his fantasies for the rest of the day. Sometimes a soldier's life is terribly hard he muses.

Joe and Carmen are giggling out loud as they drive off down the road. "Why did you tell him we were married and on our honeymoon?" asks Joe.

"Oh it just seemed like a good idea at the time," she replies. "After all if I hadn't been able to distract him and he had seen you waving your dick about in broad daylight he might have wondered what was going on. Anyway it got him thinking about sex, and that certainly distracted him."

"Distracted. He was almost paralysed by your tits. I though he was going to have a heart attack or cream his fatigues on the spot. You're really wicked do you know that?"

"The dirty bastard even copped a feel after you'd paid him off. By the way $5 was much much too much."

"I know, but I was a bit anxious to return to what we were doing before."

"What was that?" asks Carmen innocently, at the same time undoing a further button on her dress and finally releasing her wonderful breasts."

"Yes, now I can see what was making that soldier so horny" says Joe, his cock rising pleasingly again in his pants. What do you think he wanted you to do to him?"

"Oh something like this I expect ..." says Carmen, once again releasing the erection from its confines, but this time slowly lowering her head down towards it.

§§§§§

Once off the main road the going is much slower. The surface is uniformly appalling, other drivers have little or no concept of left or right, and animals roam at will across the tarmac. But it's a hot bright afternoon. The countryside is varied and attractive. The windows are down, the radio is on and Joe is sitting next to a beautiful and highly accomplished sexpot. There's a fleeting moment of concern as he thinks of Maria and then of Lansky, and wonders what he's got himself into, but it doesn't last long.

She warns him that, once in Trinidad, she'll have to spend most of the time with her family, but promises to find a few moments to show him the sights. She asks him about Maria, and what she would think if she knew what Joe was up to the moment he was out of her sight. He repeats what Maria said along with her caution that Lansky might not be so tolerant. "I think she's right," says Carmen thoughtfully. "He certainly is possessive but there's no reason he should know. And frankly a 50 year old man should expect a women 30 years younger to want more than a very occasional screw."

"Why does he keep you? And why do you stay?" asks Joe.

"I think he keeps me because he can. I'm a sort of trophy that he shows off to his friends and associates. It's a status thing. If you get to his position and don't have a mistress then people will think there's something wrong with you or you're queer. And why do I stay? Frankly it's a lot better to have a Lansky bother you a couple of times a month than it is to have to fuck two or three different men a night or to parade your pussy to a bunch of jerk-offs in the front row. I have a nice apartment and a small allowance. I'm doing a course in economics and history at the university. But it *is* lonely. I only have a couple of girl-friends and no men friends at all."

'Why not?"

"Cause all they want is to jump my bones"

"So?"

"That's not the deal. Lansky pays for me and I'm available exclusively for Lansky."

"Em what about what we just did?"

"That's different. We didn't fuck."

"You mean manual or oral is OK, but not intercourse?"

"That's about it?"

"Oh" says Joe in a disappointed voice.

"Come on" says Carmen. "You've got Maria whenever you *need* to go all the way. But I'll try to stop you getting too horny while you're away from her or at very least save you from having to do it yourself!"

She laughs, kisses him gently on the cheek and then sidles back across the seat to her side of the car and looks out of the window.

"Look. Sugar. Isn't it beautiful?"

Joe looks at the mile after mile of the tall thick bamboo like stems with their sparse green tops. "Not particularly," he says. Or at least not to my eyes".

"It what it represents" says Carmen. "It's Cuba's past, present and future. It's brought us all our prosperity and all our problems this stuff. Just over a hundred years ago we were largest sugar producer in the world. It was the sugar planters like Carlos

Manuel de Cespedes that first abolished slavery and first fought to liberate Cuba from Spain."

"Now some would say you're fighting to liberate Cuba from America."

"Yes, and that's because of sugar too. We let the US dominate the sugar market at the end of the last century. According to my father by 1890's we were the US's third largest trading partner in the world after you British and Germany. The trouble is that we let sugar become just about our *only* crop, and we've been increasingly dependant on the US ever since. Now US corporations own most of the sugar production and two thirds of the farm-land that grows the cane. It's a real struggle for independent sugar planters like my father to survive."

"So what would happen if the Americans pulled out and stopped importing sugar?"

"It would be a catastrophe. Cuba couldn't survive. Or at least not without opening up new markets very quickly. But why should America want to do that? It's not in their interests."

"They might see it as being in their interest if Cuba was communist," said Joe.

They had driven through Cienfuegos a lively looking city set on a bay, with ship yards and fishing boats lining the water front. Now, heading south-east, they are keeping the blue waters of the Caribbean to their right while inland the land rises from the flat central plain they'd crossed to the foothills of a range of low mountains, the Sierra de Escambray.

"Tell me about the history of this area" said Joe.

"Well Trinidad was one of the first three settlements on Cuba. That's to say Spanish settlements. There had been Indians here for a couple of thousand years before Columbus arrived. Did you know that Columbus got it completely wrong? He thought he'd discovered China, and that he'd be able to open up a trading route to India for Spain. A couple of people in his party disagreed and argued that Cuba was an island but Columbus wouldn't have it and threatened to kill them if they said anything when they were back in Spain. Anyway about 20 years later the Spanish returned with 300 troops and started to wipe out the local Indians. They were the first Conquistadors, but the trouble was there wasn't

71

much gold here. So they started farming. Mainly tobacco but also sugar which they'd brought with them. But farming needs lots of labour, and what with the policy of killing off the natives, and the fact that the Spanish had brought smallpox with them, there weren't enough locals to cultivate the land. So what do they do? They import muscle from Africa. And the first of our lot arrived in 1524.

"By then Trinidad was a thriving port, and market town. There was cattle ranching, tobacco farming, and sugar. Cortez used it as a base for his invasion of Mexico. But it was sugar that created the wealth. At one time there were more than 50 mills along the valley here and Trinidad produced a third of all Cuba's sugar."

Now they're driving along right next to the sea with golden sands stretching out before them. "Can we stop for a swim?" asks Joe. And they pull off the road to section of beach hidden by a line of shrubby trees. Joe strips naked and runs into the water, diving headlong into the lapping waves. Turning to float on his back he watches Carmen as she steps out of her dress and walks down to the water's edge. She has a classically beautiful body with large but firm breasts, thin waist, slender shapely legs and a well rounded behind. It's the first time Joe has seen a naked black woman apart from the shadows of the stage of the Shanghi, and the sight is intensely arousing.

They swim together for a while and then lie in the late afternoon sun on a rug from the car. After running his hand gently along her arm and over her stomach and licking the salt off her breasts Joe discovers she is serious about the no intercourse rule. But she takes pity on his bursting erection and slowly deals with him by hand.

Afterwards, side by side, looking out to sea with the sunlight glittering on the water Carmen asks Joe a favour. "My parents don't know about Lansky … or about my previous 'career' choices. They're a bit old fashioned about things like that. So I'd be grateful if you wouldn't mention them. As far as they are concerned I've been working as a waitress in various bars and restaurants in order to pay for my university studies".

"And who am I? Asks Joe, and how do I come to be driving a brand new expensive American car?"

Maria thinks for a moment, "I suppose you'd better be my new boyfriend. You work ... let's see, in a casino. It won't make you very popular with them but I don't suppose that matters much. And the car? Perhaps you've borrowed it. It's always best to tell the truth when possible," she says without any hint of irony.

Trinidad turns out to be charming, with a maze of narrow cobbled streets leading up to a church and square on top of the hill. The houses in the town centre are simple old Colonial–style, generally built out of wood, and never more than two stories high. They are set close to each other so the impression is of a terraced street. Carmen takes him on a quick tour of the town before directing him down onto Jesus Maria street to a substantial corner house, modest from the outside but, looking through the open door, Joe can see spacious high ceilinged rooms and furnishings that look like the inside of an antique shop. Carmen wants a bit of time alone with her family before Joe is introduced. So they arrange a rendezvous the following day, he deposits her suitcases in the hall, and drives off in search of his hotel.

§§§§§

Outside Havana and Santiago there's not much realisation that the Cuba is in the throes of a revolution. Actually, truth be told, there's not much realisation in the two major cities either. Everyone vaguely knows there is an underground opposition movement – but that's largely because, when you have a repressive totalitarian regime, any opposition has to be underground. And everybody knows that Fidel Castro is up in the mountains with his small band of armed revolutionaries. But if you told any Cuban that in less than a year they'd be in charge, you'd be laughed out of town. Funny that.

Revolution Cuba '58

PART 3

Spring

Chapter 12

Trinidad at night appears even lower wattage than Havana. There are no street lights at all outside the central area. And those that do exists confer only a shadowy glow on their immediate vicinity. Large numbers of youths inhabit the streets and instantly congregate round any visitor, offering rooms or directions to 'best restaurant in town". At first it's intimidating. Joe has left the car outside the windowless edifice that passes for a hotel and is walking vaguely in the direction of the main plaza by the church where he remembers seeing bars and eateries. But soon he finds the locals friendly especially once it's clear he can cope in their language. The town is teeming with life. Everyone it seems is on the street or on the porches of the houses that line them. There seems to be a folk music festival going on inside a large municipal building. He settles down at a bar next door and orders beer and food. The evening is warm, the atmosphere glorious. So why does he feel the glimmerings of dissatisfaction?

Here he is on a beautiful tropical island. Not yet 22 years old. A well paying if not overly respectable job. An exciting radical and tolerant girlfriend. An ex-prostitute companion. Cold beer. Succulent local fish. What more could he want? But suddenly Joe realises he's homesick. He laughs out loud to himself. Who in their right mind would be homesick for the damp gloom of Deptford in March when they could be in the balm of the Caribbean?

And then he recognises that it's not the place he's homesick for, but the people. His family. And even his father. They'd always had a rather rocky relationship. Frank is a man of decided opinions and intolerant of those that do not share them. All his life he's worked in the docks on the Isle of Dogs. The aristocracy of manual labour he calls it. He's always been a dedicated union man, often shop steward or branch secretary. Joe has listened interminably to his views on the evils of capitalism and the dignity of the working man. He also listened to his mother decrying the latest work to rule or picket or strike which for her will mean even less money with which to provide for her family.

On the one hand Joe is proud of his old man. On the other he's intensely irritated by his inflexible views. The introduction of the national health service was a disaster because it allowed doctors to work privately. National ownership of *all* the means of production must be in the hands of the people – run by worker's committees not boards of directors. There shouldn't be a *minimum* wage, there should be a *maximum* one based on the average earnings of manual labourers and no-one – businessman, lawyer, doctor, politician – should be allowed to exceed it. Grammar schools should be abolished and public schools razed to the ground and everyone should go to a technical college and be taught car mechanics and brick-laying. It went on and on and on.

It wasn't in any sense pure Marxism. Frank was a member of the CP but largely because the socialists were too wishey-washy for him. But *his* communism had nothing whatever to do with the Soviet Union or Eastern Block. It was no use saying look what's happening in Hungry or Czesclovakia, Frank would simply shrug and say what they do is their business I want to overthrow the system in England. Line up the toffs and send them down the mines. See how they like it. That's how we'll get rid of the class system.

Nothing Joe could ever say to him made a tuppeny-ha'penny worth of difference. "How about abolishing the *working class*?" he'd once suggested. "If we give everyone a good education and encourage everyone to try for a good white collar job and make houses cheap enough for people to buy, and encourage everyone to invest their savings in shares, then everyone will become middle-class eventually".

"Bloody bourgeois clap trap," shouted Frank. "If everyone's middle class who'll sweep the streets and collect the rubbish and run the sewage works? You'll end up having to import a whole lot of coloureds from abroad like they're talking about now to run the busses."

Joe smiles again at his father's unthinking racism. Not based on prejudice for the colour of people's skin. Indeed he'd fight tooth and nail if anyone in his union branch was discriminated against because of their skin colour. But Asians in Asia, Africans in Africa, West Indians in the W'indies, the English in England. That's how he saw the world. Even the odd Taffy, Paddy or Jock that appeared down the docks was looked on with some suspicion. Certainly the Irish had no business being out of Ireland. No business at all. Indeed intercourse between countries at any level seems an anathema to him. What do we need to import all this stuff for? We can grow most of it at home and if we have to do without bananas then we'll do without bloody bananas. Britain should be self sufficient. It was as if Adam Smith had never existed.

Frank was always uncertain of how to deal with Joe. He taught him to box and was proud that he excelled in a working class sport. But he couldn't understand why Joe so wanted to go to a grammar school when he passed his eleven plus. His older son, Joe's brother Frankie, had done perfectly well at the secondary mod, had left at 15 and had followed his father into the docks. It was only the intervention and absolute determination of the boys' mother that Joe should have the best education possible that finally persuaded Frank that the battle wasn't worth the candle. And in a curious way he was proud when Joe passed his exams and stayed on into the sixth form.

'It's all right as long as you don't go off to some namby-pamby university. They should be abolished, the lot of them," he tells Joe and anyone who will listen over a beer down the Rose and Crown one Sunday lunchtime. But even with the possibility of a full grant, Joe can't see how college can be afforded and instead of deferring his national service, he signs up as soon as the summer term ends.

But for every irritating memory of Frank there's a happy one. Playing football on Hilly Fields. Walking down by the river at Greenwich. Pointing out the cranes and derricks that load the barges, and then across the muddy Thames to the docks where Frank works with the big cargo ships that carry the goods around the world, imports and exports that has put the 'Great' in Britain. Though as Joe grows older he forbears to mention how at variance is the international trade that gives Frank his living with his world view of splendid isolation.

§§§§§

Carmen's father Rodriguez turns out to have decided views as well, though somewhat opposite to Frank's.

They are sitting round an elegant oak dining table in the Colonial house on Jesus Maria street the following evening. Carmen has met Joe in town in the morning and passed on the invitation. Her father is a big man. Well over six feet and broad with it. Probably only in his mid-40's he looks much older. What hair he has left is curly grey. He and the rest of the family are immaculately dressed. A servant brings in food that has clearly been prepared by a cook. Grace is said. Polite questions are asked about Joe's background and family and job at the casino which he's able mostly to answer truthfully. In turn he asks about sugar planting and the season and the workforce. He learns that there is a large population of *Guajiros* – peasant small holders – who work in the cane fields for a couple of months a year particularly during the harvest when the cut cane has to be transported to the mills within 48 hours to stop it fermenting in the tropical heat. The rest of the time the *Guajiros* are subsistence farmers, generally on unproductive hilly land that they have no rights to.

Rodriguez is not a fan of trades unions. Each year, he tells Joe, the planter must assess the quality of the crop and anticipate the likely price he can get for it. Then and only then can he work out how much he can afford to offer his workers. If the workers were organised and collectively bargained for a standard wage it would be holding the planter to ransom. The planter might then go out of business and the worker would be the one to suffer. To Joe it sounds rather simplistic free market thinking.

"Doesn't that give the planter huge power over the workforce" asks Joe. "The natural incentive will always be to pay as little as possible and to maximise profits. And that means that the *Guajiros* will always be on the poverty line."

"They have the freedom to take their labour elsewhere, or indeed not to work at all if they don't think the rewards are sufficient."

In other words the freedom to starve themselves and their families since there *is* no other work to go to thinks Joe to himself. "What determines the market price of sugar?" he finally asks.

"It's set in Chicago in the commodities market there. Traders assess demand and supply and fix a price. It's fairly stable unless something untoward happens. If a hurricane wipes out part of the crop there'll be an undersupply and so the price will rise."

"What would happen if, say, the Cuban government bought all the sugar produced on the island at a fixed price so the planter and the worker knew exactly what they could expect, and then the government released the sugar onto the US market at the most beneficial price. In other words if all the planters worked co-operatively instead of competitively and you had some central planning?'

"That sounds damn near communism" says Rodriguez. "It would be a disaster. It would skew the market and eventually the US would look elsewhere for its sugar. Somewhere where there would be real competition driving prices down.

"But what I don't understand" says Joe "is where this freedom lies for you in the present system. You have the freedom to pay your workers the lowest wage you can get away with. And you have the freedom to invest or not invest in new machinery. But you don't have the freedom to determine the price you sell at. There is only one market out there. As you've already said, the price is set by the US commodities traders. Yes theoretically you could seek new markets in Europe or Asia, but that's a bit like telling the *Guajiro* he can take his labour elsewhere. In the short term there really isn't anywhere else for you, or for him, to go."

Rodriguez doesn't answer immediately. He looks Joe up and down, "I have to say, son, I just don't agree with you. If it's free market versus central planning give me the free market every time. Now, enough of this shop talk over dinner. Let's adjourn out onto the porch for a brandy and cigar, and we'll rejoin the ladies a little later."

There's an almost audible sigh of relief from Carmen that serious political disagreement between Joe and her father has, for the moment, been avoided. And she seems far less surprised than Joe that the old fashioned English habit of the sexes separating after dinner seems to be alive and well in Southern Cuba.

Outside a box of fine Cohiba's is produced and the ceremony of sniffing, crinkling, cutting and lighting takes place. Joe is not a big fan of cigars. He never really took to cigarettes. Perhaps the smell of his father's habitual Old Holborn roll-ups or, on special occasions, green-packeted Woodbines put him off. But he likes the smell of a good Cuban cigar even if after half an hour's puffing his mouth feels numb and tastes like he's been chewing a pair of three day old socks.

Rodriguez steers the conversation back onto Joe's prospects and ambitions which, since he has none in particular, is not an easy subject to maintain for long. He's asked how long he's been 'going out with my daughter'. He seizes on the 10th of December when he first met her at the opening of the Riviera. Then her father beats around the bush a bit, reminding Joe that the family is Catholic, and that Catholics have very firm views about things like sex before marriage. Clearly he can't bring himself to actually ask if this Englishman has honourable intentions but that's what he's driving at.

To divert the subject Joe asks about the 'cultural' mix of the local population hoping not to give offence by speaking directly of race. But Rodriguez seems to think Joe is as asking if he'd mind a white boy marrying his black daughter."

"Cuba's a funny country" says Rodriguez. My forbears are from Africa. And yet here I am a catholic with an old Spanish name. Almost anywhere else in the Caribbean if you have black skin you are in the majority. Your father or grandfather may have been a slave but now it's by and large your land. In Cuba we haven't been slaves for hundreds of years but we are the minority and it's certainly not our land. There are three classes here. White Spanish, Black African-Caribbean, and the mixed race that's the result of the first two groups intermingling over the years. But the blacks generally remain the lower class citizens. People like us are OK. We've got money and a position. But generally you'd prefer not to be black in Cuba. So to go back to your question how would I feel about my daughter marrying a white boy ... the answer has to be that while I'm proud of my heritage and background, for her it would mean greater acceptability, and for my grandchildren greater integration into Cuban society."

Joe is lost for words. He wasn't in any way asking how the planter would feel about him marrying his daughter, but he couldn't exactly tell him that. The image comes to him of Lansky and Maria listening in to the conversation. Or Carmen waiting for business in a hotel bar. It's amazing how demure she looks here in front of her family. Just like a good little Catholic girl waiting for her wedding night to lose her virginity. If he father had any idea of what she'd been doing to Joe in the car yesterday .... Unwelcome carnal images are floating into Joe's mind. Another change of subject seems to be in order. He sips his brandy – imported from France like the wine at dinner he noted - and wafts cigar smoke around his head.

"Tell me about the rebels. Are they strong round here? Do you think they'll ever overthrow the president?"

"Pah. That bunch of bearded half-wits" sneers Rodriguez. "All they do is make trouble for us all. "They create instability and instability is bad for business. It makes the US nervous, and it makes the markets nervous. There's 60,000 troops in the army and what, 100 or at most 200 rebels. They haven't a hope. Not a hope."

"They've done surprisingly well so far haven't they?" asks Joe. "The army hasn't been able to wipe them out in over a year. They've got American journalists and TV crews visiting their camp every other week and sending back glowing stories about how Castro's so great and how the government's so corrupt. And what about support in the cities? The July 26 Movement seems to have branches everywhere, they even kidnapped Fangio in Havana last week and then released him."

"Yes that was a pretty stupid stunt" says Rodriguez. Whoever dreamed that one up ought to be shot. It may look different in the city. But down here there's no support for the rebels. I personally think some of President Batista's men go a bit

81

too far, but the only way to stop terrorism is to stamp it out straight away. And if that means stringing a few people up by their balls to discourage the others, then so be it. And anyway can you really see the US allowing a bunch of communist thugs to take over a near neighbour and important trading partner?"

"At the moment I don't think Washington has any idea of whether Castro and Ceinfuegos and even for that matter Guevara, are capitalists, liberals, socialists or communists. In fact from what I hear I'm not sure if the rebels themselves know." says Joe.

"What makes you think that?"

"Well Castro seems to have been very careful to distance himself from the *Partido Socialista Popular* – the communist party. "

"But what about the letters the rebel Amando Hart was carrying when he was arrested last month?" says Rodriguez. "I heard on the radio that they proved the whole rebel movement was communist inspired."

"Hmm. I'm not sure you should believe everything you hear on the radio. It's not exactly impartial. I've no idea personally what sort of government Fidel Castro might be planning, but I do think he has a lot more support than many people imagine and I also think that your president has an uncanny knack of shooting himself in the foot. Whenever it looks as if he's winning the propaganda war, his troops go and shoot up another bunch of people. Amazingly no soldiers are hurt, but the locals are all killed, leaving no wounded, no prisoners and no witnesses. And people then tend to believe the rebels' version of events that it was a massacre of innocent people dressed up to look like a legitimate fight against terrorists."

"Are you two still arguing about politics" says Carmen coming out onto the porch and sitting down next to Joe. "For heavens sake it's a lovely night. Let's speak of something more agreeable. Joe, I've never asked, do you ride?"

"A bit" he replies. "I had a few lessons when I was a kid on holiday down in Kent. But I've never ridden a Western saddle like you use here."

"You mean you do the rising trot rather than the ball-crusher" laughs Carmen.

"Daughter, watch your language" scolds Rodriguez only half seriously.

"Well how about coming riding with us tomorrow. Dad's going to take me up the valley to look at this year's crop. Do you want to come along. That would be OK wouldn't it she asks her father?

"Yes, join us. But I warn you you'll be pretty sore by the end of the day if you're not used to riding. It may be the two of you will want to turn back early by yourselves. Meet here at 9.00 tomorrow morning?"

Chapter 13

The valley they ride up the following morning is glorious. Much of the countryside on the journey from Havana to Trinidad had been scrubland. Low and flat and dull. But the *Valle De Los Ingenious* is fertile and green. Trees line the northern slopes as they rise up into the Escrambray hills. A dirt road follows the river along the valley floor, and to the south lies the cultivated acres of sugar cane alternating with grassland and grazing cattle.

"It all used to be sugar at the end of the 19th century," said Rodriguez, "but so much was destroyed in the wars for independence that the big plantations moved away to Cienfuegos and Mantanzas Province."

An army patrol in an ancient open back truck lumbers up the dirt road and stops the three riders. The sergeant takes Rodriguez aside and speaks urgently to him.

"He says to be on the look out for rebels in the area" Rodriguez reports back. "Apparently a splinter group has formed in these hills. The garrison here is small and they don't have the resources to search them out. Once you get up into the mountains there are no roads but trails known only to the *Guajiros*. Personally I think he's exaggerating. Why would rebels want to come here?"

Precisely because the Sierras are so impenetrable thinks Joe, and remembers back to his time in Cyprus when he was the one in uniform, searching out groups of rebels in the Troodos mountains. Highly mobile men on foot or horseback are almost impossible to track down once they leave established roads. An army platoon crashing through the undergrowth not knowing where it is going makes an easy target. Mind you a troop truck crawling up a valley is not that difficult to hit if you know what you are doing.

They continue their inspection of Rodriguez's plantation. One sugar cane looks much like another to Joe so he's pleased when they stop at an overseer's hut for an early lunch. Rodriguez is reluctant to let the couple go off on their own after the

Sergeant's warning but Carmen pleads with her father, pointing out that she probably knows the hills better than any rebels and, anyway, she has Joe to protect her.

So, after lunch, they part company and Carmen leads Joe up a steep trail heading into the Sierra foothills. After a while they pause and look back through a clearing. The valley is laid out below them, and beyond across the cane fields he can see the Caribbean glittering blue in the distance. To the right they can just see the tower of the church in the Plaza Mayor in Trinidad.

"It's beautiful here" says Joe, "why did you ever want to leave to go to Havana".

"It's beautiful but boring. Nothing ever happens. All anybody talks about is sugar or cattle. The whole area is caught in some sort of time warp. If I stayed they'd have married me off to the son of some other planter and I'd be bringing up a hoard of children with my life half over. You saw what my father was like with you last night. Every man of an even vaguely eligible age is immediately sized up as husband material. I may not have made great choices in the city, but I have certainly seen sides of life that just don't exist here. And now I'm at the university I'm actually using my mind for the first time."

The trail rounds a bend and, through another gap in the trees, they find themselves looking directly down to the valley a hundred or so meters below. The army truck is making its way back down the hill, with troops holding rifles at the ready standing in the back. Suddenly shots ring out and the soldiers return fire randomly, not knowing where the attack is coming from. Then, from both sides of the road, armed men appear, perhaps five in all, and start firing directly at the truck. The driver has the presence of mind to accelerate and since he's heading down hill, the vehicle gathers speed and rushes past them.

The action is over almost before it's started. "What a shambles" says Joe. They broke the most elementary rule in the book. They set up the ambush on opposite sides of the road, so once the target had passed they were shooting at each other."

"Yes," said Carmen. But it does prove the Sergeant was right and that there is a rebel group operating here. It's about the most exciting thing that's happened in Trinidad for a century."

They ride on, now heading away from the main valley, following a little stream that flows down towards the larger river. After 10 minutes or so Joe can hear the sound of rushing water ahead and, as they emerge into a clearing, he sees a high waterfall pouring down from a sheer cliff face above.

"This was always my favourite secret place" says Carmen. "I used to come here all the time as a child and let the water splash down over me."

"Well, come on. You can do it again now" says Joe. And he dismounts with some relief, walking bandy legged for a few steps till his body adjusts.

He ties up his horse, goes over to Carmen, still mounted, and holds out his arms to catch her as he swings a leg over the pommel and jumps down. Once in his arms he holds her for a moment and then kisses her full on the lips. It's the first time they've kissed, despite their intimacies in the car two days before and, thinks Joe, it's a wholly pleasurable experience.

Horses secured, they walk through the clearing to the base of the waterfall. It's only a thin stream of water,, but falling from a considerable height. It's hot, even under the partial shade of the trees, and Joe strips off shirt, boots. trousers and pants and moves straight into the cool shower. Carmen undresses more slowly. She's wearing a loose white linen shirt which, when removed, reveals a white bra which, if possible, serves to enhance her breasts. She shakes off her riding boots and slowly pulls down her jeans. Now in only bra and pants she turns towards Joe. The memory of the recent kiss and the slow strip has teased him as she intended. And despite the cool water cascading over him, his penis is on the rise. Buy the time Carmen has removed bra and pants and joined him under the waterfall it's fully perpendicular.

"Can't you control yourself at all?" she laughs.

"It's entirely your fault" he replies. If you didn't have such a delicious body I would remain quite limp."

"I don't think it's got anything to do with me" she says. "Any naked woman would do just as well. I just think you're a horny bastard."

They embrace under the cascade, gliding hands over wet backs and arms and breasts and buttocks. They're standing on a flat rock and Joe lays her down just away from the main stream of water, but with spray splashing over them. He kneels at her feet and parts her knees. He licks the water off her calves and thighs, moving his head ever nearer the focus of his desire. She moans gently to signal acceptance and puts her hand on the back of his head, drawing him more firmly to her.

Later, they lie beside the waterfall on a blanket unrolled from a saddle. In the warm sun they sleep in each other's arms, contrasting black and white naked bodies laid out in the clearing. And that's how the rebel soldiers find them as they move back into the hills after their unsuccessful ambush of the army patrol. Had the horses whinnied as they approached the clearing Joe or Carmen might have stirred or woken, but the animals made no sound. The four men were able to walk right up to the sleeping couple, and, suppressing laughter, to surround them. It may be that they would have liked to gaze on Carmen's naked form longer, but they had pressing business. And with guns pointed, one loudly cleared his throat, waking the sleepers with a start.

There's nothing like the experience of a slow awakening from a post orgasmic doze in the warm afternoon sun and looking round to see a canopy of leaves and the soft spray of a waterfall nearby. And this, for Joe and Carmen, was certainly nothing like that experience. Instead of a canopy of leaves and the soft spray, the first thing they saw were the barrels of four rifles pointed at them, each held by a desperate looking and decidedly unshaven man in a grubby approximation of battle fatigues.

"Wake up sleeping beauties" said one of them. "We need your horses and your help. We've a man wounded down the trail and we've got to get him up to our camp. "

Carmen was the first to respond. Unabashed and unashamed she rose slowly and looked with amusement at the men ogling her body. She said simply "Well give us a moment to get dressed and we'll see what we can do". Realising, perhaps somewhat belatedly, that it's rude to stare, the men averted their eyes and their guns while she donned her clothes. Joe reached for his pants and jeans and asked: "How badly wounded is he. How far to the camp is it, and why didn't you simply take the horses while we were asleep"

"Erm, we're not too sure exactly where we are" said the spokesman in some embarrassment. We need you to help us out of here. All these trails look alike, and we came in much further up the valley. Our comrade is shot in the leg and so can't walk. He's lost a lot of blood and is quite weak, but the wound looks clean so he will probably survive. I think we are about two hours march from the camp but it's hard to be sure."

Joe looked at the position of the sun and did some quick calculations. Say half an hour to pick up the wounded man from wherever they'd left him below, half an hour back, and then two hours up country. It would be growing dark as they arrived, and there'd be no question of getting back to Trinidad that night.

"What's your father going to think if we don't show up tonight?" Joe asked in English.

"Go spare and call out the Army, the police, the national guard and every *Guajiro* he can find for ten miles around." She replied in the same language.

"That's what I thought. I think we'd better arrange for you to go back alone once you've pointed us in the right direction." She nodded her assent.

"Right said Joe in Spanish to the rebel soldier." We'll help on one condition."

"You are not in much of a position to make conditions" he relied fingering the bolt on the rifle."

"Except that if my girlfriend isn't at home with her father this evening, by tomorrow these hills will be alive with the sound of the biggest army operation since the last war of independence. He's a personal fiend of the governor of Sancti Spritus province, and had dinner two nights ago with Colonel Cowley" he said utterly untruthfully, but naming the most vicious and most feared of Batista's henchmen. "Plus since we know these trails and you don't there would be nothing to stop us going round in circles until your companion bleeds to death and we've stumbled on an army patrol. What I propose is this. We take both horses and collect the wounded man. Then my girl will set us off on the right trail to your camp. Then you will allow her to return home on her horse. I will stay with you as a hostage, and tomorrow or the next day will return to Trinidad with my horse. But I want your word as a man of honour that you'll keep your side of the agreement."

The rebels looked at each other then nodded briefly. "You have my word" said the spokesman.

It took less time to get down the trail to where they had left their wounded companion than anticipated. He was not in good shape. The bullet had severed a fairly major blood vessel and he was still bleeding profusely, with his trousers and a shirt one of them had wrapped round the wound dripping with blood.

"We have to stop the bleeding before we move him" said Joe, summoning up the little knowledge of battlefield first aid he'd got from his National Service training.

The blanket that had so recently served as a bed for the naked couple was now torn into strips. With a borrowed knife Joe cut away the man's sodden trousers and saw, with satisfaction, an exit as well as entry wound. He wrapped layer after layer of blanket round the leg and they heaved him up onto Joe's horse. Faint from loss of blood it was touch and go whether he be able to hang on, but he grabbed the pommel of the saddle as tightly as he could and they set off back up the trail. Carmen had ascertained from the men whereabouts in the mountains they were heading and soon she led them out above the tree line and pointed them in the right direction, outlining which landmarks to head for and which to avoid.

"How are you going to explain my absence and the loss of the horse" asked Joe as Carmen turned to go.

"I don't know. I'll think of something. Look after yourself, and don't get brainwashed into joining them. They're a very smelly bunch" she said, "and I don't think you'd get much sex in the mountains unless you like goats or men".

She turned and was soon out of site heading back down the trail, while Joe walked beside his horse towards the revolution.

Chapter 14

If Joe was unused to riding, he was certainly unused to walking. The trail was steep and dusty. The sun was hot and dry. Joe could feel his feet starting to blister. But the scenery was impressive. As they zigzagged upwards he could see the coastline spread out behind and the peaks of the low mountains looming above. The rebels kept up a stiff pace, not speaking much, occasionally passing a water canteen between them. From time to time they passed evidence of habitation. Low huts made from wood and mud, roofed with palm fronds. It seemed a pretty remote place to live Joe thought.

Once over the peak of the hill they'd been climbing the going became easier as they headed downwards again along a high valley between two distant hills. Occasionally now they were in shadow as the sun began to disappear below the western peak. They'd been walking for the best part of two hours and the men now seemed confident they knew where they were going.

"How much further?" asked Joe.

"About another mile or two" said their leader.

And sure enough within twenty minutes they left the trail they been following and set off up a steep ravine to their left. Even the horse found it tough under hoof, and the wounded man who had been slumped forward in the saddle at best semi-conscious now grunted in pain and lifted his head to see what was happening. A few moments later they were just about to enter a large grove of trees when a man armed with a rifle rose in front of them. "Stop" he commanded and then, seeing who it was, said "OK come on. What happened? Who's hurt?

They took the wounded man to the centre of a clearing under the trees where a camp fire was burning, and bundled him off the horse. Other men emerged from the shadows and undergrowth round about and ran forward to help or quiz the party.

Joe felt a bit redundant so he sat down near the fire, resting after the arduous walk, and removed his shoes to see what damage he'd done to his feet. When he left Havana he hadn't been expecting either to go horse-riding or to find himself hiking up in the sierras and so he was wearing only a fairly flimsy pair of baseball boots.

As he looked around he could see evidence of a sloppy military encampment. There was one simple *Guajiro* hut like the ones he'd seen on the trail which seemed to serve as the headquarters . A number of small tents were pitched round the outside of the clearing interspersed with sleeping bags or blankets laid out on the ground. There were rucksacks or kit-bags lying around. String tied between two trunks bowed under the weight of drying clothes. An animal carcass - a sheep or a goat, was being spit-roasted over the fire. A few rifles were in evidence. A group of perhaps ten men had gathered round the new arrivals and were now examining or offering advice to those examining the wounded man.

"Joe? Joe Lyons? What the fuck are you doing here?"

Joe looked up to see a vaguely familiar face peering out from behind a wispy beard. For a moment, out of context, the man was impossible to place.

"I can't offer you iced tea today I'm afraid. But we've got some locally grown coffee which is not too disgusting if you drink it quickly and hold you nose. But how *did* you get here? And why."

"Basically I walked" said Joe, "because your men commandeered my horse after they succeeded in shooting each other while making pig's ear of an elementary ambush. But more to the point, what's the renowned student leader and attacker of presidential palaces Faure Chomon doing up here in the hills? I thought you were a city type?"

"Well, the money you helped to liberate from the casinos was enough to get me to Miami to collect a group of exiled comrades and bring them back with a few guns to join this group here. Actually almost all of us are graduates of the *Directorio Revolucionario* - the armed student faction of the July 26 Movement. We're beginning to think that Castro might be right and that the revolution is going to have to come from the peasants and not the intelligentsia, from the mountains and not the cities. But you still haven't explained what you were doing riding about the hills like some plantation overseer?

"Oh not the overseer, the plantation owner, " said Joe. "I'm escorting his daughter who is a friend of Mayer Lansky's. We were out for a little ride when your lot came on us"

"So you are still working for the mob then?"

"Sadly there's not much evidence of the mob in the Riviera casino. I hardly ever get to rub anyone out, and fresh concrete boots are in short supply in Cuba."

The two smile at each other. Faure gives Joe a guided tour of the camp and introduces him to the local leader Eloy Gutierrez Menoyo, and an American ex-marine with the pleasingly piratical name of William Morgan. Joe and he are relieved to be able to communicate in their native English .

"I've been down here for five months or so" says Morgan. It's not such a bad life. Enough to eat. Lovely scenery. A good cause. But we are desperately short of guns and they are not too hot on tactics,"

"I'll say they're not" replies Joe. They tried to ambush the patrol tuck as it was going down hill, positioned on either side so they were always in danger of getting caught in their own cross-fire. In fact I'm pretty sure that's how your man got hit. From what I could see the army troops were firing in completely the wrong direction."

"What would you have done?"

"Well for a start they should have tried to attack when the truck was going up-hill, preferably at the steepest, narrowest point. Then at least it will be going slowly and you should be able to get a few shots in before they can drive off. Secondly if you are short of ammunition you need to target the front and forget about the guys on the back. One or two shots through the windscreen is quite likely to make the truck crash even if you don't actually hit the driver. Plus you're more likely to get the radiator or something in the engine which will force them to stop. Obviously you keep everyone on the same side of the road to avoid friendly fire, but I would have had one person, preferably my best shot, separate, up in the rocks above or ahead to give covering fire and distract the guards."

"You seem to know a bit about it" said Morgan.

"Yes, but from the other side. In Cyprus the British were the saps in the trucks. So we were taught a great deal about when we would be most vulnerable. The slower you go the more exposed you are. If you're actually forced to stop you're sitting ducks. Really that's what your guys should have done this morning if they'd had time to prepare. Get some decent obstruction – a tree or a large rock - onto the track just round a blind bend. The truck has to stop. Half your force is ahead and half to the back. Whichever way the troops run you've got them covered. And if you're lucky you might even manage to capture the truck as well as some guns."

"What would we want a truck for? You may not have noticed but the roads are a trifle narrow hereabouts."

"Not here, down there. Drive it off the road, cover it up. Take the distributor cap with you so even if they do come across it they can't move it. Then you've got some transport when you need it later. Because it's an army truck it won't immediately arouse suspicion so you can take it right up to a road block or barracks, and it will help you get away if you need to leave in a hurry."

"You fancy a new job? " asks Faure who's been listening and following some of their English conversation. We could always do with some new tactical thinking?"

"No I'm not a soldier anymore" says Joe. "I'll gladly offer advice if I can, but this isn't my fight and I'm staying out of it."

"Actually you might be able to help without getting directly involved " says Menoyo. We have been planning an assault on the local barracks but it's too well guarded most of the time. What we need is to get most of the soldiers out on patrol at the same moment and then we might have a chance of going in. We have people wanting to join us but we don't have enough guns for them. We have to capture more rifles from the armoury at the barracks."

As night falls they settle round the fire and plan the operation. The barracks is at a small settlement named Manacaslznaga about five miles out of Trinidad on the road to Sancti Spiritus. It has about 50 troops stationed there who habitually patrol in platoons of ten or twelve usually with two vehicles.

"So it's divide and rule" says Joe. You have to get patrols going off in two different directions, and then you have to find a major distraction at the barracks itself to divert attention from you goal which is the armoury. Of course one problem with the plan is that most of the guns will be out with the troops".

"We can live with that" says Faure. "We need the ammunition most of all and any rifles will be a bonus.

§§§§§

Joe is lying on a borrowed blanket looking up at the stars. It's a cloudless night and with no lights for miles around the layers of light come drifting through his vision. What other life forms and civilisations are out there, scattered among the planets and galaxies? How many of them are fighting for freedom against their own oppression? Joe remembers how later in the evening Faure had questioned his assertion that this was not *his* country, and not *his* fight. "It's everybody's fight. It's everybody's business. If you stand idly by and watch as your fellow humans torture rape and murder it makes you complicit. You cannot have a civilisation unless it's based on the rule of law. And if you allow a dictator like Batista to set aside the law and let his henchmen brutally oppress the population without doing anything about it. It makes you as bad as them."

"No it doesn't" Joe had argued, "If the army took control in England and started doing what Batista is doing here then, yes, I would feel the need to oppose it. But I wouldn't expect you, as a visiting Cuban in London to have to join in. Not your country. Not your fight."

"It's my world and oppression is oppression wherever it rears its head. Yes I may not have such a strong personal interest in it, but if I knew people who lived there – people like Maria or her mother – then I would have that personal connection and I would think it my business to join the resistance. "

"Ah but you're an idealist and I'm a pragmatist" says Joe. "I don't want to risk being killed or having my balls crushed or my fingernails removed. I want a long and happy life and to die an old man in my bed."

"How much happier a life reflecting, as you lie on that deathbed whenever it may be, that you have achieved something really worthwhile in your lifetime. That you have made a difference. That you have done the right thing. That people are better off as a result of you. It may be that, like this ant here, you are only one in a vast colony of people working together to towards that goal. But it is your duty as a human being to push towards that ideal."

"And what of the other innocent people you hurt along the way in your revolution? The civilians killed by reprisals for your actions against the state? The people killed in the crossfire of your gunfights? The soldiers just doing a job, blown up, ambushed, shot. They're human beings too. They have a right to life. They have wives, mothers, sons, daughters who will grieve their death."

"Soldiers who support a corrupt regime that murders and tortures the population have no rights. No rights at all. And when you sign on as a soldier you know the risk you are taking. It may be slightly different for a conscript, but not for a paid army. Anyway, tell me" said Faure changing the subject, "have you ever killed anyone?"

"Yes" Joe had said. "In Cyprus. You know the Greeks were fighting for an end to British rule of the island. I don't think Britain was as corrupt a ruler as Batista, or even the Spanish when they ruled Cuba, but Cyprus wasn't our country and I had a lot of sympathy for the Greek independence movement. The trouble was that it was indiscriminate about who its targets were. They killed a Turkish police officer in Paphos, no doubt justifying it in the same way that you justify killing Batista's troops. And Britain thought 'hang on we can't have these Greek chappies going around bumping off the Turks just because they're working for us.' So they brought in a new bunch of soldiers and sent us up into the mountains to round up the EOKA rebels. So there am I, doing my national service ... a conscript, suddenly flown in to a conflict that was nothing to do with me and where my sympathies were by and large for the other side. And it all changed. The training takes over. They go on and on and on about how dangerous it is patrolling in the mountains, and how the guerrillas are just itching to kill you. And so when you meet one face to face you don't think about it. You pull the trigger first."

"And that's what happened. You pulled the trigger first."

"Essentially. But it wasn't quite as simple as that. We were on patrol in Land Rovers up in the Troodos hills. Quite like these mountains but with many more trees. We come round this corner and there's a huge tree down completely blocking the road. There's a sharp drop to the left and a sheer wall to the right. The only way to go is back. So the word is being passed to the last driver in the line to turn round when they start shooting at us. I'm in the second Landy. We can't go forward, can't go back. In fact we can't go anywhere. The bullets are flying about bloody close to our heads. So we abandon ship and drop down into the trees below the road. I start to move back towards the last vehicle and get separated from my mates. Suddenly I'm alone in this bloody forest. The firing on the road above is slowing down but there is still a load of noise everywhere. So I push on until I recon I'm level with the last of the transport. Gun up, heart racing I scramble up to the road and poke my head above the parapet. First thing I see is I've overshot the line of Land Rovers ... they're up the road 20 yards to my left. Second thing I see is this young bloke about ten feet away. He's on his belly, gun in front, taking potshots and my mates and Solihul's finest vehicles. I don't think twice. My rifle's already raised. I just pull the trigger. First shot hits him in the leg. I can see the surprise and the pain. I can see the blood welling out of the wound. And he looks round and stares straight at me. And I get the shock of my life. I know him. I've seen that face a thousand times. He's young. About 19. He's got short brown hair. He's got prominent ears with large lobes, and not much of a chin. I know him because …he's me. I know it sounds stupid, but at that split second I'm convinced it's my own face I'm looking at. And I also see he's moving his gun round towards me so I fire again. And again. I empty the entire clip into him. I watch each bullet punch into him. I see the blood flow. I watch him die there in front of me. Just feet away. Of course it's not me any more. It's just a young Greek partisan. Fighting for what he believes. Fighting to overthrow oppression as he sees it. Fighting for freedom. But I'm in tears. Sobbing my heart out. I've taken a life. I've killed a boy just the same as me. I've killed a bit of myself."

"You didn't have any option" says Faure after a long pause. "He had a gun. He would have shot you without a second thought."

"Actually he wouldn't" says Joe. "He didn't have any bullets left. There was a bloody great fuss about the whole thing. We weren't supposed to be shooting up the locals. We were supposed to be keeping the peace. My patrol captured the others who'd attacked us and later found a load of weapons hidden nearby. But there was only one fatality. And he'd got seven of my bullets in him. And his gun was empty. And at the enquiry it was even suggested he was surrendering not attacking. But I was cleared in the end and even commended for going round the back. 'First rate tactical thinking' they said, and drew a veil over the fact that I'd drilled a defenseless man full of holes."

"Does it still bother you?"

"Bloody right it does. I still wake up in the night staring into the barrel of this gun, that's just popped up from below the road. I always know my own gun is empty. Sometimes I'm trying to get it round, pointed at him, sometimes I'm trying to push it away to surrender. Sometimes the British Army squaddie shoots me. Sometimes he doesn't. But it's still the same bloody nightmare.

And Joe looks at the stars and ponders on what Faure has said about standing idly by. It's not my fight. He says to himself again and again. I'll help them. But I'll not kill for them. And he falls asleep.

Chapter 15

Joe drives Lansky's Dodge up to the sentry at the gatehouse of the barracks. As military installations go this is a pretty ramshackle arrangement with a mesh and barbed wire fence surrounding the perimeter, a small collection of huts in the compound, a palm-leaf roof to keep the mid-day sun off the motley collection of vehicles and, apparently, only one soldier on duty in the small sentry-box.

Carmen leans across Joe and smiles at the man whose expression immediately transforms from utter boredom to total interest.

"We want to see the commanding officer." She says.

"Why?"

"To report on rebel activity"

"I'll have to see if he's available" And the man grabs his gun, deserts his post, and walks slowly towards one of the huts.

Joe smiles at Carmen. She doesn't return the compliment. Since he arrived back in Trinidad the previous day she's been surprisingly cool towards him. It seems she was shaken by their kidnap, and shares her father's view of the rebel movement. He described his adventures and the rebels' camp to her in fairly glowing terms and found her unimpressed. She's of the view they should go straight to the barracks and report the whole incident. Joe appears reluctant, only finally agreeing after much arm twisting.

The sentry returns and raises the barrier, waving them through to the Captain's hut. He greets them still buttoning up his uniform and rubbing sleep from his eyes. It's clear he's been enjoying an extended siesta.

His office is sparsely furnished with an ancient desk and a fan that makes no appreciable difference to the sluggish air. He finds two chairs and they sit before him. He produces a note-pad and a pen and begins to compile a report, directing his attention mainly at Carmen rather than Joe. Probably only in his late 30's he looks 50. Mixed race. Dark balding hair, bad teeth, bad breath and the expression of one whose career has passed him by and all he can look forward to is monotony and paperwork and the fear of his superiors.

But the Captain does raise a spark of interest when it's clear they know the whereabouts of the rebel camp, and when Joe tells him that he learned of their plans to move on in the next day or two he becomes almost animated.

"It should be a simple job to surround them" Joe says. "There's only one guard to the main entrance to the clearing. If you sent one patrol round the back of the hill and approach from two sides you should be able to cut off any escape route. I expect you'd be able to capture them easily without any casualties. It would be quite a feather in your cap to take an entire rebel division. Show those commanders in *Oriente* how it should be done. Probably mean promotion at least."

Fishing has never been easier. The captain has swallowed the bait whole, while wholly failing to notice the barbed hook. He produces maps, asks Joe about the rebel's guns and ammunition, and is impressed to hear that Joe has served in the British army. Joe compliments the Captain on his barracks and his men, and is duly rewarded with a tour of inspection.

It's even more of a shambles than it looked from the outside. Clothing is strewn around the sleeping quarters, half eaten food rots on plates. Privates fail to salute or even acknowledge the officers. Most, it appears, live at home in the surrounding area, only keeping a token force to guard the barracks.

"What sort of heavy weapons do they allow you to keep here?" asks Joe innocently.

"Just a couple of machine guns. They're old but effective".

"Yes but heavy " suggests Joe "I wouldn't want to have to carry them up into the hills. It would cut down on manoeuvrability. You'd spend you time having to defend them rather than being able to mount a mobile attack. I'd say speed and surprise were your best weapons."

On the way back to town Carmen is surprised. "I thought you supported the rebels. Now it seems you've handed them over to the army. It doesn't bother me, but I'm surprised at you."

"Well, I got to thinking what they might have done to you if I hadn't been around," says Joe. "And anyway I'm not sure our Captain will find it quite so easy to take them as he thinks."

Next morning Joe is due to collect Carmen at 10.00 for the drive back to Havana. At 5.00am he's nestling the Dodge into a small opening at the side of the railway tracks off the road between Manacaslzenga and Condado. On the short journey out of Trinidad he's had to pass the barracks. The dim bulbs that illuminate the perimeter show no sign of any of the military vehicles that had, the previous day, been parked in the shade.

Away from the Barracks it's still dark with just the glimmer of dawn appearing over the hills to the East. The car is facing along the railway tracks and Joe gives three quick flashes on the headlights, counts to 60 and then flashes the lights again.

Less than five minutes later the passenger door opens and William Morgan slips in. They have a few moments animated conversation and Joe hands over some sketch plans he's made.

The Dodge purrs back down the road but again pulls off along a narrow track this time a few hundred yards from the Barracks. Joe, carrying a pair of binoculars, climbs up quietly through the undergrowth to a vantage point overlooking the sentry box where he'd stopped the previous day.

It's a long wait with nothing to see. There's hardly any traffic. Finally at 6.30 a *Guajiro* appears in ragged trousers and straw hat astride a donkey. He stops at the sentry post and a sleepy looking soldier emerges. There's a moment's conversation, a flash of blade and the soldier crumples back into his box. The barrier is raised and two lines of six men emerge from the undergrowth crouching low and run into the compound. Silently one group takes up defensive positions while the other moves out of Joe's sight behind the huts. Through his binoculars he sees the door to the dormitory open and a soldier appear. There's a shot and he leaps back inside. Moments later more shots ring out, this time from the dormitory windows. Then other soldiers appear and fire towards the rebels. It's clear the Captain has not left the barracks entirely unprotected, though it could be only a token force.

Joe sees smoke rising from the hut that serves as a mess and kitchen, and soon flames are crackling up. A missile flies through the air and crashes against the dormitory hut with the sound of breaking glass and the thump of exploding petrol. Moments later a sheet or pillowcase is pushed through the door on the end of a rifle. The rebels cease fire and eight soldiers emerge out into the dawn light holding their rifles up in surrender. A man who Joe can now make out as Menoyo orders them to line up against the perimeter wire facing away from the camp. Another collects their rifles and is left to guard the line of men. Another few shots ring out from the back of the camp. Then, moments later, come the first group of men staggering under the weight of tin boxes and two heavy machine guns.

Joe goes back to the Dodge, starts the engine and heads for the barracks. He pulls up just beyond the entrance and reverses up to the sentry box where he can see the body of the unfortunate guard slumped in a pool of blood. It's a matter of seconds for the boot to be lifted and the metal ammunition cases and the two machine guns to be placed in the roomy interior. Joe drives swiftly off.

At 10.00 he's outside Rodriguez's elegant home in Jesus Maria street. Carmen's father shakes him warmly by the hand and thanks him for both protecting his daughter and for informing on the rebels. "It's a funny thing," says Joe, putting her suitcases into the empty trunk, "but I saw smoke coming from the direction of the Barracks when I drove past there half an hour ago. I do hope the captain didn't leave the place unguarded when he set off into he hills to round them up. "

The journey back to the city is uneventful.   Carmen is quiet for most of the time, and has certainly lost her skittish flirtatiousness.   Joe, looking forward to seeing Maria again, doesn't mind. That electric sexuality on the journey down and under the waterfall has evaporated. Now they sit companionably side by side. Carmen suggests a detour via the regional capital Santa Clara. "It's worth seeing. And you probably won't ever get back there again" she says, little knowing the significance that

Santa Clara is to have on Joe's life and the on future of her country.

§§§§§

Indeed, who would suppose that by the turn of the year this small provincial city in the centre of the Island would prove the tipping point for the revolution. Graced with a University and a high-rise hotel – all of ten stories – there's little else of importance in Santa Clara. Oh, except for the railroad. The railroad on which Batista was to gamble his presidency, and to lose it so spectacularly.

Revolution Cuba '58.

PART 4

Late Spring

Chapter 16

Havana is buzzing. The sights, smells and sounds of the city assault Joe as they did when he first arrived. But now the buzz is political.

A senior judge has issued an indictment for two of Bastista's most notorious henchmen who are alleged to have been involved in torture and murder. It's all over the local papers. It's all over the Miami Herald. It's talked about on the radio and in the bars.

Joe has acquired a 'local' in the inappropriately named O'Reilly street. There's nothing remotely Irish about it, and no Guinness available in the pub. But it is true the décor could have been imported from Dublin or even Paris with is long elegant wooden bar running all the way along the back wall. There are high stools fixed to the floor along its length and a selection of etched glass mirrors and racks of upside-down bottles in front. The rest of the floor is littered with wooden tables and chairs where customers can sit and drink coffee or orange juice in the morning, beer at lunchtime and rum Mojitos or Diquaris throughout the evening.

There are no windows, just huge arches along the two outside walls. They have large wooden louvered shutters than can be manipulated to keep direct sunlight out, or opened fully in the early morning or evening to connect the inside directly to the pavement life on the street outside.

It's known by everyone as Marti's, though whether this is in honour of Cuba's national hero and first independence fighter Jose Marti or of its current owner, is unclear. He's a large jolly dark-skinned man referred to universally as Marti though whether that's his real name or he's simply nicknamed after his bar is equally unclear.

Unlike the Bodeguita del Medico two streets away where famous Americans like Ernest Hemingway hang out, Marti's is more of a local for locals. The odd tourist finds his or her way here, but by and large it's Vieja residents that play chess or dominos at the tables or gather to discuss the latest turn of events. And because a smattering of M26/7 supporters also gather at Marti's, it's a fertile place for gossip, and an invaluable source of information and stories for local journalists and foreign correspondents.

Joe's working pattern for the Riviera is irregular, but usually concentrated in the evening. Occasionally he'll be given day-time runs, but more usually he wakes when Maria leaves for work, and then sleeps again until ten or eleven. Cooking facilities are primitive at the apartment and so he generally heads down to Marti's for a late breakfast of eggs and bacon and local bread. Joe has tutored Marti to make a passable pot of tea, with proper loose tea-leaves and boiling water poured into a pre-warmed pot.

This idiosyncrasy one morning attracted the attention of a gnarled American sitting at the next table. The inability to get a decent cup of tea aboard is bemoaned by English ex-pats the world over, but it's rare to find an American understanding, let alone sympathising. His name turned out to be Matthews, a Lain-American correspondent for the New York Times. Joe had heard his name mentioned because he'd achieved a notable scoop the previous summer by getting the first major interview with Castro up in the Sierras. Now he is held to be a generally reliable source of information, able to keep a foot in both the Government and the Rebel camps.

A morning or two after his return from Trinidad, Joe and Matthews are discussing the President's fury with his renegade judge.

"Batista apparently summoned him to the presidential palace and ordered him to withdraw the indictments" says Matthews. "But the judge cited the constitution which guarantees the independence of the judiciary and refused to do it. Next day there's a presidential decree suspending the constitution! And Batista himself throws out the indictments. The judge, sensibly, flees to Miami and causes a stink in the US press. The US Ambassador here seeks clarification and is told by *El Presidente* not only does the constitution remain suspended, but that this summer's elections have been postponed indefinitely. This proves too much for Uncle Sam who at last realises that the regime here is a full-blown dictatorship and suspends arms shipments. All in all it's boiling up into a nice little diplomatic crisis."

"There's certainly not much press freedom here," says Joe leafing through the local papers. "This report about guerrilla action in the Escrambray mountains is complete rubbish. I've just got back from there."

"Really?" says Matthews pricking up his ears. "What's the version of the story you heard?"

Joe fills him in on events pretty much as they unfolded but leaving himself out of the picture. The local papers were calling it a skirmish between rebel forces and an armed patrol in which at least one rebel was killed or wounded. A major assault on the rebel position in the hills was said to have followed with a number of prisoners taken and valuable military equipment captured. The report mentioned a small fire at the barracks but not of the attack on it. There was no mention at all of the death of at least one soldier, the capture of up to ten others, or the loss of rifles, two heavy machine guns and sizable quantities of ammunition.

Maria is also agog with Joe's tales of the rebel encampment and of the attack on the barracks. Within 48 hours the Cuba Libre, an opposition free sheet, is being distributed with the full story, and Matthew's piece in the New York Times appears accusing the military of blatant censorship and disinformation and making much of the rebels' chivalry towards the daughter of a local plantation owner who was kidnapped and released un-harmed.

Maria welcomed Joe back with open arms and, to his relief, open legs, pointedly declining to ask him anything about his relations with Carmen. Lying on the bed on the evening of his return, the tale of Rodriguez and his daughter's pro-government views seem enough to satisfy her curiosity. But she can't get enough details of Faure and Morgan and Menoyo and by the time he's describing the attack on the army post she's growing visibly excited. Joe looks at this woman and feels an unaccustomed pang in his heart. Beautiful, radical and sexually excited by stories of rebel fighting. It's a pretty rare combination and one to be savoured. So he savours her in the best way he knows, slowly undressing, caressing, nuzzling, fondling, exciting and, finally, joining.

Afterwards she tells him of the plans the Movement has been making for an all out national strike the following week. It has the backing of Castro and the Sierra part of the July 26 opposition. And on a given signal there will be armed uprisings across the island. In the meantime no taxes are to be paid, government executives and the judiciary are to resign on mass, members of the armed forces are to be declared criminals, and workers from all sides of society are to walk out, crippling transport and shutting down utilities and power stations. But Maria is worried.

"The leadership of the National Directorate – the city branch of the Movement don't want the Communists, the PSP, taking part. Castro says it's open to **all** Cubans to strike but the *llano* leaders won't have it. I fear a split that will just weaken the movement."

Sure enough on April 9th, the day on which the strike is called, little appears to happen. Joe walks over to Marti's amidst the usual morning roar of busses. Trains seem to be running normally. The lights remain working. The Batista sympathising unions ignore the call. The PSP feel side-lined and angry and also disregard the day of action. Few civil servants and no judges are foolish enough to resign. Sporadic attacks on military or government bases are ruthlessly suppressed by Rolando Masfeerrer who's civilian-based death squads now seem to operate without restriction under the suspended constitution."

"It looks like a severe setback" says Mathews, sipping a cup of Joe's tea. The problem with the July 26th Movements is that they have no overall leader, and no defined command structure."

"The problem is the PSP surely" says Joe. "Any revolution needs the support of the workers, and the radicalised workers in Cuba are communists, not members of the trade union movement."

"Yes but Castro has a real quandary defining the nature of his revolution. On the one hand he's got advisors and lieutenants like Che Guevara who are known communists, and who are pushing for a Marxist state, and on the other hand he needs to keep the Americans sweet. And he knows that the cold war and paranoia whipped up by Joseph McCarthy will make them run a mile from a communist Cuba. In fact they'd probably use military force to prevent it going that way in the first place."

"Even if that means continuing to prop up a corrupt regime led by a dictator who suspends the constitution, cancels elections, and gives free reign to men who delight in torturing and killing children?"

"That, in a nutshell, is Washington's dilemma. As usual with your English perspicacity, you have cut right through the crap and put your finger on the core of the problem. "

Joe and Matthews laugh. But Maria doesn't when Joe meets her later. The strike was effective at the Cohiba cigar factory largely, Joe suspects, because most of its employees are members of, or sympathetic to, the Movement. But she's distraught about the failure of the strike overall and believes it's a major setback.

"How many more men and women and children will have to die before this hateful man is overthrown?" she cries. "Why can't they see that it's only by remaining united we can triumph over the corrupt government?"

"How would you feel about living under a communist regime?" asks Joe steering the subject away from the strike.

"I don't know. I've never thought about it. I suppose if it meant good schools and free access to doctors, and a decent wage for all workers it couldn't be worse that what we've got now. But why do you ask. Fidel is not a communist. And those bastards in the National Directorate certainly aren't."

"No but Che is. And Raul Castro probably is. And a number of others in the Sierras according to your mother."

"Anything would be better than what we've got now."

"Hmm, I'm not so sure people in Poland or Hungary or Czechoslovakia would agree with you. Life's pretty tough there. And *their* governments don't much like opposition either. It's a police state in many ways similar to this one. The only difference is that this police state is based on corruption and American capitalism while over in Eastern Europe it's based on corruption and Soviet Communism."

"Then why are you prepared to help the movement?" asks Maria.

"Because I also hate what Batsista is doing to your country, but more important ..." Joe pauses.

"Yes?" says Maria.

"More important it's the best way I know to get into your knickers."

For a moment it looks as if she's going to be righteously angry with his flippancy. But her face softens and she moves over to kiss him.

§§§§§

In Washington they may have been having second thoughts about the Batista regime, but in Havana it is as if nothing has changed. The daily stream of airliners continues to arrive from Miami and New York. They disgorge dollar-laden tourists eager for sultry sensuality, along with brief-cased businessmen eager for the rich pickings of the tropical island. The expensive cars continue to roll off the docks on their way in. The cigars and sugar continue to be loaded up on their way out.

And business is good. Lansky's Riviera, in common with all the other big hotels in town, is booked out. The casino is humming with the sounds of hundred dollar bills changing hands. There's a long waiting list for a table in the restaurant and even hefty tips to the Maitre D. wont get you a seat.

But Joe has discovered that Lansky himself had had a bit of a setback. The gossip in the hotel's back-rooms was that he'd been arrested when he got off the plane in the US back in February by detectives investigating the murder of "Don" Umberto Anastasia. There was little surprise that this mafia hit man had himself been rubbed out the previous Autumn, left lying in a pool of blood in the barbershop of the midtown New York Park Sheraton Hotel. Unfortunately in his pocket were documents connecting him to a number of Cubans involved in the Havana hotel and casino trade. One went by the name of Roberto 'Chiri' Mendoza while another was Santo Trafficante Jr, a Lansky associate, and one of the group that had backed Big Tony against Joe in the tennis court fight before Christmas.

Joe knew 'Chiri' Mendoza personally. He'd been detailed to 'entertain' him on a visit to the Riviera one evening. Jake Lansky had explained his duties like this: "We have a number of VIP guests who we have to entertain. Some we like, some we don't. None do we trust. Your job is to be nice as apple pie to them. Get them drinks on the house all evening, arrange chips for the casino, best table at the Copa room, even sort them out a girl for later if that's what they want, but watch them like a hawk. One half of you is looking after them in case there's someone else around who doesn't like them, and the other half is making sure they don't get frisky with any other guests."

In spite of these somewhat tortuous instructions Joe generally found that 'entertaining' duties were far from onerous. The VIP's were generally unusual people who, after the first four or five drinks, had good stories to tell. Mendoza was no exception.

"I want to see how the whole operation works" he told Joe. "I've just landed the concession to run the casino at the new Hilton Hotel here in Havana, but it's going to cost me a million bucks a year, and I need to be sure it's going to pay."

After a few more beers 'Chiri' is telling Joe how the Hilton came to be built. "It's not one of the American jobs. It's Cuban. It's owned by the Hotel and Restaurant Workers Union. It will provide their members with jobs and it's a good investment for the their pension fund. They've sub-contracted the marketing to the Hilton chain, and they're sub-contracting the Casino to me. There are just two problems."

"What are they" asked Joe on cue.

"First no-one runs a casino in this town without Mr Lansky's agreement, and second no-one runs a casino in this town without the President's agreement. The difference is that the President's agreement is even more expensive to come by."

So when Joe hears that Chiri's name also comes up in connection with the New York shooting of 'Don' Umberto he's not particularly surprised, though he does wonder what the Cuban was doing there. Curiously it's Lansky himself who answers the question.

Despite owning the Riviera, Joe's boss still retains close links with the Hotel Nacional. Jake Lansky continues to oversees the casino there, and a good deal of business is still conducted round the hotel's pool where Meyer has his own personal cabaña and where he holds court at lunchtimes. Joe is sometimes summoned to drive Lansky on from there, either to the Riviera, or home to Teddy, or sometimes to Miramar and Carmen's.

One afternoon he's waiting within earshot of Lansky and his associates and overhears the following account of Mendoza's New York visit.

"You know hat that dumbfuck was doing?" Lansky asks rhetorically. "He's heard that George Raft had been hired by the Capri to act as 'meeter and greeter' and thinks he'll go one better at the Hilton. Who can he get that's better known than a Hollywood has been? How about a sports star. What sport do they go nuts for down here in Cuba? Baseball. So Chiri only goes and arranges a meeting with the world's most famous ball player to put the proposition to him. Trouble is he fails to find out DiMaggio doesn't gamble and doesn't drink. So ten minutes into this meeting in which he's talking about the Yankee Clipper being a personal guest of Present Batista and all, Joe turns to him and says he doesn't think his endorsing betting and alcohol would be a great example to set for the youth of the American nation. And so Chiri is kicked out with nothing to show for his trip except a five minute yak about the tribulations of playing mid-field."

The group around Lansky erupt with laughter and someone asks the little man about his own problem in the Big Apple.

"Huh, those stupid cops" says Lansky. "You know the only charge they could find to throw at me was vagrancy. I mean there was I with a hotel reservation, an airline ticket back here, a trunk full of luggage and a thousand bucks in my pocket and they try to pin a vagrancy rap on me! Anyway after I got bailed out they gave me a tail. So there's this stupid flatfoot dripping with rain sitting in the foyer of the hotel waiting for me to make a move. So I thinks I'll have a little fun. I goes over and sits next to him and starts taking about the weather, and how wet it is for the time of year. And then I ask him if he knows where I can get some chickens. 'Chickens?' he says. 'Chickens' I say, 'Well' he says 'I think they do chicken at the 57th street Deli. 'No' I says 'I want live ones'. 'Live ones' he says as if I've suggested some kinda sexual perversion, 'Live chickens? How many?' 'Oh' I says 'between one and two hundred a month. Beef I can get,' I say, 'lamb, seafood, no problem, but fresh chickens in Cuba?! Impossible."

Lansky by now is doubled up with mirth, and the others are laughing so loudly that they're attracting stares from others round the pool. Even Joe is having difficulty keeping a straight face at the image of the man suspected of being America's top crime boss sitting in a New York hotel complaining to a plainclothes detective of the difficulty of getting good quality chicken in Havana. Meyer Lansky is, he reflects, a man of many contradictions.

Chapter 17

Lydia has re-appeared at the apartment, back from another trip to the Sierra Maestra, with news of a dramatic restructuring of the revolutionary leadership.

Fidel Castro, distraught over the failure of the national strike had summoned the entire disparate leadership of the M26/7 to a meeting in the mountains. Over three days they had discussed how to move forward.

"Everyone from the *llano* seemed to have entrenched positions while everyone from the *sierra* seemed flexible and pragmatic" Lydia tells her daughter and Joe over late night rum on ice. "It was Che who broke the deadlock. He blamed the National Directorate for condemning the strike to failure by excluding the PSP. And he called on the main three directorate leaders to resign. Of course they refused, so they put it to a vote among the members representing the entire movement, and it was carried. Salvador, Daniel and Faustino have been dismissed and command of the *llano* has been moved to the *sierras*. It was also decided that Fidel himself would become general secretary of the political side of the movement as well as commander in chief of the military side."

"Wasn't there some resentment from the other commanders, from Che or Raul or Camillo about this coup? Asked Maria.

"Not at all. They seemed pleased that there would now be one strong effective leader. Che called it a 'decisive meeting' in the building of the true revolution"

But Lydia also reports on renewed activity among the army and fears of a major offensive. "We desperately need information about what they are planning and when they are planning it" she says. "Is there any chance that Batista may have confided in his American friends like Meyer Lansky do you think?" she asks Joe.

"I don't know, but I can ask," he replies.

Asking Lansky anything so direct is not going to be easy. Joe discusses the problem with Herbert Matthews in Marti's the following morning. Matthews has also heard rumours about an all out assault on the guerrilla positions in the Sierra Maestra, but is equally ignorant of the date. He promises to ask around and suggests Joe quizzes Lansky associates rather than the top man himself.

In fact getting the information turns out to be easier than Joe expects. Two days later he's driving Lansky across town and mentions a report in the local paper about Fidel's consolidation of power over the revolutionary movement. Does that not make the American businessmen more fearful of their investments?

"Nah" says Lansky from the back of his Dodge. "The army are about to rub that lot out altogether. By the first of June there won't be a revolutionary movement."

"Why the first of June?" Joe asks innocently.

"Because that's a week after the army move in" says Lansky. "And if 10,000 troops and the entire air force can's wipe out a bunch of ragged-assed *banditos* in the hills in a week I'll give this guy Castro a free room at the Riv."

Joe rushes back to report the news to Lydia but she has already left, carrying less precise information back to the rebels.

"We have to let them know" Maria says. "But who can take the message?" She looks at Joe with those wide moist eyes that make his heart melt.

"Maybe I could find a reason for a visit to Santiago" he says. "After all I haven't seen the east of Cuba yet."

Thus, the following evening, they are at Havana's central station. Lansky has been surprisingly flexible in giving Joe time off at short notice. Maria has given Joe details of who to ask for in Santiago to help him get through to the rebel's lines. Matthews has given him a letter of accreditation as a New York Times stringer and asked for any first hand accounts of preparations for the anticipated battle. Joe has a rucksack hastily packed with warm clothes, and a new pair of expensive American hiking boots bought that afternoon from the biggest department store in town, and some food for the journey.

The station, an elegantly facaded building down by the docks in the old town, is heaving with people. Huge engines bellow steam and smoke into the high glass ceiling. Joe and Maria embrace passionately. "Come with me" he says.

"I can't. I promised my mother I would work for the Movement in the city and not with the rebels in the mountains. After my brother's death it wouldn't be fair to her. But you be careful. And hurry back. I'll be waiting for you. I love you,"

Joe is equally surprised and delighted at the last three words. He hugs her tighter to him and whispers that he loves her too, and runs his hand over her smooth neck and back and wishes they'd had time for a last session before he had to leave.

The guard is whistling the final passengers on board. They kiss and part. Joe leaps onto the train, slams the door closed, pulls down the window and leans out.   As if in a Hollywood film Maria walks then runs down the platform waving at the departing train as Joe blows kisses from the open window.   It's both extremely silly and wonderfully romantic.

The carriage is crowded, hot, smelly and uncomfortable. The tacks are uneven and Joe finds himself gripping the armrest for dear life as the train clatters and jolts over the worst sections. Heading East from the city the scenery is the same as on the trip to Trinidad – flat and dull. Joe tries to read, but the light soon fades as the sun sets behind them, and the dim overhead bulbs provide insufficient power.   In the gloom Joe reflects on what he's doing – carrying messages to the rebels – a hazardous and potentially lethal occupation. But his cover is good. He's an accredited journalist, following in the steps of many others who have visited the guerrilla   encampments.   The lure of the *Barbudos* is undeniable. There's a strong romanticism about living in the hills, defying authority, fighting for justice and against oppression. His experience with Faure and the Escrambray rebels has given him a taste for adventure and the adrenalin of action.   But it was certainly not what he had planned. After Cyprus and Suez he had no appetite for military life or for the business of killing. But then Joe is philosophical.   The winds of life blows this way and that, he muses. You can, if you choose, steer a pre-determined course, tacking left and right,   fighting the elements to   arrive at a particular destination, or you can run before the wind, letting it take you where it will. Almost everything that has happened to him since leaving Miami has been serendipitous – meeting Lansky and gaining an entrée to the rich hotel and casino tourist world of Havana – meeting Maria and seeing at first hand the struggle of the workers, the pain of oppression and the politics of opposition.

Yet he remains to be convinced of the type of society envisaged by the rebels if they do win their revolution and dislodge Batista. His reading of Cuban history shows a succession of authoritarian regimes, often overthrown after violent struggle only to be replaced by another, equally bad. And Eastern Block communism is hardly a good model.

The motion of the train puts Joe into a semi-slumber, punctuated by noisy stops at provincial stations. Matanzas, and Santa Clara, before midnight, then Guayos and Camaguey in the small hours. Shortly before dawn, around Las Tunas, troops board the train, moving from carriage to carriage demanding papers and generally throwing their weight around. Across the aisle and two rows down the carriage Joe has noticed a petite, olive skinned woman of about thirty. The two soldiers working their way down the carriage appear to be paying her an unusual amount of attention. At first Joe thinks it's her sex. But soon their voices are raised, demanding she come with them. The situation is becoming heated. The woman is refusing; the soldiers insisting. One grabs her roughly by arm and pulls her from her seat, hitting her round the head with his other hand. She slaps him in the face and, quick as lightening while he's still reeling from surprise, she grabs her bag and makes off down the carriage towards Joe. The two soldiers are now after her and almost without thinking Joe rises from his seat, blocking their way and says in a pastiche upper-class English accent "I say, old boy that's no way to treat a lady."

There's another moment's hesitation and then, unable to use any other weapon in the confined space, the private lashes his fist out at Joe's face. Joe dodges the blow and in return hits him hard on the point of the chin. Before he has time to recover Joe grabs the backrests on either side of the aisle and, using then as levers, kicks the guard hard in the chest, pushing him away, back down the carriage. He falls back and trips over his companion,

117

knocking him to the floor. Joe reaches up for his rucksack and follows the woman's path down the carriage, At the end, one of the doors is open. Joe looks left and right and then jumps down beside the tracks.

The train looms above him, the great metal wheels inches from his head. They are not in a station, though there are lights some way down the track. There is no sign of the woman. There are noises from inside the carriage so Joe moves away from the train towards the undergrowth beside the tracks. The two soldiers from the carriage appear in the open doorway and call to others on the ground. Joe wants to know how many are in the patrol altogether, and he's relieved when only two others appear, hurrying along the track.

You stupid idiot he thinks to himself. Why did you have to get involved. That wasn't your problem. Now look at you. Hiding beside a railway track with Batista's troops out to get you.

But there isn't much time for reflection. The patrol has found the woman and they're dragging her along beside the tracks. They shout to their companions on the train that there is no sign of the *hombre*, and continue up towards the engine at the front. Joe waits a moment then dodges under the couplings between two carriages to the far side of the train. Now he can follow the two soldiers and the captured woman in relative safety. When he reaches the engine he can see it is beside a water tower and the pipe on the wooden arm is just swinging back to the side. There's a conversation between the train driver and the soldiers, but with the hissing of steam from the cylinders Joe can's make out any words. Eventually the two guards complete their inspection on the train and jump down. The driver is given the all clear. He releases the brake and opens the valve. As the fire glows in the cab, great plumes of black smoke rise from the funnel. The huge connecting rod moves slowly from piston to wheel, building up the torque required to turn it under the weight of the massive engine.

Now is Joe's chance. One leap and he'd be beside the train and up onto the step beneath the door. One twist of the handle and he'd be back inside the carriage. One minute more and the soldiers would be receding into the distance and he'd be home free. So why, then, is he still crouching down by the track waiting for the train to pass?

There's a small hut on the other side of the track beneath the tower, possibly used by engine drivers waiting as they take on water. The four soldiers shove, push and pull the woman towards it. Once they're inside Joe follows silently. Through a crack in the shutters he can see the inside illuminated by a dim electric light bulb. The hut has been turned into a make-shift guard house. There's a table with a bottle and glasses and bits of food. A wooden bench opposite has been serving as a bed. The woman is pushed onto a chair beside the table and her hands tied behind her. The men demand to know her name. She refuses to answer. One slaps her hard across the side of her face. Her bag is searched papers are found and examined. Joe hears the name Sanchez spoken and sees the woman does not deny it. She is quite attractive with short dark curly hair. She's wearing a practical dress made from a cheap but tough looking material, a boy's jacket, and extremely unfeminine stout leather shoes. The soldiers talk among themselves evidently trying to decide what to do next. It appears they have captured someone important and should take her to their headquarters. But then she is a woman and surely a little fun might be had before they hand her over? The latter thought seems to prevail because one man moves to the bench and rearranges the blanket while another moves to the woman and begins to rub his hands over hear breasts. Emboldened he feels down inside her dress and under her bra. She maintains an expression of complete boredom. But the fondling of her mamaries has clearly been enough to excite him for he now walks round to the front and unbuttons his trousers inches away from her face. With his penis released, he grabs her hair and pulls her head towards him, forcing himself into her mouth. For a moment there is a look of near ecstasy on his face which rapidly turns to agony as two things happen in quick succession. First the woman bites down as hard as she can on the protuberance in her mouth and wrenches her head to one side to increase the damage her teeth do. Second a projectile hurled by Joe flies through the air and smashes the light bulb. Now in darkness there is confusion. The felatee is howling in agony while the other three soldiers are asking what the fuck is going on. One, unwisely, puts his head out of the door to see if there is anybody there. There is. And Joe brings down a heavy length of wood hard on the top of his skull before scurrying away from the door round to the back of the hut. Two soldiers grab their guns. The third grabs his injured and bloody dick and feels round for some bandage or dressing. They pull their unconscious comrade back inside and close the door.

Two men with rifles in a confined space when under attack from without can't do a lot except poke the gun barrels out of a window hoping to find a target. And as the first rifle duly appears Joe, crouching below the window ledge, grabs it, pulls it hard away and then shoves it back with all this strength, hears a reassuring crack as butt meets bone, and then pulls the weapon away again, this time finding is comes freely through the opening.

One unconscious, two injured, one gun out of four captured. It's a start. But he's now lost the initiative. He hears the voice of his old NCO during training. "Keep moving. Keep 'em guessing. Irritate and destroy until they make the mistakes." So Joe moves round the hut until he's away from either the window or door then raises the rifle, aims and fires. The bullet hits one side of the corrugated tin roof and goes right through coming out of the other. The sound inside must have been shockingly loud.

"If you want to escape with your lives, come out now with your hands up." he shouts. It's corny, it's clichéd, it's melodramatic, it sounds as if it's straight from a poorly scripted Western, but in the circumstances it's all he can think of. Unfortunately it doesn't have quite the anticipated effect.

"Fuck you" shouts one of them back. "You put down the gun and we may let you live. If not we kill the woman. Very slowly.

It's a standoff thinks Joe.

Chapter 18

Looking round in the pre-dawn light Joe searches for something that could give him some sort of advantage.   In the distance down the tracks are lights which could be Las Tunas station and the town beyond. The engine driver's hut stands in a clearing at the end of a dirt track guarded by a wire fence and open gates. It is about 10 feet from the base of the water tower which rises on stout wooden legs some 20 feet up to the bottom of the metal tank which it supports. One of the legs has a ladder of iron rungs running up to a gantry which gives access to the hinged wooden arm which can be swung out over the tracks carrying the long canvass hose pipe to fill the tanks of steam engines below.

In a moment Joe is at the base of the tower, securing the end of some stray rope to a wooden railway sleeper. Moments later he's climbing up the iron rungs of the ladder. It's risky because it is within sight of the hut's window.   But he's reasonably confident no-one will be looking out. After all the last person to do so is now nursing broken jaw or smashed cheek-bone.

Up on the gantry at the base of the tank Joe has a commanding position and good cover. He throws the end of the rope as far out over the arm as he can manage, grabs the free end, and hauls up the railway sleeper. It is tough work, the sleeper is heavy and the rope's friction over the wooden arm considerable. Eventually though the sleeper is dangling down on the end of the rope, lowest point about ten feet above the ground. Joe now swings the wooden arm round so it is suspended a few feet above the corrugated iron roof of the hut.

All at once there comes a cry of pain from the woman inside the hut and almost immediately Joe lets go of the end of the rope he's holding, releasing the sleeper which crashes down onto the tin roof creating a decent sized hole before disappearing inside. "Bingo" he says to himself, hoping it has landed on one

121

of the soldiers rather than their captive. Next he runs back along the gantry and unties the cord that holds the canvass hose in place. It swings free like a giant elephant's trunk, dangling above the hut roof. One more pull on an adjacent line opens a valve and the water thunders down from the tank above through the hose, across the wooden arm and down onto the roof. A small adjustment and Joe has the contents of the water tank cascading through the hole in the roof filling up the room below.

He stretches out full length at then end of the gantry, rifle trained on the hut's door. Moments later it opens and, as he expects, the woman is pushed out as a human shield in front of the soldiers. But one thin woman is not much of a cover for three fully grown men. And as they have no idea from which direction an attack may come   they are singularly unable   protect themselves. Joe aims carefully. He's back at the army rifle range a .303 Lee Enfield in his hands. "Bring the sights up slowly and then squeeze, don't pull the trigger" whispers his instructor in his ear .

The second soldier screams in pain as the bullet rips into his leg. The third runs flat out down the track towards the gate. Joe wastes one bullet , missing the moving target in the dim light, before turning his attention to the man still holding the hostage. But he need not have worried. For all her size the woman is fighting like a lynx. They've unwisely untied her hands and she prods a thumb hard into his eye and then knees him viciously in the groin. As his legs buckle from under him she grabs his rifle and swings it by the barrel round her head, crashing the stock with a ringing crack into the side of his head.

"Look out" shouts Joe from above as he sees the fourth soldier crawl from the sodden interior of the hut and raise his rifle in the woman's direction. Joe fires first but is unable to get a clear shot. The woman, however, reverses the captured rifle, fires once, expertly slams the bolt up and back, ejecting the spent cartridge, then forward and down, ramming the new bullet into position. In a second she's fired again, again reloaded, and run to safety on one side of the door, gun at the ready. She checks that the man she's shot is truly out of action before turning her attention on the soldier Joe hit in the leg. She removes his rifle from within reach and checks him for other weapons. By the time Joe has stemmed the flow of water and climbed down from the tower, the woman has tied him up, and wrapped a mass of material from the hut round his leg wound.

"Why didn't you finish him off?' asks Joe joining her. "After all you make a pretty good job of his friend here." He points to the dead soldier who has a bullet wound in the arm, presumably from Joe, as well as one in the chest and one in the centre of his forehead clearly from her marksmanship.

"So he can tell his comrades that the Fidelistas do not kill in cold blood. If they attack us we will fight back, and we will win. But if they desert the army they can join us to overthrow the corrupt dictator ."

She takes a deep breath calming herself, letting the adrenalin subside. "By the way Mr Chivalrous Englishman, thank you for your help. That was a clever trick with the water. I'm Celia."

"Pleased to meet you I'm Joe" They shake hands formally. "But aren't we forgetting something, the one that got away. I don't think it's far to the town and he's bound to be back with his friends before long."

"Ok" she says. "Follow me then" And grabbing as much ammunition as she can find from the pouches of the three soldiers, she picks up her captured rifle, pulls her bag from inside the hut and sets off at a run over the tracks and into the cover of the low trees on the other side.

§§§§§

After an hour's walk at a rather brisker pace than Joe would have chosen, they halt. They've been heading south east, with a golden sunrise breaking the sky ahead and to the left of them. Celia shows Joe a map as they share water and the remains of Joe's train supper from the night before.

Having established that Joe is also heading towards the Sierra Maestra, Celia outlines the problem they face. First they

123

have to skirt around the south of Las Tunas where the alert will have been raised for them. Then they have to go 75 kilometres along the main road to Bayamo which, after Santiago, is the main regional garrison town for Batista's gathering forces, and then they have to find their way through the government lines and across the mountains to the rebel positions, a further 60 kilometres as the crow flies, but the best part of a week's hike if crisscrossing mountain passes and avoiding army lines.

Once Joe understands that Celia has been on the rebel side since before the Granma landed, he outlines the message he is taking. "It simply can't wait for two weeks to be delivered" he says. "We must find some transport".

"That could be easier said than done" she replied. "There'll be road blocks all around Bayamo and into the foot-hills, and all trains will be stopped and searched. It was pretty silly of me to have taken such a risk last night, but I to was in a hurry to get back. You know the dates of the advance, but I have details of the troop disposition and plans."

"What's this train line here?" says Joe pointing to a line on the map running parallel to the south from Joabo to Bayamo and then branching off into the Sierras.

"It's a freight line, and the trains are even more closely guarded than the passenger ones. Often they have soldiers onboard all the way."

"But it goes through hardly any towns, and avoids the main road. Even if we didn't travel by train, at least we could follow the tracks."

And so it's agreed. They head south picking up a small road out of Las Tunas at Cautro Caminos. There's very little traffic. Once, around 11.00, a dilapidated cart drawn by a decidedly mangy horse stops and carries them ten kilometres or so. The driver looks askance at the rifles. Though they're wrapped in a blanket there's little disguising what they are. Celia offers the man a generous number of Paesos to forget he's seen them. Otherwise they move off the road into any available cover whenever they hear an engine for fear it could be an army patrol.

By the late afternoon they reach the railway line just short of the village of Ganboa. "I think we have to take a chance any get some supplies here" says Celia so they hide the guns and go into the town, buying bread, cheese, fruit, two more blankets and filling Joe's water canteen from an iffy looking well. He also buys a bottle of the cheapest rot-gut rum and they set out again. According to the map, the road follows the railway for about six kilometres. So they stick to the road until it branches off to the east to join the main highway. Just beyond the junction they see a deserted looking *guajiro* hut on a rise above the road. Climbing up the find it bare but relatively clean and dry and settle down to their meal. The rum was intended as an emergency pick-me-up, but soon half the bottle is gone and they're laughing over the events at the water tower. "If you could have seen the expression change on that soldier's face when you took that huge bite out of his cock" giggles Joe. "One moment he's like the cat that got the cream, the next it's like he's been stung by a scorpion.".

"It was about the same when you dropped that beam through the roof. They'd just decided that I needed a little bit more softening up when suddenly there's this massive crash and it's like god's chucked a thunderbolt down from heaven. It misses one by a whisker and he moves over to the hole to see what's going on and gets a ton of water right in the eye."

"That was pretty good shooting of yours," compliments Joe. "I've never seem a woman handle a rifle so well."

And so Celia tells him of her training with the rebels and exploits since she started to support the opposition after the first attack on the Moncarda barracks, before it was even known as July 26th. Movement. She'd been in Mexico as the invasion was planned and had been furious with Castro for forbidding her, as a woman, to come on the Granma. As soon as she'd discovered where they were in the Sierras she'd joined them and been by Fidel's side almost ever since.

It seems she knows the mountains well, having hiked round them when a girl guide in her home town of Manzanillo. She'd started off as a courier for the guerrillas, but had graduated to Fidel's secretary, personal assistant and, as far as Joe could judge, his occasional lover. Certainly she is besotted by him. So much so that even lying next to each other under a single mosquito net, a matter inches apart that night, he didn't attempt even the merest of exploratory touches. Sex with Celia was decidedly not on the agenda.

He lay awake for a while, his mind roaming over the day's events. She had asked him why he'd obstructed the guard on the train and risked everything for her. And he didn't know the answer. It was just instinctive. He didn't like men throwing their weight around with women. In his area of South London it wasn't done. He's been brought up to believe that women were the weaker sex and that they should be respected and protected by men. He'd been taught to give up his seat on a bus for any woman, young or old, to hold open doors for women and to let them pas through first. And above all not to force yourself sexually on a woman. Even getting her drunk in the hope of loosening her morals and her bra strap was held to be "caddish" behaviour by his father and by a surprising number of his contemporaries. His image of women as the weaker sex, had, it is true, received a bit of a jolt when he'd crossed the Atlantic. The American matriarch seemed alive and well. Maria and Carmen and certainly Celia all seemed tough and purposeful and able to hold their own intellectually and, in the latter's case, physically too. But if his intervention between Celia and the soldier had been completely automatic, the choice *not* to get back on the train when he had the chance was less so. By then the sense of adventure had taken over. The wind was Easterly, and there was no question of coming about and steering any other way. Joe's die was cast. His metaphor was mixed and possibly clicheed. But he was definitely on the road to revolution.

Chapter 19

The next morning is cloudy, which will make travelling easier. They find some water from a stream for a quick wash and are on the road before 5.00. It's a long, long slog. Joe's new boots are rubbing. Not badly, but enough to provide painful blisters. And once your feet begin to hurt, every thought you have is focused on that pain.

A village comes into view in the distance. Again hiding their rifles at the outskirts they go in to buy bread and fruit. Walking back up the main street Joe has in idea. There's a garage, not yet open for the day's business. It's not much more than a large shed with big double doors at the front. But there are no other houses or shops near. Joe asks Celia to wait for a moment and skirts round the back looking for another entrance and finds a door at the side. The rickety lock gives way easily and he's inside peering among the oil cans, rusty machinery and cars in various states of repair. And then he sees it. In one corner. Not new. In fact decidedly ancient. But in one piece and looking in working order. It's not a model Joe is familiar with, but one bike is much like another and Joe has spent much of his youth watching his father take his old Triumph 500 apart and put it back together. Joe himself had a BSA Bantam when he was 16 which he rode all over the south of England before he seized the engine.

Now he undoes the petrol cap and shakes the tank: there's fuel inside. He switches on the petrol to the two carburettors, searches out the ignition switch and pulls out the kick start. It's a big twin cylinder engine and he has to bring his full weight down to turn it over. It declines to start. He checks the controls and sees the choke lever. "Idiot" he thinks to himself. He closes the choke all the way, opens the throttle a little and jumps down on the kick start again, Immediately the engine fires, making a huge noise in the confined space. Joe leaves it to idle and searches quickly for various pieces of equipment including a small petrol can. With these secured in the ancient leather panniers, he takes a $20 bill from his wallet and leaves it protruding from under a stone next to the bike. Then he pulls open one of the main double doors just wide enough jumps on the bike pushes it off its central stand, pulls in the clutch, pushes the gear lever down, and edges out into the forecourt. There are few people around at this early hour and no one takes any notice of the bike emerging from the garage, nor of the small woman who climbs on to the pillion.

"Your steed, m'lady" jests Joe as they pull out of the village back to where they left the guns.

"We can't go on the roads. We'll hit army blocks every ten kilometres" she replies.

"We're not going to," he says.

And they retrace their route back to the railway line. Joe looks for a suitable place, changes down, guns the engine, and shoots up the bank and onto the tracks. At first he tries riding along beside the tracks over the end of the sleepers, but it's extremely hard to steer. And on embankments there's the danger of a steep fall if he misjudges. So shortly he stops and puts down a small log beside the rail, and eases the bike's wheels over it, stopping again to pick up the wood which he hands to the already laden Celia.

"Why do we need to carry this?" she asks.

"Because if a train comes we're going to need to get back over the rail in a hurry" he replies. And indeed the danger of their position is apparent. On a straight stretch of track they would be able to see a train approaching perhaps a mile away, but anywhere with a bend and it could be on them before they know it and the noise of the bike would probably drown out the sound of the steam engine. But for now both are relieved not to be walking. It's a pretty bumpy ride as the cinders and stones between the railway sleepers are not flush. So the bike is going bump bump bump, jolting the passengers every second or two. Joe finds the faster they go the harder is the ride, and he's fearful for the suspension and front forks. So they settle down for the optimum speed which turns out to be around 10 miles per hour – only just over double walking pace.

After an hour or so he again puts down the log, crosses the rail, and steers the bike out of sight into a clump of trees.

They eat bread and fruit and discuss their progress, agreeing that while the bike is better than walking, it's by no means perfect. Joe studies the map and sees a series of small roads marked.

"We'd be much faster on these. And we're getting close to Manzanillo. Could you find your way through?"

"Possibly, though I mainly know the main roads, not these little farm tracks. And there's always the chance of running into a patrol."

At that moment they hear a train approaching, and within moments it's clattering past them, engine labouring under the weight of the freight cars behind. They both think of the panic there would be if they were still on the bike in between the two rails, trying to get the wheels over the log and the rail. It decides them to try the road whatever the additional risk. Joe checks the petrol again and estimates that they will need a refill within twenty or thirty kilometres.

As they set off again the sun breaks through the clouds and suddenly it's magic. Bowling along country lanes on a powerful motor-bike, wind rushing though hair, sun on face, beautiful girl behind. It reminds Joe suddenly of a Sunday afternoon before he'd joined the army. Out on the Sussex Downs, his little Bantam struggling up the steep Ditchling beacon with his girl-friend on the pillion, arms around his waist, looking out over the English Channel, and then roaring down to Brighton for fish and chips on the front, a go in the penny arcade on the pier and a chaste kiss before the ride back to London up the A23.

Now he can again see the sea, but this time it's the royal blue of the Caribbean. Now the girl behind him is a wanted terrorist, they're carrying two stolen rifles, and they are heading straight for the largest concentration of troops on the island for decades.

The small road turns into a larger one, bringing traffic from Las Tunas to Manzanillo. Again they stop and make some preparations. Joe finds some saplings and forms an elongated front bumper which he attaches to the bike's frame. Celia takes the rifles out of the blanket, slings one across her back, and places the other under Joe's right arm, barrel resting on the handlebars, pointing forward.

They've got ten kilometres to go on the main road before they can turn off on smaller tracks. They're roaring along at 50 miles an hour when they turn a corner and see the road block ahead. It looks as if this is just a truck with a handful of soldiers stopping traffic and checking papers. Joe slows down as if he's preparing to stop. But a sharp eyed guard sees the rifle over Celia's shoulders, raises his own gun and shouts for them to halt.

Celia fires at him and misses, but the bullet is near enough for him to duck out of the way and throw himself to one side. The other troops, now alerted, begin to raise their guns and take aim. Joe changes down, opens the throttle and the bike accelerates hard. They're ten yards from the soldiers. Celia is working the bolt to re-load. Joe is looking for a way through. The troops have put out a series of oil drums to stop the traffic. There's room for one car to pass in the middle, but that's where the soldiers are concentrated. For a moment he heads straight at them and then swerves to the left and then to the right and aims the bike in-between the two end drums. There's not quite enough room to get through, but the makeshift bumper now comes into its own, hitting the metal with a booming crash and pushing the two drums apart. The bike squeezes through the gap. Celia fires again. The soldiers change their aim and prepare to shoot. It's touch and go whether they will hit the now retreating target. Joe opens the throttle again and the worst thing happens. Nothing. The engine coughs and splutters. They're out of petrol. "Shit" he swears loudly, and then his brain functions again. He reaches down to the fuel lever on his left and pushes it all the way up praying that, like his old Bantam, it operates an emergency tank. The left hand cylinder fires again, and though it's clunky and uneven the bike moves forward. To switch the right hand tank to reserve would mean taking his hand off the throttle. Celia, like a Red-Indian in a western, has freed the rifle from under Joe's arm and is aiming it wildly behind in the vague direction of the troops. Joe can hear their truck starting and now risks taking his hand off the throttle and switching the right hand fuel feed over to reserve. Now both cylinders are firing properly in tandem and the bike roars away down the road, with Celia grabbing his shirt and holding on for dear life.

"We've only got enough petrol for a few miles" he shouts. "They're bound to catch up.

The land is flat and there's no cover, but after five minutes they round a bend and see a cane field in the distance.

"If we can make it to there," shouts Joe, "we could hide the bike."

They fly down the road until the tall sugar cane is looming next to them. Joe slows and searches for an entrance between the fronds big enough for the motorbike. He sees a gap he hopes will be wide enough, slams on the brakes, slews the back wheel round at forty-five degrees and lurches over the verge and into the plantation. The make-shift bumper that was so effective with the oil cans at the roadblock also works here, pushing the shoots apart and allowing them to squeeze in. Once they are ten yards or so from the road they stop. He cuts the engine, lowers the foot rest, and they leap off. Celia is reloading the rifles. They run back to the road and look at the hole they've made into the cane. Joe pulls a couple of flattened stems upright again to disguise the entrance and they look about to find the best vantage point. In the distance they can hear the whine of the truck's engine.

They soon find a pile of old leaves and branches which they dive into, pulling them over their bodies. The field is slightly lower than the road and looking out they are eye-level with the tarmac.

"Go for the tyres. Nothing else" instructs Celia.

The truck comes into view round the bend and moves towards them. They wait until it is almost parallel before firing, pulling their respective triggers simultaneously. Both bullets find a target. Two tyres blow out at the same moment. The vehicle lurches left and then right. The driver fights to control it but they're going too fast and he slews down the bank on the far side of the road. The front wheel hits an obstruction, and the vehicle overturns and continues sliding along on its side, finally coming to rest with a jolt against some rocks about thirty yards down the road.

"We need to be nearer" says Celia, abandoning their cover and running down towards the vehicle, hugging the edge of the cane field. Joe follows a little way behind.

The overturned vehicle is relatively small, not much more than an long-wheelbase Land Rover. It has a metal cab and a canvass tilt over the back. There is no movement from the driver, but as they take up positions Joe and Celia see the back flap rise and a number of bodies start to disentangle themselves.

"Don't shoot" she says to Joe. And boldly walks across the road to within a few feet of the tuck, waiting, rifle raised, as the soldiers emerge. She shouts: "You're surrounded. If you want to live, surrender now."

The soldiers are clearly too dazed from the crash to put up any resistance and as they emerge from the back Celia lines them up on the ground a few feed away, piling up their rifles.

"OK, Go and check on the driver " She tells one. "Joe, cover him will you."

Joe moves round to the front of the truck and watches as the soldier kicks in the broken windscreen and pulls the driver and passenger out. The is former is unconscious, the latter dazed and confused.

Eventually they join their comrades round the back under the watchful gaze of Celia and her rifle. A first aid kit is located and treatment applied to the most seriously wounded. There are six troops altogether. And Celia duly collects a pile of five rifles, one pistol and about 250 rounds of ammunition.

Joe checks the engine of the truck and is pleased to see it's petrol. At gunpoint he details two of the soldiers to push the motorbike out of the cane field and back across the road. He cuts the truck's fuel line a short way after it emerges from the tank and pushes the end in to the bike's tank, allowing the petrol to flow slowly through. Then he fills the petrol can he acquired the previous day. Celia meanwhile has tied the spare rifles together and secured them on the back of the bike behind her seat. The bullets are put in the panniers. Less than ten minutes after the start of the action, they are ready to leave. Celia gives her little speech about the rebels not having any personal gripe with individuals in the army, and inviting them to desert and join the revolution against the corrupt dictatorship.   No one immediately takes up the invitation, though now they seem to be out of danger the soldiers are clearly impressed with her efficiency and relieved at her clemency.

Finally Joe takes a cigarette from one of the soldiers and lights it. As they mount the bike and start to move off, he throws the cigarette into the pool of petrol that's been collecting since he finished filling the can. There's a dull roar and a sheet of flame leaps up. The unarmed soldiers hurry out of the way, pulling the unconscious driver with them. As the bike moves off down the road, there's a satisfying woomph of explosion as the rest of the fuel in the truck's tank goes up.

"We make a pretty good team" he shouts to Celia over the noise of the wind. "We should do this more often".

Chapter 20

Whether it's down to good luck or to Celia's good judgement, they don't encounter another patrol for the rest of the day. Once they're off the main road, a series of small tracks takes them from the Guacanayabo plain up towards the foothills of the mountains. It's a wonderful sight. The line of blue hills rising ahead of them, filling the horizon as far as they can seen in either direction.

On one level they are simply a picturesque mountain range but on another, Celia argues, they represent something profoundly romantic and profoundly Cuban. These hills have been the cradle of the revolution. She shouts above the noise of the engine and the whistling wind telling Joe how, for more than eighteen months, they have been home to the gradually expanding rebel band. It was to here that the handful of survivors of the disastrous Granma landing first retreated, retrenched, and set up camp. It was here they eeked out an existence, constantly on the move until they'd forged themselves into a semblance of a fighting force.

As the light fades Celia and Joe set up camp for the night . They'd stopped at Canabancoa and bought some fresh meat, vegetables, herbs and a cheap pan. Now, a few miles up the road towards the hills, they make a small fire and cook up a stew. As it simmers slowly Celia fills Joe in on the early days of the rebel army. The first big task, it seemed, was persuading the local *Guajiros* to shelter them. "The peasants had two main enemies. First the army's rural guard who patrolled the mountain villages meeting out vicious assaults on the local population while maintaining a network of informers by threats of torture and of death. Then there were the overseers of the local land owners who kept the equivalent of their own private armies and who harassed the *Guajiros*, often forcing them off the land on which they were squatting."

Into this mix came Castro and his band of ragged rebels. They handed out summary justice to informers and were, at first,

as feared as the other two groups of oppressors. But slowly –
perhaps on the basis of "my enemies' enemy" - the Guajiros came
to trust the rebels and rely on the small sums of money they paid
for food and shelter. Certainly the army became increasingly
reluctant to enter too deep into the Sierras, and some of the
overseers actually changed sides and put their forces at the
disposal of the *Barbudos.*

Meanwhile the myth of the guerrillas was spreading to the
plains and recruits started to arrive at first as a trickle and then as a
flood. The biggest problem, Celia explained, was getting
weapons for them. Every skirmish with the army that resulted in
captured guns was a success. Every one that failed to capture a
weapon, a failure. Che Guevara had been assigned to set up a
training camp, and new recruits were sent there to learn the basics
of guerrilla warfare. "The trouble was that he also provided them
with political indoctrination as well as military techniques" said
Celia. "And that might have been OK but Fidel thought it was
becoming more and more Marxist and less and less Cuban.

"Isn't Castro a Marxist?"

"No I think he's politically pragmatic. He passionately
believes in the overthrow of the dictatorship. He certainly
believes in the removal of American imperialism, and if pressed
he would probably agree to many of Che's ideas for land reform,
giving the peasants a real stake in their country. Don't forget
Fidel came from a massive land-owning family. His father had
20,000 acres of sugar and forestry plantations. And while he was
still a teenager he was out trying to unionise the workers on the
estate."

"But that's a long way from leading a guerrilla army in the
hills?"

"Yes. I think the Jesuits were partly responsible, He went
to two Catholic schools where they taught him to think and to
argue. When he got to university to study law he found the whole
of academia as corrupt as the political system. He got involved in
radical politics abroad. He was in Bogotá during the revolt which
followed the killing of the Trade Unionist Gaitan. He helped
found the Ortodoxo reform party, and was about to stand as a

candidate for the lower house in 1952 when Batista seized power again."

"And he's been fighting Batista ever since?"

"Pretty much, though the July 26 attack on the Moncada barracks was the first armed action."

"And what's the current strength of the rebels?" asks Joe.

"Here in the Sierras, about 300 armed," says Celia. "Or 307 if we get through with our guns."

"Three hundred!" exclaims Joe, appalled. "But Batista's sending 12,000 men. He's got the latest American Sherman Tanks. He's got an air force. The rebels will be annihilated."

"That shows that you don't know either their determination or this terrain. Tanks are useless in the mountains. Planes can't see through trees. I grant you the Rural Guard are experienced fighters in this area, but most of Batista's troops are new recruits. They don't want to be here, and will desert and join us at the earliest opportunity."

Joe hopes she's right. But rather doubts it.

The following day he sees for himself what Celia meant by the difficulty of the terrain. The bike, which Joe has discovered is an elderly German BMW, makes light work of the switchbacks and passes. But there's so much cover that one or two snipers could hold up a military convoy almost indefinitely. There are deep ravines dropping almost vertically, and dense impenetrable tropical forest.

There's a biggish town, Bartolome Maso, in between them and their destination Las Mercedes. Celia deems it too dangerous to go through the town, which, she says, will be swarming with troops. However she's unsure they'll be able to get the bike over the narrow trails that are the only way round.

"Theoretically where a horse can go, a motorbike can too" says Joe, "but not necessarily something as big and clumsy as this. Now the little Bantam I had in England with some trail tyres would get up almost anything."

In fact the BMW performs better than expected. Joe keeps the revs high and slips the clutch a lot and the powerful boxer engine keeps going where others would have stalled. The weight of the rifles on the back prevents the rear wheels from spinning too much. On the steepest parts Celia gets off and walks alongside, and on two occasions they tie a rope between the bike and a tree ahead with Celia adding her slight weight, pulling as a counter balance. After about two hours hard climbing, they're over the ridge and heading down into a slight valley with the road to Las Mercedes ahead of them.

There's now a view in front down across the plains to Manzanillo and the sea, with the Sierras rising up steeply to the south. It's breathtaking country, and once the bike's back on the narrow road they purr along nicely in the afternoon heat, rising all the time up into the hills. Suddenly, turning a corner, Joe has to slam on the breaks. There's a tree lying across the road, blocking it completely. As they come to a halt, three men with rifles and beards, in grubby camouflage fatigues, rise up from one side of the road and demand to know who they are and where they are going. Celia quickly establishes her credentials, and the rifles they are carrying ensure a welcome and free passage. The rebel soldiers help manhandle the bike round the felled tree. Joe is impressed with the efficiency of the operation. Looking back down the hill he realises the men would have had the bike in sight for at least the past ten minutes. Had it been an army patrol they would have had ample time to prepare an ambush, or to have disappeared back into the trees if it looked too strong to tackle.

It's now only a matter of five or six kilometres to the forward camp at Las Mercedes. Celia is sniffing the cool mountain air. Joe is looking forward to resting after the bone shaking drive. The village itself is nothing to write home about. A collection of shacks with palm frond or corrugated iron roofs. But on the road out there are sentries posted, one with a relatively new looking field telephone. They are waved through and are soon climbing on a steep track again, the BMW in first gear with engine roaring. Next moment they're on the level and the bike shoots forward immediately in front of a man standing watching their progress. There's no time to swerve, though Joe tries, and he feels the front wheel passing over an obstruction. The man yells with pain and jumps back, narrowly avoiding being hit on the backside by the butts of the rifles slung across the back of the bike.

"Fuck me" he shouts at Joe. "you drive a bike almost as badly as I do. You've run over my fucking foot." Then, seeing Celia on the back, he says, "Oh, it's you Sanchez. I might have known. What is it? Orders from Fidel to wipe out his chief lieutenant."

"Hello Che" she says, smiling. "Meet Joe Lyons. He's an Englishman and he's been helping me bring you some new guns. Now please look after them nicely. It's been hard work getting them up here."

"English....no wonder you can't steer a fucking motorbike." says the man with distinctly un-Cuban accent.

"Bloody Argentines" responds Joe without thinking, "Always standing around in the bloody way."

It's one of those moments that could go either way. There's a flicker over that youthful bearded face as he decides whether he's offended or amused. Not many people dare to insult him these days. But then he's been rude both about Joe's driving and his nationality. And the man has brought him new guns. And he's carrying Celia Sanchez on the back of a vintage bike. So all in all ...Che smiles and pats him hard on the back.

"Welcome. Anyone that's got up here on an R12 can't be all bad. Though British bikes are better. I drove all over South America on a Norton 500. We called it La Ponderosa, the powerful one."

When he smiles Guevara's face lights up. He is startlingly good looking. His hair is long, almost over his ears, his beard is straggly and thin. He's wearing relatively clean army fatigues and a soldiers' cap with a single star on the front denoting his rank of *Commandante*.

Come and have some coffee and tell me the news from the *llano* he says to Joe and Celia, and leads the way over to a hut besides which is a camp fire tended by a strikingly beautiful black girl who soon moves away to inspect the hooves of a mule that is tethered nearby.

They settle down to talk. Che lights a cigar. Joe savours the coffee which is hot and sweet and extremely welcome. He tells Che everything he's found out through his American connections of Batista's likely advance date, and of the speculation over the numbers expected to be involved. Celia outlines her intelligence which involves Batista's forces using the navy to land troops all along the shore to the south of the Sierras, and to increase air strikes on the rebels' positions.

Che nods thoughtfully. "That's all useful information. We guessed they were building up for an assault soon though we weren't sure when. May 24th or 25th. That's four days away. We'll have to work hard to increase the defences. How long are you staying English? Do you play chess? The English are supposed to be good at chess. And I want to hear more about the R12 and how you got it here. I'll be back about sunset. Share a meal with me. In the meantime explore the camp.

And with that, Che Guevara walks off to organise his defences. Joe watches the retreating figure with a feeling of alarm. It looks as if he has little choice but to stay with the rebels and see it through.

§§§§§

So there they are. 300 lightly armed rebels pretty much surrounded by more than10,000 government troops. Batista's army is bristling with the latest American supplied weapons. He even has tanks, an air force and a small navy. The rebels have a motley collection of superannuated rifles and machine guns and insufficient ammunition for either.

Now if you were a gambling man which side would you back?

The trouble with a narrative in which you already know the outcome is that betting on the result is no fun. What may be quite interesting, however, is to consider how the President and his generals could ever have been so woefully incompetent as to lose.

Revolution Cuba '58

Part 5

Early Summer

Chapter 21

Joe looks round the camp. It is, frankly, a shambles. Some people have put up tents, some just have sleeping bags and mosquito nets, others only a blanket. There's a haze of wood smoke and the pungent smell of cigars. There's rubbish and grime and makeshift lines with washing drying in the evening breeze. Near one campfire a large man is hacking up the carcass of what looks like a goat before adding it to a big cauldron-like pan. Other than that it's almost impossible to make any sense of who's who and what they are doing or why. There are assorted weapons lying around. Joe recognises a number of M1 Garands of the type they captured from the regular soldiers. But there are also Carbines and Thompson sub-machine guns and a number of other rifles and automatics that he can't identify.

Celia says she has to go and find Fidel who is apparently in another camp a short distance away. She kisses him chastely on the cheek, thanks him for his help, and walks off into the woods. Joe perambulates, checking out the lie of the land and looking for a corner where he can park the BM and make his own modest camp.

There's something undoubtedly exciting about being in the heart of the mountain rebel camp. But there's also something unnerving too. Joe reminds himself that, gathering to the North and the West, are thousands of government troops intent on wiping them all out. This is certainly not a safe place to be. But what are his options? He could try to find a way back down with the bike and hope to get through to Santiago with the aid of his reporter's accreditation. This would assume that no general description of the man who beat up the soldiers by the train in Las Tunas or at the check point by Manzanillo had been circulated to the troops actually in the Sierras.

That may or may not be a safe bet given the general scale of the current army manoeuvres. But the consequences if they were looking for him would be pretty catastrophic. He could, probably, stay with the rebels, and take his chances in any ensuing action. That sounded much more fun, but was undoubtedly more dangerous. And, as he reminded himself, it still wasn't his fight. He felt naturally sympathetic to the underdog, and naturally opposed to the bully-boy tactics of the government. But this is Joe from Deptford. Adventurer at large. Not a dedicated Marxisist revolutionary set on bringing down the capitalist system.

While Joe is musing on his future he spies a small patch of spare ground at the southern edge of the camp. It's between two trees, with a view out over the valley and no other people in the immediate vicinity. He goes back to the bike and pushes it slowly towards 'his' space. Once there he unties his rucksack and few possessions and spreads them out on the ground beside the bike. His worldly goods at that moment consist of a thick blanket with a zip along two sides enabling it to turn into a sleeping bag. A mosquito net which has already proved essential on the nights outdoors after leaving the train. He's got a spare pair of trousers and a pair of shorts, a shirt, T- shirts and underwear. Wrapped in one of the T-shirts is Big Tony's automatic pistol and about 40 rounds of ammunition. Feeling this is the right place for guns, he checks the weapon, ensures the safety catch is on, and tucks it into his belt. Then he sits down on his blanket a looks out over valley at the setting sun. Suddenly a woman's voice behind him makes him jump.

"It can't be that damned Englishman that's fucking my daughter can it?"

Joe turns and sees Lydia leaning over the bike's petrol tank. "I hardly recognised you with your clothes on", she smiles. Joe scrambles up and moves to give her a hug. She's wearing clean and, amazingly, ironed battle fatigues in a fetching olive green. She takes him on another tour of the camp, explaining that they'd moved there just a few weeks before because of the increasing troop activity below. "Yes, I wondered where the cigar factory and the blacksmith's and radio station you told us about had gone" said Joe.

"I'm still baking bread" she says, "but it's a pretty makeshift oven now. Che told me he'd bumped into an

Englishman on a motorbike carrying guns and Fidel's woman. But I couldn't believe it was really you. What are you doing? Where on earth did you get the bike?"

Joe retells his adventures as they gaze out over the mountains watching the sky changing colour. By the time he's finished the sun has dipped below the peaks. "Come on" says Lydia, we're due for supper at Che's. And it wouldn't do to keep Zoila waiting".

"Zoila?"

"Zoila Rodriguez. Che's current mistress. She's a peasant girl from Las Vegas de Jibacoa. Stunning. Keep your hands off!"

"Yes, mum" laughs Joe, and remembers the beautiful black girl he saw brewing the coffee earlier.

They walk over to Che's encampment but the *Comandante* is not back yet. Zoila turns out to be extremely shy, but asks them to sit by the fire and wait.

"So what did you make of Celia Sanchez?" asks Lydia.

"She's a pretty determined woman. An amazing fighter, and she seems unafraid of anything" answers Joe.

"Yes, she been with the Movement a long time. Before '56 she was the leader in Manzanillo. After the Granma disaster she set up a recruitment camp right under the nose of the army on the edge of the city. She reckoned that no-one would be looking for rebels within a few hundred meters of the local prison which was swarming with troops. But she personally recruited and armed forty new fighters and eventually got them safely up into the hills here. It doubled the size of Fidel's army at the time. And now she is the unofficial historian of the Movement. She keeps every document for posterity, no matter how dangerous or incriminating."

"If you ask me she's a complete pain in the ass"

The voice comes from the gloom of the trees. Joe and Lydia look up to see Che approaching. "She keeps on and on at us to form a battalion of women fighters here, and now Fidel's made her a member of the General command we all have to listen to her."

143

"And what's wrong with women fighting for the cause " bridled Lydia.

"Nothing at all, except that they play havoc with discipline. All the men spend their time either thinking about taking them into the woods for a fuck, or actually doing it."

At which moment Zoila sashayed into sight and gave Che a hug and a kiss. The others burst out laughing, and even he had the good grace to see the irony in what he'd said.

"Isn't that one of the biggest problems you've got maintaining a force of this size?" asked Joe. The men need some R & R, especially after a fight, and there's not many facilities up here. No bar, no brothel, and not many local girls for them to chase after?"

"Yes, that's true. And we've had a few cases where locals were raped and we've had to deal with it severely."

"How severely?"

"They've been shot. The revolutionary court has invariably sentenced them to death".

"Can you afford to lose recruits so readily?" asked Joe. "After all they're just young men with urges, and like it or not rape tends to be one of the consequences of war."

Che looks into the fire for a moment as Zoila hands round some food.

" Ever since we arrived on the Granma and first established a base in these mountains iron discipline has been vital. To start with we've had to win over the local *Gaugeros*. At first they thought we were no better than the army or the land-owners. But slowly we've shown them that in the revolutionary army we do not steal or rape or pillage. We buy our food and supplies. We respect their wives and daughters. We are on their side and working for them against a corrupt regime. But it's true, politics doesn't mean much when you are so poor you are hungry most of the year.

"So how do you deal with informers? Presumably the army tries to buy information from the locals and if they are as poor as you say they are, then it must be very hard to stop them selling you out?"

"There is truth in what you say." Che looks wistful for a moment. "Yes we have had to establish rigid discipline among the locals too when it comes to secrecy and our own security."

"You mean you've also executed informers." Says Joe. "But surely that makes you just as bad as the army in the local's eyes?"

"We've had to execute traitors. We'd never have survived otherwise. Right from the outset, even in Mexico when were preparing the Granma people we trusted were discovered to be agents of Batista and were selling our arms to line their own pockets. And when we arrived here in *Oriente* there was a local man called Eutimo Guerra who'd been with us almost from the beginning as a guide. He knew these mountains like the back of his hand. Suddenly one day he asked permission to visit his sick mother. Fidel even gave him money to help him on his journey. But his journey took him straight to the enemy who promised him wealth and a military rank if he betrayed us and killed Castro. When he returned to us after the "visit" we welcomed him back as a brother. Then things started to go wrong. Although we were on the move all the time the enemy always appeared to know our position in advance and they attacked us mercilessly. One night I remember it was very cold and Eutimo asked Fidel if he could have his blanket. Fidel said there was no point in them both being cold, but that he could share it. So the two of them slept side by side under the one blanket and two top coats all night long. The one on whom the hopes and success of the revolution depended, and the other who was prepared to sell out his comrades for forty pieces of silver."

"So what happened?" asked Joe.

"Eutimo couldn't bring himself to assassinate Fidel. He lay there all night next to him with a 45 pistol and two hand grenades and murder in his heart. But he funked it. A few says later his treachery was exposed and he admitted what he done. He even told us that he'd flown over the mountains in a spotter plane pointing out our positions to Major Casillas – a murdering bastard member of Batista's forces.

"So you executed this Guerra character," said Joe.

"Yes. And he expected nothing less. He fell on his knees before Fidel and asked simply that we kill him. He said he knew he deserved death."

"Who pulled the trigger?"

Che looked up at Joe and fixing him with a stare that seemed to penetrate his soul. "I did. I ended the problem by giving him a shot with a .32 in the right side of the brain. The bullet exited in the right temporal lobe. He gasped a little while and then was dead."

This was said quite matter-of-factly. But the surprising anatomical detail was chilling. Joe knew that Che was a doctor … or at least a medical student who had not fully completed his qualifications, but here he was describing the final moments of man's life with almost complete detachment. Che had pulled the trigger, Che had killed him in cold blood. Yes he may have been a traitor, he may have deserved to die, he may even have begged for death, but it still seemed an extraordinary way to describe the act.

"And did that act as a salutary lesson? asked Joe finally.

"Yes, we drew up a code which we called swift revolutionary justice. Fidel decreed that desertion, insubordination and defeatism would all be capital offences."

Joe stared at the fire and at the man, wondering at the zelotry or at last the sheer single-mindedness that had driven him.

As if reading his thoughts Lydia said "What you must understand Joe is that this was a turning point for the revolution. Celia has told me all about it. At the same moment that Eutimo's treachery was discovered she and the rest of the national directive of the July 26th Movement had come up here to the Sierras for its first meeting with the Granma survivors. Although they looked on Fidel as a natural leader, mostly they believed in insurrection in the towns and cities .. the *llano*. They couldn't see how a small bunch of unwashed and unshaven fighters in the hills could possibly overthrow Batista's massive army. But Fidel was adamant. The focus of all revolutionary activities MUST be on the fighters. He persuaded Fausino Perez and Amando Hart, but many of the others were pretty unimpressed."

"You say you were a small bunch, but how many were you then?" Joe asked. "Herbert Matthews who I know a little from Havana says you had "several thousands" of supporters."

"Eighteen" said Che.

"Eighteen!?

"Eighteen. While Fidel was speaking to Mathews Raul kept marching them backwards and forwards, making it look as if there were many more. And we sent messengers to Fidel with news from our "other divisions". That was actually me and two local peasants."

"But Herbert says Fidel spoke of 50 telescopic rifles, and that you operated in units of 10 to 40 men while Batista had columns of 200?"

Well it's true that Batista did have columns of 200" said Che with a smile. "And it also true that we operated in a unit of 10 men, and that would have gone up to 40 if we had had 40 men available. And as for the telescopic rifles, I'm not sure how that information came about. Fidel personally had one rifle with a telescopic sight of which he was immensely proud. I suppose he might have said he *wished* he had 50 of them, and that somehow got lost in translation."

"It was a pretty good propaganda coup" says Joe admiringly.

"Yes, it was certainly worth a number of small victories against the army. But I'm not sure what it's really achieved in the long run. That interview came out 15 months ago. And the US is still propping up Batista. Washington is still selling him arms. The CIA is still trying to play both sides off against each other. Now, enough shop talk. What about this game of chess. Pawn to king four ..."

Chapter 22

The following morning it becomes clear, as Joe had feared, that there is to be no easy way off the mountain. The army has been moving troops for days and has sealed off the area through which Joe and Celia brought the bike. Scouts report that the rebels are now completely encircled over a wide front. Inland, to the north and the east, up to seventeen battalions are spread out on the planes and into the foothills, each with its own tank company. To the west and the South, the mountains run down to the sea where naval and air patrols cut off any possibility of escape.

But Batista's men appear to show little appetite for actually engaging the rebels who, did they but know it, have only six lightly armed columns each with fewer than 50 men. As Joe looks out from his vantage point on the top of the mountain he can see why. The terrain is virtually impenetrable for regular troops with motorised support.

One of Che's key duties besides commanding the 8th column, is to run a training camp for the new and raw recruits who continue to arrive. Over their late night game of chess he had quizzed Joe on his army background and then asked if he would help out kicking the mainly peasant volunteers into a semblance of a fighting force. Remembering his days in Cyprus Joe suggested the best training and the most economical use of ammunition might be to organise a succession of harrying raids on the army's most forward positions. His plan is to take two rebel soldiers and get them as near to army patrols or guards as possible, loose off a couple of rounds each and beat a hasty retreat back up the mountain.

Che agreed to the idea, seeing it would provide some actual experience of engaging the enemy in a fairly risk free way. So Joe sets about organising a series of war games in the woods to brush up on field craft before moving down the hills towards the actual enemy.

Over the coming days he finds many of the rebel recruits willing and eager to learn, but generally pretty incompetent. Men and boys who have done little more than cut sugar cane all their lives now have some trouble grasping even the most basic of military principles. But he perseveres and within a week is ready to send out his first three raiding parties. Two are accompanied by rebel veterans, while he goes with the third. His two boys seem scarcely old enough to shave – probably no more than 14 or 15 years old. One, Raul, is big and awkward and appears to have little imagination or ability to extemporise. The second, Pedro, is short and wiry and light on his feet and does seem able to think for himself, but he appears rather cocky. They have both been loaned rifles for the raid with the warning that if they fail to bring them back their military career and probably their future ability to father children would be over.

The three move off down the hill following a winding path. They speak to the look-out sentry at the edge of the camp who has seen no sign of enemy troops all day and has no idea of their position. So Joe and his companions proceed cautiously, searching for cover wherever it presents itself and stopping regularly to listen for any sound which could give a clue to enemy positions. Twice planes appear from the east and buzz over the mountain while Joe pushes Pedro and Raul deep into the undergrowth. After moving for a couple of hours they reckon they should be approaching a road which might just have some military traffic. It is slightly further than he expected, and more of a track than a road, but they find a vantage point with sufficient shade to protect them from the baking mid-day sun and settled down to wait. Joe has been over the plan with the boys numerous times. Any patrol that comes through is likely to have several vehicles. Under no circumstances are they to attack the leading one. Indeed they should wait until the last truck or jeep is well past before firing. Then, immediately, Pedro is to set off 50 meters up the hill before stopping to provide cover. Joe and Raul will then criss-cross each other on the way up to Pedro's position, alternating in giving each other cover. In no circumstances will they simply run off into the undergrowth. Well, that is the well-rehearsed theory anyway.

After nearly an hour's wait Pedro signals that he's heard the sound of an engine. Soon Joe and Raul can hear it too. But not just one or two engines … dozens of them. Shortly a convoy comes into view winding up the track from below. But what a convoy. It is led by a full sized tank with two armoured cars behind, and then truck after truck of troops. From their vantage point the three can see about a quarter of a mile of roadway. Soon its entire length is full of vehicles, with more appearing every moment. Within ten minutes the leading tank has reached them and they can see the observer's helmeted head sticking up out of the turret just a few meters below. The thought apparently occurs to Joe and Raul at the same moment that this is not a hornet's nest that they want to stir up under any circumstances. Both lower their guns and snake further back into the undergrowth. But not Pedro. He is inching *forward* his rifle raised, looking to take a pot shot at the exposed head in the tank. Joe's heart sinks. It is just exactly what he didn't want to happen. The image unfolds of the tank brought to a halt, and the entire convoy, unable to move forward, stopping dead with the troops swarming out of the trucks and fanning out over the hills to confront two boys with clapped out rifles and ten rounds of ammunition apiece, and Joe with his pathetic little .38 automatic .

He frantically signals to Pedro to move back, but the youth can't or doesn't see. In slow motion Joe watches him pull back the bolt on the rifle pushing the cartridge up into the chamber.   He sees him nestle down on the ground just as he's been shown in training, raise the rifle, take careful aim and slowly, oh so slowly, squeeze the trigger. Joe expects to see a puff of smoke from the rifle's barrel just a split second before the sound of the shot echoes round the valley.

In fact what he hears is the dull click of the trigger coming down on a dud cartridge. And it is a sound that is almost completely muffled by the growling tank engines and the dozens of heavy trucks that are, by now, beginning to pass below. Certainly none of the troops heard anything, nor did they see a clearly surprised Pedro shuffling back under cover.

Fifteen or so minutes later the last of the long line of trucks comes into view and Joe signals silently to Raul and Pedro to take up their sniping positions again. The two boys move cautiously forward and this time wait for the end of the convoy to pass. Bringing up the rear behind the last truck is another tank which wouldn't provide any sort of target. So Joe hopes they will aim at the final truck just before it becomes obscured by the tank. And he is pleased to see this is what they do. The truck passes, the tank comes into view the boys aim, fire, reload fire again and, before anyone knows what has happened, Pedro has crawled back into the bushes and set off up the hill towards the rendezvous point.

Joe has just time to see that at least one of the bullets had reached it's mark as a soldier falls back holding his arm with blood flowing. Then he is back in the bushes waiting for Raul to pass him. He sees Raul stop ten meters further up and turn to provide cover . Joe scrambles up past him and in turn stops ten meters higher up. In fact with just eight rounds of ammunition in the rifle neither Raul nor Pedro were realistically going to be able to provide much covering fire had the troops been on their tail. And nor would Joe with the puny hand gun. But this is a training exercise and it is important the boys follow orders. So when Joe and Raul had passed each other five or six times, they should have found Pedro waiting, rifle at the ready, surveying the scene from his higher vantage point. But they didn't. There is no sign of him at all. From below there is the sound of sporadic firing as the soldiers responded to the sniper attack. But as Joe surmised they probably have no idea where from where shots have come and no commander is going to order his few troops to disperse into the heavy undergrowth where there might be a sizable ambush waiting. The most likely and most sensible thing to do is to pop off a few rounds in all directions hoping to keep any concealed gunmen at bay while the truck disappears round the bend and, hopefully, out of range. And this, indeed, seems to be what has happened until, from below comes the heavy *whooof* of a big gun firing, followed immediately by the explosion of a shell. For some reason the tank has opened fire. But on what? And why? And above all where the hell is Pedro?

Joe speaks urgently to Raul and then moves back down the hill. He is looking for another vantage point that will give him a

151

view of the road so he moves off the path that they had followed just moments before. Eventually he comes to a gap in the trees and cautiously peers out. A hundred feet below he can see the truck that they'd fired on now stationary, blocking the road, a bullet hole through its windscreen, and troops taking cover behind it. The tank, which can't get past, is manoeuvring into a position that will enable it to shoot up into the undergrowth. Now the soldiers open fire, all aiming, as far as Joe can see, for the spot where the three of them had sheltered earlier while waiting for the ambush. And then he can see why. The small figure of Pedro is crouching there and, as he watches, he sees him hurl a small object in the direction of the truck. Immediately comes the explosion of a hand-grenade followed almost immediately by the bigger bang of the truck's fuel tank exploding. Pedro then fires a number of shots in quick succession before retreating back into the bushes. The troops, believing they are under a sustained attack, flee the burning vehicle and run off up the track towards the rest of their convoy. The tank, seeing itself trapped, roars into action barging the burning truck out of the way and pushing it over the side of the road into a small ravine below. It too then follows the retreating troops round the bend and out of sight. Moments later there comes the sound of someone running up the hill to Joe's left and a sweaty and somewhat scared looking Pedro appears. He has his rifle slung across his back and is carrying another gun along with two ammunition pouches attached to which are a number of grenades.

"Look what I've captured" he says proudly seeing Joe.

"Look what you've done" replied Joe furious. "You've made us the target of an entire battalion who could be swarming over this mountain in seconds and probably calling up air strikes to bomb the fuck out of us. This was supposed to be a training exercise, not a one man war against the whole of Batista's army. Now come on, let's get going before they're on to us.

The two climb higher, pushing their way through dense scrub, until they come upon a bemused Raul who has remained precisely where Joe instructed, despite all the noise from below.

"Well done Raul. You're exactly where you should be unlike this fucking maniac who wants to get himself and us all killed."

In fact Joe was having some difficulty being angry with the now rather crestfallen Pedro. To start with it appears that the troops are not prepared to pursue them up the mountain, and although an aircraft does appear twenty minutes later and circles round for a while it is clearly unable to spot them, and after firing a few dozen rounds in entirely the wrong area, it disappears off in the general direction the column has taken. Once they are certain they are not being followed the three rest in a low cave and Pedro explained his actions.

"I was running up the hill just as you instructed when I looked over at the road and saw two soldiers had been sent back to look for us. They were on their own and I thought I've got seven bullets left surely it's worth a go at them. So I turned left and slithered down the hill onto the road lower down. They came round the bend and I fired on them. I hit one but missed the other who ran off to get help. So I grabbed the wounded guy's rifle and ammo and suddenly realised I was cut off. I couldn't get back up to our path the way I'd come, it was too steep so I had to go forward towards the tank and try to find my way back to our original ambush position. The trouble was the tank gunner spotted me and lobbed a couple of shells at me. Then I fired at the truck's windshield, tossed a grenade at it, watched it explode, and then legged it here. I did all right didn't I?"

§§§§§

"Apart from disobeying orders and endangering the entire operation he did pretty well," Joe reported to Che when they arrived back at the main camp later that evening. "He's obviously quite fearless, a reasonable shot, and he did single-handedly destroy a truck, put a number of men out of action, and capture a rifle and some grenades and we did all get back in one piece. So ultimately I think he'll make a useful soldier for you."

But when Che summons Pedro it doesn't appear he has heard any of Joe's positive assessment. He unleashes a long tirade, laying into the young man, accusing him of insubordination, reminding him it is an offence against the revolutionary code and could be punished by death, telling him the revolutionary army has no place for egotists. On and on he goes while Pedro stands there, his head bowed, utterly deflated, thinking he was to be praised by the CO, but finding instead he is more likely to be cashiered if not shot. Joe considers it prudent to say nothing. This is after all Che's call, and if he feels that rigid discipline is more important than impetuous bravery that is for him to determine. But he does feel just a little sorry for Pedro, especially when Che demands he hand over his newly captured rifle.

"Next time you go into combat without a gun. If you are so good at getting weapons off the enemy you don't need to take the few we have here. Now go." And with a wave of his hand he dismisses the boy.

"You probably think I was too harsh" he says a few moments later to Joe. "But I've found that there are dozens of these young men who come here expecting glory and fame, and it's as well to get them in the right frame of mind from the start. By the way, English, you don't have a rifle do you?"

Joe shakes his head.

"Well now you do. If you want it. You should know how to use it. It looks like one of yours".

And Che hands over the newly captured gun which Joe can see is, in fact, far from new. It's .303 Lee Enfield. The gun used by the British army in both the first and second world wars, and one with which Joe trained and fired in competition at Bisley during his national service. As a piece of engineering it is solid and well made, and reputedly the fasted bolt action rifle ever produced . As an object of war it has iconic status for Joe.

Che can see him admiring it, running his hand over the stock and butt. "Now all you have to do is to make up your mind whether our fight is also your fight too." he says.

And Joe knows he's right. He can't go on sitting on the fence for much longer.

Thanks" he says simply. "I think this will need cleaning and oiling." And he walks off to his small corner of the camp with his prize.

Chapter 23

Still Batista's army doesn't come. Days turn to weeks as the rebels wait for the all out assault that has been promised and predicted. Instead all that happens is the army is, meter by meter, kilometre by kilometre, squeezing the circle and forcing the *Barburdos* into an ever smaller space. But at a snails pace. Meanwhile the raids on the army from the hills continue daily. Wherever troops move, snipers take pot shots at them. Castro has ordered a series of landmines to be laid which, day by day, take their toll both on vehicles and, equally importantly, the soldiers morale.

Air-raids are a constant feature. But the Cuban air force is poorly equipped and the rebels almost impossible to spot under the canopy of trees. As a result the planes fly over, strafe a piece of open ground and then fly off without inflicting any real damage or casualties.

Food and supplies continue, somehow, to be getting through the enemy lines. The diet is dull but adequate, and Lydia's bread when she bakes it is excellent. Joe finds himself increasingly drawn to the Argentine *Commandante*. Guevara is a fascinating companion. Most of the time he is intelligent and witty, with a considerable depth and grasp of political theory. He had travelled widely across South America and his tales of the road were always fascinating. He seemed to enjoy the Englishman's company – and certainly enjoyed beating him at chess which he did with almost tedious regularity. It provided Joe with access to the man that few others in the camp were afforded. To most Che was a remote and forbidding character – a revolutionary zealot and a scarily strict disciplinarian. But to Joe he sometimes seemed a little boy lost. His chronic asthma was a real disability and one which he forced himself to overcome with such steely determination that he appeared, on the surface, hard as nails. But Joe detected a soft centre. Che talked with real affection of his family in Buenos Ares, and in particular of his mother – another Celia. His relationship with his father had been difficult. Che clearly felt he'd let him down by not completing his medical training and taking off across the continent on his motorbike. But the travels had clearly been the making of the revolutionary. For the solidly middle-class boy who had wanted for nothing now to have to live with no money, and experience at first hand the real poverty of the people was a seminal experience. But Joe also felt that in his nature there was a real restlessness. An inability to settle to any task for long. A force driving him ever onwards, even if the direction he was travelling was not always the best thought out.

§§§§§

One morning Joe asks Che if there is a grand plan and if so what it is.

"Essentially it's to lure the army further and further into the mountains where they can't operate properly and we can. As you've seen their tanks are useless beyond the foothills. And once they leave their trucks behind they have no real advantage over us at all. In fact because we control the higher ground we have the advantage. The reports we receive suggest the commanders are squabbling among themselves and the troops don't want to be here in the first place."

"But we're going to have to engage them at some stage in an actual battle aren't we"

"Not unless it's at a time and place of our choosing. For the moment we can hold out pretty much indefinitely and simply wait for them to make mistakes or push in too far."

Joe knows the rebel commanders meet regularly to discuss the tactics. One afternoon they assemble at Che's camp. Juan Almedia, Camillo Cienfuegos, Ramiro Valdez, Crescencio Perez and, of course, Fidel Castro himself. Even from a distance he's a charismatic figure. A head and shoulders taller than the rest. Smartly dressed in pressed green fatigues and his trademark forage cap, tortoise-shell glasses, black beard trimmed neatly. He wears his rifle slung over one shoulder and a belt with leather

157

cartridge pouches round his waist. At his side Joe spots Celia
carrying papers and pens. Secretary, note-taker, message writer,
she's recorder for posterity of every minute detail of the
revolution.

After the meeting she sees Joe in the clearing near Che's
botha, and comes over and kisses him on the cheek. "Come and
meet Fidel" she says.

In fact the great man is distracted and hardly acknowledges
the Englishman. But Joe is still thrilled to have met him in person
and shaken his hand.

That evening while Che and Joe are playing chess around
the camp fire. Joe quizzes him on his political ideology:

"Do you see yourself as essentially socialist or
communist?"

"Well the second is just an extension of the first" he
replies. "As long as you believe in equality, real equality, then it
doesn't matter what you call it. You empower the humblest
person in society and give them work and dignity."

"But how do you achieve that equality? Do you simply
strip away all the wealth of the capitalists and entrepreneurs and
just hand it out to the people? Or does the state take over all the
enterprises and run them on behalf of the people. And in either
case is that going to be an efficient way to run factories? Look at
what's happened in eastern Europe, it's hardly been a major
economic success story."

"In eastern Europe and in the Soviet Union people do not
starve. There you do not have wealthy land-owners growing ever
richer on the backs of the peasants they are exploiting. You don't
have labourers bonded into economic slavery. You don't have
your country's natural resources being shipped abroad and sold
there for a thousand times more than they paid you for them. It's
a corrupt imperialistic system and it's going to be history."

Joe changes tack a bit: "Can your post-revolutionary Cuba
survive economically without the markets in the US, particularly
for sugar, and without American business investment here?'

"Yes of course Cuba can survive without the US. In fact I
believe it would be far far better off without it. But even when
we've nationalised the American owned businesses, they'll still

want to buy our sugar. And even if they don't, there are other markets. And crucially we've got to stop being so reliant on sugar. You can't have an economy where all your agricultural workers are unemployed for half the year. So we have to diversify. And we have to have factories where we produce real things that people need from raw materials that already exist here."

"It sounds a bit as if you want to push Cuba back into some sort of peasant economy from the middle of the last century. Where are you going to get the petrol to run the tractors, or the electricity to power the mills? How are you going to pay the wages of your workers?"

"Why should we have to pay wages? Why should we have to deal in money at all. What's so good about material incentives? What's so great about the "free" market, about supply and demand. All they do is perpetuate inequality. I tell you what I dream of. I dream of a society where everybody earns the same ... or at least earns according to his or her needs. So a man with a dependent family might earn three or four times as much as someone doing the same job but with no dependents. In fact I'm not at all sure we need money at all. Let's abolish it altogether. Give people what they need, according to their needs."

"But why would anybody bother to get up in the morning and go to work? Why would they sweat under the hot sun cutting came, or put in a long day in a factory unless it's to earn money?"

"But that's exactly the point. They shouldn't *have* to work in a factory or break their back cutting came *in order to* earn sufficient money to live on. The *living* bit should be guaranteed and they should work because they want to work. Because work is inherently and intrinsically good. It's the nobility of labour. It's in the national interest not in the private interest.

"I tell you what I'd do" says Joe laughing, "I'd make you president of the National Bank and Minister for Industry after the revolution, and see how you got on with such idealistic theories."

Che laughs too, and moves his rook down to the eighth rank pinning Joes's king. "Check-mate I think."

159

§§§§§

There are some English speakers in the camp, most notably two American GI's who have deserted from the US naval base at Guantanamo, 50 miles to the West of Santiago. They are young and politically naïve and their reasons for joining the rebels seem more to do with boredom with the US military routine and a wish for adventure rather than any revolutionary ideology. They tell Joe that other Americans have arrived to join the rebels but soon left after finding living in the hills with the most rudimentary of sanitary facilities and a diet consisting mainly of stewed goat not to their liking. For the rest, the rebels are an extraordinary cross section of Cuban society. There is a smattering of lawyers and lecturers, artists and intellectuals, and there is a larger number of peasants, most unable to read or write. But the bulk of the band is made up of what Joe thinks of as the lower middle classes. Shop-keepers, clerks, bureaucrats, artisans and factory workers. It is, he reflects, a long way from Marx's *lumpen proletariat.*

Perhaps the most extraordinary thing about this disparate group of people though is how well they gel together. Yes, there are occasional squabbles, and fights do break out from time to time. But on the whole everyone believes passionately in the cause. Most have friends or neighbours who have been killed or tortured by Batista's thugs, and many have lost members of their immediate family. But the real sense of common purpose seems to be instilled by Castro and his *Comandantes.* They spend a lot of time with the men, talking, discussing, planning, encouraging. On the surface there is only the loosest of discipline. It's a million miles from the square-bashing sergeant-major-shouting hierarchical approach of the British army. But as Joe discovered from his earlier discussion with Che, swift revolutionary justice awaits any defectors or traitors to the cause or, indeed, anyone moving too far out of line. One man was quickly executed for raping a local girl. Somehow, though, it's not the fear of discipline that drives the rebels, nor yet the imperative of the political crusade on which their embarked, it's more the camaraderie and wish for approval in the eyes of Castro and his compatriots. Che recalled how proud he was right at the start of the campaign when his bravery in combat was recognised by Castro and when later he was promoted to *Comandante* after the battle of El Uvero. He also recalled the bleak despair he had felt early in the campaign when Castro had castigated him for leaving his rifle and ammunition in a peasant's hut in the hope of escaping more easily from the surrounding troops. Nearly two years later he can still recall Fidel's exact words: "You have not paid for the error you committed because the price you pay for the abandonment of your weapons is your life. The one and only hope of survival that you would have had, in the event of a frontal clash with the Army, was your guns. To abandon them was criminal and stupid."

If there is one hierarchy among the rebels, Joe discovers, it derives from experience of fighting, battle honours and bravery. Much of the talk around evening camp-fires is of previous actions. Fallen comrades are venerated, especially if they died gloriously capturing a machine gun or taking a military outpost. Already the legend is being forged of how the revolution was fought and won. And there is a firm elite growing. An aristocracy, a royal family among the revolutionaries. Essentially you had to have been on board the Granma when it landed in Cuba after it's turbulent voyage from Mexico, to be part. Certainly Fidel's most trusted lieutenants all were. And rather like the descendants of the original Mayflower settlers in New England the boat would have to be of cruise liner size to accommodate all those who subsequently claim to have been on board.

Joe himself, untested in battle, is regarded as a curiosity by the soldiers around him. The tale of how he ran over *Commandante* Guevara's foot on his motor-bike while bringing Celia Sanchez and a cache of rifles to the rebels has spread around the camp, and some ostentatiously move their feet out of his way when he passes in mock tribute to the event. His role in training new recruits also lends him a certain respect, as does his evident access to Che. But the rebels are wary of foreigners – some even of Argentineans though they'd be careful of saying so too loudly – and the veterans tend to keep together like older boys in the school playground, who can never believe that the next generation of callow youths can ever live up to their prowess.

His esteem did rise fractionally when Lydia brought him a hammock she'd requisitioned from somewhere on her travels. Most men slept on the ground. Most of the "officers" had hammocks. It was, Joe reflected, a definite move up in both senses of the word.

He was pleased to see Lydia who had made another risky cross country trip from Havana, and had again mysteriously managed to sneak through the army lines to reach the mountain encampment. She brought news and letters from Maria who Joe was missing both emotionally and sexually. Havana remained much the same as ever Lydia said. One long rum-soaked party dancing to the music of the conga but heading nowhere. Speculation about the rebel's communist inclinations continued both among the moneyed American classes and also among the various factions within the Cuban opposition movement. The failure of the April strike and the constant reassertion of the army's "final" assault on the rebel stronghold had buoyed up Batista and his government. Sporadic bombings and subsequent roundups, arrests and tortures were routinely ignored in both the Spanish and English language newspapers.

Maria sent gossip of friends, news of work-place intrigues, and a few paragraphs of erotic thoughts to stoke Joe's memories and fantasies. For fear of the letters falling into army hands and compromising both their carrier and the movement she said little of her M26/7 activities. But she did praise Joe for his role in rescuing Celia about which Lydia had evidently told her. In a coded paragraph at the end she told him she was proud of him and what he was doing but worried too about what his future might be. It was his decision, she said, but she implored him to take care.

Reading the letter again by candle-light before bed that night Joe also wonders about his future: entrenched among a bunch of ill-armed and generally inexperienced rebel soldiers; surrounded on all sides by the military might of a vicious Latin American dictatorship; day by day watching the noose tightening; waiting for the final showdown in which he would, inevitably, be

162

caught in the middle. His prospects, he concludes, look decidedly un-rosy.

Chapter 24

Throughout June the news of the Army's advance is worse and worse. They have been moving steadily up from the south. Two battalions cross the main range of the Sierras and, by June 19th, are approaching the small town of Las Vegas, squeezing the rebels between the troops which had been guarding the Northern escape routes from the mountains. The revolutionary commanders estimate that now they control just four square miles of territory round the peak of San Larenzo.

Each day raiding parties are sent out to harry the advancing columns, usually with good results. Home made bombs and land-mines hold up motorised convoys while snipers pick off stray troops before retreating back up the mountain. Every day come reports of 10 or 20 troops killed or seriously wounded with almost no corresponding casualties on the rebel side.

Life in the camp is tense. June 14th is Joe's birthday. He is 22. No one knows. He receives no cards or presents. How different from those sunny days in the Deptford of his youth when groups of school-friends would come round for parties and his mum would serve jelly and ice-cream and Madeira cake with icing and candles. A birthday was the result of weeks of excited anticipation. What presents would he get? Would it be sunny? Who should he invite to his party? Would his dad be able to get off work early and come too? The delicious pain of knowing it would be over all too quickly and there'd be another year to wait for the next one. He remembered once, when he was about eight, asking in all seriousness why he couldn't have two birthdays a year instead of one.

Now it means nothing. No one else knows or cares. At least they didn't until early in the evening he was passing Che's botha and the Argentine invited him over and handed him a cup of sweet Spanish wine and announced "It's my birthday. I'm 30 today".

Joe half remembers some statistic from a school which says that in any group of 30 people there is a 50-50 chance of two of them sharing the same birthday. He didn't understand then how it could be possible and certainly didn't now. But the co-incidence of a shared birthday is strangely bonding and Joe and Che stay up long into the night reminiscing.

A week later Joe is again summoned to Che's botha, but this time it's not a social occasion. Fidel has heard news that a group of rebels has fled from the advance party marching on Las Vegas, leaving behind vital bomb-making equipment and ammunition. Che hands Joe a note from Castro ordering an investigation and instructing him to "send boys from the school to recover the munitions and then use whatever men you have to hold whatever terrain is left of Las Vegas inch by inch."

"I've already sent out three patrols today and can't spare any more men until they're back", he tells Joe. "So I want you to take some of your trainees down to the town and find out what you can. Don't engage the enemy unless you absolutely have to, but try get the ammunition back, look out for some good defensive positions. I'll either come myself or send re-enforcements later."

Although less than two miles away, it's an hour's scramble over difficult terrain from the camp to the town, all the while looking out for army patrols. It's a hot clear day and the rain-forest seems alive with wild-life. Parrots screech overhead while exotic butterflies and insects flutter about their business. Joe is leading a platoon of 15 men and boys, the youngest probably no more than 14. All but one is armed, but with the oldest and worst of the captured guns. The one unarmed man is Pedro, still smarting from having had his Lee Enfield taken from him, and eying Joe suspiciously as if he had been responsible for the dressing down he was given by Che.

Peering out from the dense undergrowth Joe can see the small town lying in the valley below. So far there is no sign of army activity, in fact there is no sign of any activity at all. But a slight ridge to the left is blocking his view of one side of the town and he asks Pedro to double back until he can see over the ridge and then to report back. "No heroics. This is just scouting. See but don't be seen. And I need the information quickly." Pedro nods silently and slips off. Joe orders the rest of the men to spread out and keep watch. In fact he's not too worried about an attack.

There's almost no way the troops could reach his position unobserved.

Within 15 minutes Pedro is back, reporting that he can only see one army truck and a jeep beyond the ridge, guarding the road in to the far side of the village. So, cautiously, Joe takes his men down into the valley to the right. The first building on the outskirts of the village is a small wooden house. Leading from it is a dirt track a hundred yards long to what looks like the main street that traverses the settlement from left to right. Joe looks at the house and decides it would make a good stronghold. There is an unimpeded view down the track, and should they need to retreat in a hurry, there's cover less than 20 feet from the back door.

Joe sends half his men further down to the right down to the right, while he deploys the rest on the edge of the clearing that forms the back yard. There is still no sign of any movement in the town at all, but someone has to be the first to cross that open space between the trees and the house. Just as he is about to move forward himself, Pedro nudges his arm. "I'll go he says".

"Ok, wait a moment," says Joe, and fishes in his pocket for Big Tony's automatic which he hands to Pedro. "Look after it".

Pedro nods thanks, takes the gun and moves forward. Joe expects him to crouch and run to the cover of the house, but instead he walks calmly out of the shrub, across the open space and up to the back door of the house on which he knocks. Joe checks left and right where he can see some of his men, rifles at the ready to provide covering fire if it's needed. But it isn't. Instead the door opens and an old wizened man greets Pedro, hears his explanation and ushers him inside. A few moments later Pedro re-appears and beckons for the rest of them to follow into the building. After ordering three men to stay hidden in the undergrowth, Joe signals for the remainder of the troop to enter the house. He runs, bent double, and they follow. Once inside he orders three men upstairs as look-outs and turns to meet his host.

"Welcome," says the man. "I thought you had abandoned us. A bunch of you *Fildelistas* were here last week, but as soon as an army patrol took a few pot shots at you, you turned and ran.

Since then we've been waiting to see who will get here first, Batista's bastards or you cowards."

Joe ascertains that the abandoned explosives are probably in a house on the other side of the village, near to the guards that Pedro reported seeing from the ridge. He sends a messenger off to report back to Che and then summons his men for a briefing.

"We're going to move very cautiously through the village to this house here," he says drawing a rough sketch map. "Along the way we will leave men at strategic points to provide covering fire if we meet resistance and need to retreat in a hurry. The objective is to get to the house without being seen or heard by the patrol, recover the munitions and get them safely back to the cover of the trees. There may be some people like this old man still in the village, but most are believed to have fled. Clear?"

They nod agreement and set off. Two men remain upstairs in the house; three are still in the woods behind; one has been sent back with the message, so Joe's troop is now ten strong.

By now it's around mid-day and the sun is pounding down. The ground is dry and dusty. The houses, when they reach main street, all seem shuttered and deserted. In fact the whole place is like a ghost town. A dog lopes lazily across the road ahead. There is some muted bird song, but otherwise all is silence. Joe's considers simply walking straight down main street and hope that the troops are confined to the edge of the town, looking the other way as they guard the road in. The image comes to him of a Western, with his men as gunslingers marching past the saloon to the rendezvous at the OK Coral, and suddenly the church clock starts to strike twelve.

Instead he positions a man on the corner of the dirt track and ushers the rest across the road and up an alley that runs parallel to the street but behind the houses. Within five minutes they are at their objective. Joe looks round carefully and can still see no sign of life. He slips up the back steps to the house, turns the handle on the door quietly, raises his gun and then pushes the door hard back on its hinges and thrusts the barrel through the opening, covering the inside. The room, a kitchen, is empty. Pedro follows him into the house and quickly explores each room in turn. He reports back that it is deserted, but that the missing boxes of ammunition and explosives are in the front room. But he also tells Joe that from the front window he can see the soldiers. Joe moves forward and looks out of the window. Two men are sat in the shade of the next house but one, playing cards, their rifles propped up against the wall. Further down the street he can see the truck and the Jeep parked together, but no sign of other troops.

"OK, lets get this stuff out of here, quietly now" he whispers. The men carry the boxes out through the kitchen and move off back down the alley, Joe checks round the house again and then follows them out of the back. They've covered a hundred yards and are almost back at the corner that leads up the dirt track to the old man's house when Joe realises someone is missing. He checks the troop and sees it's Pedro. "Damn" he says to himself. He orders the box carriers to get the munitions safely back into the hills behind the village. He leaves one man on the corner of the alley, and another on the opposite corner of the house but guarding the street, and then slips back to look for his missing charge.

Before he gets back to the house two shots ring out in quick succession. They are only small calibre, but in the almost complete mid-day silence they sound like a small nuclear explosion as they echo and reverberate round the deserted buildings.

Seconds later Pedro shoots out of the back out of the house where Joe has spotted the sleepy soldiers. He's running hell for leather, with a huge grin on his face, and carrying the two rifles that had been leaning up against the wall. Joe is unable to decide whether to be angry or admiring. Before he can make up his mind a volley of rifle shots opens up along main street. Pedro and Joe reach the corner where they've left their two look-outs and Joe peers round the far side of the house looking down the road towards the truck. Almost immediately shots sound and bullets zip past him. He pulls his head back behind the wall in double quick time.

"Damn," he thinks. "We've go to cross main street before we can escape back up our track and into the foot-hills. And main street now looks like sniper alley. Cautiously he edges his rifle round the side of the building and fires a shot up the street; whisks it back, pulls back the bolt, and fires again. Then he risks another look. In the distance he can see soldiers hugging the houses to the side of the road and a couple of men clambering into the truck."

He turns to Pedro and the other youthful rebel. "Go and see if you can find anything that will provide us with cover to cross the road. A nice tank would do, but failing that an ordinary car or even a horse cart or hand-cart. Otherwise we're stuck here, and they'll be calling up re-enforcements as we speak."

The two youths slip off and Joe moves round to the rear of the house and tries the back door which is locked. One bullet later and he's inside, climbing the stairs and peering out of the front window along the street. A number of troops are now in the back of the truck, rifles pointing forward as it starts up and begins to move down the street. Immediately comes a volley of covering shots from the ground troops. Joe knows that the moment he uses the upstairs window he will attract their fire, but somehow he has to stop the truck. He waits until it is clearly in view about twenty yards away and already blocking the sight line of at least one rifle. Then he smashes the window-pane and fires his first shot into the truck's windscreen, his second into its radiator, a third into the leg of one of the soldiers on the back and, steadying himself, a final shot into the truck's front tyre. Then he drops down onto the floor and snakes towards the door, just as a small machine gun opens up on his window smashing the remaining glass around the room and slivering splinters of wood off the frame.

Back down stairs Pedro and his companion are back reporting they can't find anything to use for cover to cross the road. But by now the rest of Joe's look-outs, alerted by the fire fight, have congregated across the other side of the main street and are waiting for instructions. Joe signals them to spread out and gestures two to get up to first floor or roof level. He risks another glance round the corner of the building and sees two men crouching behind the cover of the truck which is now stationary and disabled in the middle of the road. A third man is helping his wounded companion back up the street. There are sporadic shots coming from the soldiers crouching behind cover further back on either side of the street.

Pedro touches Joe on the arm and points to a can he's holding. "This any use?" he asks. "It's petrol."

"Yep," says Joe. "Go and find some bottles, some rags and some matches." Pedro scuttles off while Joe draws breath and tries to think of a plan. It was bloody stupid to have got himself into this situation. Throughout the operation he's tried to keep an escape route open at all times. And now here he is, pinned down by a dozen troops, unable to cross the main road to safety. What is needed is a diversion and possibly a move that would give him the initiative.

The sound of shots comes from across the road and he looks up to see that two of his men have found good strategic positions on the roofs of houses opposite. They are loosing off occasional shots to keep the enemy back behind cover. Now it is a stand-off he thought. They won't move to let us cross the street and we can't cross the street until they move.

After a while Pedro and his companion return with bottles which they fill with petrol, stopping the tops with rags. Time passes slowly with the occasional shot being exchanged. Eventually Joe decides on a plan of action. He again signals to his men across the road, speaks urgently to the two men on his side of the street, and then with Pedro in tow, moves quietly back along the alley, past the house from which they had recovered the ammunition, past the back of the house where Pedro had shot the guards and up to the next cross roads. Joe knows he has circled round behind some of the troops, but he doesn't know how many. If he moves up to the intersection on main street he might be able to cross safely while attention is focused down the street towards the disabled truck. On the other hand there could be troops to the right as well as the left, and if they try to cross the road they'll be caught in the cross-fire. What to do for the best?

There's not much time to reflect. Suddenly there's a splintering of glass and a whoomph as the first of the Molatov cocktails lands in the street. Joe gestures Pedro to look right while he flattens himself on the ground and inches forward to the corner of the house, looking to the left. Now he can see down main street. There's the truck in the middle of the road and two soldiers in the shadow of buildings on either side. A second explosion

170

follows, narrowly missing the stationary vehicle. Joe fires three rounds in the direction of the soldiers on the opposite side of the road, a third cocktail comes flying over and this times hit the truck square on. The one bang of exploding petrol is rapidly followed by a second as the lorry's fuel tank explodes.

"Look, they're retreating," says Pedro touching Joes arm and pointing right. Indeed the jeep that had been parked by the side of the road is now disappearing down the road towards the outskirts of the town.

Joe and Pedro are not the only ones to have noticed. The four remaining soldiers are also watching their only hope of escape vanishing. In front of them are four or five gunmen positioned on roofs and in upper windows. Somewhere beside them are people flinging petrol bombs at them, while to their rear are Joe and Pedro. They are outnumbered and surrounded and it takes only a second for all four to throw down their weapons and shout out that they are surrendering.

Twenty minutes later Joe is back at the house of the wizened old man with his troop guarding the four prisoners. They have little information to impart. They were ordered to guard the road into Las Vegas until the rest of the battalion arrives. They don't know how soon that will be, but quite soon. There were just ten of them, with one truck, one jeep and some rifles and sub-machine guns.

Joe gives them the standard revolutionary message that he learned from Celia Sanchez. The war is against Batista and his corrupt government, not against individual soldiers. They are free to go. They must leave their guns and ammunition behind and not re-join their platoon. If they want to do any more fighting their can join the rebels where they will be welcome. The men mutter about the rebels chances against the combined advancing battalions of Colonel Mosquera and Major Martinez, and say they would prefer to return home to their families. Joe orders two of his men to escort them to the northern edge of town and prepares to move the rest of the troop back into the hills.

Once again Pedro taps him on the arm. "Surely we could take the rest of the platoon? They only have six men and one of those is wounded. We have more. And we could do with their guns, especially the submachine guns and the ammunition, and even the Jeep?"

Joe considers the idea. His orders were to recover the detonators and ammunition and report back on the situation in the town. This he's successfully done. But Castro's wider orders were to hold the town at all costs, and there's no doubt removing or capturing the remaining army presence in the town would fulfil that command.

He reassembles the troop and orders them to move cautiously towards the western edge of the town where the army post is situated. They are not to cross Main Street for fear of being cut-off as Joe had been earlier. He and three others will go down the street itself, while the rest will make their way through the alleys behind the houses and stores. With the guns taken off the prisoners they now have better quality weapons and much more ammunition than before, including some hand-grenades.

The move to the edge of the town is without incident. If there is anyone still living there, they are very definitely keeping hidden. From the last house Joe can see a road-block about 100 yards down the road. There is the Jeep parked in the shade of a tree, and four or five men moving around behind a line of concrete filled oil cans. Approaching the post is going to be difficult as there is little or no cover between it and the last house. Joe orders five men to skirt round to the south and see how near they can get from that direction and positions another man on the roof-top above. Then, without any real hope of hitting anything, he fires four or five rounds to let them know they're under attack, and hears his bullets ricocheting off the oil drums. Fire is returned towards the general direction of the town, but it's clear they don't know where the rebels are positioned.

"Now, how to get near enough and make use of the grenades or petrol bombs?" thinks Joe to himself. At his side is Pedro again. "I think I could sneak up to them from the North, if there is plenty of fire from you here, and the others to the south" he says.

"It's too risky. There's no cover to speak off. If they spot you you'd have no chance. What we need is a full scale diversion.

At that moment comes the whistle of something moving rapidly through the air followed almost immediately by a huge bang. A crater appears in the road halfway between the road-block and the village, as earth and stones shoot up into the air and rain down all around.

"That's interesting," thinks Joe, "shells or a mortar but where's it coming from?"

"There's our diversion" says Pedro, running across the street and then haring off along the northern edge towards the soldiers.

"Damn" exclaims Joe and signals the men around him to open fire. A dozen rifles and a captured sub-machine gun open up, spraying the oil cans with lead, but not doing any more than frightening the troops behind them. Another shell explodes, this time fractionally nearer the road-block than the town, further distracting attention from Pedro's fool-hardy hundred yards dash.

And then he is within grenade throwing range. Joe watches as the youth stands up to his full height, pulls the pin and lobs the projectile over the row of oil cans. There is a momentary lull, two shots ring out from behind the defensive line, Pedro lurches back, and falls to the ground as the grenade explodes.

For a moment there is silence and then another shell whistles over, this time finding it's range nearer to the building sheltering the main group of rebels.

"Look, quick, up here" shouts the look-out on the roof. Joe runs up the stairs on the double and peers out of the attic window over the low balcony. It gives him a clear sight a mile or two out to the West, and what we sees makes his blood freeze. Re-enforcements he was expecting, but not this! Almost every square inch of the plane seems to be filled with advancing troops. Hundreds of trucks are lined up along the road all overflowing with soldiers. In front of them are armoured cars and rubber-wheeled light tanks. And at the front of the column is a full sized tracked tank with its cannon pointing right at them.

"And that way, look, it's our men" said the look-out.

Joe looks round through the town down main street. There, at the far end, are some twenty rebels preceded extraordinarily, by a donkey. Joe rubbs his eyes and looks again.

Yes there is no doubt, heading right towards an entire army battalion is Che Guevara astride a mule!

§§§§§

Joe runs back down the stairs two at a time. He orders two men to see if Pedro is still alive and can be helped. The others he tells to wait for as long as possible and then pull back into the hills behind the first house they'd come to. He himself sets out east along main street towards the rebels shouting loudly "hold your fire …. it's us".

Guevera, when he reaches him, is wheezing horribly. He is clearly in the throes of one of the serious asthma attacks that Joe knows plague him from time to time. "Welcome to the liberated town of Las Vegas, *Commandante*" Joe said. "Unfortunately there is a small problem. Half Batista's army is a mile or so down the road, heading this way and I've ordered my troop to retreat. We got the ammunition, the explosive, and the fuses and we've captured a few more weapons, but I'm afraid the town is lost."

At that moment the sound of a car engine can be heard heading towards them. As Che's rebels raise their rifles, Joe looks round and sees Pedro at the wheel, steering erratically along main street. "Wait, hold your fire" he says. Pedro drives up to the group. He is clearly badly injured. His chest is covered in blood, his face is pale and screwed up in pain. His eyes focus on Joe. "Here, I promised to return this", and he hands Joe back his little automatic. "There are also some rifles in the back, and this may be useful…" He points to an elaborate army radio transmitter in the Jeep, and weakly lifts a small book with cardboard covers. Joe takes it from him and looks inside. "I think it's a code book" he says turning to Che. "With luck we might be able to intercept and decode the army's communications."

"You have done well" says Che to the wounded Pedro. "By your actions and bravery I hereby promote you to full membership of the revolutionary army. I also award you your pick of the captured rifles to carry in future engagements."

Pedro's eyes gleam with pride, but it is all too clear to the group standing round the Jeep that he won't be taking part in further engagements of any sort. With a smile still on his face he slumps forward over the steering-wheel, eyes staring sightlessly through the wind-screen.

"I think it's time to get out of here" wheezes Che, as another shell explodes nearby. He dismounts from the mule and climbs in to the passenger side of the Jeep. "English, you drive. Comrades, put Pedro in the back, we'll bury him on the mountain. And you …" he says to one of his lieutenants, "…take this radio and see if you can get it to work. Pretend you are one of the troops guarding the town. Tell them to stop that tank firing. Say there are no rebels here and that they are only hitting their own men. But tell them the road in is heavily mined and they should proceed with extreme caution. That should hold them up for a little while. Then take the radio and code book back to the camp and guard it with your life. Right, English, let's go. I need to find a doctor's house or a pharmacy to get some medicine for this damned asthma."

Che grins at Joe: "And on the way out you can explain how you managed to bring down the entire goddamn Cuban army onto one simple little mission to recover some explosives …"

Chapter 25

The code book and short wave radio turn out to be of real importance. The army had only recently changed their encryption system and the book provides the key to their top level communications. It enables the rebels to monitor all troop dispositions and plans for attack. Good intelligence had long been one of Castro's strong points. In the two years in the Sierra Maestra he built up a network of informers and scouts and messengers. Hardly could an army platoon commander fart than the news was relayed back to his headquarters by a breathless runner. But now the information comes straight to them from an even wider front. And, more importantly, with the captured transmitter they can issue erroneous orders. Advance lines suddenly find that the Cuban air force is inexplicably dropping napalm bombs on them rather than the rebels. It does nothing for the morale of the troops or their commanders.

In fact Joe discovers that Radio is playing a major part in the wider battle against the Bastista regime. One day he's walking round the camp when he comes across a massive aerial poking up through the trees. Out of curiosity he follows the cables back to a camouflaged tent a few dozen meters away. Some way down the hill a small generator is providing electricity. In the tent is a high power transmitter and a rebel announcer pumping out information. When in Havana he'd heard of Radio Rebelde, and knew that many in the wider M26/7 relied on it for information. Castro broadcasts frequently, giving vent to hour long diatribes against the corrupt regime and urging all true patriotic Cubans to oppose it by whatever means. At other times the announcers simply run through the official government reports of skirmishes and actions between the army and the rebels and correct the propaganda. From a small start earlier in the year, Radio Rebelde has proved a significant rallying call against the government, and attracts a huge audience desperate for impartial news.

§§§§§

A few days after the fall of Las Vegas, Che is summoned by Castro to a meeting of the *Commandantes*. Army radio traffic has revealed that Colonel Sanchez Mosquera's 11th battalion is "resting" in a valley at Santa Domingo. Though as Che later reports back to his troop: "What the bastards have got to rest *from* is a fucking mystery. They haven't done anything except sat on their fat arses being driven here in a convoy of trucks."

The orders are that the rebels will surround the valley on three sides and either drive him back or capture the men. This, Joe thinks, is somewhat optimistic. Fewer than 300 lightly armed rebels against a thousand strong army battalion with artillery and air support. But given their position there is not much alternative. Everyone, save a few left behind to guard the camp, is expected to take part, and Joe appears to have been accepted as de facto commander of his small platoon of trainees.

His men are ordered to take up positions on the upper reaches of the Yara River at the head of the valley. It's the most likely, and indeed currently the only, route for the army to penetrate the top of the Sierras and the rebels' strong-hold so Joe knows they're there as a last line of defence if all else fails. Part of him wishes he was more in the thick of the fighting, another part is relieved not to be in the danger of the front-line. There's a spirit of grim determination among the rebels, and rousing homilies from Castro and Che and the other *Commandantes* instil a genuine passion for their cause and a belief they can vanquish the vastly superior forces.

The immediate news when they reach the river is not good. Mosquera, safely back at his command post some miles away at the Estrada Palma Mill, has summoned up another battalion, the 22nd, to do his dirty work. Under their commander, Major Villavicencio, they've split into three companies and are advancing up along the river.

The main advantage of Joe's position is that he can see right down the valley and is able to watch as events unfold. The terrain is rugged. Too rugged for vehicles. At the base, the valley is perhaps a kilometre wide, but it narrows to less than half that at the top. It's steep so advancing troops are always going to be moving uphill, and it has thickly wooded steep sides which provide excellent cover for the rebel forces. In fact as Joe looks down early on the morning of 28th of June, he wonders who on earth would even think of trying to take a 1000 men up the valley without any cover at all. "First I would call in the air force and bomb the hell out of the hills," he thinks to himself during the hours waiting for the action to begin. "Then I'd order a major artillery barrage in case there was anyone left, then I'd deploy troops as far up on the hill sides as I could get them so they would have the advantage in height , in fact, no, even then I wouldn't order my men to walk up the exposed valley floor".

But to his amazement that's just what Villavicencio does. In broad daylight his companies begin to move up on either side of the river. "Into the valley of death …" thinks Joe. And almost immediately there is a huge explosion. A massive land-mine – perhaps 70 lbs of TNT, has been detonated under the first company. Immediately rebel machine guns open up, scything into the disoriented troops.   The column's formation has been completely destroyed. Soldiers are running this way and that. There are cries from the wounded. Some first aid is being given but there seems no attempt to evacuate the injured. Troops are firing randomly into the hillsides seemingly unable to identify the source of the heavy machine gun fire.   Then into the melee Castro's men start firing mortars and for a while all is smoke and noise and confusion.

The action is too far away for Joe and his platoon to join in. Though just technically in range of his Lee Enfield, there seems little point in wasting ammunition when the machine guns are doing the job so effectively. But just then a runner appears with orders from Guevara. Those at the head of the valley are to move round along the ridge to the west and then down towards the river to try to cut off a possible retreat of the third column. This is not massively welcome news to Joe. It means having to climb back up into the hills, cross the river, skirt round through dense undergrowth to the top of the valley and then follow the ridge along for about a mile before dropping down to the valley floor. And then they would be sandwiched between the retreating remnants of the 22nd and the fresh troops of Mosquera's 11th battalion which, so far, have taken no part in the fight.

It's a long hot hard climb through the trees up to the ridge. Joe's men, though, are young and fit and apart from carrying rifles and ammunition have almost nothing else with them, so move freely. It's late afternoon by the time they have joined up with a second rebel platoon and moved back down into the valley and into position. There have been constant bursts of gunfire as the rebels continue to tie down the troops. Across the river Joe watches as a new army column moves up to relieve the beleaguered first company. No sooner have they joined forces than a further wave of mortar shells rains down on them from the hill side. Castro's well positioned machine gunners are also finding their targets. The troops are tied down, unable to advance up the valley and apparently uncertain what to do next.

The third company, whose retreat Joe is supposed to be preventing, is nowhere in sight. The bank of the river here is much steeper than opposite, There is nothing that resembles a proper path and anyone moving up or down stream has to clamber over giant boulders and rocks and, occasionally climb up the side of the valley to get round deep pools in the fast flowing river. It's ideal territory to defend, and almost impossible to attack. He positions guards up to the right to look out for the missing column, and also downstream to the left in case Mosquerra decides to send re-enforcements along this bank of the river.

The sun has now dipped behind the high westerly ridge and Joe wonders what's going to happen next. The regular army, he thinks, is in an improbable but impossible position. Two companies of around a hundred men each are pinned down across the river, the third, on his side, is in the wrong place to help them and is evidently following earlier orders to press on. There is only an hour or so of day-light left and if they don't retreat back to the main battalion at the Mill they're going to be at the mercy of the rebels all night long. The same thoughts have evidently occurred to Villavicencio as shortly afterwards his men begin to move back, leaving the dead and the wounded behind and some even abandoning arms and ammunition.

Joe anticipates that the order to withdraw will also have been communicated to the third column on his side of the river and sure enough they soon appear, moving as rapidly as the

179

terrain will allow along the river bank. The rebels wait until they have congregated are in a wide-ish clearing and then open fire from cover of the trees above. Joe nuzzles down tight to the ground, legs splayed, rifle strap wound round his left arm, head bent at an angle over the sights. He fires, feels the kick of the recoil against his shoulder, moves his right hand up from the trigger feeling for the bolt. He lifts it, slides it back watches as the spent cartridge case flies out of the side, feels the new bullet pushing up into the chamber, slams the bolt forward and down as his hand continues back down to the trigger guard. Through his sights he sees a melee of people. There is gunfire from all around. Half the troops have stopped and are returning fire from whatever limited cover they can find. Of the rest, some are simply running full pelt downstream clambering over rocky outcrops away from the action, while others are moving back up the valley in the direction from which they have just come. Joe shifts his body to pick out a target among those retreating to his left. He fires and sees a man stumble and fall. Two immediately behind him trip over the man's body. Another bullet in the chamber, another running target, another soldier falls to the ground. But now the returning fire is getting heavier. A machine gun has been set up on the river bank and bullets are zipping around the heads of Joe's platoon, some ricocheting off the trees and rocks behind which they are crouching. Joe signals them to fall back and find new defensive positions. Despite the odds of more than three to one in the Army's favour, Joe reckons his little troop can hold them up almost indefinitely. It's a brave or foolhardy soldier who will follow them in to the unknown of the undergrowth. But the machine gun is bad news. Joe skirts round a little to the right and peers out to see if he can get a clear shot at it. There's a gap between two rocks. Flat down on the ground again, just like at Bisley, tense, rigid, cradling the Lee Enfield. It's not a man he's aiming at, it's the concentric circles of a paper target. He nudges the barrel over millimetre by millimetre until the centre of the circle is fully in his sights and then caresses the trigger. "Don't pull it" says the voice of his instructor. "Don't even squeeze it. Just focus on your index finger. Feel the blood moving through it, now bend the joint a fraction more …" there's a loud bang next to

Joe's ear, and a kick to his right shoulder. The machine gun stops suddenly. "Good shot" says someone, though Joe can't distinguish whether it's his instructor at the rifle-range or a fellow rebel in the Santo Domingo valley. He's already pulling the bolt back, snaking back into the cover of the undergrowth and looking round for his men.

Amidst the smell of the cordite and the clattering bangs of different calibre gunfire Joe notices the sky has tuned flamingo pink as the sun's dying rays reflect off the fluffy clouds. So much beauty above, so much mayhem below. A white flag is waving from his side of the river. The remaining group of soldiers has surrendered. Of the original column of a hundred men, five are dead, thirteen or fourteen wounded, a couple critically, while thirty or forty soldiers have simply disappeared into the hills, most abandoning their weapons in their flight. Joe's rebel group of 25 has nearly double that number of prisoners! A runner is sent to inform Castro of the outcome of the battle on this side of the river, and to ask for new orders. Ammunition and guns are collected. The captured troops are set to work patching up their wounded and burying their dead. Sentries are posted, though Joe thinks it's unlikely that Mosquera would try to send support into rebel held territory at night. But assuming that half of the 22nd Battalion escaped, the first day's action added to Mosquera's completely fresh troops of the 11th, there are still more than one thousand five hundred soldiers waiting a few miles down the road to tackle the 300 rebels.

Joe and the others search among the army packs for food and water and settle down to wait for daylight to bring the decisive part two of the battle of the Yara river.

§§§§§

The following morning is overcast and provides good cover for the air-force planes that appear shortly after dawn. Joe hears them first. A low rumble in the distance. Then they come into view from the open end of the valley following the fast-flowing river up towards its source in the hills behind. On the first two runs they strafe the valley floor, bullets kicking up dust and smashing into rocks. Those that hit the water look like stones sent skimming across the surface. But they are nowhere near worrying Joe or his group concealed in the trees higher up the bank.

On the second run the planes drop Napalm. Globulets of petrol bursting into flame on contact with the ground. It's surreally beautiful. Fire spreading up from the rocks and water of the river. Steam rising from the surface. Some foliage is burning and smoke is rising. But with no wind it's not causing any discomfort or danger. Then, across the river, there's movement. As the planes roar off up the valley, figures are breaking cover and stumbling down to the water's edge. Why are they coming out into the open where they'll be sitting targets? Then Joe realises they must be prisoners that Castro's men have taken, and they're being pushed out into the open to stop further Napalm runs. Should he do the same with his prisoners? He doesn't like the idea of putting anybody in such direct danger. In fact all his instincts are to protect all those under his command, friend or foe. But he sees the logic of the move and, not for the first time, wonders at the steely-hearted determination of Castro and his commanders. Rebels who will execute their own men for relatively minor infringements of the revolutionary code will obviously not think twice about using captured troops as hostages or decoys. Yet it sits oddly with their often expressed views about most of the soldiers in Batista's army being ordinary Cubans forced into fighting for the dictator against their will.

As Joe is pondering the dichotomy he hears the planes in the distance again. It's decision time. Shall he too force the prisoners under his control out into the open where they could be horribly burned and maimed if the pilots don't recognise them early enough and abort the bombing in time. He looks over to where the group is gathered under the trees. Mostly in their late teens and early twenties they're a fairly sorry looking bunch. He'd spoken to a number the previous evening. Some were young conscripts forced into fighting while others were poor peasants who'd been seduced by the offer of regular meals and money. But none, he reflected, really wanted to serve Batista nor fight their fellow countrymen. No, he wouldn't send them out to face the Napalm. They could stay under the cover of the trees and take their chances there. But he did want to get his men higher up and that would be impossible with the prisoners in tow. He ran over to the group under the trees and spoke to a sergeant. "I'm releasing you. You can go back to your army unit if you really want to, or you can stay and fight with us, or you can simply disappear over the hills and try to get home. It's up to you."

A look of relief spread over his face. He had clearly thought Joe was about to order them out into the open. He spoke quickly to his men. Half a dozen moved forward asking to stay with the rebels, the rest disappeared instantly into the undergrowth.

The rumbling of the planes engines now reached a crescendo and they lined up for another bombing run. Almost in slow motion Joe sees the viscous liquid being released from the tanks under their wings and raining to the ground where it bursts into flames. Meter by meter it moves towards the group of Castro's prisoners who are frantically waving and shouting down by the rivers edge. The leading plane finally sees them and realises what is happening. The pilot hesitates for a moment then banks steeply to the right just as the trailing fireball reaches the exposed men on the ground. A few are caught by the flames and plunge into the fast flowing waters of the river, taking their chances with the rapids and the rocks.

At that moment the rebel machine guns opened up on the planes from the far bank of the river and all is pandemonium and confusion. The smoke and smell of the Napalm drifts over to Joes position, the clatter of the machine guns fights for dominance over the roar of the aircraft as they strive to gain height. One rebel bullet finds its mark and disables the rudder of the fighter. The pilot struggles to steer clear of the trees on the ridge but just clips a tall pine. It pitches the plane forward into the undergrowth where it explodes with a massive boom that echoes down the valley. Then in the comparative silence that follows Joe can hear the rebels from three or four hundred meters away across the other side of valley burst into applause and cheers. Instantly his own group joins in, celebrating the triumph of the lowly foot-soldier against the power of the airborne killing machine.

The combination of the hostages exposed on the river bank and the loss of a plane to rebel ground-fire halts further bombing runs. Instead, a short time later, the army again begins to move up the valley. If their commanders have learned anything from the events of the previous day they appear not to show it. Once again two columns advance in the open, and one again Castro's men have laid land-mines, one of which explodes with devastating effect just as the leading soldiers reach it. This time, though they put up more of a fight, seeking better cover and using mortars and their own heavy machine guns against the rebel positions.

Joe's orders arrive by runner in mid morning, instructing him to maintain his position on his side of the river just in case Mosquera again tries to send men up that bank. It turns out to be a lengthy frustrating wait. Apart from taking the occasional long-range pot shot at army positions across the river, there is nothing to do. Those columns continue to take a battering from Castro's riflemen who all but surround them. The only retreat is across the river but it's too deep to ford and too swift to swim. And anyway Joe's recruits would be there waiting. He's pretty pleased about how they've performed. He knows that most are itching to get involved in the thick of the battle on the opposite bank, while a few have decided guerrilla warfare is not for them, and are itching to get away from the mountains and back home to wives and girlfriends and family. As the hours tick by Joe too begins to think about sex. Well that's not strictly true. He thinks about sex a lot, but in the rebel camp there's not been much he can do about it except exercise his right arm regularly. And whatever the temporary pleasure of masturbation it's not exactly a fulfilling emotional experience and it certainly lacks the warmth of a female body with it's mysterious and exciting smells and curves and hollows. No, Joe is missing Maria. And it comes as a bit of a shock to him. He's not before had that butterflies-in-the-chest feeling that signals more than the magnet-at-the-end-of-the-cock imperative which usually drags him helplessly towards the female sex. He wants to see her. He wants to see her soon. He wants to see her urgently. He begins to think of Havana and Maria and how he might be able to get back there.

Joe is shocked from his reverie by the appearance of a messenger in the late afternoon. His platoon has been ordered back to the main camp in the hills..

§§§§§

Through ineptitude or cowardice Mesquera has failed to commit his own battalion to the fight. Indeed he actually ordered them to fall back from the advance base at the Palma Mill to their headquarters at Santa Domingo, effectively conceding victory and abandoning the 11th to their fate. And they were duly routed. After being pinned down for much of the day some surrendered, but most fled. Castro had captured quantities of arms and ammunition, taken prisoners, gained a decisive victory, and opened up a route out of the Sierras down the Yara Valley. And Mesquera was reckoned to be one of Batista's more able generals!

But one victorious battle does not a revolution make. The rebels are still massively outnumbered and control only a tiny mountain top in Cuba's most easterly province. Somehow they've got to break out and sweep across the country to Havana, humbling the might of the government forces and carrying the people before them. And they've got less than six months to do it. You still want to risk a hundred Pesos on their chances?

Revolution Cuba '58.

PART 6

Mid-Summer

Chapter 26

On the trek back to the camp Joe comes across Lydia among another group of rebels. They fall into step and she tells him of her part in the action. She was in the thick of the fighting, positioned with Castro's main force across the river from Joe, dodging bullets and firing back at the enemy.

They share supper and sit in Joe's corner of the camp. "We can do it," she says. "We can really beat the bastard. Small groups of dedicated patriots will always overcome a demoralised army that doesn't believe in what it's fighting for and doesn't want to be killing its fellow countrymen."

"Small is the operative word" replies Joe. "Three hundred against ten thousand. That's pretty poor odds, even given the terrain."

"Cuba's first revolutionary leader, Jose Marti, said in the 1880s "Victories in war depend on a minimum of weapons and a maximum of morale". And that's as true today as it was then. And actually Batista has done us a favour. By encircling us and pushing us together into such a small area he's actually concentrated our force for us while his army's lines are hopelessly extended over a huge area."

They talked into the night, Lydia fired with revolutionary fervour and still high on the adrenalin if the battle earlier that day. They were sitting on Joe's blanket, looking out over the Sierras with the stars and moon above them and, as the temperature dropped, she nuzzled up to him for warmth. He put his arms round her shoulders in a protective gesture and she shifted his right hand gently so that it was resting against her left breast. After so long a period without sex, the feel of a woman's bosom beneath his hand was instantly exciting. He moved his fingers slightly, in a gesture that might be taken as simply getting into a more comfortable position, or could be read as a tentative caress. To his surprise she responded instantly, pressing his hand harder against her body and turning her head round so her face was pressing against his. He rubbed his bearded chin against her smooth skin, and risked a little chaste kiss. She turned her head further round and kissed him properly, holding him tight against her and feeling beneath his shirt for his bare flesh.

They fumbled with buttons and underclothes and moved their hands urgently over each others bodies. Lydia was on fire and before he fully knew that it was happening, she was straddling him, pushing him up and into her, rocking back and forth on top of him, bringing him to a rapid and explosive climax.

Later, as they made love again at a pace more suited to her pleasure, she whispered in his ear: "isn't it every man's fantasy to have the daughter *and* the mother?"

"Only if you can have them together at the same time in the same bed" he laughed back.

§§§§§

Next morning Che is in ebullient mood. "It's out greatest victory yet. It just shows what the power of the power of a guerrilla army fighting for a righteous cause can achieve. And Mosquara! What a corrupt, lazy, cowardly bastard. I'm not sure he'd have won even if he's sent the whole of his 22nd to support the 11th, But to leave them there without any proper back-up. He should be cashiered and shot for cowardice."

Guevara has come over to Joe's little spot on the edge of the camp and is looking out over the mountains. When Joe awoke, Lydia was gone. Now Che is sitting on the blanket, smoking a fat Cuban cigar and drinking locally grown coffee. He hands Joe a cup and hears his debrief. "Yes, you did well at the river. I think you were wrong to release so many prisoners but I see that you thought guarding them was endangering your own men". Joe has slightly edited the version of events, and played down his humanitarian concerns in favour of protecting his men. "And you came away with a good quantity of guns and ammunition and 6 new recruits. Not bad for a Limey and a bunch of trainees."

Joe is pleased by the praise, but still a bit surprised that the *Commandante* is sitting drinking coffee with him when there must be rather more pressing matters to attend to. Eventually Che gets to the point.

"I have to ask you to take on a new assignment. It will mean leaving here and it could be dangerous. So it's not an order, just a request for you to volunteer."

Joe is becoming more curious by the minute.

"You know that Fidel's brother Raul left the main rebel group some months ago to open up a second front in the Sierra Cristals north and east of Santiago. Well, he's been pretty successful. He's built up a force of over 200 men, he's got an armoury, hospitals, and schools and has been harrying the army at every opportunity. But the May offensive has been hard for him. He's dangerously low on ammunition and he embarked on a new policy without consulting Fidel or any of us in the top command."

"And what is this new policy?"

"It's to take as hostages any Americans found within his territory, demanding that the US stop supplying Napalm and providing refuelling facilities to Batista."

"Wow," said Joe, "that's pretty provocative".

"Yes, and pretty effective too. In the last few days he's seized American and Canadian nationals from the Moa Bay mining company, the Nicaro mine, and the United Fruit Company's mill at Guaro. Then two nights ago he hijacked a bus outside the US base at Guantanamo with 24 American sailors and marines aboard. It's been all over the American press, and has put our movement on the map like nothing since the Matthews interview in the New York Times."

"But isn't is a bit like trying to capture a tiger by grabbing its tail? Surely you want the US to end its support for Batista, not to come to his aid. The last thing you want is Uncle Sam sending a couple of divisions up here. They'd do the job a bit more thoroughly than Mosquara."

"Exactly. So Fidel had made a public announcement on Radio Rebelde ordering Raul to release the hostages. But he needs to get written orders and a personal letter to him urgently, outlining his full views about hostage taking. Now we've opened

189

up a route out of here we need a fast messenger, and when I told Fidel I had a motorcycle at my disposal he jumped at it. I've got others who will take the note if you ..."

"No that's fine," interrupts Joe, "I'd be honoured to go, and I'd like to meet Raul. He sounds like a rather decisive sort of fellow."

"Good, then I'll arrange for some gas and a map for you. I'll be sorry to see you go. I've enjoyed our talks and games of chess even if your end game is painfully slow," smiled Che, "And perhaps you could take some rolls of film to be developed. Get two sets of prints. Give one to our local M26/7 contact in Santaigo and tell them to keep them until after we've triumphed. I think they'll be important archive documents. The other set and the negatives you can keep and give to me when you next see me."

Joe wonders once again at the ability of the Argentine to find time to play chess and worry about photography in the middle of fighting a revolutionary war. But he doesn't ponder for long. He hurriedly packs up his few possessions and hands over his prized Lee Enfield to the best of his trainees. By the time he's had a quick breakfast a messenger has arrived with Fidel's letter to his brother, along with other papers and orders.

The bike fires second kick, and by nine o'clock Joe is negotiating the rocky trail back down the mountain. He pauses on a bend and looks back to the camp where he's spent the last few weeks. It's been a good time. Yes there's been the looming presence of Batista's army a few miles away, but somehow unreal. It's been more like the camping trips he used to go on with the local Deptford Scout pack in his youth, all marshmallows and stories by the camp-fire, only with guns instead of marshmallows in the Sierras. He's met the charismatic Fidel Castro and got to know slightly the enigmatic Che Guevara. He's tested himself again in battle and come under fire in three or four engagements. He's once more overcome the fear of death or serious injury, done his job efficiently, and rather relished the adrenalin rush of battle. And, thinking of last night's tingling tryst with Lydia, reflects that he's also rather complicated his personal life.

But generally he's not sad to be leaving. The thought of a hundred miles or so on the bike will blow away the cobwebs and, if he's lucky, after delivering the messages to Raul Castro, he might be able to find his way back to Havana and Maria.

After a hair raising ride down the mountain, the going gets easier in the foothills. Che's map marks a way through where, theoretically, there won't be many army patrols. By mid-day he's making good progress along a dirt road heading almost due east, skirting round the city of Bayamo, planning to cut north of Santiago which remains a major Army stronghold, and to get into the Sierra Cristals by way of Palma Soriano.

It's another perfect tropical day. Sun beating down from a cloudless sky, cool breeze in his face, the big twin cylinder engine purring beneath him. If Joe believed in a God, he'd certainly agree that he was in his heaven and all was right with the world.

So the sound of a gun firing and the whistle of a bullet flying close over his head is a nasty wake-up call. He looks round and sees an army Jeep in hot pursuit behind. He twists the throttle, pulls in the clutch and kicks down on the gear lever. The bike leaps forward and accelerates away. But this is not a good road for outpacing a jeep. It's narrow and twisty and gravely. Already Joe has felt the back wheel skidding out from under him on the lose surface. This is not the moment to lose it on a bend and find himself face down on the road with several hundredweight of bent BMW and an army patrol on top of him. So if he can't outrun them he'll have to outsmart them.

Round the next bend Joe sees a narrow track leading off to the right. Changing down again as he approaches, he slams on the rear brake, twists the bars slightly to the right, and feels the back of the bike sliding round under him. Just as he's at right angles to the main road, he pulls the bike upright and guns the engine. The back wheel spins against the gravel, finds purchase, and thrusts the machine forward up the narrow track. There's cover ahead, an old *Gaujero* hut with thatched palm leaves for roof and walls. Joe edges the bike round the back, kills the engine, and free-wheels to a stop next to a pile of firewood under a makeshift cover. In the silence he can hear the jeep approaching the entrance to the track along the on the road below. He looks round for something to cover the bike with and sees, standing just a few feet away, the evident owner of the *botha*. He's wearing ragged trousers and a

191

torn shirt, and has a machete hung from his belt. In his hand is an ancient, battered, but still effective-looking double barrelled shotgun, and it's pointing straight at Joe's head.

"Buenas dias," says Joe smiling at the stony faced man. "I could use some help. The soldiers are after me".

"Why should I help you?" grunts the man through toothless gums.

"Because they're heartless murdering bastards and we should stand together against them."

"My son's in the army," says the man, and spits a globule of phlem from the side of his mouth onto the ground by Joe's right foot.

Damn, he thinks, that was the wrong opening gambit, now I've got problems, The sound of the Jeep which had passed by the entrance to the track can now be heard executing a three point turn and coming back along the road.

Without warning the Gaujero lowers the gun and reaches forward next to the bike and the woodpile, pulling out an old canvass tarpaulin. "Use this", he says.

Joe pulls it over the BMW and throws a couple of palm fronds on top. His host gestures that Joe should climb underneath as well. The jeep engine is getting louder as it approaches up the track. Through a hole in the canvass Joe sees the man turn and walk back to his *botha*. Two soldiers climb out of the jeep and look around suspiciously. One is carrying a submachine gun the other a rifle.

"Who's here?" shouts one.

"Just a poor peasant," replies the man from within the hut.

"Well come out with your hands up," relies the soldier. A moment later the man appears at the open door.

"Where did the motorbike go?" demands the soldier.

"What motorbike?"

"The one that came up your track."

"Not this track," says the man. "Though I did hear an engine going down the road a while back."

"You're lying." says the soldier, as he moves over to the hut, reverses his rifle and drives the but into the man's stomach. As he doubles up in pain the soldier kicks him hard on the shin and, when he's collapsed on the ground kicks him again, this time in the face.

"We know he's here, now tell us where you're hiding him."

The man on the ground grunts in pain. Joe raises the canvass. "Stop. Leave him alone, it's me you want."

As the two soldiers turn to face him, Joe raises his automatic and fires at the second soldier who's holding the machine gun. Instantly he turns and points the gun at the first man who's trying to get his rifle back round into firing position.

"Drop it or you're dead," says Joe simply.

The soldier hesitates for a second, glances at his colleague writhing in a pool of blood on the ground, and then throws down his gun. Joe gestures him back, away from the weapon and goes over to check the wounded man and retrieve the sub-machine gun.

"Are you OK?" he asks the *Gaujero* who's now struggling to his feet and wiping the blood off a cut lip.

"OK. I kill these bastards now, yes?"

"No. Don't do it. It makes you as bad as them. We'll fix the Jeep so they can't go anywhere and I'll give you a ride out of here on the bike. Unless you really want to stay?"

The man surveys his hovel. "What, leave this beautiful home?" he laughs, looking round at the squalor around him.

"I tell you what," says Joe, "We'll sell it to these soldiers." He goes over the wounded man who's clutching a bleeding arm. "Give the *Gaujero* your money. Every Peso. Come on hurry up or I'll put as hole in the other arm." The man fishes about in his trousers for a few grubby notes and some change.

"Now you.'

The other man pulls out a purse and hands it over.

"OK. Now into the hut both of you. Let's see that arm. Hmm take your shirt off and wrap it round the wound. I don't think you'll bleed to death."

Joe asks for rope and ties the two soldiers back to back in the middle of the room, making sure that they should be able to slip their knots after an hour or so. Then he goes to the jeep and lifts the bonnet, unclips the distributor cap, removes the bakerlite and brass arm beneath and tosses it into the undergrowth.

The peasant, who says his name is Sergio, finds a sack from a corner of the hut and puts in it the weapons and ammunition they've taken from the soldiers. Joe tops up the bike's tank from a jerry can in the back of the jeep and they're off.

"I've never been on a motorbike before," says Sergio. It's much more fun than a mule. By the way, thank you for the money."

"It's only right that you should have some compensation for the loss of your home".

"Yes, but that wasn't *my* home. It belongs to my neighbour. And it doesn't even really belong to him because it's the property of the land-owner."

Joe laughs. "Won't your neighbour get a bit of a shock when he come home and finds two soldiers trussed up inside?"

"I never liked him much,' comes the laconic reply.

"And why did you help me and not the troops. I thought you said your son was in the army?"

"Stupid, that boy. I think he's soft in the head. I told him not to fight for that bastard Batista, but would he listen?"

Joe laughs out loud as his new found companion directs him down narrow mule tracks eastwards towards the Sierra Cristals, and the next chapter in his increasingly bizarre adventure.

Chapter 27

With Sergio to guide him, Joe makes good progress around Palma Soriano and into the foothills of the Cristal mountains. The peaks here are much lower than the Maestra, and the hills more spread out.

Before long they are stopped by a rebel patrol and guided to Raul Castro's headquarters at Mayari Arriba. To Joe's surprise this is no makeshift mountain campsite, but a large, well appointed Spanish colonial house in the centre of a small village. Joe parks the bike outside the wrought-iron railings and walks up the path to the front door. There is a bell-pull which sounds deep inside the house. He half expects a liveried butler to appear and ask for his visiting card. However the door is opened by a strikingly attractive woman with long black hair and freshly applied rouge lipstick. But instead of the flowing dress she should have been wearing to compliment the setting, she's in an olive green rebel uniform. But not the usual grubby threadbare and torn combat fatigues of the mountain troops. No, this one is spotlessly clean, freshly pressed and, amazingly, looks tailor made. It fits her like a glove, has elegant shoulder-pads and gathered seams and tucks.

Joe stands there, mouth open, not quite sure what to say. When he finally gathers his thoughts he asks limply: "Is Raul at home by any chance?"

The woman continues to amaze by replying in good English with a trace of an American accent, "No, not at the moment, he out inspecting his defences. Can I help?"

Joe explains his mission, and the woman, who Joe estimates to be in her late 20's, introduces herself. "Welcome, I'm Vilma, Vilma Espin. Do come in. Raul should be back in an hour or so. Can I get you a drink, or some food." And then looking more closely at the rather grubby men in front of her she wrinkles her nose slightly and wonders if they might like a shower.

Sergio declines the offer and says he will wait outside and guard the bike. Joe jumps at the chance – the first shower or bath he's had in all the weeks since leaving Havana.

In an elegant bathroom he toys with the taps and dials hardly able to believe that such luxury still exists. Naked beneath the huge shower rose, he lets the hot water cascade over him and wash away the grime of the mountains. Vilma has taken his clothes away to be washed and had found him a clean T-shirt and jeans. And so it is a well scrubbed and fairly presentable Englishman who arrives back down stairs twenty minutes later.

"Where did you learn your English?" he asks Vilma.

"At school in Santiago and then in the States at MIT. I did a year's post-graduate course."

"In what?"

"Chemical engineering'" she said matter-of -factly.

"And how did you find you way into this line of work?"

"You mean helping to run the revolution?" she laughs. "Well my father was an executive with the Baccadi rum company in Santiago and we lived in a nice house and I went to a private Catholic girls school, and was perfect little rich kid. Then I went to the University of the Oriente and began to listen to what the professors and lecturers were saying about what was happening to my country. And I started to see what the workers who supplied the sugar to make my father's rum were being paid, and what conditions they lived in. And after a year in America living among the pampered elite of Boston and New England I was questioning my whole upbringing and way of life."

"But that's still a long way from taking up arms to overthrow the government?"

"Yes, but I was travelling in Mexico and heard that Fidel was in exile there after being released from prison so I went to visit him. That's where I met Raul and Che for the first time. And they changed my life. After that I went back to Santiago and started organising the resistance for the 26th July Movement, and running a number of safe houses. But things became a bit hot after a while and I had to leave so I came up here to join the second front."

As she told her story Joe was thinking about just how widespread in Cuban society ran the support for the overthrow of the government. This was not like the Russian or even the French revolution, where the proletariat rose up against the capitalists or the upper classes. Here in Cuba there were people from the lowliest peasants and factory workers to the highest professors, lawyers and even rich Chemical Engineering graduates all united in the one cause. And once again Joe wondered if they knew what they were letting themselves in for. It's one thing to create a popular movement to overthrow the government, but it's quite another to find a replacement which will be supported by, or popular with, those original disparate opponents.

But while he is pondering this there comes the sound of a car's engine outside.

"That will be Raul," said Vilma.

Joe looks out of the window and sees a smart grey four wheel drive Toyota Land Cruiser skid to a halt. Bouncing out of the drivers seat is a man in his late twenties wearing a light coloured Stetson and sporting a pony tail. Had a country and western song been playing Joe wouldn't have been surprised. The sheer incongruity of the scene strikes him: the brother of the leader of the Cuban revolution, wearing a cowboy hat, driving a Japanese jeep, and calmly commanding the second front from a Spanish Colonial Villa in the hills above Santiago with a price on his head half of a dictator's army after him. This was the stuff of Alice in Wonderland.

Raul Castro is shorter and slightly thinner than his brother and has earnest baby-face features that make the battered pipe he is smoking look incongruous. He welcomes Joe after Vilma had introduced him and ushers him into an elegant room dominated by a large desk covered in papers.

"So I see my brother's not so keen on my new policy of taking hostages," he said after he had seen Fidel's letter. "It is essential to declare categorically that we do not utilise the system of hostages however justified our indignation may be about the political attitudes of any government" he reads out loud .

"Well that's all very well, but I've got them now. The question is what to do with them."

"Does Fidel say they've all got to be released at once?" asks Joe.

"No, he just says that although he's sure I am managing the situation with great tact, I must keep in mind that in matters that can have weighty consequences for the Movement I must not act on my own initiative. Whatever that means."

"According to Che the concern is that Washington is still officially neutral in this war and what they don't want to happen is for the US to come down firmly on Batista's side."

"Neutral!" exclaimed Raul. "Neutral. They're supplying tons of Napalm to Batista, which is being put into US made bombers, which are being refuelled at the US base here and flown over OUR country to be dropped on OUR people. The same people who are being shelled by US made Sherman tanks and shot at by US made rifles and machine guns. And you call that NEUTRAL?"

"Calm down Raul, you'll give yourself a heart-attack" says Vilma who's been listening to the exchanges. "What Joe is saying is that there can be a considerable difference between Washington's official diplomatic line and what it allows the military to do. And as for the CIA, well they've always been a third force that may or may not back the military or the diplomatic agenda."

"Well where does that leave us. We've got a bunch of hostages that Fidel says we shouldn't have taken. But if we return them it makes us look weak, and makes the Americans think they can push us around in the way they've been doing to Cubans for centuries, plus they still go on re-fuelling Batista's planes in Guantanamo."

"Well," says Joe thoughtfully, "how about releasing them but not releasing them?"

Raul and Vilma look at him as if he's crackers.

"What I mean is release some, perhaps the oldest or those with a medical condition, and keep promising to release the rest when certain concessions have been gained. It makes you look humanitarian, it accepts implicitly Fidel's no hostage stance, it doesn't make you look supine to Uncle Sam, but it does enable you to use your bargaining power to the full."

The expression on the listeners' faces changes from astonishment to admiration.

"Yes," says Raul, "we could string this out for weeks or even months. It's a good idea. But what we need is someone to negotiate with the American consul in Santiago."

"As the Americans would say," adds Vilma, "an honest broker."

They are both now looking squarely at Joe. "You think *I* look honest?" he laughs.

"Well relatively honest. And you do have the advantage of speaking American ... even if it is with a funny accent".

"But how do I get through into Santiago. I thought the city was swarming with troops?"

"Well, you could phone up Park Woolam at the US consulate, tell him you are coming, and ask him to arrange safe passage."

"Phone him up," says Joe in amazement, "from where."

"Well, from here. We do have the telephone you know. We're not some third world country stuck in the stone-age. This is Cuba mid-way through the twentieth century. We have all the benefits of modern American technology: refrigerators, air conditioners, Sherman tanks, B25 bombers!"

All three burst out laughing, and it's a while before Joe can extract a phone book and look up the number for the consulate. As he dials he's still astounded that in the middle of a civil war in the headquarters of a key revolutionary leader the public telephone is working. But then, he reflects, it was only a month or so since he left Havana which gave every indication of being a modern thriving metropolis. It's just that the weeks in the mountains have rather coloured his perceptions.

The girl on the switchboard at the Santiago consulate is business-like and firm. No, she can not put Joe through to Mr Woolham. He's busy. Perhaps he might like to submit his request in writing..."

"I'm currently in the mountains with the rebels who are holding a number of US citizens hostage. I'm not sure that there is any paper here, and anyway there is a certain urgency about this, They might start killing them unless you pull your finger out …"

"There's no need to take that tone with me, sir" says the receptionist sniffily. "And if you are so remote how is it that you can make a telephone call?"

"Well, this is not some third world country stuck in the stone-age. This is Cuba mid-way through the twentieth century," parrots Joe, "We have all the benefits of modern American technology: refrigerators, air conditioners, Sher ….Shirley Temple ice cream," he corrects himself quickly.

The woman at the other end, while convinced she has a complete nutter on the line, is also conscious that these are unusual times in Cuba, and that her chances of a good posting back to Washington could be irreparably marred if he IS telling the truth and the hostages all get killed because of her.

"Hold one minute, sir. I'll see if Mr Woolam's assistant is free.

Eventually, after being passed three times round the Consulate Joe is able to persuade someone in authority that he's serious, and they promise to speak to the local Army commander about guaranteeing Joe a pass to get through into the city. He's to call back two hours later.

§§§§§

The following morning, after a night in a bed! with ironed sheets! and another shower, Joe is back on the bike heading South. Sergio has insisted on coming too. He has relatives in Santiago that he wants to visit, and he says he knows all the roads around about. Though since he's now thirty or forty miles from his home and his only previous means of transport seemed to be a mule, Joe is a bit puzzled about how this can be. However he's glad of the company, and thinks there may be strength in numbers when it comes to negotiating at army check-points.

The previous evening Raul had taken Joe around to a number of houses in the hills where the hostages were being held,

All seemed in good health and are being well looked after, albeit under heavy guard. Joe provided paper and pencil and got one member from each group to write a short note to attest to the fact that they were still alive.

Raul also showed Joe a number of other facilities he'd established including a hospital and a several small schools. "The hospital was initially for our own rebel troops who were wounded in attacks," he said, "But in between engagements we try to treat as many local people as possible."

Indeed the building, a converted local store, had simple but modern looking facilities and a ward with 14 beds. Inside it was teeming with children and adults who had clearly come from surrounding villages. "We've got nearly 20 doctors, two dentists and two pharmacists working in the villages we control" said Raul proudly. "Most of the local *Campesino* families have never been to a doctor before. Their children are usually suffering from stomach disorders and parasite borne diseases. They're so grateful for our help that when our wounded are brought in they come with gifts of food and honey to feed them."

It was an impressive undertaking. Nearby the medical centre was an operating room in a wooden shelter with a corrugated iron roof. Apart from health service, the second front had also established a network of teachers and class-rooms. "Many were teachers before we liberated the area" said Raul, "and amazingly the government continues to pay their salaries!"

The contrast between the remote villages in the Sierra Cristals and the bustle of Santiago, when Joe eventually gets there, is vast. Sergio and he had met some delays on the road down from the mountains while one army post phoned another to verify their credentials, but eventually they got through to the outskirts and gazed down on a city nestling in a sunken valley, someway inland from the coast, but with a huge natural harbour. Like Havana the only outward evidence of an ongoing revolution are the presence of armed troops dotted throughout the streets, and an occasional convoy of army trucks rumbling along. Otherwise all is normal. Indeed after they have found somewhere to park the bike near the US consulate, Joe is immediately approached by two or three prostitutes and at least one man offering dirty postcards and his daughter and even his daughters friend if the price is right. Sergio tells them to fuck off in a torrent of toothless Spanish, and before long the two are sitting in the air-conditioned waiting room at the Consulate.

"Are you sure you want to come along to this?" Joe asks Sergio. "It will all be in English, and probably rather boring."

"I've never been in an American office building," he replies. "I'd like to see what it looks like. Anyway I'm your bodyguard now."

Joe smiled at the thought of Sergio being able to protect him from the heavily armed marines who are on duty throughout the building. But he agrees to let him come anyway. He looks enough like a rebel to give me some veracity, he thinks.

The waiting room is crowded with Santiagans seeking exit visas to the US. While they are waiting Joe glances at a day old copy of the Washington Post. The hostage situation is front page news with two senators demanding that effective help be given to Batista unless the Americans are released within 48 hours. The US Ambassador in Havana, Earl T Smith, is also quoted making bellicose noises, while the Secretary of State, John Foster Dulles was trying to be a bit more emollient. Joe recalls a conversation with Herbert Matthews in which the correspondent said he believed that Ambassador Smith in Havana and his technical junior, the Santiago consul, were at logger-heads over support for the Cuban dictator. During coffee at Marti's bar Matthews said he'd heard the Santiago consul was being specifically allowed to report direct to Washington without his dispatches going through Havana – an extraordinary departure from normal diplomatic protocol.

When they are finally ushered in to the consul's office, Park Woolham is sitting in a plastic covered upholstered chair behind a huge modern desk entirely clear of clutter. Behind him is a large brass relief eagle and the Stars and Stripes draped from a flagpole. On the opposite wall is a portrait of President Dwight D. Eisenhower. By Woolham's side stands a man in a crew-cut and sharp suit who is introduced as the vice consul Robert Weicha.

Joe starts the conversation in Spanish for the benefit of Sergio, but is quickly asked to switch to English to avoid any "ambiguities or misunderstandings". He tells the Americans he is an accredited journalist who had been gone to meet the rebels of the second front in the Sierra Cristals for an article when the hostage crisis erupted. He outlines Raul's offer to release half a dozen of the hostages and says he believes there could be a staged release of the others as certain concessions are made. The key demand is for an end to the refuelling of Cuban air force planes at Guantanamo. But crucially the rebels also want the US to obtain an assurance from Batista that US military aircraft would not be used against them. Woolham replies with the official Washington line that the US will not be blackmailed into helping the rebels and that, since there is an official arms embargo, the US couldn't be supplying fuel or ammunition to the armed forces.

Joe glances up at the vice consul in the crew-cut as he hears this and sees the younger man shifting uncomfortably. There's either something the consul doesn't know that his assistant does, or Woolham is lying through his teeth and Weicha is not much of a poker player, he thinks.

"Look," he says out loud, "frankly I don't give a stuff about the diplomatic niceties of the US's relationship with Batista or about the arms embargo, or whether the military or the CIA is, or is not, officially, or unofficially, refuelling the planes or loading them up with Napalm. What I do know is that Fidel Castro and, more importantly here, his brother is convinced they are. And Raul Castro's got the hostages. And they are obviously not going to release them without some concessions. So it seems to me it might help to move this on if you could give Raul some assurances that he'll actually believe."

The US consul sits thoughtfully for a moment. "Young man," he said smiling, "I think you might be better off sticking to journalism. You're far too direct to be a diplomat. Usually we'd beat a round the bush for twenty minutes or so and then reach the position you've just got to in three. Now I don't know what we're going to talk about for the next quarter of an hour!"

It was Joe's turn to smile. "How about the differences in nuance between your attitude to the rebels and that of your ambassador in Havana. The word is that Mr Smith is much more of a Batista supporter than either you or the State Department."

Woolham for a moment paled, and then forced a smile back onto his face. "Boy. I was right first time. Much too direct. OK, we'll stick to the hostage situation. Much as I appreciate your coming here and all, I think that I should really be negotiating with Senor Raul Castro himself rather than a newspaperman who just happened to be 'passing by'. What would you say the chances were of me being able to take a US chopper up to the Cristals and meet him face to face, and even see how our people are faring?"

Joe thinks for a minute, impressed that Woolham has seen through, but nevertheless is playing along with, the charade of his being a visiting reporter rather than an active member of the rebel forces. "I might be able to fix that," he says. "I'll need a little time. When could you go? Day after tomorrow?"

Chapter 28.

Joe finds a public telephone box in the Plaza Delores and puts a call through to Mayari Arriba. He quickly establishes that Raul would be happy to have the opportunity to speak directly to Park Woolham and is given a map reference where the chopper could land. Another phone call to the Consulate confirms the arrangements

Next stop is a camera store where they promised to develop film and provide two sets of prints in four hours. Having first established that the owner is no fan of the government Joe hands over Che's rolls of film.

Afterwards, with a little subterfuge, he complains of toothache and asks Sergio to accompany him to a dentist. Only when they have found one does he own up that he is proposing to have a set of false teeth made up for his companion. Sergio sits uncomplaining in the dentist's chair while a cast is made of his gums. He's clearly never before been in a dentist's surgery and Joe tries not to think of the means by which he had had his teeth removed in the first place.

Afterwards Sergio goes off to try to find his missing relatives while Joe picks up the photographs and heads for the contact Che has given him. The imposing headquarters of the Santiago Rotarians club seems an unlikely spot to find M26/7 activists, but the club's secretary himself welcomes Joe and, after the briefest of acquaintances, finds him a hotel room for the night and arranges for him to join a number of 'like minded friends' for dinner that evening.

Joe fills in the time before dinner by writing to Maria and, in a coded way, telling her his news. He hopes, he says, to be back in Havana in a few days time and is missing her terribly.

Half a dozen of the Movement's Santiago leaders are gathered in the back room of a small restaurant off the Plaza Delores. Travel after dark is trickier in the city because of the sheer number of army patrols out on the streets. General Cantillo rules the regional capital with a rod of iron from his headquarters at the infamous Moncada Barracks. The talk is of the blatant murder of two sisters by police in the city in reprisal for a rebel attempt on the life of the defence minister. Joe listens attentively. But once the talk moves to the activities of the *Burbudos* in the Sierras, he's the centre of attention. He gives a blow by blow account of the Battle of the Yara river and Mosquerra's failure to send in his battalion as re-enforcements.

Several present disagree with Che's assessment that the Colonel is merely a coward. Of all Batista's military commanders Mosquerra is held to be the most able, the most cunning, and the most ruthless. And what Joe quickly realises is that, here in the centre of the very province where the rebels have been winning victory after victory for eighteen months or more, no one can see how they can deliver a knock-out punch against the might of the army. On the *llano* the view remains that it is only civil insurrection that will finally unseat the dictator.

"But at what cost?" asks Joe, "If every time you strike at a political or military target they simply round up innocent civilians and murder them, you have to ask 'is it worth it?' At least if you join the rebel army you know the risks you are running and you are not putting innocent lives at risk."

This remark causes howls of protest. The army in the Sierras has routinely rounded up and shot innocent peasants in reprisal for the guerrilla's activities. And, it is pointed out, guerrilla actions themselves have not infrequently resulted in the death of civilians. Any action against the government whether in the *sierras* of the *llano* will inevitably result in innocent lives being lost – but the alternative, simply allowing Batista and his secret police to grind down the country, is worse.

The topic if conversation is easier when they move on to the US and its hopelessly mixed policy over Cuba. The Santiagans agree that the official suspension of arms shipments to Batista is being openly flouted by the military in Guantanamo. And while the US may not be supplying *new* tanks and aircraft, spare parts for the old ones are still routinely being sold. Meanwhile the dichotomy over whether Washington should throw its diplomatic weight behind the pro-American dictator or risk backing the communist-leaning rebels remains unresolved. Joe's speculation of a rift within the State Department is supported. The Secretary of State, John Foster Dulles, is thought to be much more concerned about events in Europe and Africa than in the Caribbean. Meanwhile there appears little backing for their Havana ambassador Earl T Smith's rigidly pro-Batista stance.

As he lies awake later that evening, Joe wonders how it will all be resolved. He thinks that Fidel and Che can probably hold off the army almost indefinitely in the hills, but can't see how they can possibly defeat them on their own terms on the planes. Urban terrorist warfare is little more than a pin-prick in the side of the regime. Censorship is so ubiquitous that few people have any real idea of what is going on, unless they listen to Radio Rebelde or can get a copy of the messily mimeographed Cuba Libra. The US is most unlikely to force Batista out and, even if it did, has nothing certain to replace him with. It's a mess, he reflects, and decides that he will accompany Park Woolham to his meeting with Raul Castro and then go back to Havana. He might contact Lansky and see if there's any work going in the Casinos. But at very least he hopes to have Maria in his arms and in his bed.

§§§§§

Next morning the sun is shining and the city looks beautiful as he leaves the hotel the M7/26 people have found for him and walks downtown looking for a café for breakfast. The pavements are thronged with people starting their day. Busses and taxis and carts clog the streets. Suddenly a blue car with the letters SIM emblazoned in white along the side screeches to a halt a few feet in front of Joe and two men leap out. They are both pointing automatics at him and they bundle him into the back seat.

"Where are you taking me?" he asks.

"Shuddup. You'll find out soon enough."

This is not reassuring. SIM, the Servicio de Inteligencia Militar, are Batista's dreaded secret police. They are known torturers who more often than not kill their victims rather than release them. In his mind Joe runs through what they might have on him and what compromising documents he light be carrying. The conclusion he reaches is not comfortable. The car roars through the morning traffic to a large nondescript building. Joe is bundled inside and marched down several corridors before being pushed into a square room, completely bare except for three chairs in the middle. If there is a window it's completely covered. The only light comes from a dimmish bulb dangling from the centre of the ceiling, He is searched, handcuffed and sat on one of the chairs and told to wait. The arresting officers take his passport and ruck-sac away with them.

The minutes tick by and Joe tells himself they are deliberately keeping him waiting to allow his mind to do their work for them. The fear of what could happen is likely to be far greater than the reality. Pain is transient. Death is a release. But he doesn't want to die and isn't that keen on pain. Most of all he doesn't want to be permanently disfigured. He's not particularly vain, but he's proud enough of his looks and his body. And at 22 he profoundly hopes that he will have a fair number of years more to enjoy them. Crucially he asks himself what he knows that could compromise anyone else. There seems little point in being tortured for information that the authorities already have. But if it's a question of putting someone else's life in danger, then he would hold out. Yes, but for how long? And if they were so brutal as to get the information from him in the end anyway, then what would have been the point of going through the ordeal in the first place?

His reflections are cut short by two men entering the room. They are in plain clothes. Both in their 30's. One is taller and thinner than the other and wears a moustache. Neither has shaved that morning and, from the smell of body odour wafting over, not washed overly much either.

"Name?" demands the thin man, who's holding Joe's passport.

"It's in my passport."

"Name?" this time the question is slightly louder with an edge of menace to it.

Joe gives his name. "As you can see I'm a British citizen. I'd like to have a representative of the UK consulate present please."

The interrogators simply ignore the request: "Address?"

Joe gives his address in Havana.

"What you doing in Santiago?"

"Collecting material for an article. I'm a newspaper reporter."

"Why are you carrying a gun?"

"Same reason you do, protection"

"Where did you get it?"

"I was working for Meyer Lansky in one of his casinos in Havana and he provided it."

"What you doing in Santiago?'

"Collecting material for a newspaper article."

The blow when it comes is quick and hard. A back of the hand slap across the side of his face. It stings rather than hurts.

"What are you doing in Santiago".

"I had business with the US Consul."

"What business?"

Joe starts to tell the story of the hostages and being asked to be an intermediary. But the moment he mentions Raul's name he's stopped.

"So you're a member of the Movement of the 26th of July and you've been consorting with known criminals and wanted men?"

"No I'm a newspaper reporter collecting material for an article ..."

Smash! The same open hand. The same side of the face. This time harder with smarting pain.

"Who did you meet last night."

"Some members of the local rotary club," says Joe using the cover he's been told about.

"They're all members of the Movement of the 26th July."

"Are they?"

Smash. Harder still this time. Bash. The other side of his face. He can taste blood in his mouth.

'Why were you meeting well known members of the Movement of the 26th July?"

"Look. You can hit me as often as you like. But the reason I'm here, and the reason I met Raul Castro, and the reason I had dinner with members of the Rotrary club last night is that I'm a reporter. I've got a letter of accreditation from the New York Times correspondent in Havana. I'm working on a story on the political situation in Cuba."

He braces himself for another blow but it doesn't come.

"Why you got photographs of all the rebel leaders in the Sierras"

"Same reason."

Smash, bash, smash. Three in a row. It's like being in a boxing ring with your hands tied, and unable to dodge the punches. A sharp headache is developing.

"Why you got photographs of all the rebel leaders in the Sierras?"

"Che Guevara gave me a film to get developed to be published in my article in the New York Times. I'm planning a follow-up on the interrogation tactics of SIM."

This time Joe's braced for the blow. But instead of a back-handed slap it's a closed fist punch full in the face. Pain shoots through him. His nose throbs and starts to bleed.

"Where were you three days ago?"

"Travelling to the Sierra Cristals to meet Raul Castro for an interview for my paper."

"How were you travelling?"

"By motorbike".

"Did you stop or were you stopped along the way?"

With a horrible realisation of were this could be heading Joe hesitates.

"Were you stopped along the way?"

"I was not stopped. I did stop to get food and fuel."

"Why did you shoot an officer of the Cuban Army and leave him and another officer tied up in a *botha*?"

"I didn't shoot anyone. Or tie anyone up. I'm a newspaper reporter. And I'm a British citizen and I demand to see a representative of the British consulate."

"I'll tell you what I think," says the fatter of the two men who's been delivering the blows and is now speaking for the first time, "I think you're a member of the July 26 Movement. I think you've been working with wanted criminals in both the Sierra Maestra and the Sierra Cristals and you came down to Santaigo carrying treasonable messages for the movement's leaders in the city."

Joe says nothing.

"But I also tell you what. I don't give a fuck. Because we've got the gun that you used to shoot a member of the Cuban army. We've got his description of you. And we are carrying out forensic tests right now. And once we have a match we are going to give you a trial and then we are going to execute you. By firing squad. And THEN, and only then, we will call the British consulate and tell them where to come to collect your body. Comprende?"

Joe 'comprendes' all too well. He might have got away with having Che's photographs in his possession. He might have got away with consorting with the top revolutionary leaders. He might have got away with meeting the underground movement's leaders in Santiago for dinner. But try as he can he can't see any way he can get out of being charged with shooting that damned soldier.

The interrogators have left him to his thoughts in the airless room that smells of shit and blood and fear. Mostly his own, he realises dolefully.

Chapter 29.

The hours drag by. Around mid-day he's brought some bread and water. He paces the room. When will he be missed? He's supposed to be at the airport the following morning to meet Park Woolham to accompany him in the chopper up to the mountains to meet Raul. But that's 20 hours away. And would the American consul actually start looking for him if he didn't show up? Surely his prime concern would be to check on the hostages and try to secure their release rather than worrying about a stray Englishman who, anyway, he strongly suspects is not all that he says. Meanwhile the speed of a 'military' trial could be pretty swift. The only surprise is that they are concerned about a forensic match between his gun and the bullet they must have extracted from the arm of the soldier, But hang on a minute. You can't get a forensic match between a bullet and a gun unless you have the spent cartridge case. The hammer striking the cartridge leaves a unique impression – or unique enough to be able to be fairly certain which gun it's been fired from, but the piece of lead that is the bullet can't by itself be matched to a specific gun, only to a particular calibre. And what were the chances of the two soldiers, once they had released themselves from Joe's knots, hunting around in the dirt by the woodpile, looking for a small brass cartridge in the hope that it might sometime later be valuable forensic evidence. Not very likely. But then why would they need forensic evidence anyway? SIM and the army are not known for adhering to such niceties. Shoot a couple of bullets into a victim and hang him from a nearby lamppost as a warning to others. That was more their usual style.

The thoughts are spinning round and round in Joe's head, and not coming to any conclusion. At about 4.00 two uniformed soldiers arrive and, without word, handcuff Joe and lead him out to a waiting army van. They sit on either side of him on a bench seat in the windowless back. It is airless and stifling. The drive, however, is relatively short. When the rear doors open again Joe can see they are in a large barracks. Moncada, he thought. The same Moncada barracks that Castro had attacked in 1953 to begin the revolution.

He is hustled along stone corridors, down steps and into a proper cell with solid iron bars for the door and a massive lock. There is, however, a small window high up in the far wall and looking through it he remembered Oscar Wilde's line about the 'little patch of blue that prisoners call the sky'. "Damn it," he thinks, "I'm a bloody prisoner. And unlikely to be a live prisoner for much longer unless something fairly dramatic happens to change my luck." But nothing does happen, and he paces up and down the small cell to while away the time.

An hour or so later the outer door clangs open and he hears the sound of feet approaching, A guard appears in front of the bars and unlocks his door. Expecting to be taken out, he rises. But instead another figure is pushed roughly into the cell. It is Sergio. "Damn, they've got him too." thinks Joe, but has the presence of mind not to say anything, and even pretend not to recognise him in case it could compromise either of them. But the ploy is worthless as a few moments later two more soldiers appear. One has his arm in a sling, and Joe recognises him immediately as the man he had shot outside *botha* where he had first met Sergio.

The two soldiers look straight at the prisoners and formally identify them to the captain. The officer turns and speaks through the bars. "You have been identified and found guilty of shooting and wounding a soldier of the Cuban army, and of abducting him and another member of the armed forces. Papers found on you prove you are members of the revolutionary force that is attempting to overthrow the legitimate government and president. You are therefore guilty of treason, the penalty for which is death by firing squad. There is no appeal and you may not contact anyone. You will be executed at dawn tomorrow. That is all."

So saying the group turns on its collective heel and marches off down the short corridor to the outer door which was loudly slammed shut. Joe turned to Sergio. "Fuck I'm sorry they got you too. How did it happen?"

"Oh, I walked into the barracks and asked to speak to the Captain."

Joe wasn't sure what was more peculiar, what his companion had just said, or how he said it. Instead of his habitual toothless mumble, the sentence had been delivered with a guttural whistling sound. And as he looked at his face he could see why. The collapsed jaw was no more. The gummy grin had gone. Instead two rows of amazingly white teeth propped apart the mouth. Sergio appeared ten years younger and 20 times better looking.

"Your teeth. You collected them. They're great. At least you'll look your best for the firing squad. And that's the main thing."

"With a little luck there won't be a firing squad." Sergio grinned.

But he would say no more however much Joe tried to get him to elucidate … neither would he be drawn on what on earth possessed him to give himself up. Instead he asked what had happened to Joe and found some water in a corner of the cell and started to wash his wounds and scrub off some of the blood that had dried on his face.

They passed a companionable few hours talking about life in the hills and cane cutting. They were given a passable meal of some sort of stew and bread. Joe laughed to see Sergio take out his new teeth before eating. "I haven't quite got the hang of them yet," he said, "and anyway I don't want to get them dirty. "

Joe was uncertain of the time – they'd taken his watch along with the rest of his possessions at the SIM headquarters – but he reckons it must be near mid-night when he hears a key turn quietly in the outer door, and footsteps move lightly down the hallway. In the dim light Joe recognises the Captain who had earlier pronounced the death sentence. Just as he opens his mouth to demand to see the British Consul, Sergio speaks up: "About bloody time. And what do you call that swill you served us for dinner … I've eaten better food from the compost heap. Are you sure you've got the right size uniforms?"

Joe stares in amazement. Then looking backwards and forwards between the two men he begins to see a resemblance. Now Sergio had his teeth, the two men's jaw-lines look uncannily similar. And their eyes are the same colour, and there is something about the shape of the nose…

"Don't tell me this is your son who's in the army? he whispers.

"Useless boy," says Sergio, but with some affection. "Never did do what he was told. But now he may be able to repay some of the trouble he's caused his poor father. Quickly put on this uniform. The guard will be changing in ten minutes and we'll use the confusion to get you out of here".

The two prisoners change quickly and in a few moments look like passable imitations of Cuban soldiers. "Remember, you are to *march* behind me. Don't amble along. Hold you heads up and your chests out. Now off we go, left, right, left, right, left …"

The captain son of Sergio leads the way out of the cell block, along dim corridors and up sets of stairs. Eventually they emerge onto a parade ground. There is almost no-one else around, and once or twice when squaddies pass, they salute the Captain.

There is a crescent moon as they cross the open space and slip into the shadow of the curtain wall that surrounded the barracks. Entering a small guard room by a side gate, the captain hands Joe a bag. In it was his ruck-sack which, amazingly, still contained his watch, his money, his passport, and Big Tony's automatic.

"I told the Captain you might be able to make a contribution to his retirement fund," says Sergio.

"Of course" replied Joe, and pulls out a $100 bill that he'd concealed in the bag's lining. "Thank you for your help. I'm really very, very grateful. If you take my advice you won't wait too long before you retire. The rebel army has Moncada as its number one target when it reaches Santiago."

He shakes the Captain's hand and with Sergio slips out of the gate which is swiftly locked behind them. No longer in step, the two 'soldiers' walk across the broad avenue outside the barracks chatting noisily as if they have just come off duty and are looking forward to getting off to a bar or home to their wives and families. But once in a side street Sergio breaks into a trot.

"Come on. I think it's best if we get as far away from here as possible."

Round another corner there's a shape in the shadows and Sergio pulls off a cover to reveal the BMW. Joe looks amazed. "How did you get this here? I thought you didn't know how to drive?"

"I don't. But I have a cousin who runs a garage in the city and he moved it for me. Incidentally he said it could do with a service, and if you're passing to drop it in to him!"

Joe laughs as he pushes the full weight of his body down on the kick start. The roar of the engine seems incredibly loud in the silent street, but in a moment Sergio is on the back and they are moving off, the twin cylinders now purring quietly beneath them.

"Where to?"

"The airport, " said Sergio, "if you want to be on that flight up into the Sierras tomorrow morning."

They head out of town. There are no road blocks, and the odd army patrol they pass waves back at them as soon as they spot the uniforms. There's a bit of waste ground at the far side of the runway and they park the bike and settle down to wait for dawn.

"So, come on, how the hell did you find me?" asks Joe.

"Well, I was waiting near your hotel when you came out, just to make sure you were OK and I saw the SIM grab you. I knew that once you were there the only way they'd let you go was to hand you over to the army. So I got hold of my son, told him about the incident at the *botha*, and how you'd come to my rescue when that pig started beating me up. He phoned the SIM and said you were wanted for shooting one of his men, and they handed you over.

"But what about the trial and the firing squad?"

"There never was a trial. My boy made up that story for the benefit of the guards on duty at Moncada. I thought it was a nice touch having me thrown in the cell and having those two identify us. Incidentally I understand they had to leave their jeep behind when they couldn't get it started after they got your ropes untied. They're now being charged with misappropriating army property."

"Surely the jeep was still there. All they had to do was bring along a new distributor arm?"

"No, by the time they had got back it had somehow disappeared. My neighbour is a bit of a collector of things that he finds lying around near his property!"

Joe lets the information sink in before slapping Sergio resoundingly on the back and thanking him sincerely. It had, he reflected, been a rather worrying sort of a day, what with the prospect of hideous torture and death by firing squad. Perhaps a period of rest and recuperation back in the safety of Havana might be advisable for a bit.

§§§§§

By 8.30 the following morning they're in the air and heading north towards the hills. The whole of the Santiago valley is spread out beneath them. Behind they can see the blue waters of the Caribbean. Along to the West the peaks of the tall Sierra Maestras unfold into the morning haze. To the East in the distance is Guantanamo and the US naval base.

Park Woolham and Robert Weicha had been at the airport early. They both raised eyebrows at the sight of the army uniforms Joe and Sergio were sporting, but nothing was said. There was time for coffee and Cuban bread before they took off. Joe briefed the pilot about where they were heading and said he'd be able to pick out the landing area when they were overhead. It was a glorious morning for flying and after clearing the area around the airport, the chopper kept low following the contours of the undulating land. Sergio was as excited as a kid at Christmas and kept his eyes glued to the window.

After twenty minutes or so they see other aircraft approaching from behind. Two air force fighters rapidly overtake them and shortly afterwards dive down towards a village in the foot-hills. Even above the noise of engine of the helicopter they can hear machine gun fire. Trails of earth are rising from the

217

ground as the bullets pepper the main street. The few people about run for cover.

"Raul says this happens every day," Joe shouted to Woolham. They just come and shoot up villages indiscriminately. It has no effect on the rebels ability to fight – they carry out any manoeuvres at night. It simply endangers civilians and increases support for the opposition."

Joe has a little trouble identifying from the air the landing area that Raul showed him from below in the Land Cruiser a few days before. But eventually he finds it and the pilot nudges the chopper down into the clearing. There's no sign of a reception committee so the Americans hang around smoking Luckies until Raul and his Toyota arrive.

He takes one look at Joe and Sergio. "I see you've joined the other side then. Didn't take you long to forget about us. I'd be a bit careful though about wandering round here wearing those uniforms. Someone might take a pot shot at you."

He welcomes the US consul and his assistant and they all leave in convoy heading for the first house where a group of hostages is being held.

The Americans have nothing but praise for their captors. They're being extremely well looked after. The food is fine. The facilities are perfectly adequate. It's a bit boring and they wouldn't mind seeing their families again soon, but they entirely understand the rebels actions in abducting them, and some are even open if their support for the revolutionary cause.

It's the same story at the other locations where the second front are holding the hostages. And by the time Raul has shown the consul the schools and hospital Park Woolham seems in a much more friendly frame of mind.

"It's highly unlikely that I can persuade Washington to change its policy of non-interference, " he says. "So I don't think they will be phoning up President Batista and telling him not to use his US supplied weapons against you guys. But I will seek an investigation into the possibility of Cuban planes being illegally re-fuelled at Guantanamo. If it *is* happening then the investigation itself might be enough to stop the practice. And I will speak to General Cantillo about the air force raids on positions here in the hills. If I can persuade him that it's civilians who are getting hurt, and that it's counter-productive in propaganda terms then we might be able to get them suspended. Now, what about a time-table for release?"

The discussion continues for some time, with Raul holding out for more concessions, and refusing to specify when releases will take place until he's seen some action on his demands. But by the end of the meeting Woolam is re-assured that the hostages are in no danger and that they will be released, though not all at once. Castro is reassured that Woolham will do what he can.

As they prepare to leave Sergio speaks privately to Joe. "I know you want to get back to Havana. And I'm missing the mountain air. So I think I'll hang around up here, and see what I can do to help out."

Joe embraces him and thanks him once again for his help. He collects the rest of his belongings from Vilma's house and changes back into his own clothes. The chopper ride back to Santiago is uneventful, and arrives in time for Joe to book himself on the evening flight to Havana. He fills the time waiting for the departure by negotiating to store the BMW in a corner of a hanger at the airfield.

By 8.00 he's on a scheduled Cuban Airlines flight heading westwards into the setting sun. Down below him are the Sierra Maestra's and Che and Fidel and the rebel forces still holding out against Batista's army. For half a moment he wishes he was among them again, eating tough goat round the campfire and conducting hit and run operations against the troops. But the thought passes quickly. It was fun while it lasted, But now he wants no more excitement. Rampant sex with Maria, yes. Work around the Casinos and international hotels possibly. But further danger, definitely not.

§§§§§

Joe's comfortable flight westwards is in stark contrast to the journey Che Guevara is shortly to make. After a number of further hard fought victories in and around the Sierras the

219

government's "summer offensive" fizzles out. The demoralised troops are largely confined to barracks, allowing the rebels much greater freedom of movement. Raul maintains his hold on the North East of Oriente province, while Castro himself controls the Sierras to the South West. So he dispatches Camillo Cienfuegos northwards, and Che westwards, with orders to disrupt communications and consolidate support. If successful they are to meet in the centre of the Island effectively cutting it in two. It's a grand plan. But the night before Che is due to leave, an unexpected army assault cripples his transport. Now, anyone else would have waited a few days, captured a couple more lorries and jeeps, stolen some petrol and moved out in comfort and style. But not the ascetic Guevera. Oh no. He simply orders his force to proceed on foot. But it's a marathon march, and they are harried by army patrols and strafed by air force fighters at every turn. It's hurricane season so the weather is atrocious. They are blighted by virulent foot rot and are plagued by insects. Yet herein lies the making of the myth. The revolutionary fanatic who bears all external hardships and dangers as well as his own personal asthmatic cross. And, leading by example, carries his small band of men along with him to ultimate victory. But don't think it was without hardship and pain.

Revolution Cuba'58

PART 7

Late Summer

Chapter 30

Joe treats himself to a taxi from the airport. He asks the driver to go via the Malecon. The sea is up and waves send plumes of spray over the sea-wall and onto the wide pavement. Lovers, out for a traditional evening stroll, scurry back when a big one breaks like children on a beach running away from the water. Window down, Joe sniffs the night air. There's nothing quite like the smell of this city anywhere. Hot, sticky, sexy, salty with a touch of hibiscus, jasmine and mixed humanity.

On the right is the new American city.... Lansky's futuristic Riviera hotel, the new Hilton, the stately Nacional, all ablaze with lights. Ahead though it's darker. Under the dim street lights lie the pastel coloured houses that line the street before it reaches the harbour. On the corner he looks up the broad boulevard leading to the Presidential Palace. Is Batista at home tonight? Does he sleep easily in his bed as his secret police torture and murder his people. Does he comprehend the breath and depth of opposition to his regime?

The taxi crawls through the crowded streets of the old town lined by faded colonial facades. Its sheer familiarity is exhilarating. Joe is glad to be home. He climbs the stairs to his room and is greeted effusively by Concha his landlady. "Your room is just as you left it. I've kept it clean. There is mail for you. You've been away a long time. What have you been doing?" Joe asks if Maria is in, but Concha says she's at a meeting and won't be home until late. He takes a beer from the communal fridge and flops out on his bed to read his letters. Suddenly he realises he's incredibly tired. He hadn't got much sleep the previous night between the escape from Moncada and the early morning rendezvous with the American chopper. He falls out of his clothes and into bed.

Later, he doesn't know how much later, he's half wakened by the connecting door being gently opened. Through semi closed eyes he sees a vision of loveliness moving across the room. Silhouetted against the window in a transparent flowing negligee, she stands beside the bed like an angel looking down on his recumbent figure. Very slowly she lets the negligee fall to the ground and stands naked before him. Her scent arcs across the gap between them. She slips in under the sheet beside him, her skin warm, soft, electrically charged. Joe is still three quarters

223

asleep, with that groggy feeling that there's a hundred ton weight pressing on his body rendering him unable to move. But it doesn't matter because Maria is moving. Her hands caress, her lips kiss, her thigh rubs. Unbidden, a memory from his childhood forces its way to the front of his mind. His grandfather had a device for treating rheumatism which he and his brother loved to play with. It consisted of two cylindrical brass tubes, each about six inches long, and each connected by a wire to a small machine the size of a hard-back book. The main element was a powerful battery attached via some capacitors or resistors or whatever to a large dial. You turned it on and held the two brass rods one in each hand. Immediately the tingle of a mild electric shock tickled you hands and started moving up your arms. Then you or your brother would turn the dial round one notch and the tingle would become more powerful. At full power it was unbearable. An exquisite torture, a cross between sublime pleasure and unendurable pain. Not unlike the sensation Maria is producing as she brings him to the brink and then lets the current subside before building him up all over again. Groggy with sleep, Joe had no concept of the passage of time. He wants the dial turned fully up, he wants the agony and the ecstasy at full voltage. He wants the torture to last for ever and to stop at once. Finally, tantalisingly, exuberantly , she lets him explode in her body, expire in her arms, die crushed under her weight. At last, lovingly, she lets him slip back into unconsciousness.

The following day he wakes late. Maria has already gone, but as he lies luxuriating in the warm sunshine pouring through the window, she returns with fresh pastries and a jug of steaming coffee.

"Why aren't you at work?"

"It's Sunday, silly. Even we factory slaves are given one day off. Not like you for whom every day is a Sunday."

"I'll have you know that up in the Sierras I used to rise at dawn, wash in icy mountain water and shoot a brace of soldiers before breakfast."

They drop crumbs all over the sheets, slosh milky coffee over the edge of the cups, lick jam off each others fingers and more intimate places, make love again, talk and talk and luxuriate in each others bodies and company. It was as if they'd never been parted. But better because they had so much to catch up on. Maria wants to hear every last detail of his adventures, and particularly of the camp. The one shadow ahead is what Joe is to say about Lydia. How do you tell your girl-friend that you've slept with her mother? Best to say nothing? But then if she finds out later...

"So tell me about Lydia. I imagine she's in her element up there. She just worships Che."

"She wasn't there all the time. She's still running messages between the *sierra* and the *llano*. But she's become a real fighter. Che says she is fearless in battle, ever urging the men on, and ever ordering them around. We were briefly together at the Yara River battle and afterwards ...""

"Yes ... ?"

"Afterwards we sat up talking under the stars and ...""

"Yes...?

"Erm ... well I don't quite know how to put this .... we were both high on the adrenalin of the battle and ...""

"You fucked her."

"How did you guess?"

"I didn't guess. She wrote and told me. Here you can read it."

She hands Joe a letter and points to a paragraph towards the end.

"I was with your Joe at the Yara River. He is a man you can be proud of. He is brave and resourceful and fought well for the cause. Afterwards he gave me comfort. Just once, and at my instigation. Don't be angry with him. He is the sort of man a mother can be happy her daughter is involved with."

Maria moves over and holds Joe tightly in her arms. "I love you" she whispered.

"Yes and I love you. You know I do."

"I didn't know, but I believe you do."

"I do, and nothing I could do with anyone else would have the same meaning as us."

"I believe that too. And as you know I'm not the jealous kind. I let you go off with that Carmen who I'll bet you fucked silly all the way to Trinidad and back."

Joe reddens at the memory.

"And that I don't mind. It even makes me a bit hot to think of the two of you."

So saying she slides her hand down to his crotch, but instead of caressing his balls or his cock, she takes a clutch of

225

pubic hair between thumb and forefinger and yanks hard. He grimaces at the unexpected pain.

"However," she says puling harder, but smiling broadly: "if you so much look at my mother again or my sister I'll pull your hairs out one by one and then take my nail scissors to what's underneath. Understand?"

Joe kisses her laughing face, and waits until she'd relaxed her grip on his short and curlies before saying innocently: "Sister … I didn't know you had a sister. Younger is she? Pretty …?"

§§§§§

The main tourist season doesn't get going until late October or early November and then stretches through the Christmas period generally ending about Easter. The Summer months, apart from being excessively hot are also the rainy season with heavy afternoon downpours and the possibility of hurricanes forming. So although the casinos and night clubs are ticking over, this is not high season for high rollers or hoteliers.

Meyer Lansky greets Joe like a long lost son but says he had just hired a new driver and there isn't anything immediately for him to do. If Joe checks in regularly he'll let him know if anything came up. Consequently Joe has time on his hands, and spends much of his day hanging round at Marti's. In exchange for the accreditation he'd been given he writes up a full report for Herbert Matthews of events in the Sierras Maestra and Cristal. The New York Times correspondent is heading back to the US for the summer but before he goes he introduces Joe to a colleague from the Chicago Tribune. George Dubois is an enigmatic figure, tall and lean, he is a Latin American specialist and president of the influential Inter-American Press Association.

He takes an immediate liking to Joe and, despite the differences in their ages, they become regular companions, chewing the fat and talking politics over morning coffee or lunchtime beer, and even playing the odd game of chess.

Dubois had been in the military, a US army colonel, and had established close connections with the State Department in Washington. It is an unlikely background for a newspaperman but he is highly regarded and apparently extremely influential in moulding public opinion in the States.

He is fascinated by Joe's adventures with Che Guevara and can't hear enough about the rebel Argentine and his politics. In

226

fact he is so interested that Joe sometimes feels he is being de-briefed rather than simply the object of journalistic curiosity.

But for Joe, Dubois is absolutely 'sound' on Batista. He hates the dictator, and loses no opportunity to denounce him and his regime's tyranny. It was his articles that had been influential in persuading Washington to impose the arms embargo earlier in the year.

"Now I see your lot are going to flog the bastard weapons," he says one morning.

"My lot?"

"Yes the UK. Your Prime Minister has sold 17 Sea Fury fighters to Cuba. Apparently they come with a large quantity of air-to-ground missiles. There's also talk of tanks coming too. "

"That's disgraceful. If even the US has stopped supplying arms to Batista, what the hell is Britain doing. How do you know about this?"

"It's all in here," says the American handing over a copy of the underground newspaper, *Revolución.* I don't know about the rest of the weapons, but I heard about the Sea Furies from other sources so I'm sure that's true."

Joe reads the article which claims that London sold the Cuban regime amphibious tanks as well as jets, which Batista had "bought for the criminal bombardment of the rural population." A full-page poster in the bulletin called for a boycott of British products, and in particular, of the Anglo-Dutch company Shell. The "President of Shell was one of the principle agents and promoters of the sale of English planes to the dictatorship," it said.

"You should write a letter to the Times," said Dubois with a smile. "Or even write a piece on your first hand account of how Batista uses his planes against civilians. You could try the Manchester Guardian, it has a long tradition of liberal politics."

The thought turns over in Joe's mind and a few days later, on Dubois' suggestion, he visits the offices of the Foreign Press Club in Havana and askes to speak to the Manchester Guardian's correspondent. It turns out they don't have one, but the secretary puts Joe in touch with someone called a 'stringer'. This is local Cuban journalist who files reports on a freelance basis. He phones the number given from a street pay-phone and, to his slight surprise, finds it is a woman who answers. After quizzing him on what he knows she said yes, she'd telex the foreign news desk in Manchester and suggest a first person article on what the Sea Furies might be used for and the effects they would have against peasants in the Sierra Cristals.

The reply comes through the next day. They'd like a thousand words. With as much detail of conditions in the mountains as possible, including transport links and medical facilities. There would be a fee of £20.

George Dubois kindly offers advice on what to include, and how to structure the article, and by the third of fourth draft Joe is reasonably pleased with the result. He arranges to meet the stringer at the Foreign Press Centre, and she shows him how to type it out on the telex machine locally, cutting a long paper tape of the result. Then they dial England, and feed the tape back into the machine which magically sends the words cluttering across the Atlantic far faster than most people could touch-type.

Maria is delighted that Joe was doing something to raise foreign awareness of the evils of Batista's regime, but she urges some caution about his new companion from the Chicago Tribune. "It's true he's been extremely critical of the president, and like Matthews he's done good interviews with Fidel and Che. But some people think he may be more than he seems. Don't forget he worked for the government for years in the Army and in Washington, And now he seems to be supporting a third force rather than the Movement."

Joe strolls down to the public library and leafs through back editions of the Chicago Tribune. It is true that Dubois' articles did all they could to highlight the corruption of the government. But it is also true that he doesn't seem to think that Castro's 26th July Movement will be an acceptable alternative. Attention, he suggests, is focusing on former political leaders who are currently in jail or in exile.

Joe decides to tackle him on the question, but there is no sign of the newspaperman at Marti's. Instead, sitting it his usual table, is another American who appears to know who Joe is, and might even have been waiting for him. "Hi I'm Bill Williamson. Jules told me I might find you here. I'm attached to the US embassy here in Havana."

"Hi." said Joe non-committaly. The phrase 'attached to the embassy' is rather a loose one he thinks.

"I bumped into someone who you met in Santiago. In fact you shared a chopper ride together."

"Oh yes..."

"Yep. Robert Weicha. Sends you his best."

Joe remembers the man with a crew cut at the Consulate who seemed to know more than his boss about the refuelling of Batista planes at Guantanamo.

"Said you had some pretty good contacts with the opposition hereabouts"

Now we're getting to the point thinks Joe. "I understood the US wasn't taking sides here."

"No more we are. Save possibly for the side of the US citizens here and the economic interests of US citizens here and at home."

"So to cut the crap as you Americans like to say. You think the writing's on the wall for Batista. But you don't trust Castro because his brother and chief lieutenant are Communists In short you don't know which horse to back?"

"That's a pretty concise précis of the situation." The American thought for a moment, while staring hard at Joe as if assessing him. "I'll bet you don't play much Poker?" he said at last.

"Can't afford to," replied Joe. "But why do you think I don't."

"Cause I think you're too goddamned direct. I don't think you'd know how to bluff."

"Oh, I'm only direct when I think there's no point in bluffing. I play chess. That's a game of bluff too. You've got to keep your opponent on his toes, always trying to work out *why* you made the move you did. Some times it may be part of a grand strategy, sometimes it may be to lure him into a false move and sometimes there may be no reason at all."

The older man looked at him with more respect. "The point about chess is that you can see all the pieces on the board at once. The thing about Poker is that you keep much of you hand concealed. And getting back to Cuba, that's what the US is doing here. It's not revealing its full hand to anyone."

"That could be construed as playing each side off against the other. Which, frankly, I don't think is much of a policy," said Joe.

"That's one perspective. The other is that we are biding out time until we see more clearly which way the wind is blowing."

"Yes but the danger is, as with any mixed metaphor, that the wind will suddenly veer off in another direction and you'll find all the cards you thought you were holding have been blown away."

"Ok, you mentioned cutting the crap. Well here's the deal. Bob Weicha thought you had some pretty good contacts within the July 26 Movement. Let's say for the sake of argument that there are some businessmen I know who think their interests would be best served by supporting that group against the president. And if, for example, they believe they should put their money where their mouth is, the question is just *how* to get that money into the right hands."

"Yes, I see that your hypothetical businessmen would have bit of a problem there," said Joe. "There are almost as many opposition splinter groups as there are prostitutes on the streets of Havana. Choose the wrong one and you could end up with a nasty sore on your dinky."

"So what would you suggest?" laughs the American.

"Well as I'm sure Jules Dubois explained to you, I'm a reporter. And in the course of my last field trip I met both the Castro brothers and Che Guevara. My strong advice is to make sure the money gets to them. In my view they are the most likely group to be able to form any sort of new government if Batista should fall. Currently they're desperately short of guns and ammunition. Now, you could find the 26th July Movement leader in Havana and channel and 'donations' through him. But you stand the risk of some or all of it being siphoned off for urban opposition. So what you need is a courier to physically take the money to the Sierras. And there I might be able to help you. I know of someone who makes the trip fairly regularly."

"When could you arrange this?"

"I'd have to see when the courier is next making a trip. I could get back to you in a day or two. Can I phone you?"

"Yes, as long as you're careful what you say. There are some at the embassy who don't need to know all the details."

Including your ambassador, thought Joe. You could hardly expect one of Batista's biggest supporters to be in favour of channelling US payola to the rebels. But he says nothing, and arranges to be in touch with the mysterious William Williamson shortly.

§§§§§

"It's the fucking CIA," said Maria later. "What the hell are they playing at? They've been supporting Batista along with all the other right wing despots in Latin America for decades, Why the hell should they now want to start funding the opposition? Especially if there are elements in that opposition who have been communists. It doesn't make sense.

"I think it's called backing both horses in the race. Then whichever one wins you can go up them and say: "jolly good show. I knew you could do it all the time. Now you're in power please don't forget who helped put you there.""

"It's dirty money and we should have nothing to do with it."

"Yes, but if the same dirty money is supporting the government, then all you are doing is evening up the score. And frankly the *Fidelistas* need the money more than the *Batistas* at this particular moment.'

Maria eventually sees the logic in this argument and agrees to try to contact Lydia to see when she will next be in Havana.

Meanwhile, a day or two later, Joe has another mysterious encounter at Marti's. This time it is a Cuban who asks if he might join Joe. Since almost every other table in the bar is free at the time, it is obvious that he has picked Joe out deliberately.

Where Williamson had been direct, this man is obscure to the point of opaqueness. He says he is called Luis, though Joe would have laid odds that wasn't his real name. He is small, with rodent like features and walks with a slight limp. He says he is a 'tax collector' though in Cuba this seldom means a civil service job. He speaks in the vaguest terms about 'redistributing wealth' and making sure that groups who really need money have access to it. And he ends with a veiled warning that it is dangerous to walk around Havana with large sums of cash.

As he leaves Joe shakes his head and asks himself what the hell that had all been about?

Chapter 31

Two days later news comes from one of Maria's relations in Bayamo that her mother will be visiting Havana shortly and would like to see her daughter. Joe phones the US embassy and is put through to Bill Nicholson: "That game of Poker you suggested ... well I think I can arrange it for next week. Can you get the stakes together by then? Good. Where shall we meet?"

Williamson suggests a bar across the harbour from Havana Vieja at the base of the Morro Rock and the Cabana fortress.

On the appointed evening Joe arrives early. Lydia had made it clear she did not want to be involved in the 'drop' so he is alone. Instead of using the new tunnel, he takes the crowded passenger the ferry over to Casablanca on the Eastern side of the harbour, and starts climbing the winding road towards the fortress. Half way up he pauses to admire the nearly completed white marble *Estuada de Cristo* or statue of Christ with its magnificent view out over the harbour and the city beyond.

The Cabana is a huge Colonial fortress, reputedly the largest in the Americas, complete with moats and keeps and towers and cobbled streets. It was built the year after the British under Augustus John Hervey and the Earl of Albemarle had captured the adjacent Morro Castle fortress and it cost so much that Carlos III of Spain reputedly tried to view it through a telescope from Madrid convinced it must be large enough to see.

Now part of it is used as a barracks and to house Batista's political prisoners while the remainder hosts tourist shops and a museum. It is a popular destination at sunset with its panoramic views across the bay, the Malecon, the Presidential Palace, the imposing Capitol building and the spread of the old city.

Joe spends a happy hour on the tourist trail before walking down a long flight of steps to the restaurant and bar at the waters edge below. He orders a beer and sits looking out over the harbour as the sun, just starting to edge down in the Western sky, throws sparkles on the water.

"Pretty isn't it? Makes you wonder why this island seems fated to be governed by autocrats who are kicked out on a regular basis in a war or revolutionary bloodbath."

Joe turns to Bill Williamson standing next to him at the bar. "Do you include the US in that list of autocrats?"

"The Spanish, the British, the Spanish again, the US, the nationalists, the Military. It doesn't matter who. They were all just as bad as each other."

"Your senators Orville and Platt with their amendment that gave the US the right of military intervention in Cuba when ever it saw fit hardly helped create stability."

"Hey, you've been reading up your history," said Bill. "Yes perhaps that wasn't a great move. I'd have favoured annexing the country lock stock and barrel like we did in Puerto Rico, Guam and the Philippines, and we would have done here but for some interfering busybody senator from Colorado called Teller passing an amendment to respect Cuban 'self determination'."

"Is that what we're doing now?" asks Joe with a sardonic smile, and a sideways glance at the brief case resting on the American's knees, "respecting Cuban self determination."

"No, we're trying to block certain hotheads who favour re-inventing the Orville-Platt amendment."

"Including one Earl T Smith, US Ambassador and, supposedly, your boss?"

"I think that merits a 'no comment'.

Williamson slides the attaché case across from his knees onto Joes in a seamless movement that not even the sharpest eyed observer could have spotted. "I trust you'll make sure that reaches the right hands," he said. "I'd hate for your sake for it to disappear!"

After he's gone Joe sits for a few more minutes staring out over the water. Then he pays for his beer and starts back up the hill towards the fortress. He plans to take a taxi into town and knows they leave from entrance to the Cabana where it adjoins the older Morro castle to the North. There is a steep roadway, little more than an extended ramp, leading from the water up to the fortress and rather than climb up the gruelling flight of steps again. He decides to walk up the incline. To his right is a sheer wall, to his left a low parapet with an increasing drop below to the rocks and the sea.

The ramp is obviously used to transport goods up and down to the restaurant so Joe is not particularly surprised to hear a car's engine straining up the incline from below. As it approaches, he climbs onto the low wall to give it room to pass. But instead it stops just ahead of him and both passenger and driver's doors open simultaneously. Instinctively Joe searches round for an escape route. It doesn't look promising. Behind is the ramp which offers no cover whatsoever; ahead the car with two men now emerging, pistols drawn.

233

There are trees and shrubs growing up the steep side of the cliff below the parapet and without thinking Joe jumps down, clinging onto the briefcase with an iron grip. He stumbles, and rolls over, coming to rest against a flimsy tree-trunk that is the only thing between him and a 30 foot fall. He glances up to see the Cuban he'd met at Marti's who called himself Luis raising his gun from the low stone wall ten feet above him. But he can also see a large round hole, perhaps a drain, leading under the ramp and into the fortress a few feet away. Finding his footing on the steep slope is hard, but he levers himself against the tree and pushes forward, diving for the opening. He is just in time. He hears the shot and simultaneously feels the bullet zing past him as he moves.

The tunnel is just over four feet high so he can move down it bent double with a slow loping run. He knows it will take several moments for his pursuers to scramble down the precarious slope and reach the entrance. But when they do he will be completely exposed. One shot along the drain would be almost certain to hit him. So after a moment he turns, draws his .22, and starts to walk backwards, eyes fixed on the tunnel entrance. Sure enough after a few moments a shadow cuts out the dim light that is penetrating. Joe fires, appalled at the massive noise the shot makes, reverberating around the confined space. The shadow moves quickly aside, and Joe uses the moment to turn and run forward, searching in the gloom for some bend or junction around which he can hide. But there is nothing. The drainage tunnel seems to be going straight in, albeit at a slight upward angle, well inside the fortress wall.

Another few yards and Joe turns, drops flat on his stomach, props the brief case up in front of him, and aims the gun past it down to the entrance. He is rewarded a moment later by seeing an arm move round and point a gun towards him. Two shots explode almost simultaneously, his and his pursuer's. The bullet coming towards him whistles overhead and then ricochets off the tunnel walls and into the distance behind him. His bullet, however, appears to have found its mark. For there is a muffled yell and the sound of a gun clattering down on the tunnel floor. Joe waits a moment and then fires another shot to buy extra time. Then he is on his feet, moving as fast as his crouched position will allow. In the semi-darkness he doesn't see the iron grid across the tunnel before he bangs into it. 'Damn,' he thinks, 'now I'm buggered. It looks as if the tunnel's completely blocked.' But feeling around he realises there is a narrower hole above and metal hoops protruding. "Perhaps it's an inspection shaft, ' he thinks, 'leading up to the surface. Quickly he takes off his belt, threads it through the brief-case handle and loops it over one shoulder and under the other arm. He thrusts the automatic into his back pocket, grabs the lower rung and hauls himself up, his other arm grasping in the blackness above for another rung. Sure enough it is there and after some inelegant moments dangling from his arms, he manages to get his feet on the rungs and move cautiously upwards.

Now, for the first time since the car pulled up in front of him he has time to reflect on what is happening. Whoever Luis is, he clearly had fore-knowledge of the transfer of money. And he was clearly out to 'redistribute' it, either to himself, or to one of the other underground movements desperately in need of funds.

He had one accomplice that Joe knew about, though there could be more. One might or might not be wounded. He is heading up into a fortress part of which is a prison and will be heavily guarded. In any case there are troops all over the place and Joe has no wish to meet them. People may already have heard the shots which had so far been fired. Generally it didn't look too promising.

After climbing perhaps 40 feet Joe feels an obstruction above. No light at all now penetrates from the tunnel entrance, and he is in total, enveloping, inky blackness. He feels carefully overhead. It is a wooden door. Made of stout planks. And it won't budge an inch when he pushes against it. But, beneath the door, the mortar holding the stones of the shaft wall feels crumbly. He scrabbles around, first with his fingers and then with a pocket knife, and is eventually able to prise a stone out and drop it down into the tunnel below. Five minutes later and he has made a golf ball sized hole. He can feel a fresh draught rushing through it, and can see a pinprick of daylight. After prising another few stones lose he is able to get his hand and arm through. At that moment he heard noises below. Two shots in swift succession, and then the sound of something being pushed or thrown along the tunnel floor. He thrusts his arm through the gap in the stones and felt about for the lock that was holding the trap-door closed. More noises below and then the breaking of glass and a woomph of petrol exploding. Smoke starts to rise up the shaft. His fingers find a bolt and start to try to lever it back. More noises of splintering glass below. Somehow they're bowling petrol filled bottles along the drainage tunnel and then exploding them he thinks. At that moment there is another explosion below and flames follow the smoke up the shaft. The bolt is moving slowly but too slowly. Joe is coughing and gasping. His feet and legs are growing hotter by the minute. The bolt slips free, he pulls his

235

hand back in, puts his face to the hole and gulps the clean air while simultaneously pushing up on the wooden door.

With the flames rising around his knees, he levers the door back and climbs out into the space above. A rapid glance round tells him several things. First he is in the corner of a large court-yard or parade ground with castellated ramparts along the seaward side and buildings on the other across the open space. Second he is staring down the barrel of a heavy duty hand-gun. And third, the sneering face peering from behind the gun belongs to Luis.

"I think you have something we want," he says pointing to the brief case dangling at Joe's side from his belt.

The situation seems hopeless. The Cuban is out of hitting range and anyway in real life you just don't go for the old movie trick of trying to disarm a man who's holding a gun on you. Not if you want to live to tell the tale. Reluctantly Joe begins to pull the belt over his head. Then suddenly from behind them on the ramparts comes a huge booming noise, like the sound of thunder echoing round the fortress. It is followed immediately by another one, equally loud. Joe jumps at the sound but keeps his eye fixed on the gun opposite. Luis jumps but looks round to see what sort of act of god is being foisted upon them. A third boom, and Joe flings the metal edged brief-case as hard as he can at his opponent's face, pulls it back by the leather belt still attached to its handle, and throws it forward again. The first blow hits the outstretched hand holding the gun knocking it aside, the second hits the man hard in the face, catching him just above the eye. Instinctively he clutches his hand to his wound . Joe, his feet still on the top rungs of the shaft, regains his balance and whirls the belt over his head, sending the briefcase up and round in an arc. Like a demented highland hammer thrower he alters the trajectory of his missile, smashing it into the side of Luis's head. Joe leaps from the shaft, grabs the fallen magnum and races off across the court-yard. Looking up to the ramparts he can see a line of cannon poking out through the wall. As he watches a man with a glowing taper holds it to the muzzle of one, and stands back as the ancient gun fires out across the bay. Every evening at sunset, Joe remembers, they fire the cannons from the Cabana. What good timing!

He doesn't have long to ponder though because he can hear footsteps behind him, and Luis shouting to an unseen person for help. Joe runs up a set of stone steps onto the ramparts themselves and looks back. The line of cannons is behind him with a clutch of tourist onlookers close by. His pursuer, clutching his head, is moving towards the steps. At the far end of the courtyard down below, is a large gate leading to the main exit, guarded by at least one armed soldier. In front, the ramparts continue on and round towards the top of the gate but with no obvious way off it. There is little choice. Joe continues running along the rampart, hoping the soldier isn't about to look up and see a man clutching a small case and a large gun. Reaching the corner he can see both sides of the gate and, as he feared, more soldiers. But to his left is a narrow ledge connecting the corner of the rampart with the outer walls of the original Morro castle. Scrambling along this, he is able to drop down into a deserted alley-way that leads into a to a maze of smaller passages. Joe chooses one at random and begins almost immediately to climb up a steepish slope. It leads eventually to a spiral stair-case and, at the top, a look-out point on the tallest North-Westerly tower of the castle. In front he can see the mouth of the Harbour. To the right the sweep of the Havana Bay. On the rocks below, the City's famous white lighthouse. Turning round towards the entrance of the otherwise deserted castle he sees two men, one with a distinct limp, crossing the draw-bridge, about to enter the maze of passages.

Joe sizes up his position. His tower provides a strategic vantage point but has the disadvantage of allowing no possible escape route. He checks his weapons. The revolver has only three bullets in its chamber. The .22 automatic has seven. Ten shots. He guesses Luis might have got another gun, and his companion is certainly armed. The thing that is slowing him down most of all is the brief-case. Looking round he finds a perfect hiding place beyond the ridge of the roof and out of sight of anywhere on the tower. He slides it into place and slowly tiptoes down-stairs.

The sun has set below the horizon and although the sky is still aglow, the light is fading fast. Joe knows he is still above his pursuers and was reasonably certain they will have to approach him from in front. As he moves silently down he tries to memorise every fork or cross passage in case he needs to beat a hasty retreat. In the event he hears the two men before he sees them. They are panting for breath as they climb the steep alleys whispering about what best to do. Peering round a corner Joe sees them still some distance below splitting up to search in separate directions. An idea occurs and he collects a pocketful of large stones from beside a crumbling wall. In a moment he can see the two will be crossing either side of a central chamber. He watches as Luis moves cautiously into view and them waits for the first sign of his companion. The moment he appears Joe tosses a handful of stones which bounce off the tiled roof above the man's

237

head. Luis, not realising who was there, fires three shots at the sound of the stones. Joe sees the second man stumble and fall silently to the ground. Joe aims the Magnum and fires. There's a kick as the recoil forces the big gun upwards. In the half light he sees the shot go wide, Luis leaps back under cover.

Now begins a frightening game of cat and mouse. Joe creeping forward, listening intently. The other man slipping from shadow to shadow. Both fire two or three shots not even certain at what they were aiming. Joe reassesses his position and decides that, with one man down, he'd actually be safer back on the tower. So he begins to retrace his steps. But the rat-like figure pursuing him has somehow found a passage that brings him out behind Joe. As he slips round a corner he sees Luis raise his gun and fire twice. The first shot misses but the second slams into Joe's upper arm. The sensation is like being stung extremely painfully by a massive hornet, while simultaneously being kicked by a mule.

Now Joe is running and Luis chasing. Down one passage, up another, banging into walls in the dark, rushing across openings hoping not to be spotted. Eventually he runs through a door and realises he's reached a dead-end. He'll have to stand and fight. His right arm is hanging limply. He fishes the automatic out with his left, but is not at all confident he can fire it accurately. He is on a wide ledge between his original look-out tower, and a second tower to the East. Beside him is a wall about three foot high separating the ledge from the drop to the rock below. Cautiously he climbs onto the wall. His back against the rising tower, out of sight of anyone following him through the door. And indeed Luis doesn't see him as he comes cautiously through the opening. Joe leaps on top of him, brining the butt of the automatic hard down on the top of his skull. But it isn't a knock-out blow and the two roll over in a heap on the ledge, each fighting to get on top of the other. Joe frees himself from the tangle of limbs and steps back. His left hand no longer holds the pistol, his right is hanging limply by his side. Luis begins to rise. Joe moves in and hits him hard in the centre of the face. It is more instinct than science, but now his training takes over. A series of quick-fire jabs from his left fist connect with the man's nose, forcing his head back. Joe swings his arm back, transfers his weight to his front foot and smashes a vicious uppercut onto the point of his jaw. Luis staggers back under the force of the blow. His calves connect with the low wall unbalancing him. In show motion, it seems, he sits heavily on the wall before his momentum carries him further and further backwards. For a moment he appears to see-saw on the edge, but then his legs rise in the air and he disappears with a back summersault into the void.

For a split second the powerful lamp from the lighthouse catches the falling figure full in its beam before he crashes onto the rocks below.

Chapter 32.

Joe stares out of his bedroom window onto the street four stories below. His arm is mending slowly. Much too slowly for his liking. After he'd retrieved the briefcase and bribed a taxi to take him home, Maria rushed him to a doctor sympathetic to the Movement. The bullet had missed the bone but done a fair amount of damage to tendons and muscle. It would be a couple of months healing he was told.

Both Maria, and Lydia when she arrived, were full of praise for his determined defence of the money. There was $25,000 in the case which Lydia transferred to various body belts and undergarments before she set off back to Santiago Province. The two women asked around among their underground contacts, but there was no knowledge of anyone fitting Luis' description working for any of the various opposition splinter groups. The best guess was that he was freelancing as a Cuban gangster.

Confined to his room for long periods while the wound heals, Joe dug into his savings and made a number of purchases. A small air conditioning unit now whirrs noisily in the corner of the room. But it means that the stifling summer months are a bit more bearable. At first Maria poo-pooed it as a piece of cissy Yankee crap. But after a few nights decent sleep she began to soften. Now, when she gets back from the steamy factory, she will throw off her clothes and stand naked in front of it, letting the cold air blast her skin. Joe determines the sizeable sum of money he spent on it was worth it just for that.

He also bought a second-hand typewriter which he's become fairly adept at using with just the fingers of his left hand. Thirdly he ordered a telephone to be installed in the hall. Concha and her family are thrilled by this new device and race each other to answer it whenever it rings. Finally he bought a powerful new shortwave radio. The main broadcasts from Radio Rebelde are on AM, but the rebels use short wave to communicate between different groups, as, amazingly, does the US embassy. Lightly coded messages can be intercepted between the consulate in Santiago de Cuba and the embassy in Havana. The staff knows that SIM always monitor their phone lines, but reckon that it is an almost impossible task to keep tabs on the hundreds of available radio frequencies.

The Manchester Guardian had sent Joe two copies of the edition in which his piece about civilian casualties from air-raids appeared. He is as thrilled as a boy with a new toy to see his name in print. He cuts out one of the articles and sends it home to his parents. The Manchester Guardian is not exactly required reading in Deptford, and he doubts that they'd have seen the original.

Armed with the radio as a source of information, his typewriter, the telephone and an air-conditioned 'office', Joe sets out to gather material for further articles and news items about Cuba. Once he is able to present himself in Marti's again he seeks the advice of both Matthews and Dubois on how he can extend his range. Apart from giving him a list of British and North American newspapers that have no full time correspondents in Cuba, they also tell him how to angle a story for different markets. Papers in the UK will want pieces about English people or businesses. So when the underground movement bombed the Anglo-Dutch Shell oil refinery in Havana in reprisal for the sale of the Sea Furies, that was one for any and all British papers.

Through Radio Rebelde, Joe monitors the progress of the Sierra Maestra rebels. During July a number small but decisive victories follow the Yara River battle. There is Santo Domingo itself, Las Mercedes and Las Vegas de Jibacou. Joe is thrilled to hear they'd re-captured the village where Pedro had been killed and he'd saved Che on his Mule from walking straight into an army battalion.

Astoundingly Mosquera is pulling his men further and further back and, as they retreat, confusing rebel signals from the captured radio and codebook mean that they are being attacked by their own side. On one occasion the Air Force napalm a retreating Army column by mistake killing and wounding dozens.

But this is nothing compared to Castro's extraordinary victory at El Jique. For weeks he besieged the army garrison, eventually persuading an entire battalion to surrender. The Commander, with whom he been at college, Major Jose Quevedo, not only turned over all his weapons to the rebels, but actually changed sides and joined them.

By mid August Castro's forces have taken 433 prisoners all of whom are released unharmed to the Red Cross. They have captured a 14 ton tank, twelve mortars, two bazookas, 33 heavy machine guns and nearly 400 rifles and sub-machineguns. For the first time they have more weapons than they knew what to do with. Since the start of the May offensive the rebels have lost just 27 men killed and 50 wounded.

Lydia, back from the front, reports that Che and his column have been dispatched to the Escrambray mountains to try to unite disparate groups of rebels there, and take control of the central Las Villas province. "They collected a small convoy of jeeps and pick-ups, but the night before they were due to leave an Army patrol captured two of the vehicles loaded with all the gas they were going to need for the journey. In they end they had to set off on foot. God knows what's happened to them..." she said, and added in a motherly tone, "Che's asthma was particularly bad, and he refused to take Zoila. She was in tears being left behind to care for his mule."

The revolution is hotting up in the *llano* too. There are a series of bombings around Havana, and a campaign of sabotage at the airport. The day after two particular explosions in the capital, the bodies of seven youths are found hanging from lamp-posts in a vicious government reprisal.

When the first of the British Sea Furies are delivered in early September Castro announces on Radio Rebelde that he's telegraphed the British Prime Minister Harold Macmillan, appealing "in the name of Liberty" to end the sales. The moment he hears the broadcast Joe telexes news of this appeal to foreign editors at a number of UK papers as a tip-off. It is his first scoop and he receives praise from all and even gets a telegram from one news desk thanking him personally. Macmillan, it transpires, rejected Castro's request.

But the occasional bit of news reporting is not a full time occupation and Joe finds himself getting restless. Mid-way through the summer the phone rings on the landing outside his door and he is summoned by one of Concha's sons. 'It's for you," said the boy," says his name is Lanky or something."

It turns out to be not Meyer, but his brother Jake. Joe had left his new number at the Riviera and National Casinos in case any work came up."

"How's that arm?" asked Jake after a few pleasantries.

"Much better thanks. It's out of plaster, and I can move it quite freely. But I'm not sure I'm up to 'protection' work."

"No, no, it's nothing like that. It's just that one of my regular watchers has gone back to the States for a vacation, and I need someone who knows their way round a casino floor for the odd evening."

Joe agrees to give it a go. Sitting in a high chair like a tennis umpire watching out for any sharp practise either from the punters or from the croupiers seems like a good option. Maria is less than enthusiastic about him returning to the world of the

Casinos, and she'd got used to having him around in the evenings. But Joe promises her a night out at the new Cabaret in the Copa room and guarantees it is only holiday relief. Maria declares herself easily bought and gives in gracefully.

As he watches thousands of dollars changing hands across the green baize Joe is struck again but the extraordinary discrepancy in lifestyles on the Island. Here are millionaires pissing money away like water. Elsewhere in the city are the Marias and Conchas working hard in factories or brining up families on less a month than these guys would give as tips in one night. And then there were the Sergios who cut cane for three months of the year and are unemployed the rest. They live not in room-serviced luxury, but in mud-floored palm-roofed huts and like many of their fellow peasants, have never in their lives been to a doctor, seen the inside of a school or even ridden in a car.

It is, he reflects, a country ripe for a communist take-over. And perhaps his concerns about what had happened in the Soviet Union and Eastern Europe are unfounded here. Perhaps Che is right and Cubans will dispense with money and choose to work just for the dignity of the activity itself and because it is their patriotic duty. But what would happen to those who didn't chose to? Would the revolutionary government be so tolerant of them?

One evening, out of the corner of his eye, he notices a punter shaking the hand of a Cuban croupier at one of the card tables. The dealer closes his palm and slides it across and into his jacket pocket. His hand comes out open and empty. Joe was sure he'd just pocketed a hefty tip. Tipping staff on the floor of the Casino is strictly forbidden. Joe looks round for Jake but he isn't about. He let it ride. Later in the staff locker room he seeks out the croupier. "I understood tipping was forbidden," he said.

"Oh yes," said the Cuban. "Don't worry I hadn't forgotten you. Here's your cut." And he fishes out five $10 bills and thrusts them towards Joe."

Joe hesitates a moment. He's clearly stumbled on an established scam. Croupiers are paying the watchers to turn a blind eye so they can receive tips from punters and help 'improve' the odds. Something in him revolts from the idea of joining in the grubby game. But he took the money saying "Look, I'm only here for a few nights, and I'll let it go this time. But when I'm on duty, don't let me see it happen again or I will have to report it."

The croupier looks dumbstruck. Amazed on the one hand that anyone would NOT want to make a little on the side themselves and on the other terrified that he might be reported and loose his job. Joe knows he is paid more than a top Cuban airline pilot or consultant physician for dealing in the Casino, and jobs there are hard to come by.

"Take my advice," he said under his breath, "start looking for another line of business. I don't think the casinos will be around for long after Castro and Guevera arrive in town." And smiling at the man's look of utter incredulity Joe goes off to find Jake.

Meyer Lansky's bigger little brother was in the back-room surrounded by piles of cheques and dollar bills. Joe knew that he was skimming off the cream, removing a percentage of the evening takings before declaring the rest in the official books. Part of the cream would go to government officials and the rest into the Lanskys' overseas accounts. Was what Joe is about to report any worse than what is happening here? No, probably not, so why mention it? Because If I don't I'm as corrupt as any of them, he thinks.

Jake greets him with a nod.

"Here, says Joe handing over the $10 bills, "you'd better add this to the takings.

"What is it?"

"Bunce that one of your croupiers gave me for not squealing on a tip I saw him pocketing from a punter. But since I am squealing I thought that morally I shouldn't hang on to the money"

"Fuck," said Jake all attention now. "I really didn't think that was happening here. Who was it?"

"No, I'm sorry, I'm not going to say. After all I did take his money. But I thought you probably ought to know that it seems pretty common practice. I mean I was actually offered the money, I didn't have to ask for it. I suspect there's a standard tariff with your regular man.'

"Yeah, Thanks for letting me know. I'll make sure he doesn't show his face back here and kick some ass among the men on the tables. Damn. You realise it means you won't be able to come back, they'll know who squealed and want revenge. But here's a hundred bucks for busting the scam. And I've got a delivery tomorrow. I'll give you another hundred if you can take care of it for me."

"Suits me, " said Joe.

§§§§§

The following morning at 10.00 Joe is back at the casino. Lansky was just counting out a wadge of $100 bills and adding them to the pile in a small suitcase.

"Christ," exclaims Joe, "how much is in there?"

"$1.3 mill."

"And where's it going to?"

"Presidential palace. Side door. An aide will be waiting for it."

"So this is a regular drop?"

"Every Monday, midday, regular as clockwork. It's from all the casinos not just here."

"But 70 million bucks a year into Batista's back pocket. That's a lot of spondulics."

"He doesn't get to keep it all. Most of it is paid out to keep the machinery of government running. And if that's what it costs for us to be here, then we just look on it as rent."

Joe took the bulging suitcase to the back door of the casino where a car was waiting. A young man was in the driver's seat. Probably the same age as Joe had been when he arrived in town all that time ago. 'God has it only been 10 months since I got here?' he thought. 'It seems like a lifetime."

They chat on the short drive over to the Presidential Palace. The youth had flunked out of college in New England and drifted south looking for work. Someone had mentioned the casinos in Havana and he'd taken the Key West ferry down to Cuba to take a look. This is his first week in the job. Driving for Lansky. He seems proud as punch.

"I wonder what they'll do with this after the revolution?" Joe said as they approached the ornate palace. "Turn it into a museum probably. With the Granma in the courtyard, and Fidel's second best underwear in a display case."

The young man looks at Joe quizzically. "Revolution? What Revolution? There 'aint going to be no revolution here, Uncle Sam wouldn't allow it."

Joe smiles to himself as he pulls the suitcase out of the trunk and carries it past the guards over to the side door. Should he tell him Uncle Sam is already covertly supporting the revolution ... a sort of half-hearted insurance policy? And probably paying premiums to a number of other underwriters too in order to cover all possible eventualities. But compared to the million-plus dollars a week that Batista gets from the mob, $25,000 from the CIA to Castro doesn't seem that much. It won't buy much cover, he reflects.

He looks up at the lighted windows of the Palace and wonders if Batista is at home. Does he too believe that 'Uncle Sam" will never allow him to be overthrown. Or can he see the writing on the wall? Joe looks across the street to where someone has daubed "*HISTA LA REVOLUTION*" in big red letters, and laughs at his own pun.

'The whole system stinks' he reflects, 'and it's time for me to get out of it.'

§§§§§

"But what are you going to do?" asked Maria in some alarm when, in bed than night, Joe explains how disillusioned he felt.

"I'm really not sure. I need a change. I need to get out of Havana. Come with me. Come to Florida, or New Orleans, or Santa Fe."

"I don't want to go to the Sates," she relies, " I hate the US. Why would I want to go there?"

"How about South America. Brazil, Chile, Argentina? Anywhere but here?"

"No. Here's where it's at. We're just beginning to win. Ever since I was a girl I've been fighting to get rid of Batista. I can't leave now just as the Movement is on the verge of triumph."

Joe looks at her perfect body and the passionate in her eyes. His heart lurches. "Will you marry me then?"

"Why, because you're bored? No. I'll marry you because I love you and because I'm proud of you. And you know what made me most proud? It was when you were fighting with Che in the Sierras. Doing something you believed in. Unselfishly. For The Cause. I'll marry you come the revolution. And the faster you help it to happen the quicker our wedding day can be. In the meantime ..." she smiled, rolling over on top of him you'll just have to make do with very sinful pre-marital sex".

Later he lies awake. Was Maria right? Had he fought at the Yara river unselfishly? For the Cause? He rather feared his motives were less pure. Hadn't he just drifted in to the rebels' camp and found he couldn't so easily get away? He'd been trained to fire guns and think tactically. Battle was an adrenaline rush. After a childhood of being made to feel he was the bottom of the class-structure pile and that he would never amount to much, he still had something to prove to himself. But one thing Maria said did strike a chord. "You were doing something you believed in." Yes. Joe does believe in overthrowing Batista. He does believe in re-distributing the wealth of the country. He does believe in chasing the money changers out of the casinos. He does believe in giving the insufferably smug United States a bloody nose. And above all he does believe in Maria. And she IS a cause worth fighting for. Perhaps his destiny is intrinsically tied to the rebels. There is only one way to find out.

Chapter 33

Joe gets off the bus in Trinidad remembering his last time there in the spring with the curvaceous Carmen. Now he has nowhere to stay thinks he might look up her parents and see if he can beg a bed for the night, and possibly borrow a horse for his journey. He has no idea exactly whereabouts in the hills to the North of the city the rebels are holed up. In conjunction with Maria he'd decided to seek out Che again, rather than join the main rebel force under Castro who are still fighting around Santiago in the East.

Carmen's mother remembers him immediately, invites him in and insists he stay. Her husband, Rodriguez is away upcountry on sugar business and won't be back for a couple of days. Joe is not too disappointed. He'd found the older man rather heavy going, especially his unreconstructed free-market capitalism. His wife on the other hand seems much more liberal. They have a quiet dinner together, still dished up by a servant, and talk about recent events.

Had he seen her daughter recently? Joe says he hasn't, but understands she is still studying at the university.

"I'm not sure "still" is quite the operative word," says her mother. "I know she only started this year. We let her father believe she was studying so he wouldn't get upset about this Lansky fellow".

"Oh, you know about Lansky?"

'Yes, I always knew rather more about Carmen than she realised, and certainly a whole lot more than Rodruigez. I mean he even thought you were her boyfriend and might be about to ask him for her hand. Anyway I think she's thorough that period now. She's no longer living in Lansky's apartment nor off his money. And I understand she's got involved in the July 26th Movement."

"That wouldn't please her father much".

"No, but I don't have any problem with it. In fact I think a new government is inevitable. It's just a question of when, and of what complexion?"

"What complexion would *you* like to see," asks Joe judiciously.

"Well, not an dictatorship headed by a former sergeant-clerk, run by the army and enforced by murderers and torturers in the secret police.'

"But an overthrow could have serious consequences for people like you. Land-owners and business people."

"The capitalists and the bourgeoisie you mean?" she laughs. "Yes, well perhaps our time has been and gone. As long as the revolutionaries don't string us up on the lampposts and as long as it produces a fairer system and we have enough food to eat and schools and hospitals for *all* Cubans then perhaps it will have been worth it."

"What sort of government do you think they do want? Rodriguez was convinced they'd be out and out communists."

"I think that's still a possibility. Interestingly the battle for the ideology of the revolution may be being fought out here."

"In Trinidad?"

"Well, up in the Escrambray hills," she said. "The Argentine Ernesto Guevara has been here a month or so after a marathon march from the Sierra Maestra. When he arrived he found there were already at least four different factions all claiming to be the true spirit of the revolution, and all refusing to accept Fidel Castro as the overall leader."

"What are the groups?" asks Joe.

"Well to start with there is a bunch of thugs calling itself the *Segundo Frente* – the Second Front – they're a break-away from the official *Directorio Revolucionario* led by Faure Chomon, and then there is our M26/7 group which has had an armed section active here in Trinidad for more than a year,"

"Our?"

"I have a red and black armband somewhere at the back of my drawer upstairs" she says cautiously. "Not that my husband knows anything about it."

"It's OK," reassures Joe. "My girlfriend in Havana is an active member, and I've met a lot of the underground people, including Faure Choman. In fact the last time I saw him he was up in the sierras here, with an extraordinary American called William Morgan."

"Yes, Morgan's still around, though he's now providing military training to the *Segundo Frente* people. It's all a real mess. Especially as they are all firmly opposed to the PSP - the communists, and when Che Guevara arrived he was welcomed by a senior PSP official who has seldom left his side. The M26/7 leaders refuse to have anything to do with the communists or the *Segundo Frente*. The *Directorio* refuses to have anything to do with Che's plans to rob banks here in the *llano*, or to enter any pact that includes the PSP. So there is no one in overall control, no unified military command, and consequently next to no ability to fight the Army."

Joe tells her that he is planning to go up to see Che and his group using the cover of his press credentials. He's immediately promised a horse and some directions.

In fact by the time he's up next morning there's a full saddle-bag prepared with food for several days, ground-sheets, blankets and, more importantly, a new-looking semi automatic hunting rifle with telescopic sights, and a thousand rounds of ammunition.

"I know you newspaper men like fresh meat" says Carmen's mother obliquely.

"That's a lot of game to kill in a couple of days."

"Who knows how long you'll be away. Take care. And come back and let me know what's going on up there."

So Joe heads out of town on his horse, making his way up the up the Valle De Los Ingenious, remembering last time he rode this way, the discussions about sugar production with Rodriguez, the rebel ambush, and sex under the waterfall with Carmen.

It's another lovely day. The worst of the rains have now passed and it's heading for Cuba's best time of year. Hot but less humid during the day, and pleasantly balmy in the evenings and at night.

Before long Joe has left the foot-hills and is climbing steadily into the mountains. After the Sierra Maesta they really only rate as hills. Only three peaks are above 800 meters. While the rebel camp on Pico Turquino was nearly 2000 meters high. But they are pretty desolate and pretty impenetrable to army patrols.

As expected, Joe is challenged before long by two bearded riflemen who appear from nowhere. He says he is looking for the camp of the Argentine, and is rewarded by one of the rebels spitting copiously on the ground. But they point him in the right direction, and an hour or so later, after several further challengers, he reaches the main rebel camp.

It doesn't appear on the surface much different from the last place Joe had encountered Che. There are groups of people sitting around talking and smoking. There are animals, particularly chickens, squawking around. There are lines of washing drying in the afternoon sun. In the centre is a circle of recently constructed *bohios*. Joe approaches one and sees Che deep in conversation with two other men seated on rough stools round a home-made table. He dismounts and tethers the horse, loosens its girth strap, and sits down to wait. After a while he hears raised voices and can see the group are having an animated discussion. Finally Che rises and shouts loudly for all nearby to hear: "You have overstepped your authority and you have lied about receiving orders direct from Fidel. You will immediately bring your men and your weapons here to this camp and place them under my command. And by the power vested in my by our revolutionary leader I hereby demote you to the rank of Captain. Is that clear?"

The target of Guevera's wrath sits with his head bowed. Then he rises slowly and brings his right arm up in a weak salute. "Yes, *Commandante*, it is clear," he mumbles and turns to leave.

"And you," says Che turning to the other man, "will tell Faure personally that I expect the forces of the Directorio to be armed and ready for action by tomorrow evening. Is *that* clear?"

"It is clear, *Commandante,* but I do not think the forces *can* be made ready in such a short time."

"Short time! What the fuck have you been doing for the last twelve months *except* preparing your forces? What would have happened at El Jique, or El Uvero, or the Yara River if I had said to Fidel ... I am sorry *Commandante,* my forces are not ready for the battle ahead. GO AWAY NOW AND MAKE THEM READY," he bellows.

The man stands and turns on his heel without saluting and walks away, head held high. Guevara paces up and down for a moment, letting his anger subside. Then he looks round and sees Joe. "Hello, English, you came back then. And on a horse this time. Petrol too scarce for the BMW?"

"Yes, I just dropped in to bring you those photographs you ordered. Some have not turned out too badly. Though I think you'd be better advised to decrease the shutter speed and close the aperture by one or two stops. You might get some in focus then."

Che smiles broadly, his previous anger vanished. "It's good to see you. Here I'm surrounded with idiots and shit-eaters." He takes the packets of prints from Joe and starts leafing through them.

"Yes, who were those two?"

The first was a guy called Borodon, the local M26/7 militia leader. He and his comrades have been bleating on about how Fidel wouldn't do this and Fidel wouldn't want that. Well, today I caught him out. I found out he's been lying about having met Castro and, as you probably heard, I gave him a real tongue lashing. It will be interesting to see if he *does* deliver his men and arms to me."

251

"And the other? He seemed more insolent."

"Yes, he's one of Faure's *Directorio* henchmen. They're all behaving like old women. 'Oh, we can't attack, this, or we mustn't risk an assault on that. We might get hurt'. Now, what's the news from the big city?

Joe fills him in on the latest rumours that are circulating, along with any hard bits of news he's garnered. "But you probably know all this already," he says. "Lydia set off a few days before me so she'll have brought you up to date. And what about the puppy? I don't see it around."

When he'd left *Oriente*, Che had left behind not only Zoila and his mule, but also his beloved dog Hombrito. The last time she'd been in Havana Lydia had found a puppy to bring him to replace it.

Che's face darkened. "Didn't you hear," he asks, "She didn't make it. She was betrayed by a man a hundred times her inferior and wounded and captured by troops. Along with Clodomira. They were killed and their bodies desecrated."

Joe feels as if he's just been landed a massive punch in the solar plexus. Lovely, lively, laughing Lydia. Dead? It isn't possible.

Che saw his expression. "She was an unblemished revolutionary" he said rather pompously, but with real feeling. "She had infinite courage. She carried the most compromising of documents. Without her communications with the rest of the Island would have been impossible."

"She was devoted to you, you know?" said Joe.

"I do. Once I tried to have her transferred from a front I was commanding near Las Vegas because I thought it was too exposed and too dangerous. She absolutely refused to go, and only left when she followed me to a new fighting front."

The news of Lydia's death has a profoundly melancholic affect on Joe, just as he knows it will on Maria when she hears the news. But how is he to tell her? He's only just arrived to rejoin the fight. Perhaps he could volunteer as a messenger to Havana in a week or so's time if the opportunity arose. In the meantime he asks Che was the plans for action are.

"Well, that's the problem." is the reply. "We're hardly carrying out any attacks at the moment. I can't get any of the groups to agree on a target. But there is something planned for tomorrow night at Guinia de Miranda. Want to come along?"

"Try to keep me away."

"I'm afraid your Lee Enfield is probably still behind in the *Maestra*."

"That's fine.   A supporter in Trinidad gave me her husband's new hunting rifle. I hate to think what he'll say when he finds out."

§§§§§

Next evening at sunset Che's column of men marches down to a small town in the valley and establishes positions in the moonlight round the local Army barracks.   As suspected the Directorio leaders have confirmed they are still "not in a condition" to join them.   Nevertheless Joe, eying up the exposed target, estimates that, in squaddie parlance, the exercise should be 'a piece of piss'.

The signal to attack is to be a bazooka shot on the curatel. But the shell falls short and explodes noisily yards from the building. The rebels duly open fire, only to find that their shots are returned with interest. Within minutes the Army has brought a heavy machine gun into action and is spraying the rebel positions. Grenades are thrown ineffectually and two more Bazooka shots fail to find their mark. Several of the rebels are hit and, within minutes, the whole exercise is beginning to look like a rout.

Joe has taken up position behind a tree twenty or thirty yards from the entrance to the barracks. Using his ammunition sparingly he is trying out the new rifle and making fine adjustments to the telescopic sights. But in the dim light it is almost impossible to find a useful target. The machine gun is protected behind heavy armour-plating, and the soldiers well concealed. He feels a tap on his shoulder. It's Che. "That idiot with the Bazooka couldn't his a barn door at ten feet. You ever fired one." Joe nodded, though in truth it was a long time since he's been received his one solitary afternoon's training with the weapon in England.

Now he slithers forward behind Che and is handed the long metal tube. He remembers it is a bit like putting a five foot drain pipe over your shoulder. The disadvantage of the early models was that you had to either stand fully upright or balance on one knee with the other leg outstretched to keep it steady, thus exposing you to enemy fire. From the wooden handle and Garang webbing, Joe recognised this as an early World War II version, designed primarily as an anti-tank gun.

He checks that Che is behind him ready to load the finned rocket-propelled grenade. He picks up the tube looks to see that the rudimentary sights are aligned. Then he rises to his knees and pushes one leg out in front.

"Ok, now."

Che loads the shell and closes the breech. Joe takes careful aim, remembering his instructor's warning that, over a distance, the grenades have a tendency to drop low. So he targets the top of the building outlined dimly in the distance ahead, and squeezes the trigger. There is an almighty roar, the shoulder restraint smashes back into his body with the force of a Welsh rugby prop forward in an open scrum. A sheet of flame flies out of the long tube along with the RPG. Its trajectory takes it upwards and for a moment he is sure it was going to overshoot. But yards from the building it drops obligingly and rams home just about lintel height. There is a loud explosion. Pieces of wood and stone and glass rain down to the ground and, moments later, come shouts from inside: "Wait. Hold your fire. Don't shoot. We surrender."

Joe thrusts the Bazooka into Che's arms and says loudly, saluting and smiling: "Good shot, *Commandante*. Realising the importance of some morale boosting propaganda Che winks at him saying quietly "Thank you English", and walks forward carrying the weapon before him.

There are only 14 enemy soldiers in the barracks and just 8 rifles. The rebel force has lost two dead and seven injured. And they've used up quantities of ammunition as well as four precious RPGs. It is not a particularly good outcome. One trophy however, is an army jeep. Che asks Joe to drive him up into the foothills near to the camp of the *Directorio's* forces. There they leave the vehicle with along with its ignition keys as a memento, for Faure and his men, of the battle in which they had failed to participate.

§§§§§

The following day as Joe goes over to speak to Che, Air Force planes appear from the North and dip down low over the mountains looking for signs of rebel activity.

"Recognise them?" Che asks, pointing. "They're your Sea Furies. Great isn't it. Even the United States, who happily sell arms to children and homicidal maniacs, even the United States has scruples about supplying a murderer like Batista. But not

Britain. Oh no. The great Harold Macmillan says he has no problem with the arms sales. Despite the fact that the tanks and planes are being used to kill innocent civilians."

"There is another way of looking at it," says Joe.

"What's that?"

"When you've taken over the Army and the Air force, the planes will be yours. And you never know when you might need them to defend Cuba against foreign aggression. And I think that's more likely to come from the US than from Britain!"

Che smiles. "Yes, that is a different perspective. I hadn't thought of that."

Joe raises the question of returning to Havana to let Maria know about her mother's death. Che says he will be sorry to see him leave again so soon after he's rejoined them, but understands. He asks Joe if he will carry some letters and documents.

So less than a week after he arrived, Joe is on his horse, walking back towards Trinidad. Memories of Lydia go over and over in his mind. Like the first time they met, in the middle of the night, with him stark naked, both holding guns at each other's heads.

And of course the bitter sweet memory of their night together after the battle of the Yara River. He will miss her. And he can't predict how Maria will take the news, and whether it will have any impact on their plans together.

§§§§§

A journey that may be relatively simple for a civilian - from Trinidad to Havana – is going to prove rather more complicated for the rebels. Support may be growing. Arms may be flowing. But across the central flat-lands the army, with its tanks and air-cover, is dominant. The Fidelistas may have had the upper hand in the Sierras, but not here. Dotted along the main highways are curatels or small strongholds of troops. None may be individually that strong, but together they form an impenetrable barrier to any possibility of marching on Havana. And Havana itself is bristling with the largest concentration of government troops on the island. So a great deal more than mere force is going to be needed if the revolution is to be secured. And time is running out. Autumn is upon us and it has to be all tied up by the turn of the year!

255

Revolution Cuba '58.

PART 8

Autumn
and
Winter

Chapter 34

The journey back to Havana seems interminable. On the outskirts of Trinidad he leaves the horse at the stables belonging to Carmen's parents and sets off for the bus station. But there is a three hour wait for the next service to the capital. So Joe climbs up the hill into the old town along the cobbled streets past the colonial traders' houses, to the Plaza Mayor and the unfinished 19th century church. It is hot in the sun so he seeks shade in the dim interior and sits facing the ornate wooden alter.

Joe isn't really much of a one for churches. His father was a devout agnostic and had never showed any inclination to bring his children up in any religion. His mother was a low-church Christian and sent the two boys off to Sunday school though more, he subsequently suspected, to get an hour's peace and quiet than for any real religious conviction. Joe himself veers between pantheism and atheism. Either God was nowhere or he was everywhere. He certainly didn't feel as if he was here in the dim recesses of a Spanish-Cuban church.

But where is Lydia now? Has she joined the oblivion of the rest of Batista's victims? Will she live on only as one of the martyrs of the revolution? Or just in the fading memories of those who knew and loved her?

The melancholy thoughts follow Joe as he walks back into the bright sunshine. The bustle of the streets is just an irritation. The colour of the surroundings is washed out. On the bus, winding its way along the coast road, the sea has lost its sparkle.

The journey is seriously delayed. One of the rebel groups has managed to co-ordinate the blowing of a road bridge outside Cienfuegos and the bus is forced to retrace its steps and mount a long detour on dreadful side roads.

It is late evening before a tired, hungry, hot and depressed, Joe climbs the four flights of stairs to his room and knocks gently on Maria's adjoining door. There is no answer. He turns the handle and goes in. The place is empty. Tidy but empty. On the bed lies an envelope with his name on it.

"Darling. Lydia is missing. They think she's been captured by the SIM. If so I fear for her life. I don't know when you will get this. But I have gone home to Bayamo to be with the

257

family and, if necessary, hold a funeral service.
I don't know when I will be back in Havana.
Wait for me. I love you. M."

Joe sits on the bed staring blankly at the wall. His first inclination is to rush off to Bayamo. But it is more than 700 kilometres away – fourteen hours on the bus, assuming that the roads and bridges haven't been mined. And Maria might be back before he gets there. And she'd told him to wait for her. He undresses and slips naked into her bed, falling asleep savouring the feint remnants of her smell.

§§§§§

The next day it is raining. And the one after. Joe hangs disconsolately around Marti's. But none of the foreign journalists is around. Radio Rebelde is crowing further victories in Oriente. Castro himself is on the air night after night proclaiming as ever: "We are at war with the tyranny not the armed forces … the revolution will go on while a single injustice remains." It is strange to hear his disembodied voice whispering out of illicit radios all over Havana, the words emanating from a dimly lit tent or *botha* high up in the Sierras.

Radio Rebelde has become required listening among both the middle and the working classes of Cuba. People gather in the streets to discuss the latest pronouncements. News of further hijackings or hostage-takings or battles won and victories gained are greeted with joy or consternation depending on the affiliation of the listener. The one thing that seems certain is that change is afoot. No-one believes that Batista can survive much longer. The only question is who will replace him. On the day of Joe's journey back from Trinidad, national elections had been held. Castro had called for them to be boycotted, and in the towns and villages Joe had passed through, the polling stations had appeared deserted except for the excessive number of troops guarding them. Yet when the official results were declared it seemed that across the country Cubans had turned out in large numbers to support the Batista candidate Rivero Aguero. Within a few days the New York Times was reporting that only 30% of the electorate had, in fact, voted and in some places the poll was as low as 10%.

Rumours were circulating of a massive fraud with bogus election papers having been printed and fixed by the armed forces.

Like the weather, the atmosphere is gloomy in Havana. Tourist numbers are noticeably down and although the music still plays, Mojitos are still mixed and the prostitutes still congregate on street corners, for Joe much of the magic has gone. And he is missing Maria. After a few days moping around he decides to go after her. He knew the name of her village, San Pablo de Yao, outside Bayamo, but not the names of any of her relatives. A look at his map shows him that Bayamo is right back in Oriente, just north of the rebels stronghold in the Sierra Maestra. He recalls it is the city that he and Celia Sanchez had avoided so assiduously on their motorbike ride back in the spring.

Memories of the BMW give Joe a plan. It's only about 70 kilometres further on from Bayamo to Santiago where the bike is stored. He could fly down to Santiago, and then ride up to San Pablo de Yao and search for Maria.

§§§§§

Two days later he's pulling the tarpaulin off the old boxer in the corner of the hanger on the outskirts of Santiago's airport.

He's left a long note for Maria in the flat in case they missed each other again, and then takes the bus out to the airport. The rain has lifted and it is a beautifully clear Caribbean day. The flight path takes them down the spine of the country and Joe ticks off the landmarks as they fly over them, Matanzas, Cienfuegos, Santa Clara and the Las Villas province where Camilo Cienfuegos' rebel column number 2 is operating. Then away to the south he can see the Escrambray mountains with Trinidad beyond. He wonders how Che was getting on, forging some control over the disparate opposition groups. The next city he can see is Camaguey followed by Las Tunas where, months before, he'd abandoned the train after helping Celia. Bayamo comes into sight beyond, with Castro's base in the Sierra Maestra to the South. And then they are descending into the Santiago valley with Raul Castro's domain of the Sierra del Cristal to the North.

From the air it is possible to see how the rebels are beginning to strangle the country. Apart from the major cities themselves, Raul and Fidel Castro pretty much control the eastern end of the Island. In the centre *Comandantes* Cienfuegos to the north and Guevara to the south are forming a pincer movement

259

around Santa Clara. It is true they are still a fair way from Havana and the greatest concentration of government troops, but if they can sever the central highway it would be impossible for the Army to re-enforce any garrisons to the east. Santiago might hold out for a while but without supply lines eventually it must fall to the rebels. Already Radio Rebelde is reporting that Castro has ordered the cessation of bus and train travel through Oriente Province.

These musings are still in Joe's mind as he revs up the big bike and points it back towards Bayamo. The seventy kilometres slip past easily, the warm breeze ruffles his hair and billows out his shirt. San Pablo de Yao isn't shown on the map, but after asking around for a bit – and getting a number of conflicting directions – he pulls into a tiny hamlet and starts looking for the bakers. It isn't hard to find. It is among the first houses he comes to. But it is firmly shut, with a black bordered sign on the door saying 'closed due to bereavement'. Joe knocks gently but there was no answer. He tries the door but it is locked. He walks round the back, but it is deserted. The motorbike parked outside has attracted a small group of gawking children though, and from them Joe soon elicits that the deceased was the mother of the baker's wife. Perhaps this wife is the sister about whom Maria had joked. But the children don't know where the baker or any of his family might be. Only that the bakery has been closed for several days and that they have to go all the way into the city to buy bread. Which was a long way.

Joe hangs around disconsolately in the afternoon heat, hoping someone might return to the business or that a more knowledgeable neighbour might appear. But none does. Eventually as the sun is setting he determines to find a way in and to look around the flat above the shop. A rotten window frame at the back gives way fairly easily and he is able to squeeze through into a pantry. Upstairs is eerily quiet and empty. He moves round the few rooms imagining that this might have been where Maria was born and brought up. A bookshelf holds a few gilt framed photos. One is a faded family portrait of a couple and their three children. The wife looks uncannily like Maria, but must, in fact, have been a young Lydia. And there is Maria in the front, aged perhaps six or seven, in between a slightly older brother and a slightly younger sister. It was a sad picture, Joe reflects, the boy and his mother both now dead at the hands of the dictatorship. Taking care not to disturb anything he looks carefully round the apartment in the fading evening light for any further childhood evidence of his fiancée. Eventually hunger drives him to search the larder which reveals tinned meat and crackers and the end of a bottle of local rum. By nine o'clock he is snoring gently on the settee after struggling with a dense biography of one of the country's revolutionary fathers Jose Marti. Perhaps it is the rum, or the early start, or the fresh-air of the motorcycle ride, but he is in the depths of sleep when a car pulled up outside, a door opens and there is a thump on the ground. Joe doesn't hear the steps on the stairs, nor the small gasp of astonishment as he is spotted on the sofa. He doesn't hear the footsteps retreating to the bedroom, or the scrape of the revolver as it is pulled from the top shelf of the wardrobe.

In fact Joe is dreaming of Maria. Confused unconnected images of her running and him following. He knows he has to catch her, to stop her, to save her. And then suddenly she turns on him and lifts a gun and points it at his head and pulls back the trigger. And he opens his eyes and there, in the half-light, is Maria, dressed all in black standing over him with a gun pointed at his head.

"Maria. What are you doing. It's me," he whispers sleepily.

"Who the fuck are you?" demands the woman in black with the gun. "and what the fuck are you doing here in my house?"

Joe blinks himself fully awake and sees that it is indeed not Maria, though the similarities are uncanny. "You must be her sister. I'm Joe. Her fiancée ... sort of"

"So what the hell are you doing on my couch?" she says, apparently unimpressed with his explanation.

Joe gives a potted run down of the events that have led him to be there, and notices all the while that the gun remains levelled at his head and the woman holding it remains entirely unsmiling. It is a surreal experience. The similarities of this women with both Maria and Lydia are marked, except that the latter both had happy faces. Even when talking about the most serious subjects there had been a sparkle in their eyes, and Joe's clearest memories of both mother and daughter were of them laughing. But Maria's sibling has no such joy about her. Even though Joe knows she is younger, she looks years older. In the half light he can see her forehead is etched with lines, her mouth is drawn and her eyes are cold and empty. He finishes his tale expecting, if not an effusive welcome, then at least some pleasantries. Instead she says simply: "Maria's not here and you're not welcome."

261

"Ok," says Joe. "Sorry. I thought it would be all right to wait here. I'm sorry about your mother too. She was a great lady."

"She was a stupid selfish arsehole whose infatuation with the rebels has brought ruin and shame on this family. I wish they'd got her years ago..."

Joe rubbed his eyes again. "I don't understand. Has something happened? Where *is* Maria?"

"Oh Maria's all right. She's the only person left in this fucking family who is all right. The rest of us are just fucked ..."

And with that the tears start rolling down her face and she lets out an awful cry. The gun sags in her hand and she collapses onto the sofa across Joe's legs, pinning him to the seat, her shoulders heaving as she fights for breath between spasms of agonised wails.

He leaves her alone for a few moments, appalled at the depths of her despair. Then he carefully removes his legs from under her and struggles into a sitting position. The figure before him doesn't notice. Tears mix with snot as they cascade down her face. Joe goes to the bathroom in search of a towel and fills a glass with Spanish brandy which he finds next to the rum in the larder. At first she is inconsolable, but after a little while she accepts the towel and downs a large mouthful of the brandy which makes her cough and splutter. Finally he puts his arm round her shoulders and pulled her towards him offering comfort. For a second she accepts the invitation but then, like a scalded cat she leaps back and pushes him away, scrabbling for the gun on the sofa but not finding it.

"Keep back. Get off me. Leave me alone you bastard. How dare you ..." and she collapses again wracked with tears. Joe moves back and, looking down at his hand, sees it is red with blood. In the dim light he hasn't seen a wound, but closer inspection shows the woman's black dress is soaked from the waist down. Red stains are seeping onto the carpet and dripping onto the floor. Without her noticing Joe quietly takes the gun, empties it, puts it back next to her on the sofa and moves across the room waiting for a semblance of calm. Eventually it comes and the sobbing subsides a little. She grasps for the gun again, caresses it, eases the trigger back and raises it slowly. Even though Joe knew the chamber was empty he instinctively starts forward: "Careful ..." But she ignores both his words and his body and continues pulling the gun upwards until the barrel is resting under her chin, pointed at the back of her skull. Then slowly and deliberately she pulls the trigger.

The anticlimax is palpable. Instead of the explosion of the bullet and oblivion there is just the dull click of the hammer against the empty chamber. For a second there is a flash of something in her eyes. Joe isn't sure whether it is extreme anger or despair or relief. But then she collapses again onto the couch in floods of tears.

In a while he forces more brandy into her hand and persuades her to drink. Slowly she becomes calm and he is able to lay her flat out on the sofa. "You're bleeding. I need to see where it's coming from." She doesn't respond, but she doesn't stop him and he lifts the hem of her full length dress and mops around with another towel from the bathroom. Up to her knees her legs are damp and sticky with blood but there is no obvious wound. Feeling increasingly uncomfortable and somewhat prurient he raises the hem further. She is wearing no knickers, and the blood is clearly coming from between her legs, But this is no menstruation. Apart from anything else her thighs are blue with bruises and torn with scratches. With surprisingly little effort he is able to persuade her to accept the towel as a dressing and begins a somewhat futile attempt to wash away the blood from lower down.

She refuses his offer to call a doctor or a neighbour, and lies motionless staring at the ceiling. Joe had a lit a lamp and can now see that her dress is torn and dirty and there are bruises rising on her face.

"Won't you tell me what happened?"

The tears start to flow again, but between the sobs she starts to speak.

"I'm sorry ... I'm sorry..."

"It's OK. Take it slowly. I don't even know your name."

"I'm Rosa. I'm married to Mario, the baker. I *was* married to Mario ....I suppose I'm a widow now ..."

As the tears flow again Joe brings a fresh towel and a glass of water, and props cushions behind Rosa as she struggles to sit up a bit.

"You know my mother was in the Movement and when they captured her they must have found out where she came from. Perhaps she gave the address under torture or perhaps they just worked it out. Anyway two days ago the SIM arrived at dawn. I was asleep but of course Mario was already up baking the morning's bread. That's how I knew they had taken him. When I woke there was this smell of burning. I went down and smoke was pouring out of the oven. The bread was burned to a cinder. Mario was nowhere. Neighbours said they'd seen the SIM cars

263

taking him away. I waited hoping they just wanted to ask a few questions, but in the evening I went into the city to the army headquarters to ask for him. They denied knowing anything about him and I came back home."

Rosa pauses and takes another sip of water.

"I was sick with worry and didn't know what to do or where to look next. But someone told me that they sometimes took prisoners to be interrogated at the jail on the outskirts of town. So this morning I went there. What a stupid thing to do ..."

And again the tears roll and Rosa sobs.

" They were quite open with me. 'Oh yes, he's here' they told me. 'But he's not being very co-operative'. So I asked them what they wanted to know and they said names. Names of members of the movement in Bayammo. Names of Lydia's contacts. Addresses of safe houses. But he wouldn't know that, I told them. He's not a member of the Movement. He had nothing to do with Lydia or her work.

"Well, they clearly didn't believe me. And they kept me in this tiny room and one man started coming in and asking me more questions which I couldn't answer. And then he started hitting me. The thing is that neither Mario nor I did know anything about Lydia's work. Very occasionally, perhaps twice a year, she'd come to the bakery and stay overnight. But she never, never, said anything about what she was doing. It was just a family visit. She'd talk about Maria and she mentioned you once, and she'd ask about people from the village and their children. But she never talked about herself or what she did or the Movement or the rebels or anything connected with it.

"Well the fat SIM man was beginning to get frustrated. After slapping me a round a bit he started talking about what he'd do to Mario if I didn't give him details. He left the room and came back half an hour later with a bowl covered with a cloth. And I remember thinking 'Oh good some food at last'. I asked if I could see my husband and the man said "Yes, but he won't be able to see you". So I said 'what do you mean?' and he brought the bowl over to me and whisked off the cloth."

Rosa, white as a sheet, looks as if she is about to throw up at any moment.

"What was it?" asks Joe with a mixture of horror and macabre fascination.

"His eyes. They'd taken out his eyes and brought them to me ...in a bowl ... "

Rosa stopped and grabbed Joe's arm, gripping him hard. "Then several men crowded into the room. One of them started fondling my ... my breasts, and another ran his hand up my thighs. And I thought to myself 'OK, you're going to be raped. But compared to what happened to Mario that's nothing'."

She pauses. And Joe said: "It's alright. You don't have to tell me any more."

But Rosa stiffens herself and grippes his arm even harder. "That's not all. It wasn't finished. Yes they fucked me. But that was like nothing. I just took my mind away and thought good thoughts while they did it. The first one hurt because I was dry but after that I didn't even feel it. But after they'd all had a turn they were all laughing and one said 'I think we should watch her having sex with her husband now'. And I thought no. Poor Mario. I can't be with him like this. And I can't bear to see his ruined face. But that's not what they meant. The man who'd spoken went out of the room and came back a few minutes later with the same bowl. And I thought good God what now. And ... and it was ... it was his penis. They'd cut it off at the base. And they forced it into my mouth. While they watched and laughed. This pathetic shrivelled piece of gristle. All that was left of the man I loved. That wonderful man. My husband....."

And again Rosa wept.

Chapter 35

For days Joe stays in the apartment above the bakers providing what comfort he could to the traumatised Rosa. She sleeps much of the time then awakes only to stare vacantly into space while sobbing quietly to herself. He asks around the village for Maria but either no one has seen her or, if they had, are not prepared to say. Indeed it is clear that anyone connected with the bakers family is regarded with suspicion and treated as if they carry the plague. No one comes to visit or to enquire about Rosa's well-being.

Eventually Joe takes the bike into Bayamo and seeks out a public telephone. He puts a call through to his own number in Havana and speaks to his landlady Concha. No, she hasn't seen or heard anything from Maria, but promises she will forward any messages.

Time hangs heavy for him. He tinkers with the bike. He reads his way slowly through the small library in the flat. He takes pleasure in cooking for Rosa, but isn't surprised that she eats hardly anything. Eventually, for want of anything better to do and thinking it might be therapeutic he persuades her to show him how the bread ovens work and how to mix the dough. After a couple of attempts which are so dire as to almost raise a smile from her, he manages to produce an edible batch of loaves. He leaves them outside the shop on a trestle table with a small bowl for coins and is surprised to find that they've gone within an hour. Clearly the journey to the baker in town really is irksome for the villagers. So the following morning he rises early and, well before dawn, has the ovens fired and the dough rising. Rosa refuses to sell the bread from the shop saying she doesn't want to have to speak to her neighbours and answer difficult questions. So again he arranges the loves on the outside table and again finds they are quickly bought.

Within a fortnight the plan is working as he had hoped. Rosa has taken charge of his shambolic efforts and has cleared the chaos he had made in the bakery. Now he is working as her assistant and before long is banished altogether from the early morning duties. He still goes on the bike into town every two or three days to phone Concha, and eventually his persistence pays off. She tells him there is a letter for him and she has forwarded it to San Pablo de Yao.

Joe waits impatiently all day busying himself with little tasks; chopping wood for the oven, mending the broken window frame through which he'd first gained access to Rosa's flat. The following morning a small blue envelope is delivered with Maria's handwriting on the front. It is tantalising.

He sits it on the table in front of the coffee pot and tries to guess what it might contain. At least she is alive and, apparently, free. But what if she has changed her mind about him? Could the letter be breaking off the engagement?

Eventually he seizes a letter opener and slit the top of the envelope, pulls out the single sheet of paper and begins to read:

Darling,

I am sorry for delaying so long in writing and keeping you waiting for news. I can't say where I am for reasons you will see in a moment, but I am safe and well and missing you madly.

It is now certain that Lydia was captured and killed by Batista's bastard SIM. No one knows what happened to her body. I miss her and mourn her, but venerate her for what she did for the Movement. It made me think of how inadequate was my part in bringing to an end this odious regime. It's not good enough to be sitting comfortably in the city holding meetings and distributing armbands and just raising money for the real fighters. I thought I was a pacifist now I realise I was just a coward. So I have joined the rebels. A small platoon of women known as the Mariana Grajales has been formed under the command of two amazing women, Isabel Rielo and Tete Puebla. We've been issued with Garand rifles and Fidel himself has taught us to shoot – we had to hit a US quarter at first 20 then 30 meters before we were accepted!

So far we've only taken part in small skirmishes, though it looks now as if we will be part of a major campaign that is being planned. I can't tell you where but it is possible that your Aunt Clare will know. Incidentally I understand she is still waiting to hear from Rome about her Beatification!

267

All this, of course, means that I can't be with you for the moment, though I miss you dreadfully and long to be in your arms and your bed. But I am sure you will understand. I genuinely believe that there is a real chance that we can overthrow the dictator, and before long now.

Anyway I hope to see you very soon and trust that with the help of your relation you will work out how to find me.

I love you I love you I love you.

Your own M.

Joe reads and re-reads the letter. His first response is enormous relief that she is OK. The second is panic that she might be injured in combat. And the third is complete puzzlement about his Aunt Clare – largely because he doesn't have an Aunt Clare. And what was all that stuff about finding her with the help of a relation. And waiting to hear from Rome?

For the next few days Joe continues to help around the bakery. But Rosa is pretty well self-sufficient, and he begins to find himself getting in her way more than being of much use. She seems, physically at least, a lot stronger. But he would often come across her staring vacantly into space, and in the night he could sometimes hear her weeping from her bedroom across the hall. She shows little interest in Maria's letter expressing herself pleased that her sister was alive, but fatalistically believing that if she has joined the rebels as a fighter she is bound to be killed. Meanwhile Radio Rebelde is reporting success after success in the Escrambray province. There has been a major battle at Pedrero at the start of December when the army had thrown tanks and several heavily armed companies against the rebel forces. Che has evidently achieved some unity of purpose among the squabbling factions in the region and they held off the assault for several days before turning the tables and forcing the army to surrender to them.

The radio reports that he has joined up with Camillio Cienfugos' forces and they have started marching Northwards, capturing garrisons and destroying communications as they go. Joe checks his map and sees that the city of Santa Clara could be their objective. It is the only major settlement that now stands between the rebel forces and the capital, Havana. As well as being strategically vital, Santa Clara is also the provincial capital and Batista has sent in huge number of re-enforcements.

While staring at the map Joe suddenly had a flash of inspiration. Could Santa Clara and his beatified aunt Clare be one and the same. That must be where Maria and her women's platoon are heading! And if Maria and Che and the rest of the rebels are heading for Santa Cara then so is Joe.

§§§§§

He told Rosa of his plans over supper that evening and found her surprisingly content that he should go. "I suppose that so many have died in this civil war that it won't make much difference that my sister and a stray Englishman will join them. My brother, my mother, my husband have already gone. What's two more lives thrown away."

After she has gone to bed Joe searches the bookshelves until he finds a history of Cuba ... and then sits up reading the extraordinary story of Mariana Grajales Y Cuello – after whom the woman's platoon has been named.

Mariana was born in extreme poverty in Santiago de Cuba in 1808, and although her family was free, almost all around her were *Cimmarrons* or escaped slaves who suffered appalling abuse. Native Cubans hated the ruling Spanish who were, in the early part of the 19th century, running the country with a despotic system not much different from Batista's. On the death of her first husband Mariana was left with four children. Subsequently she entered into an enduring relationship with one of the heroes of Cuban history Marcos Maceo. Together, Joe read, they had nine children. The writer of the hagiography imbued both parents with all the virtues, teaching their offspring all the

> *"highest ethical and moral values, emphasizing honesty, justice, goodwill, hard work, dedication, personal fortitude, anti-racism and solidarity with those who fought for justice and freedom. They also taught them to love nature, be delicate with women and act like gentlemen in the presence of men.*

269

Mariana also trained them to fight with machetes and to venerate the principles of freedom and the struggle for independence:

"This type of home training and education helped the boys become brave warriors, and every single one of them fought on the battle field for Cuba's liberty."

In fact the home training and education resulted in every one of her nine sons as well as her husband being killed on the battlefield in the war against the colonial oppressors. But it was on that battlefield that Mariana herself impressed both as a fearless fighter and an indefatigable nurse to the wounded.

It was clear why the current revolutionary women's platoon had named themselves after her but, muses Joe, Mariana's experience of seeing so many of her nearest relatives perish in the fight is hardly propitious. Rosa may be right, the outcome of the Battle of Santa Clara could be decidedly dodgy.

§§§§§

Nine o'clock the following morning sees him once again astride the BMW heading north-west to Las Tunas and Camaguey. The roads are surprisingly empty of both civilian traffic and army activity. But every time he approaches a major bridge or viaduct he finds traffic backed up for hundreds of yards down the road. The ploy of blowing the bridges is clearly working. In most cases cars could eventually find a way round, but it often means a lengthy diversion or a hair-raising fording of streams and rivers. It is much easier for the bike. To start with Joe can overtake the long lines of cars by judicious use of the verge. And the powerful machine makes it relatively easy to get back up steep valley sides where other vehicles flounder of fail. To his surprise he isn't stopped once, either by army check-points or rebel patrols. The occasional burned out truck or car and low-level passes of air force fighter-bombers above gave the only indication that there is a civil war on. And by the time he's reached the outskirts of Santa Clara in the late afternoon all looks pretty much normal.

He makes his way to the centre of the small city and checks into the Gran Hotel – an imposing ten story building, in fact the tallest in town. It is relatively expensive, but after the 250

270

mile journey Joe decides to treat himself, and reckons that the main hotel will be a good starting place to find out what is going on. In fact it proves rather more difficult than that. Either nobody knows what is happening or they aren't saying. There also seemed to be an unusually large number of fat men in army uniforms staying at or visiting the hotel. Joe tries to strike up a conversation with the receptionist and then later with the barman trying to ascertain how near the rebels are thought to be and from which direction they might come, but in response all he gets is nervous glances and professions of ignorance. The punters at the bar are of no greater help either, possibly feeling inhibited by a group of drunken and loud officers in the far corner.

At around 11.00 Joe goes up to his room. It is freezing. The air conditioning seems to be on full blast and as he goes to turn it off, the knob comes away in his hand. He calls down to reception and a few minutes later there is a knock at his door. Standing there is the young looking under-manager who had been at the hotel reception when Joe checked in.

"Is everything OK sir?" he asks.

"Yes thank you, fine," replied Joe. "It's just that I can't turn off the air-conditioner."

The young man walks into the room closing the door firmly behind him and makes a cursory inspection of the large metal unit underneath the window.

"Erm I couldn't help overhearing you asking about the whereabouts of the rebel forces ...." he starts. "I thought you should know that this hotel is a favourite of the SIM in Santa Clara and that General Del Rio Chaviano who's the regional army commander keeps a suite here. May I ask what you interest is in knowing the whereabouts of the *Barbudos*?

Joe chuckles to himself to hear the now rather outdated description of Castro's army as "bearded ones". He looks the under-manager up and down wondering if it is safe to speak openly to him. He sees a teen-ager not so many years younger than himself. A handsome olive skinned Cuban with probably no more love for Batista and his forces than the rest of the population.

"My fiancé has joined up to fight and I think they are heading towards Santa Clara. I haven't seen her for weeks and I am desperate to find her," he says, hoping to appeal to the young Latino's romantic nature.

"Well, of course I know nothing directly myself," said the youth fishing out a small screw-driver and reattaching the loose knob, " but in this job you can't help overhearing things."

"Yes?"

'And one of things I've heard is that the President has decided to make his last stand here. He believes that if Santa Clara falls then he will have lost the country."

"But that's crazy," said Joe. "Havana is bristling with troops. The main barracks at Camp Columbia with its own airfield is almost literally impregnable."

"Well that's what they are saying, and Batista has ordered massive re-enforcements here into this city. There are already three thousand troops here and many more are on their way. In fact I hear that an armoured train is about to leave Havana with hundreds of guns, millions of rounds of ammunition and vast quantities of explosives. With that the army should be able to hold up the rebels for months."

"You seem very well informed," said Joe. "How do you know all this?"

Instead of answering directly the young man asks Joe what he knows about the rebels. Joe tells him he's met Castro and knows Che Guevara fairly well and, as a journalist, has spent some time in the rebel camp.

Immediately Joe knows which way his sympathies lie as the young man's eyes open wide at the mention of Castro and Guevara.

"Erm, well at night I have to work the switch-board after the day telephonist has finished her shift. I'm not very used to the new machinery, and some times I must get the wrong plug in the wrong hole and I can't help overhearing what's being said," he smiles.

"This General that you say stays here, does he really have militarily sensitive conversations over open lines from his room?"

"Yes, he's so arrogant that he either thinks no-one is listening or he simply doesn't care."

"But what's he doing here? Why isn't her running the war from his Barracks."

"Chaviano likes girls. Several girls at once in fact. And he finds it easier to procure them here. In fact it is my job to make sure they are available every night. Usually that's not too difficult because there are always hookers hanging around the hotel. And I can make it a condition on their being allowed to work the bar if they also work the General. But he's beginning to get a reputation for violence and they are getting more and more reluctant to go to his suite."

Joe digests the information, not sure how or if he can use it later. "Thanks for your help." he said finally. "By the way do you know if anyone has a short wave radio that will pick up Radio Rebelde in the hotel?"

"I believe the hotel electrician is an expert on radios. And he is generally to be found just before mid-night in his workshop on the fifth floor. If you go past Chaviano's suite 515, and down the corridor through the door marked 'Staff Only' and knock three times on the second door on the right, I am sure he will be able to help you out."

As the under-manager leaves, Joe chuckles to himself at the incongruous image of life on the fifth floor. At one end in a luxury suite the regional army commander is fucking himself senseless servicing a succession of whores instead of planning the defence of his city and the defeat of the rebels, while just down the corridor hotel employees are huddled round a radio bringing the latest news of government defeats and revolutionary triumphs instead of serving guests and servicing the hotel's air-conditioning units.

§§§§§

The electrician's room is just as Joe had imagined it. Rows of modern metal Dexion shelves full of tools and cables and fuses and diodes and other spare parts. And beyond, a small windowless room with a narrow single bed, chest of drawers and small wardrobe. But in here are gathered half a dozen or so men clustered round a makeshift radio its valves glowing in the dim light. And from the speaker comes the disembodied voice of Carlos Franqui, Castro's chief propagandist and head of Radio Rebelde. He is reporting that, after four days of fighting, the town of Formento some 50 kilometres from Santa Clara has fallen to Che Guevara and his troops and that they have even captured an army tank. In Oriente Fidel Castro is besieging Maffo, while there are pitched battles for control of Trinidad and Spiritus Sancti in Escrambray.

The group of M 7/27 sympathisers in the electrician's room look suspiciously at Joe. Again he has to explain his connection with the rebels and the time he had spent with Che. Eventually they make space for him on the end of the narrow bed, and as Franqui's broadcast finishes, they set about tuning the radio across the spectrum of frequencies seeking further transmissions from the rebels. Distant indistinct voices could at first be heard behind the wall of static and then come into focus as the dial is moved back and forth to find the clearest position. More often than not the messages are coded and therefore of no interest to the hotel listeners but on one occasion Joe thinks he recognises one of the voices and asks the tuner to wait a moment. A second voice is now heard saying:

> *"....tell me what sort of tank you captured, The messenger who was there told me he had seen it but he couldn't recognise what kind it was. Now over to you Guevara." "Well Camilo ..*

"Good god it's Che Guevara and Camilo Cienfuegos." said someone. "Shush ..." said several other voices.

> *"It's a caterpillar tank. Its markings are slightly burned but it's very pretty. It's American made and I think it's going to be useful. I don't know if it's a C-37. I though the C-37 was rather different. That's all I can tell you about the tank. The mechanics here are working on it..."*

The listeners round the radio burst into spontaneous cheers and applause and Joe misses the next few sentences. But once he's got them quieted down again he hears Guevara's voice, with the gently mocking tone he knows so well, saying:

> *"I heard you telling Fidel that you were going to take Santa Clara and I don't know what the hell else, but don't butt in there because it's mine. All you have to do is to stay over there, where you are."*

There is more banter about attacking the city and it dawns on Joe that the rebel commanders have no idea about the re-enforcements the army have already brought in, let alone the armoured train that is transporting an arsenal of weapons and ammunition.

"How can I get a message to Che?" he askes the electrician. "do you have a transmitter?"

"Only a very low power job that would reach to the other side of the city ... not over the plains to Formento or wherever he

274

is now. And anyway I wouldn't know what frequency to contact him on."

"Yes you do," says Joe. "This frequency we're listening to now. And what about extending the aerial? This is this is the tallest building in town. Surely if we could get an aerial up onto the roof a short-wave transmission should cover 50 or 70 kilometres?"

It's worth a try," said the electrician, I could try to rig up an antenna tomorrow, and see if there is any other way I can boost the signal."

The following night Joe again exits the lift on the fifth floor and follows three attractive if tarty looking women as they walk along to suite 515. There are already the raucous sounds of a party going on behind the closed door as he proceeded down the corridor to the service exit. The electrician has been as good as his word and has somehow trailed a long cable down from the roof, through various ducts and into his room. He is already tuning across the bands seeking out anyone else who is on the air.

"You'll have to begin transmitting" said the electrician, "but be careful what you say. If it's too obvious it could be picked up by the SIM and they could pinpoint it as coming from here."

Joe thinks for a moment and then pulls from his pocket a crumpled piece of paper. He opens it up, puts on the headphones, presses the transmit button on the mike and says, "Pawn to King four. Kings knight to bishop three. White's move. Queens bishop to bishop three. Over." And he releases the transmit button. A few moments later he repeats the sequence of words and again he waits for a response. Over and over he recites the first three moves in the chess game he's carried with him, until at last a muffled voice came through the static: "king's pawn to king's pawn two. Over." It was unmistakably the voice of Che.

"Kings knight to bishop three. But why go on, you know the Cuban wins. Over" said Joe.

"I can't remember where it was played though? Over."

"Well, it wasn't Buenos Aries. It was in my country, Nottingham in fact. 1936. Capablanca won in 30 moves. Forced Vidmar to resign. I have some information for you. Where can I find you. Over."

"Depends where you are?"

"Santa Clara."

"Well take the bus to Baez – it's about 40 kilometers south east of you. Don't come on a horse or a motor-bike it simply attracts attention! I'll have someone meet you at Baez. Over and out."

Joe makes his was down to the hotel lobby and, while the night clerk is otherwise occupied, slips into a small side room marked Hotel Switchboard. There, as he expects, is the under manager patching through calls. He summons Joe over and hands him a pair of Bakelite headphones which he plugs into a spare socket. Immediately Joe can hear the slightly slurred voice of a person he takes to be General Chaviano. He is ranting to a subordinate, complaining of just about everything, but especially the hardship of military life. Yes, reflected Joe pretty damn hard. Headquartered in a top hotel with room service providing whisky and food and girls by the bucket load. A bit of a contrast to the austere camps in the mountains that the rebels have been living in for the past two years.

Chaviano's conversation also touches briefly on the armoured train, estimating its expected arrival about a week hence. Before turning in Joe grills the under-manager for any other details that he's picked up and might be relevant or helpful to the rebels.

The following morning Joe is walking back from breakfast when he sees a man sitting in the lobby with a pot of coffee in front of him and two cups. Also on the low table is a large scale map of the area. Joe asks the man if he can look up Baez and the two fall into conversation. The man introduces himself as Antonio Nunez and turns out to be a Geography Professor from Santa Clara university. He expresses some interest that Joe should be travelling into a rebel held area and while searching in his pocket for a pen, inadvertently pulled out a red and black arm-band – the secret symbol of the July 26 Movement.

"I'd put that away quickly," said Joe. "This place is crawling with Army and SIM officers."

Antonio quickly hides the armband and explains to Joe that he has been due to meet a contact from the movement who was going to help him find Camillo's or Che's men. He thinks he could be useful to them in explaining the topography of Santa Clara along with his observations of where the troops are positioned to defend the city. The story strikes Joe as a bit unlikely, but then he reflects that he himself was on his way to meet Guevara with even scantier intelligence about the armoured train. So he suggests that Antonio might travel with him by bus to Baez and from there see what transpired.

Joe checks out of the Gran Hotel, thanking Guillermo Domenech, the under manager, for his help and seeking permission to leave the BMW in the underground car park for a few days more. He walks though the city's busy main square looking appreciatively at the pretty girls, wondering about Maria. Antonio meets him at the bus station and together they find a rickety old vehicle which is scheduled to leave for Sancti Spiritus in half an hour and will drop them at the highway exit nearest to Baez from where they will have to walk for a kilometre or so to the village itself.

Antonio turns out to be a good companion. Just a few years older than Joe, he has a lively mind and easy manner and is full of tales of the resistance in Santa Clara, so the journey passes quickly enough.

When they arrive in Baez the place is all but deserted. It is a small village with a main street consisting of a dozen or so characteristic wooden 'dilapidated-colonial' houses, and a couple of side streets of even less pre-possessing homes. The two wait in the shade of the warm afternoon sun having bought a bottle of water and some bread from the general store. Eventually a battered Chevvy pick-up burbles down the street driven by a boy who looks not a day over 15. He calls them over. Che's forces, he explains, had that day liberated the town of Placetas about ten kilometers to the North and are now headed towards Caibarien forty kilometres further on, up on the north coast. Joe and Antonio bundle into the front of the pick-up and they roar out of town in pursuit. The youth is wide eyed with the excitement of the escapade. He'd lived in Placetas all his life and joined the rebels just as they approached his town. It had taken four days of fighting for the army to surrender. They had captured 150 rifles and ten machine guns as well as ammunition and grenades.

As they enter Placetas the church bells are ringing and people are actually out in the streets waving banners and shouting "Long Live Free Cuba". Their driver waves wildly and shouts back revolutionary slogans. He points out the police station, the town hall and the army barracks where the government forces had held out, and he shows them the cemetery where *Comandante* Guevara had set up a heavy machine gun post. He himself had seized a rifle and taken pot-shots at mobile patrols from a tall building before the surrender was announced.

"It's an important town" says Antonio to Joe. "It controls the central highway and stops the possibility of the army sending any re-enforcements from the south. What's particularly interesting is that Guevara has gone on to Caibarien, skirting round Santa Clara. He obviously wants to isolate the city and control all the surrounding countryside before attacking it."

Joe feels a quickening of his pulse as he sees the jubilant citizens of Placetas celebrating in the streets and hears the boy describing the battle. He remembers those dark days in the summer when the rebels were completely surrounded and vastly outnumbered by Batista's troops in the Sierra Maestra. Now they have broken out and are slowly but surely moving through the country, with the government forces laying down their arms at every turn. The truck tops a rise and Cuba's Atlantic coast-line can be seen in the distance and the words of the civil war song come unbidden into Joe's mind:

> *Hurrah! Hurrah!*
> *We bring the Jubilee!*
> *Hurrah! Hurrah!*
> *The flag that makes you free!*
> *So we sang the chorus*
> *From Santiago to the sea,*
> *While we were marching thro' Cuba.*

The pick-up skids to a halt at a rebel road-block a couple of miles from the coastal town. The driver explains he is bringing guests to see the *Commandante* and is waved through. A hundred yards further on they come across an assortment of vehicles littering a lay-by and batches men resting in the early evening sun. Their uniforms are filthy and stained, their hair and beards long and unkempt. But they are clearly buoyed up by victory, smiling, laughing talking loudly. Food is being served and the three newcomers are invited over to share some. Che, they are told, is out surveying the territory and preparing for an assault on the town the following morning.

"You know what tomorrow is?" asked Antonio. "It's Christmas day." Strange place to be celebrating Christmas."

A short while later a small US army-issue Jeep roars to a halt nearby and Che jumps down and walks over to their group. "English," he says and embraced Joe. "I hope you are going to stay for a bit this time. You keep coming and going. I can't keep up with you."

"*I* keep coming and going" says Joe with mock surprise. "What about you. One moment you're hiking in the Sierra Maestra, the next moment you're on a camping trip to the Escrambray Mounains, now I find you round a camp-fire in Las Villas – what is this some sort of boy scouts outing to see Cuba in the open air?"

Che laughs and introduces Joe to a plumpish rosy-cheeked woman in green battle fatigues who had been with him in the Jeep.

"This is Aleida," he said, "My assistant." But the woman had already gone over to Antonio greeting him like a long lost friend. "This is one of my tutors from the University" she said, and then to Antonio: "I haven't seen you for ages. What are you doing here?"

Antonio explains his mission and how Joe had helped him to find Che. Within minutes the two men are pouring over the maps that Antonio has brought, plotting a way through the army defences in to the heart of the city. Joe askes Aleida about her work for the movement and discovers that, like Lydia, she had been a courier, moving messages and sometimes munitions about the country. She had met Lydia one or twice and was sad to have learned of her death. Joe asks if she knows the whereabouts of the Marianas women's platoon and is told that they are very much Castro's creation and have been training and fighting with him in the Oriente. "There's been a lot of opposition to them from the men," she says. "Some didn't think they should be fighting at all and some that they should have the inferior or older weapons. But Fidel has been adamant that they are as brave as any of the men – and a good deal braver than some – and so should be treated absolutely equally."

"But are they expected here in Las Villas province?"

"I don't know, it's possible he will have ordered them up. I think he'd like them to be in the vanguard when the rebel forces reach Havana."

"And when will that be?"

Aleida didn't answer at once. Instead she looks over at Che and in an instant Joe realises that she is far more than his "assistant". The look she gave him spoke of a much more intimate relationship. "That depends on how quickly Ernesto can take Santa Clara. It's going to be a tough nut to crack. And we don't know anything about the re-enforcements that Batista has brought in."

"Well we do know a bit," says Joe, and explains about the telephone conversation he's overheard with General Cantino. Quickly Che is summoned over and he quizzes Joe about every detail he has of the armoured train, and then askes Antonio to show him where the railway lines run through the city. "We have to stop and preferably capture that train," he said. And then gesturing to Joe and Antonio continued: "And I want you two to work out how to do it and then to carry out the operation."

Joe looked at Antonio. Antonio looked at Joe. And both knew that the other was thinking: stop and capture a fully armoured train carrying three hundred or more troops, and protected by heavy calibre machine guns and probably the odd Howitzer or two!!

"Piece of piss" said Joe out loud.

Chapter 36

The camp is astir before 4.00 the following morning with the fighters checking their weapons, packing up their few possessions, and forming columns to march down to the positions that Che has assigned them. There are only about 50 men in the group with Joe and Antonio, but Che has told them the total force is about 300 strong, and fairly well armed.

The assault on Caibarien and the outlying garrison at Remadios conformed to what has become standard rebel procedure. They take up positions in the dark on any available high ground surrounding the enemy position. At the first sign of dawn they unleash a fusillade of bullets. If they can get near enough they lob petrol bombs against the walls and if they have the ammunition, they fire bazookas at the doorways and windows. The Army troops quickly find themselves pinned down and have the option of sitting out a sustained assault hoping for re-enforcements, or surrendering quickly. The conscripted soldiers have increasingly little stomach for battle, and on Christmas Day decide they would much rather be at home with family or loved ones than facing the onslaught of the rebels. In any lull in the firing one of Che's lieutenants shouts down to them to surrender, promising they will not be harmed if they give up their arms quickly.

By lunchtime both Remedios and Caibarien have fallen to the rebels and, as at Placetas, the townsfolk immediately welcome in the *Barbudos* and the Revolution. They line the streets cheering, and it is all the liberators can do to stop them attacking the captured troops and torching the barracks.

Joe has been issued with a rifle but took little part in the assault. Indeed Che had asked him to hang back and look after Antonio who, as an academic, has no military training whatsoever and had never even fired a rifle before.

As the main force moved down to the port of Caibarien, Joe and Antonio remain in Remedios with a small group who are guarding the captured troops and arranging for their weapons to be moved on. Local families have brought out food as a makeshift Christmas meal and one denizen of the town proceeds to offer his own seasonal gift. Joe and Antonio look up to see an extraordinary sight approaching along main street. On the back of a flat-bed truck are two cases of rum and a dozen women who had clearly come straight from the local brothel. The bordello owner is offering the drink and the girls as a gesture of his admiration to the rebels who, unsurprisingly, fall on both booze and broads with alacrity until the platoon leader, Enrique Acevedo, intervenes. "We're fighting a revolution here" he screams at them. "leave them alone and remember your duty." A few of the men sheepishly move away from the women, but two or three simply ignore the order and already have their trousers round their ankles preparing for entry. "What shall I do? Enrique asks Joe. "What would Che do?" replies Joe, "And what will he do to you if you don't maintain discipline?" Enrique's hand instinctively hovers over his crotch to protect his balls before he pulls out his revolver and fires three shots in the air. Having gained the attention of his mutinous men he summons up all his authority and tells them the next bullet will be for them unless they obey orders immediately.

Late in the afternoon Joe and Antonio hitch a ride down to Caibarien and seek out the *Commandante*. They find him cursing and swearing as a medical officer bends over him with bandages and dressings. "What happened?" asks Joe in alarm. "Are you shot?" Are you badly wounded?

Che looks up sheepishly. "No, I fell off a wall and I think I've dislocated my shoulder. This brainless medic here says it must be bandaged up and put in a sling and I am not to use it under any circumstances. I wouldn't mind except that now I can't drive my Jeep."

"So you're looking for a driver then?" volunteers Joe.

"Yes I am. I would have preferred a proper Cuban, but I suppose in the circumstances I will have to put up with an Englishman."

For the next two days Joe chauffeurs Che around as he visits his forces, and lays plans for the assault on Santa Clara. The man isn't still for a moment. He personally oversees every last detail, working out how and when they will get the troops and arms and ammunition into place. With Antonio they plot a route following a series of back roads and tracks which will bring them onto the University campus to the North East of the city. From there they will fan out in different directions to attack the various defensive positions. Joe meanwhile studies the route of the train lines into and through the city. It is, he discovers, the forth largest metropolis in Cuba with about 150,000 inhabitants. The government forces, bolstered by the troops on the train, amount to between four and five thousand men. Che has some two hundred and fifty men divided into eight platoons, as well as 100 men from the Directorio. They are, reflects Joe, appalling odds. But not much different from anything the rebels have experienced over the past two years since landing on the Granma and consolidating their positions in the Sierra Maesta.

After two days of planning all is ready. They set out on the night of the 27th of December, moving by moonlight through the fields and down to the university. They meet no opposition, but discover that the army occupies the strategic Capiro Hills which overlook both the road from the university to the city centre as well as the train line which runs from north-west to south-east through the city.

Given an hour off from driving duties as Che discusses his plans with his captains and lieutenants, Joe explores the university and discovers, to his delight, a large school of Agriculture, complete with associated farm equipment.

That night with three men in civilian clothes, he takes two large tractors out of their shed on the edge of the campus and, with the aid of one of Antonio's invaluable maps, heads north out of town. Skirting around to the west he comes upon a stretch of track leading off to Santa Domingo which looks unguarded. Swiftly he nurses the tractors down to the line, attaches steel hawsers around the rails, and with the big engines revving noisily in the quiet night, pulls two long sections of track up and drags them away clear of the line. By dawn he and the men are safely back on the campus.

The next day the attack on the city begins in earnest. For once Che abandons his usual tactic of night-time assaults. Now in broad daylight, yard by yard, the rebels battle from the university towards the city centre. Bullets ricochet around their heads accompanied by the thump thump of small bore artillery from Batista's US made tanks. It is all Joe and Aleida can do to stop Che grabbing a rifle in his uninjured hand and leading the assault personally. But they manage to persuade him that in this engagement his place is, like a general of old, behind the lines, keeping an overview of the campaign and providing re-enforcements when necessary.

"We must concentrate the fighting among the houses and shops," he shouts to anyone listening, "then their tanks won't be so useful."

Late in the afternoon Joe askes for a moment with him and outlines his plan for immobilising the train. "We already severed the track to the north-west now we must do the same to the east. I need ten or a dozen volunteers who are not afraid of taking risks."

Che nods his approval at the scheme and orders half a platoon to go with Joe. Under his direction they quickly load up two trailers with rifles, a machine gun, petrol, bottles and a field radio transmitter. These they cover with tarpaulins, and on top of those they pile bales of hay from the university farm. The trailers are hooked up to the same tractors that saw service the night before and, finally, the troops wriggle beneath the tarpaulin. Taking a slightly circuitous route Joe leads the convoy away from the university and down into the centre of town, praying that two hay-wains will not attract too much suspicion in a city surrounded by agricultural land.

The plan seems to be going well. The streets are all but deserted. The main fighting is still concentrated on the eastern road from the University which leads down into the city centre, and to the South of the city where the Directo troops have formed a second front. By circling round to the north, Joe's two tractors are now coming up behind the enemy's front line position. The tractors and their trailers move in convoy. As a local, and one whose accent would provoke no suspicion, Antonio is in the leading vehicle while Joe drives the second. As they cross Marti street and round the corner a fearsome sight meets their eyes. There, blocking the road ahead, is a complete line of tanks facing the opposite direction. Antonio looks at Joe who shrugs. Doing a U-turn with two trailers will be a difficult manoeuvre and is bound to arise suspicion. But they can't go forward without passing the barrier. Antonio slows but continues moving forward until he is within ten yards of the roadblock. Then he does what any driver facing severe congestion at a grid-locked city junction would, he sounds his horn. Loudly. Several times. Finally a head appears in the turret of one of the tanks and a soldier looks out in amazement. "Go back, you stupid peasant" he shouts. This as an army road block. You can't get through.

"This is a public highway and you are blocking the road," shouts back Antonio. "I need to get this hay to the cattle down in Manicagua. If you would just move your tank to one side we can squeeze through and get out of your way."

The soldier's head disappears down into the tank's interior and a few moments later to Joe's amazement the engine starts and the vehicle inches forward out of the way. 'Well it just proves that if you don't ask, you don't get' he says to himself as he follows Antonio's tractor through the gap. Whistling tunelessly and being careful only to look straight ahead, he is just parallel with the tank that has moved when the turret re-opens and the soldier's head again appears. "Wait a moment" shouts the soldier. Joe's blood freezes but he eases the gears into neutral and pushes back the throttle slowing the engine so he could hear what was being said.

284

"Bring us some beef from the farm. We're on short rations here!" Joe pushes up the hand throttle, slipped into gear and turns to the soldier with a smile. He mouthed assent knowing anything he said couldn't be heard over the tractor's engine and then waves cheerily as he lets the clutch out and moves forward.

A few blocks further on and they turn into a cul-de-sac at the end of which is the train line. Swiftly Joe orders the men hidden beneath the hay in his trailer to come out. They pull down the bales and arranged then in a wall across the road. Having removed the stash of guns and ammunition they unhitch the trailer and push it over onto its side behind the straw bales. Now they have some cover to protect them from any attack along the street. Joe joins Antonio who is pulling down the fence that separates the end of the road from the railway. He forces the big tractor up onto the slight embankment, unhitches his trailer and moves 80 yards or so along the down the line. Out come the steel hawsers again, and Joe helps to wrap one end around the metal track and attach the other to the tractor. With a roaring of the tractor's engine and a screeching of metal a section of the track is wrenched away. But now there is another sound. Rifle fire. An army patrol has turned into the street and is shooting at the rebel's barrier. Joe motions two men to lay charges under the track just ahead of the break and, with Antonio and three other men, he jumps up onto the tractor and heads off up the line, the wheels bumping over the uneven railway sleepers. Rounding a bend they see in the distance the imposing front of the armoured train, stationary in the City's main station. Seconds later Guards on the train see the tractor and open fire. Antonio secures the steering wheel so the wheels are pointing straight ahead and leaving the hand throttle slightly open jumps down onto the side of the track. One of the volunteers passes round petrol bombs he's been carrying in his back-pack while a second lets off short bursts from his sub-machine gun. Joe and the other two walk slowly behind the tractor, using it as cover. Eventually they are near enough the train to light and hurl one of the petrol filled bottles which lands with a satisfying whoomph a few yards in front. Antonio and a second man have skirted round the side and two more petrol bombs explode against the metal of the driver's cab.

The locomotive has clearly been left with steam up, and Joe can hear the stoker desperately shovelling coal into the fire to increase the pressure. More petrol bombs explode and shots are ringing out from both sides – those from the rebels simply bouncing off the heavy steel armour, but making a considerable din. After a minute or two the engine driver opens the valve and lets off the brakes and the huge beast starts to move forward. The train and the tractor are now just yards apart and heading directly for each other. Joe's group abandon their positions behind the tractor and seek cover by the side of the railway line. There follows a huge crash as the front of the train smashes into the tractor and tosses it aside as if it were made of cardboard. On cue the contingent of rebels that had remained with the first tractor now start firing at the train from down the track. The locomotive slowly picks up speed in apparent haste to get at them. With soot and smoke bellowing from its funnel, steam hissing from the pistons, and the fire glowing in the cab as the stoker piles on more and more coal, the leviathan lumbers down the line towards its own destruction. The locomotive isn't going very fast when it runs out of track, but the sheer weight of the twenty-two steel plated carriages behind increases its momentum and keeps it moving inexorably forward as its front bogies plough into the shingle and bump over the sleepers. The noise of grinding metal and escaping steam mixes with the rat-a-tat-tat from the rebels' machine gun and the explosion of the Molotof cocktails as they thud against the side of the train.

One it has come to standstill, the locomotive is lying diagonally across the track, the second carriage twisted and tilting, and the two behind that derailed, Joe signals to the group's sapper who immediately detonates the explosives which now lie under the centre of the train. It isn't an enormous bang, and it has little effect on the heavy re-enforced steel carriages. But it achieved precisely what Joe and Antonio had intended. It scares the living daylights out of the troops within.

Wave after wave of petrol bombs are hurled at the carriages containing the soldiers, and the very armoured plating that had protected them now turns their sanctuary into an oven.

Before long one of the big doors slides open and two or three rifles are thrown out. An arm emerges waving a white handkerchief, while voices tried to shout "surrender" over the surrounding din. Joe orders the machine gun forward to cover them and supervises the frightened troops as they jump from the train and hand over their guns.

As soon as he can he gets on the walkie-talkie and reports their success to Che's headquarters at the University, asking for re-enforcements to secure the captured train against a possible counter-attack. But he is told that the rest of the rebel platoons are pinned down in fierce hand to hand fighting against targets across the city and wouldn't be able to get through until at least the following day. But they did promise to contact the Directo forces which have been battling for entry to the city from the south and who are, theoretically at least, a good deal nearer to Joe's position.

Joe surveys the scene. More than three hundred government troops and officers are lined up three or four deep along side the train, guarded only by one man with a machine gun and a second who is piling up the surrendered rifles. A short way back down the track, behind the straw barricade, half a dozen rebels are still holding off an assault from down the street. Meanwhile sporadic firing is now coming from up the track in the direction the station from which the train had come. Antonio agrees with Joe's assessment that it will be difficult for their small force to hold the train AND guard the captured men. Of the two the train and its weapons are clearly the more important. But now fate takes a hand. Many of the soldiers emerging from the train are volunteering to come over to the revolutionary forces. Joe and Antonio select a group of what they hope will be the most trustworthy. Half this contingent they send to re-enforce those fighting behind them, and the rest they put in charge of marching the remainder of the captives to a nearby building and guarding them once there.

Next they set about inspecting the weapons they have captured. It is a veritable arsenal. There are machine guns, sub machine guns, rifles, bullets, grenades, rocket propelled grenades, and even anti-aircraft guns. The most mobile of these Joe deploys strategically around the train with the heaviest pointing up the track towards the station from where he expects the main counter-assault to come. It is now shortly after mid-night. The attack and capture of the train have taken some five hours in total. But it is going to be a long wait until day-light.

Chapter 37.

It is just before dawn that the counter-attack comes. Batista's forces have formed a stronghold around the station and there have been sporadic shots from that direction throughout the night. Now troops from there are moving out along the track towards the crippled train. Joe has mounted a heavy machine gun on the last carriage and placed men with automatic rifles on the roof further up. He's also deployed a small group on each side of the track using whatever cover they can find. They have grenades as well as sub machine guns and rifles. The small troop behind the straw bales and overturned trailer are still successfully defending their original position, and have set up a further defensive barricade guarding the track running away to the south-east. Even though in total Joe has fewer than 30 men, they are now relatively well armed and still jubilant about taking the train in the first place. All in all the position seems fairly secure. He had ordered the machine-gunner to wait until the first wave of troops is well in range before opening fire, and when he does they quickly scatter. The second attack is better planned. An empty guards-van has been pressed into service and is being pushed ahead of the attacking force, providing cover for them to get within range of the train. A cannon or mortar begins to fire over the top of this – missing it's mark by some way, but still showering shrapnel around and causing alarming explosions.
 A volley of grenades finally halts the lone guards-van sixty or seventy meters down the track. But it still provides good cover, and now a sustained gun-fight brakes out with both sides in well defended positions. Joe considers the situation and decides the best course of action is to deploy ten or a dozen fighters to circle round behind the van and neutralise it. But he doesn't have ten or a dozen people spare. Indeed every one is fully committed in his current position. But during a brief lull in the firing just as first light is breaking he hears his name being called from behind and he creeps back, hugging the side of the armoured train until he is out of the line of fire of the enemy rifles. There is a sight for sore eyes! A platoon of re-enforcements is waiting for orders. Joe doesn't recognise them as Che's men and judging by their fresh looking uniforms he guesses the men have got through from the Directo's lines to the south. But then, in the half light he does a double take. These aren't men at all. They are women. The Marianas! In all the activity of the last 48 hours Joe had put Maria

to the back of his mind. Now here in front of him is her troop. He surveys the group, his eye running over each face in turn. And there she is, her long hair cut short and partly covered by a forage cap, she was wearing ill-fitting green fatigues instead of her usual flowing skirt, but unmistakably Maria. She is clearly as surprised to see him as he was to find her. It is one of those movie moments when the rest of the world seems to stand still, while the main characters run towards each other in slow-motion. But what was the protocol of greeting your lover and fiancée in the midst of battle? He wants to hug her, kiss her, fondle her, run his fingers through her hair, tear her clothes off and make passionate love. There and then. On the track beside the train. With bullets flying about.

Instead, he calmly continues his conversation with the commanding officer and then turns to her and offers a soldierly embrace such as he would give to any comrade-in-arms he had not seen for some time. But their eyes do meet for a lingering moment and convey their longing more eloquently than any words could ever do.

The moment is quickly over and the women's platoon disappear silently into the dawn light, their orders to circle round to the right and attack the flank of the army troops now dug in behind to the stationary van. Joe orders his men to wait until their counterattack starts and then lay down sustained covering fire. But before the Marianas are in position, a low drone can be heard from the sky behind. Looking up they can see a formation of fighters approaching. Joe orders his snipers off the roof of the train and under the cover of the armoured plating. The planes dip low half a mile from their target, then follow the railway along, opening fire with machine guns and small calibre cannon as they approach the train. The bullets and shrapnel bounce off the steel but made a frightening din. However as the planes pass over they continue firing, their shells thudding into the wooden guards van and the army troops dug in behind.

The rebels watch delighted as Batista's British-bought Sea Furies do their job for them and destroy the army's position. The Marianas take advantage of the confusion and hurl grenades in their general direction while Joe orders the heavy machine gun to rake the enemy. Realising their retreat is cut off, within minutes a white flag is raised and the entire contingent numbering around 50 men surrenders and is marched off to join their compatriots in the nearby hall that Antonio had commandeered the night before.

Joe arranges for one of the anti-aircraft guns to be set up in case the planes return and sets about organising logistics, reenforcing his positions and raiding the train's stores for food. He had taken temporary possession of the commanding officers' quarters on the train, and now lies down on the narrow bunk-bed for a moment's rest. Within seconds he's asleep, exhausted by the night's activities and the stress of the battle.

§§§§§

Joe wakes to find Maria kneeling by the side of his bed holding his hand and looking silently into his eyes. For a moment he is back in their rooms in Havana Vieja, on the lumpy horse-hair mattress with the scent of her body beside him as she teased and tempted him with irregular Spanish verbs. Then hours would melt away as they lay in each-others arms, luxuriating in the glow of their passion. Now in Santa Clara in a claustrophobic darkened compartment on an armoured train during a short lull in the battle there is neither the space nor the time for niceties. They couple quickly and urgently, almost violently. Instead of tenderly exploring every inch of each others nakedness they remain fully clothed, just pushing aside sufficient material to allow access. Somehow, though, this is a culmination of every time they had ever had sex. This brief moment expresses more eloquently than ever before their longing and their love. It bridges the long gap since they had last held each-other, and it lays down a store for however long they might subsequently be parted. There are no cooing endearments, no protestations of undying love. None are needed. Silently and sweatily they perform the basic physical act that is at once utterly mundane and at the same time the ultimate explosive expression of their relationship.

Afterwards, Maria pulls up her combat fatigues and slips out into the corridor without a backward glance. Joe waits for a moment and then follows her into the bright sunshine of morning to continue the battle and find out what fate has in store.

§§§§§

Che had been on the radio with orders for them to move back towards the city centre leaving just a small group to guard the train. The army is tenaciously holding out in a number of places including the main railway station and the Gran Hotel in the central park square. The Marianas are to rejoin the Directo's forces and attack the station, Joe is to try to take the hotel. He leads his troop across the river and towards the park. Everywhere there is chaos. Broken glass litters the street. Cars are overturned and burned out. Shop windows are smashed. Few people are about, but those that are shout encouragement to the revolutionaries and offer them food and drink. Some even hand over petrol bombs to be used in the next round of the fray.

It takes less than fifteen minutes to reach the square, which is dominated by the ten story hotel on the western side. But the moment the troop makes its tentative way towards the park, shots ring out from the top of the hotel. The army has evidently taken over the upper floors and positioned snipers on the roof giving them a panoramic view of the park and city centre.

Joe orders his group to fall back and they skirt round on side streets away from the square itself. Eventually they come around to within sight of the rear service entrance of the hotel. While three riflemen provide covering fire Joe and the others run across the street to the door which, surprisingly, opens to their touch. Cautiously they slip in, expecting at any moment to come under fire. But there is no-one around. The lobby is empty, the reception deserted. The lift doors are open, but the power has been switched off. They move cautiously up the stairs to the first floor still meeting no resistance and still finding no people. But here the stairs leading to the upper floors have been blocked. Furniture is wedged so tightly into stair-well that it can't be moved from below. Someone suggests setting fire to it on the basis that the flames and smoke would travel upwards and help to flush out the enemy. Joe agrees and moves back to the ground floor, making his way into the small room with the telephone switchboard where less than a week ago he'd been listening into the conversations of an army general. A light is flashing on one of units. He puts on the headset and answers the call with a mock official accent:

"Hello, reception here. How can I help you?" The rebels behind him bust into laughter.

"Who is that?" asked a frightened voice from the other end.

"The revolutionary forces under the command of Ernesto Guevara. Who's that?"

"I'm a hotel guest. There are about fifty of us. We're trapped here on the fifth floor. The SIM and the army are on the roof above and they've cut the elevator service and blocked the stairs. Can you get us out?

291

"We'll try. Are there any hotel staff around there?

The guest went off to look while Joe shouted to his men to wait before setting fire to the furniture in the stairwell. But it was too late. Petrol had already been poured on and set ablaze.

A young man's voice comes onto the phone, slurring slightly. "Hello this is Guillermo Domenech, the under-manager. Welcome to the Gran Hotel. This is a great day for Cuba and a great day for freedom and …."

"Hang on a minute Guillermo. This is Joe, your English guest from last week. Listen we didn't know there were any guests still in the hotel and we've set fire to the barricade on the stair-well. I don't think we can stop it now. Can you get the guests out any other way?"

"Of coursch we can't get out another way. Otherwise we've done so days ago when the bastards trapped ush in here." he slurred. "Since then there's been nothing to do but drink wishkty and listen to the shooting in the street. And now you've set fire to my hotel and we're all going to die. It'sh not fair. Not fair at all."

Joe pulls the plug on the conversation and looks round urgently for a solution. The fire is now blazing so fiercely that the hotel fire extinguishers have no effect on it. He peers out of the back door and looks across an alley to the Clovis Theatre next door. From the upper floors the gap between it and the hotel is only a few feet as air conditioning units jut out between the two.

"Quickly," he shouts, leading his men over the alley and into the theatre. They pant up the five flights of stairs to the top of the building and pile into the projection room. Here they are directly opposite one of the hotel windows, and out of sight of any snipers on the roof.

"Can you make it across?" someone asks Joe.

"I'll have to" he replies, and squeezes out through the window onto the metal top of the air-conditioner. The gap to the widow opposite is only about five feet, but there is a fifty foot drop to the alley below if he miscalculates. Being careful not to look down he leaps across smashing the hotel window with his boot, and falling in among a shower of glass. He summons Guillermo and the guests from the corridor where they have been holed up drinking whisky and eating tinned fruit, and leads them into the room. A few object, saying they would rather take their chances with the SIM than risk falling to their death on the concrete below, but by now the smoke from the fire in the stairwell is billowing out into the corridor and there doesn't seem to be much alternative. One by one the guests are passed across the gap, including a baby and an exceedingly large woman who only just squeezes through the window. When they are almost all through Joe quizzes the drunken Guillermo about access to the roof and where the snipers are positioned. With two men in tow he climbs into the smoky hotel corridor, and up the stairs towards the tenth floor restaurant and the roof terrace. Again they met no resistance but the heavy metal door leading to the roof is locked from the outside. Joe places two grenades by its hinges, pulled the pins and makes a hasty retreat as the explosions reverberated around.

The battle on the roof lasts only minutes but it is fierce and dangerous. The dozen or so SIM snipers are spread out around the edge and, when the rebel attack comes from the stairwell in the centre of the roof, they have no cover. But neither do the rebels have much. However the abundant supply of grenades captured from the train help. Joe tosses them all round the roof from the safety of the stairs and then rushes out with his two men, spraying bullets round and diving for what ever cover they can find. One of Joe's compatriots is hit in the arm. But in the relatively close quarters their sub-machine guns are more useful than the sniper's rifles. One man had run out of ammunition and was trying desperately to clip a new magazine into his rifle. Joe doesn't think twice, he points the Thompson at him and squeezes the trigger. The response is immediate, the chunk of wood and metal in his hands leaps into life. He fights to keep the barrel down as it spits bullets. He can see the body in front of him recoil as it is hit. He can see the holes in the man's uniform and then the red stain of emerging blood. He can see the surprise and horror on his face as he realised he is badly hit and will almost certainly die. He watches as the man sags at the knees and collapses to the ground. And then Joe watches no more. He swings round, looking for the next source of danger, mentally calculating how much ammunition he has left. A bullet whistles past his face so close he can feel the wind on his cheek. And he turns and fires again, and watches another man die in front of him.

Almost before the fight has started it is over, and the bodies of the 'enemy' lie in bloody heaps around the roof. Young men. Not much older than Joe himself.

As he makes his way down from the roof through the smoke and across the rickety air conditioners to the Clovis theatre he wonders, not for the first time, just what he is doing there. Yes, of course there was the battle against a dictatorship and its abuse of power, its torture, rape and mutilation of its citizens. But you can find similar abuses in hundreds of countries and at almost any point in history. In principle it is right and proper that you should oppose tyranny and support freedom at every opportunity. But regardless of Maria, Cuba is not his country. The revolution would be happening whether or not he is there. And if he is seriously wounded or killed, which seems like a pretty fair possibility, how will that have benefited the human race or, indeed, the Cuban people? And here he is terminating other people's lives. Killing them. Dead. Yes, if he didn't shoot them first they would certainly kill him. But he is still taking someone's life. The most precious, the most sacred thing they possess. Arguably the *only* thing they possess. He remembers suddenly that it is the last day of the year and the prospect of a pint or two in the Cranbrook Arms in Deptford seems, suddenly, infinitely more appealing than dying painfully and uselessly on the streets of a foreign city.

The sombre thoughts don't last long though. Back in the square with the smell of cordite drifting across the city, with smoke rising from burning buildings and vehicles, with his small troop of guerrillas looking for leadership the adrenalin starts to flow once more and again he is in the thick of it. Caught up in an adventure he can't control, trapped in a narrative of someone else's choosing. A pawn in the game of chess that is the Cuban revolution. It is rapidly heading for the end-game, but will there be more sacrifices required before check-mate can be called?

Chapter 38

Joe orders a short rest. Someone has somehow found sticky pastries and fresh coffee and they sit in the sun in the park. The field radio has been left at the train and so they have no way of reporting that the Hotel had been liberated or of getting new orders. But suddenly Joe thinks of Maria and wonders what is happening to her at the station. After a short discussion with the others it is agreed to try to get there to offer whatever help they can, or any rate re-join the main group of rebels. From his brief stay in the city the previous week Joe knows it is some distance to the north – at least half a mile. With army and SIM snipers still in isolated positions walking the streets would be dangerous, so they look round for transport. Cars lie abandoned all about and it isn't long before they have an elderly Oldsmobile and a slightly newer Chevvy up and running. The troops pour in and, with guns pointing out of every available window they move off, the V8 engines growling beneath the bonnets.

It was the easiest mid-morning drive anyone had taken in Santa Clara for years. The roads are entirely devoid of other moving vehicles. The main problem is navigating round those that have been abandoned or burned. But after just a few minutes they are within sight of the railway station where, it quickly becomes apparent, the battle is still in mid flow.

The army has fortified the main building and packed it with troops. Their rifles and machine guns have a commanding view across the piazza in front. There is no available cover to cross the open space, and no apparent way round the side or the back.

The guerrillas besieging the position are commanded by Roberto Rodriguez, known by all as El Vaquerito – the little cowboy. Joe had met him in the Sierra Maestra and heard how, months earlier, he'd arrived barefoot at the rebel stronghold and Celia Sanchez had found him a pair of boots whose leather was ornately tooled. These, with his big straw hat, made him look like a Mexican cowboy which spawned his nickname. Since then he had shown such a blood-thirsty tenacity in fighting and total disregard for his own personal safety that Che had put him in charge of Column 8 – known as the suicide squad. As a warrior he may have been single minded and humourless, but as a person he was utterly beguiling. He was about Joe's age but much

295

shorter and slighter. He had an infectious laugh and told the most outrageous stories, but with such conviction that it was impossible to discern fact from fiction.

Now as Joe approaches him he is sizing up the enemy position and trying to calculate the chances of success from a frontal assault. Joe estimates them as nil. The fighters would be mown down by the army's machine guns long before they reach the building. But the rebels have been held up here for nearly 24 hours and Roberto is itching for action.

"At least let's try to find some diversion to distract them." suggests Joe.

The idea is considered and it is agreed that Column 8 would wait until Joe has rigged up some sort of explosive device. Then the Marianas and Joe's platoon will provide covering fire. Joe looks over the two American cars they had hot-wired and asks one of his men to make some modifications. He can see the women's brigade in their positions across the main street leading up to the station, but it is impossible to reach them without making a major detour to get out of range of the enemy's guns. A messenger is sent on the journey to advise their commander of the plan, but Joe has to be content to look for Maria among the combatants who occasionally stick a rifle around the side of a building a let off a few shots towards the station. From a distance the women look identical in their green fatigues and forage caps. But eventually Joe spots a figure who he was sure is Maria. He raises an arm in salute and blows a kiss in her direction before she disappears back behind cover.

A short while later the big Oldsmobile is lined up in one of the side streets, the space behind its radiator grill packed with explosives and grenades. The difficulty is going to be to keep it going in a straight line. Even lashing the steering-wheel wouldn't necessarily prevent it from veering away from its target. Someone was going to have to remain in it until as late as possible and then leap out right in the line of the enemy fire. Joe was definitely NOT volunteering. But Roberto did, without a moment's hesitation. It is agreed that the other car will follow the Oldsmobile as close behind as possible and provide cover for the 'suicide' squad which will then attack the building head on and, theoretically, simply walk through the gaping hole that the initial explosion will have made.

Joe watches as the two cars are readied and move off. The Chevvy keeps some way back from the Olds. Roberto, in the front car, rounds the corner, points forward in direct line with the station, ties up the steering wheel, wedges down the accelerator.

and ducks down out of sight. As the car leaps forward, the second car appears from around the corner and follows in its wake. Immediately the army's machine guns rattle into action concentrating their fire on the two vehicles. Joe's platoon and the Marianas move cautiously into the street to get clear shots at the enemy round the side of the two cars and Roberto's squad, bent low, run behind the big Chevrolet. Joe is still carrying the Thompson sub-machine gun that has proved so valuable on the roof of the hotel. But here it is all but useless. The station is two or three hundred yards away and although the Tommy gun had a theoretical range of twice that, everybody accepts that it is of little use beyond 50 yards. And its key advantage of spraying bullets around at close range is a positive liability if there is anyone between you and the enemy. Joe crouches down, slides the selector on the left side of the gun to singe shot and aims wide of the advancing troops.

By now the Oldsmobile is approaching the point where Roberto has to leap out if he is to have any hope of saving his life. Joe watches as the driver's door opens and the slight figure rolls onto the ground. But at that moment a lucky bullet from the station must have hit the explosives because there is a resounding boom and the car disintegrates in a ball of flame, with debris raining down all around.

Immediately the Chevvy following behind accelerates, screeches round the burning mess of metal that had been the Olds, and proceeds to head straight for the main doors of the station. It leaves the foot-soldiers that had been using it as cover dangerously exposed. But not one runs for cover. To a person they continue moving forward straight into the line of fire that now rattles forth from the defensive positions. Joe knows they will have to be re-enforced if they are to have any hope of taking the building and he urges his men forward, cautiously hugging the front of the buildings that line the avenue up to the station. There is a pandemonium of shooting and smoke and explosions, like a malign monster firework that has ignited itself on the ground and is now spewing out bangs and sparks in all directions. Ahead through the smoke he can see other figures emerging from across the street. The Marianas have also realised the vital need to re-enforce Roberto's Column 8 but, instead of seeking cover as they advance, they are now running straight towards the enemy guns down the middle of the road. Suddenly terrified for Maria, Joe also breaks into a run. There is a tremendous crash which announces the arrival of the Chevvy at the station doors. Amid the sound of grenades exploding and guns firing Joe leaps over bodies and debris in the street and follows the rapidly diminishing group of rebels through the splintered doors and into the building. All is chaos and confusion. The men in front of him turn left so he goes right. Through a waiting area piled high with furniture to barricade the windows he runs, and into an office, possibly the station master's. In an instant he sees two soldiers turning from the window, struggling to raise their rifles in the enclosed space. Joe aims his stocky weapon and pulls the trigger, tensing his left hand to pull down on the wooden grip as the burst of fire forces the barrel upwards. But nothing happens. Or to be more accurate one shot rings out passing the first soldier harmlessly to his left. "Damn" thinks Joe "I've left the selector on single shot. Now I'm fucked."

Joe watches as the surprised guards continue to raise their guns to take aim at him. Images flood into his mind. The first is his recurring nightmare from the Troodos mountains. Here he is again staring down the barrel of an enemy's gun. Or is it that the enemy is staring down the barrel of his gun. Which is which? And then suddenly he's not in Cuba or in Cyprus but on a cricket field somewhere in Kent. Cricket wasn't big were he grew up in Deptford but despite the ribbing of his father and brother he'd signed up one summer holiday for a local club and learned the rudiments. He was a passable bowler but never got the hang of batting. And his memory now leads him to one of his more disastrous encounters at the wicket. Going in at number ten or eleven he simply had to stay there while the better batsman at the other end mopped up the few runs needed for victory. But on his fist ball Joe had broken the golden rule and prodded at a benign delivery outside his off stump. Without moving his feet and getting over the ball to play it down onto the ground, his bat was angled up, and when the ball hit it, it rose gently off the face and into the air, offering an easy catch to gulley. Joe watched the ball spinning towards him. He watched the fielder moving into position, his hands cupped for the catch. And then he roared out at the top of his voice. **"NO"** so loudly that the startled fielder, looking up, took his eye off the red leather and promptly dropped it, letting it fall harmlessly to the ground through his outstretched arms. With some presence of mind Joe waved at his partner at the other end of the wicket and said, rather more quietly, "get back", as if to pretend that his terrified NO had been a legitimate call to stop him running into trouble. But in reality it had been pure funk that, unsportingly, enabled him to keep his wicket and, subsequently, allowed his side to win the game.

298

Now, in a gun battle in a revolution on a Caribbean island three and a half thousand miles away Joe does exactly the same thing. He bellows **"NO"** at the top of his voice and then a split second later adds still in English "touch those guns and you die!"

The startled soldiers look at the crazed revolutionary shouting to them in a foreign language. They look at the machine gun in his hand pointing straight at them. They don't know the selector is on single shot. And even if they do, there is still good chance that he can get off two single shots before they can kill him. And anyway the game's clearly up and the assault on their stronghold has been successful. So they glance at one another and nod, and lower their guns and then drop them on the floor and put their hands up.

The tension subsides. Joe finds he's still breathing. He can feel his heart racing. He looks round. The shooting is subsiding. The assault has been successful. One of his men comes in and asks if he's OK. Joe tells him to guard his captives and walks outside where the hot sun is still shining, oblivious to the carnage below. Joe first sees the mangled body of Robero. Riddled with bullets as he jumped from the car, and then smashed by the force of the explosion. He mentally salutes him for his bravery and his sacrifice. But Joe's attention is elsewhere. There's the body of a rebel lying a short way off. It's a woman. One of the Marianas. The sick sensation of dread rises in his chest. On one level of his sub-conscious he tells himself it's Maria. On another he argues it can't be her. He's only thinking it is, to prepare and protect to protect himself; to make the discovery all the sweeter if it's not her. He should run over to see. He can't. His feet are like lead. He shuffles across. She's on her side. Her back's towards him. There's blood on the ground. He kneels, puts his hand on her shoulder and gently, oh so gently, turns her onto her back. Through his tears he sees her face. Through his sobs he sees her eyes flutter open. Through his misery he sees the dark red stain spreading from her chest. He lies on the ground next to her as if they were side by side in bed. She's able to raise her head and he slips his arm under it and nuzzles up, his cheek against hers. The most stupid banal words come from his lips: "You should have been more careful. You should have kept to the side." She simply smiles and manages to move her head slightly to plant a brief kiss on his lips before whispering. "No.... It's all right .... Don't cry. It was meant to be. It was worth it. I'm sorry to leave you though. But you know part of me will be with you for ever." Her eyes close and her breathing is faint. Joe kisses her, keeping his lips pressed against hers until he can feel there is no more breath in her body. He closes his eyes and holds her tightly as she slips away from his grasp, and heads away for eternity.

§§§§§

The next thing he knows is that a hand is gently shaking his shoulder. He looks up into the penetrating eyes of Che. "Come on, English, you can't lie here in the street all day there's work to be done," he says gently. Joe disengages himself and looks round. A squad of rebel soldiers and sympathisers is tending the wounded and removing the dead for burial. "Who was she?" asks Che.

Joe tells him it was Lydia's daughter, and his fiancée. That she was a Movement organiser in Havana and that it was through her that he got involved with the revolution. Che is sympathetic, and eulogises the heroism of the Marianas. He also praises Joe for the capture of the train. "I think it's won us the city" he says. "And when he knows that Santa Clara has fallen, Batista will realise that the game is up. But I have to get messages through to Havana. All communications are down. Have you still got your motorbike?"

And so, an hour later, Joe is in the underground car park of the Gran Hotel, siphoning petrol out of cars and filling the BMW's tank. His mind is numb, trying to readjust to the idea of a world without Maria. On the road he winds up the big bike and is soon doing 80, swathing through the countryside, as the sun sinks slowly down ahead of him, reflecting its last translucent glow off the clouds.

It's *such* a fucking beautiful country, he thinks as he zips up the central highway, hits the ring road outside Havana and dives under the tunnel. The lights are all on along the Malecon. The waves are lapping gently at the embankment walls. Music is drifting from the pastel painted houses and bars, the rhythms audible over the throb of the boxer engine. Joe picks his way through the labyrinth of streets and drives out to Batista's military headquarters at Camp Columbia. There's a delay while guards check his credentials and finally he's summoned in to the august presence of Major General Eulogio Cantillo. Joe knows he's the de-facto head of the regime's armed forces, and former commander in chief of the Army in Oriente province. He sees

300

before him a sweaty slightly overweight man of about 50, with a ludicrous looking pencil moustache who's drinking milk from a large glass. He hands over the dispatches from Guevara, but Cantillo quizzes Joe personally about what's happened on the ground in Santa Clara. The city, Joe tells him, is all but completely in rebel hands, and Che and Camillio Cienfuegos are preparing to march on Havana while Castro launches a final assault on Santiago de Cuba which is now surrounded and besieged.

"I know", says Camillo surprisingly. "I met Castro there on Christmas eve."

"You met Castro?" asks Joe, amazed.

"Yes, he tried to persuade me to surrender Santaigo straight away."

"Well, I suppose I'm here with a note from Major Guevara to persuade you to surrender Havana straight away. With respect, sir, the battle doesn't exactly seem to be going your way."

Cantillo smiles wearily. "You could say that. But as you know it's not exactly down to me. Thank you for bringing the dispatch. I'll inform the president directly."

And with that Joe is ushered out. As he gets back on the bike to head back to the city centre, he sees half a dozen large unmarked planes lined up on the side of the airfield being refuelled and readied for take-off.

As Joe drives back slowly through the streets of Havana he tries to reconcile the scenes of normality with the carnage he'd witnessed in Santa Clara just a few hours earlier. Here all is natural. Street lights blaze, music blares, hustlers guard their pitches and bemoan the relative lack of tourists. The Tropicana night-club is open for business, offering a new spectacular entitled *On the Way to Broadway*. Limos and brash automobiles pull up outside the glitzy international hotels. Suddenly Joe has a yearning to return to the Riviera, and see if Lansky is still around. To warn him of what is on its way. First though he needs to go home and change.

§§§§§

For once the shower runs hot. Concha and her family are delighted to see him, but devastated about the news of Maria's death. They want all the news of the revolution and to know when the rebels are likely to arrive in Havana. They ply Joe with best

301

Havana Club Rum which helps a little to take the sting out of the missing Maria. Walking through her room and seeing her things isn't as big an ordeal as he had anticipated. He's already said good bye to her. He'll have time to grieve later. Now he is numb.

He cuts a strange figure in his white Tuxedo and black bow tie and cuberbund on the bike out to the Riviera. It is after ten when he arrives there and he'd expected the party to be in full swing. But the Copa room is half empty. Apparently there had been a rush of cancellations for the New Year's Eve party over the past couple of days as Americans ditched their vacations or returned home early.

Meyer Lansky is upstairs in his suite. nursing a severely swollen knee and a painful ulcer. He greets Joe as a long lost son. But the little man still refuses to believe that the game is up.

"Cienfuegos and Guevara will be here tomorrow or the next day" Joe insists. "Get out while you can. When the revolution hits the streets of Havana the prime target is going to be American businesses and especially the casinos."

"I aint runnin'," declares Lansky. "I've never run from anything yet and I aint startin' now. Anyway where would I go? Everything I got's tied up in this hotel. They're not exactly going to welcome me back in the old US of A. And anyway, it doesn't matter what sort of government is in charge here, they're going to need American greenbacks, and the best way to get them is from the tourists. And the tourists come because of my hotel and my floor show and my casino."

As the clock ticks towards midnight Joe tries in vain to explain both the puritanism of the revolutionary leaders, and how the average Cuban sees the US and Batista as being inextricably linked.

At twelve Joe goes back down to join the muted celebrations in the Copa room. He dances with Teddy Lansky and when the band strikes up Auld Lang Syne the small group of revellers don cardboard hats and pop Champagne corks and blow whistles in an effort of jollity. Joe is fairly drunk by now and raises his glass to toast the toppling of the "ancien' regime". A few of the waiters and other Cubans applaud. Teddy Lansky smiles wanly.

It is after three when he staggers out onto the street. And it is like going from a wake to riot. The cold of the air-conditioned hotel gives way to the warmth of the tropical night. Car horns are blaring, people are streaming out onto the pavements. The cry goes up "Batista has fled – Long Live the Revolution". A trio of drunk Cuban girls seized Joe and kiss and hug him. All around people are dancing and singing. Down the street there is the crash of glass as someone smashes a shop window. A man lifts the trunk of his car and fishes around for a tyre iron. With it firmly grasped in both hands he raises it high above his heat and brings it down with all his might, smashing the parking meter next to the car. "Death to tyrants" he says in a slurry voice and turns his attention to the next meter along the street. Others take up the chant and in a moment the parking meters, whose takings everyone knows have long been siphoned off to pay Batista's henchmen, become the material personification of the hated regime.

Joe asks around to find out what has happened and is told variously that Batista has died in a suicide pact, has been personally shot by Castro, has robbed the national bank, and, more plausibly, has taken off with his family and closest advisors in half a dozen planes bound for Miami or the Dominican Republic. Joe remembers the unmarked aircraft he'd seen on the tarmac at Camp Columbia. As he finally climbs the long flight of stairs to his room he reflects that this new years' eve it really is out with the old and in with the new.

Revolution Cuba   '58

PART 9

New Year

Ok, ok. Here our tale should end. After all it's no longer 1958. The New Year has dawned, and with it frantic calls from news desks around the world to correspondents in Havana and Latin America for copy on the revolution. Everyone agrees that Batista has fled. Indeed his arrival in the Dominican Republic has been reported. But no one seems any too sure what is happening on the ground in Cuba itself. Rumour has it that Major General Cantillo has been left holding the reins. Some believe he's done a deal with Castro and will hand over the army to the rebels when they arrive in the capital. Others, including it subsequently turns out Castro himself, believe that Cantillo has tried to double-cross the rebels and was plotting a military coup of his own with other high ranking officers. Whatever the truth there's a power vacuum, and journalists are struggling to come up with many hard facts. The Guardian's Alistair Cook is typical. Filing from New York he writes:

> **"Batista is gone, probably for good. His hand-picked President, Dr Aguero, who was duly approved by a rigged election on November 4 is plainly unable to form a Government....And Castro, the Boy Scout Napoleon with the "beatnik" beard has in two years converted 40 audacious guerrillas into a conquering army capable of disrupting the life and economy of Cuba and dictating the character of the next Government."**

Don't you just love it: "The Boy Scout Napoleon with the beatnik beard..." what a turn of phrase!

But just as we started our tale shortly before 1958 ...surely it's permissible to beg a further indulgence and allow us to foray into 1959 for just a few more pages. To dot some "i"s and cross some "t"s. After all can we really leave Joe to wake up in his lonely bed without Maria but with a crashing hang-over? I promise we won't stray too far into the new year and the new regime. We'll stop well short of the mass reprisals, with Batista supporters being lined up and summarily executed. We won't go into how Castro moves seamlessly from opposing a dictator, to becoming one himself. We won't speak of his wholesale conversion to communism of his embrace of the Soviet Union. And I promise we won't discuss the abortive Bay of Pigs episode, nor how the British Sea Furies, in Castro's hands, did indeed help foil the invasion. No, we'll just have Joe tie up a few loose ends and then send him on his way back home to Deptford.

Chapter 39

The telephone ringing outside Joe's bedroom door sounds like a jack-hammer fighting a pneumatic drill on a corrugated iron roof. His mouth is dry, his eyes are red, and his head is splitting.

"Yes?" he says when he's managed to wrest the receiver from its cradle and get it pointing the right way up.

"Yes, that's me. Who? Foreign desk? Yes that's right there has been a revolution. Yes they were partying in the streets last night, smashing up parking meters and foreign airline offices. .... that's right I said parking meters. They're seen as a symbol of corruption here. Where have I been? I've been in Santa Clara. Yes that's right there was a battle....three thousand rebels dead? Rubbish. There were only three hundred rebels in the attack in the first place. Certainly twenty or thirty may have been killed but no more. ... The government said what? Che Guevara dead? Well he certainly wasn't when I saw him at 4 o'clock yesterday afternoon. He was very much alive and planning to march on Havana today or tomorrow. What, three or four hundred words? Yes I suppose I could. Can you give me a couple of hours?"

Joe puts down the phone and lies back down on the bed holding his head in his hands. A short while later Fidel's voice comes floating across the landing. Joe reaches over and turns on the radio by the side of the bed and grabs a pen and paper to take notes. Castro is calling for an immediate general strike throughout the country and a mobilisation of rebel forces in Santiago and Havana to stop the putative Cantillo Junta in its tracks. "Revolution, Yes," he shouts, "Military coup NO!"

Joe feels his way downstairs and along the street to Marti's bar. He orders a small vodka in a double tomato juice, a large black coffee, and several sticky pastries. After an hour or so he has slightly less of a headache and a semblance of a story. It is short on facts, but long on colour surrounding the taking of the train in Santa Clara.

After battling with the telex machine in the foreign press club Joe walks through the old town, over to the central railway station, and along to the docks. A family of American tourists is disembarking from a taxi and looking round for the tender that is to take them back to their cruise ship moored in the harbour. They are complaining about the chaotic scenes in the streets and at the guns that seem to be everywhere. Joe falls into conversation with them.

"Is it always like this here?" asked the husband. "I'm amazed they get any tourists at all."

"Only on mornings after a revolution," jokes Joe. And then seeing their blank look of incomprehension: "You do know that Batista fled the country last night and that the rebels are in charge?"

"Gee no. We'd no idea. We left the ship first thing and hired a taxi to take us round. We couldn't understand what all the fuss was about and why there were so many broken windows and stuff. You mean we landed in the middle of a revolution? Gee"

Joe smiles and asks about their ship. It is a British vessel, The Mauritania. Formerly a trans-Atlantic liner, now reduced to doing winter cruises in the Caribbean and summer duties in the Med. On an impulse Joe asks the ships' officer piloting the tender if there are any jobs which would allow him to work his passage home. An hour later he is on board being interviewed by the purser for a position as a waiter and bar tender. Several Cuban crew members had, it appeared, jumped ship to join the revolutionary party and the purser is short-staffed for the trip back up to New York. The position is Joe's if he wanted it.

The tender takes Joe back ashore and arranges to collect him and his luggage the following day. He isn't sure what's made him take the decision. Something is telling him that his job in Cuba is done. He's seen history turn a page, indeed he'd even given it a little push himself. But like a guest with a post-party hang-over, he isn't particularly keen to help clear up the mess the morning after. And everywhere he goes reminds him of Maria. He will probably learn to live with the aching void she's left, but surely it will be easier if he puts some distance between himself and her home.

With the afternoon wearing on, he catches the bus across town to the Rivera to collect the bike which he had drunkenly abandoned the night before. Entering the lobby he can hardly believe his eyes. Instead of elegant American matrons and tuxedoed gamblers, the place is peopled by peasants fresh in from the countryside. Many wear the black and red armband of the revolution. Some carry machetes, some have guns and cartridge belts. One even has a small pig which is snuffling round under the ornate arm-chairs. They look magnificently incongruous and rather uncomfortable in the rococo-ornate surroundings. But they all have a defiant air about them, as if to say "all this is ours now and there is nothing you can do about it!"

In the dining room Teddy Lansky is mopping the floor, her sleeves rolled up and the bottom of her slacks wet with soapy water. "The staff have deserted us to join the celebrations," she said. "Our American guests have been told by the embassy to stay put, so we're doing what we can to look after them. But the peasants have taken over the lobby and are trailing mud all over the place. And for Christ sake: a pig in reception!! Meyer's in the kitchen."

Joe pushes through the swing doors to find the man, who once referred to himself as "bigger than U.S. Steel", hobbling around concocting some sort of meal for his guests. He seems genuinely sorry to hear that Joe is planning to leave the following day. "Write me, do you hear. And come back and stay. They'll always be a room for you here. Once there's someone in charge to speak to we'll sort all this out and it will soon be back to normal."

Joe shakes his head sadly and watches the diminutive figure disappear into the dining room. He likes Lansky, he decides. Not just because he'd helped him when he'd first arrived, but because there is no guile in him. He is the first genuinely amoral person Joe has met. He really does not think that anything he does is wrong. Breaking the law bootlegging ... well it was a stupid law, and if there is demand for booze, then it is the American way to supply it. Rubbing out the odd opponent? Well, they doubtless deserve it. And anyway they'd probably have had a pop at Lansky if he hadn't got to them first. Dropping off suitcases of cash to keep a dictator in power? Well it is just business. In some places there is a city or state tax, in Cuba it is the same, you just paid it rather more directly, straight to the government. And anyway it is the cost of doing business. Lansky is at heart an accountant for whom the bottom line is everything. Anything that interferes with business or affects profit has to be fixed.

Joe smiles quietly to himself as he revs up the bike and heads up the Malecon. There is just one major character flaw, he reflects. The man has no sense of timing. He'd invested heavily in his hotel just as the Batista regime was crumbling, and now he can't see the writing on the wall, and won't be told by anyone that the letters they are forming are the words : "Get the fuck out of here before it's too late".

§§§§§§

Joe spends the rest of the day sorting his affairs. Paying Concha off for his and Maria's room; turning his remaining cash into traveller's cheques; and arranging to sell the BMW. He is still uncomfortable that he'd effectively stolen it from the rural garage all those months ago. So he sits down and writes a note which he addresses to the garage hoping it will be passed on to the bike's original owner. In it he outlines, with only the occasional exaggeration, how the bike has helped win the revolution, and he encloses a further $50 bill.

He spends the evening at Marti's saying good-bye to old acquaintances. Matthews wasn't there, but Joe writes him a note too, thanking him for his help and his friendship.

The following morning the radio announces that Camillo Cienfuegos and Che Guevara will be arriving in Havana in a few hours. Camillo was to take over the main military stronghold at Camp Columbia, while Che was to station his men at the La Cabana, the colonial fortress on the Moro rock. Joe has a few hours to kill before he drops off the bike and embarks on the Mauritania. After watching the triumphal entry of the rebels into the city, he drives out through the tunnel to the fortress. He recalls the extraordinary fight he's had with the Cuban who'd been after the CIA's money. He never had discovered who the man was or why he attacked him.

There is a party mood among the rebel soldiers who are billeting themselves in the Cabana. The prison block which had for so long incarcerated political detainees and opponents of the dictatorship, is now full of Batista's men and members of his secret police. Che proves easy to find. He is sitting in the commander's office with a panoramic view of the bay and the city. He is leaning back in his chair, his feet up on the desk. He is wearing the iconic beret with its single star at the front, and he is smoking a characteristic Cohiba cigar.

When Joe enters he doesn't move except to raise a hand in greeting.

"Ah, English. Reporting for duty, or come to tell me you're leaving? Wait, let me guess. It's the latter isn't it.

Joe nods. "Yes, I've come to say good-bye. But also to congratulate you on your victory, and to wish you good luck. Winning the peace is often as difficult as winning the war."

"Yes, I think you're probably right. But we have an amazing opportunity here to start afresh. And I believe we can create a society unlike any other the world has known."

"You know that if it's purely communist you'll be ostracised by the US?"

"I know and I don't care. They really are corrupt, you know, the Americans. Politically, economically and morally. We have to go it alone without them."

"Have you considered a mixed economy? The British style of socialism. All the major social institutions and vital industries nationalised, but the free market operating elsewhere?"

"The free market? It's never free. Capitalism always has to be constrained or it becomes monopolistic. And it *always* exploits its workers. Outright ownership of the means of production for *all* workers. It's the only really fair way."

"Does Fidel agree with you?"

"I think you'll be surprised at the type of regime he will instigate. He's much more radical than he's let on so far. He's a clever politician. You'll see. But what about you? What are you going to do?"

"I don't know. But I just feel that it's time to move on. It's been a fascinating year, and I love this country, but I don't want to outstay my welcome."

They embrace and part. Joe looks back to see Che standing at the window, staring out over his new domain. He admires the man for his steely determination and utter single-mindedness. It was those qualities that made him such a brilliant guerrilla commander. But Joe wonders if they are really what is needed in a politician or government minister. Somehow he can't see the bearded rebel wearing a suit sitting down at a conference table to negotiate treaties or sugar production quotas. There's a restless Peter Pan quality about him that will somehow keep him perpetually seeking some unattainable nirvana just over the next hill or just beyond the next battle.

§§§§§

The Mauritania slips its mornings and heads northwards out of the Havana bay towards the United States of America. A waiter in a starched white jacket brings out a tray of drinks for passengers leaning over the stern rail watching the sun set over the city, etching the sky-line in pink, white and blue. The waiter pauses for a moment before going back inside to his bar. Silently he says farewell to the city and the country, and to the woman he loved who gave her life for her nation's future.

But one image more than any other sticks in his mind. Just before embarking he'd been walking down one of Havana's side streets, making his way towards the dock-side. Approaching a corner he has a powerful feeling of deja-vu. There's a smell in the air that that assaults him. This smell is different to Havana's habitual hibiscus and jasmine and lemon, mixed with sea salt and exhaust fumes. No, this is another odour on the mid-evening breeze that's not so pleasant. It gets stronger and, as he turns the corner, it blasts him full in the face. The road he's turned into is wide and lined with trees and lampposts. Traffic moves down it at a sedate pace. There are few pedestrians, and none on his side. There's something wrong. Something incongruous. And he looks up to see it swaying gently in the soft wind. A body. On the end of a rope. Hanging from a lamppost. A ghastly gallows. But this time the corpse is not a civilian. This time it wears the uniform of the secret police, SIM. And this time no patriots will come to cut it down.

The End

Revolution Cuba '58

Fact,Fiction
and Sources:

I am particularly indebted to the following authors and their works on which I have drawn heavily for character details and historic narrative:

Robert Lacey: *Little Man – Meyer Lansky and the Gangster Life.*
Jon Lee Anderson: *Che Guevara – A Revolutionary Life*
John Dorschner & Robert Fabricio: *The Winds of December*
Carlos Franqui: *Diary of the Cuban Revolution*
Che Guevara: *Reminiscences of the Cuban Revolutionary War*

I would also like to acknowledge the invaluable work of two historians of the period:

Hugh Thomas: *The Cuban Revolution*
Herbert Matthews: *Revolution in Cuba*

I am also grateful to many other authors whose works have been of assistance in building up a picture of Cuba in the 1950's, particularly:

Julia Sweig: *Inside the Cuban Revolution*
Rosalie Schwartz: *Pleasure Island – Tourism and Temptation in Cuba*
Andrew Sinclair: *Che Guevara*
Tete Puebla: *Marianas in Combat*
Fidel Castro & Che Guevara *To Speak the Truth*

Joe, Maria, and Carmen are fictional, but almost every other character or major player is, or was, real. For those that are interested in specifics or sources, the following may be helpful:

Part 1 End of '57. Chapters 1-5

There are numerous references to Meyer Lansky, (including a woeful 1999 made for TV bio-pic staring Richard Dreyfus) but by far and away the best and most authoritative source is Robert Lacey's magisterial biography *"Little Man"*. It is Lacey who tells us that Lansky preferred the Dodge to other flasher cars, and provides many of the details for the Riviera hotel. Big Tony is fictitious.

Descriptions of Havana's uninhibited pre-revolution night life can be found on the Web and in Rosalie Schartz's Pleasure Island. Details of the show at the Shanghai are culled from a contemporary article by journalist Jay Mallin.

Part 2. Early '58 Chapters 6-10

Maria may be fictional, but her descriptions of the formation of the M26/7 and the pre-'58 background to the revolution are factual. See sources above.

Faure Chomon was leader of the Directorio Revolucionario – a militant student group operating in the *llano* – the 'plains' or cities as opposed to the *sierras* – the 'mountains'. As such he was suspicious of Castro – if not actually opposed to him. The attack on the presidential palace is well documented. The kidnapping of the Argentine motor racing champion by the M26/7 actually happened.

Part 3. Early Spring Chapters 11 - 15

Trinidad exists as described. There was a small group of rebels, the *Segundo Frente* or Second Front operating from the nearby Escrambray mountains at this time. It included an American, William Morgan, who was later executed, in 1961, for allegedly conspiring against Castro.

Part 4. Late Spring Chapters 16-20

Marti's is a conglomeration of a number of Havana bars. Herbert Matthews was a respected New York Times correspondent who shot to prominence through his interview with Castro. He concedes in later books that he did, indeed, vastly overstate the number of rebel troops then in the Sierras.

Lydia and Celia Sanchez were both real, and both heroines of the Revolution. Lydia is lauded by Che Guevara in his essay *Lydia and Clodomira*. Celia Sanchez remained at Castro's side long after the revolution, indeed until her death in 1980. She's often referred to as Cuba's 'first lady', and some have speculated whether she was rather more than a secretary to Fidel. (See "Towards the Gates of Eternity: Celia Sanchez Manduley and the Creation of Cuba's New Woman" by American academic Tiffany Thomas-Woodard – available on the Web.

314

Part 5. Early Summer. Chapters 21-25

There is at least one source for the story of Che arriving on a Mule at one end of Las Vegas while a battalion of Batista's army was approaching the other end. And the rebels certainly did obtain an army radio and codebook which gave them a major advantage – but that probably happened a day or so after the loss of Las Vegas. Pedro is a fictional character, but his treatment by Che is typical of that of a number of rebel volunteers. The battle of Yara river happened very much as described.

In spite of Batista's appalling human rights record, Britain did sell Cuba Sea Fury fighters at a time when even the US had imposed an arms embargo. However there is good evidence that Batista's planes were being refuelled at the US Guantanamo base and supplied with Napalm.

Part 6 Mid Summer. Chapters 26-29

Raul's policy of taking US hostages is true. The disagreements between the US Consul in Santiago de Cuba and Ambassador Earl T Smith in Havana is also well documented. Smith was an unreconstructed Macarthyite hater of Communism. He believed fervently that the only way to prevent a communist take-over in Cuba was for the US to intervene financially and even militarily to prop up Batista. He was, of course, right about the eventual political make-up of Castro's government, but his preferred solution was opposed by Washington and by most Cubans.

Part 7 Late Summer Chapters 30-33

The CIA seems to have been equally split, with one faction financing the rebels and another giving active support to Batista. Several sources document sums of cash being paid by the CIA to the rebels. Robert Lacey is the source of the story of the regular payments from the casino owners to Batista. Guevara arrived in the Escrambray mountains after a gruelling march across country to find virtual anarchy among the various rebel factions. It was part of the constant jockeying for power between Castro's *sierra* force and various rebel groups in the *llano*. It was by no means certain that Castro would eventually dominate, and is a tribute to his political and propaganda skills that he did.

Part 8. Autumn and Winter Chapters 34-38

The rather gruesome details of rape, torture and dismemberment by Batista's secret police come directly from an interview with Tete Puebla, commanding officer of the Mariana Grajales women's platoon (see *Marianas in Combat*). The story of the Gran Hotel in Santa Clara comes from Dorschner and Fabrico's excellent *Winds of December* for which they interviewed Guillermo Domenech who was a clerk rather than manager at the hotel. It took rather longer than I allowed to clear the snipers on the roof – they were still entrenched a day or so after Batista had fled and the revolution was won. The armoured train was captured by pulling up the track, and was a pivotal point in Batista's realisation that the game was up. Che Guevara did fight and win the battle with his arm in a sling after falling or jumping from a roof. Cantillo did take over briefly after Batista fled, but his duplicity was punished by Castro and he was imprisoned for 8 years. He died in Miami in 1978.

Part 9. January Chapter 39

Lacey has the story of New Years Eve at the Riviera, and Teddy Lansky's comments about the unwelcome guests in the foyer. The smashing of parking meters is well documented, and subsequently the mob trashed many of Havana's casinos and other American owned businesses.

The story of the American family touring the city on New Year's day without realising there had been a revolution comes from Dorschner and Fabrico. They were on a cruise aboard the British registered Mauretania.

Castro's decision to relegate Guevara to the Cabana fortress rather than allow him to take the much more important Camp Columbia is one of the curiosities of the conclusion of the revolution. Che seems to have accepted the decision without rancour, and it was probably due to the fact that he was a foreign national and an avowed communist. Despite having triumphed, it seems that Castro was keen, in public at least, to continue to distance himself from the communists within his movement. It makes his personal conversion over the subsequent months all the more remarkable. Che did, indeed, later head the national bank, but there's no evidence that he tried to institute his novel ideas of abolishing wages for work which Andrew Sinclair ascribes to him.